Praise for
Pretty Poison

"A fun and informative reading experience . . . With a touch of romance added to this delightful mystery, one can only hope many more Peggy Lee mysteries will be hitting shelves soon!"   —*Roundtable Reviews*

"A fantastic amateur sleuth mystery . . . will appeal to men and women of all ages . . . a great tale."   —*The Best Reviews*

"Peggy is a great character . . . For anyone with even a modicum of interest in gardening, this book is a lot of fun. There are even gardening tips included."
—*The Romance Reader's Connection*

"The perfect book if you're looking for a great suspense . . . *Pretty Poison* is the first in the Peggy Lee Garden Mystery series, and I can't wait for the next!"   —*Romance Junkies*

"Joyce and Jim Lavene have crafted an outstanding whodunit in *Pretty Poison*, with plenty of twists and turns that will keep the reader entranced to the final page. Peggy Lee is a likable, believable sleuth and the supporting characters add spice, intrigue, and humor to the story."   —*Fresh Fiction*

"Complete with gardening tips, this is a smartly penned, charming cozy, the first book in a new series. The mystery is intricate and well-plotted. Green thumbs and non-gardeners alike will enjoy this book."   —*Romantic Times BOOKclub*

FRUIT *of the* POISONED ✽ TREE

Joyce and Jim Lavene

BERKLEY PRIME CRIME, NEW YORK

THE BERKLEY PUBLISHING GROUP
Published by the Penguin Group
Penguin Group (USA) Inc.
375 Hudson Street, New York, New York 10014, USA
Penguin Group (Canada), 90 Eglinton Avenue East, Suite 700, Toronto, Ontario M4P 2Y3, Canada
(a division of Pearson Penguin Canada Inc.)
Penguin Books Ltd., 80 Strand, London WC2R 0RL, England
Penguin Group Ireland, 25 St. Stephen's Green, Dublin 2, Ireland (a division of Penguin Books Ltd.)
Penguin Group (Australia), 250 Camberwell Road, Camberwell, Victoria 3124, Australia
(a division of Pearson Australia Group Pty. Ltd.)
Penguin Books India Pvt. Ltd., 11 Community Centre, Panchsheel Park, New Delhi—110 017, India
Penguin Group (NZ), Cnr. Airborne and Rosedale Roads, Albany, Auckland 1310, New Zealand
(a division of Pearson New Zealand Ltd.)
Penguin Books (South Africa) (Pty.) Ltd., 24 Sturdee Avenue, Rosebank, Johannesburg 2196,
South Africa

Penguin Books Ltd., Registered Offices: 80 Strand, London WC2R 0RL, England

This is a work of fiction. Names, characters, places, and incidents either are the product of the authors' imagination or are used fictitiously, and any resemblance to actual persons, living or dead, business establishments, events, or locales is entirely coincidental. The publisher does not have any control over and does not assume any responsibility for author or third-party websites or their content.

FRUIT OF THE POISONED TREE

A Berkley Prime Crime Book / published by arrangement with the authors

PRINTING HISTORY
Berkley Prime Crime mass-market edition / May 2006

Copyright © 2006 by Joyce Lavene and Jim Lavene.
Cover art by Dan Craig.
Cover design by Lesley Worrell.
Interior text design by Stacy Irwin.

ISBN: 0-425-20967-9

BERKLEY® PRIME CRIME
Berkley Prime Crime Books are published by The Berkley Publishing Group,
a division of Penguin Group (USA) Inc.,
375 Hudson Street, New York, New York 10014.
The name BERKLEY PRIME CRIME and the BERKLEY PRIME CRIME design are trademarks
belonging to Penguin Group (USA) Inc.

PRINTED IN THE UNITED STATES OF AMERICA

10 9 8 7 6 5 4 3 2 1

1

Tobacco

Botanical: *Nicotiana tabacum*
Family: N.O. Solanaceae

*Native American tribes believed in the healing power of tobacco
and smoked it regularly. According to myth, smoking the pipe kept
the scattered tribes from becoming enemies. They used the dried
leaves for removing poison, a practice still in effect, and to draw
the pain from insect stings.*

"I CONFESS THAT I didn't want to come here when I heard
what my topic was supposed to be." Dr. Margaret Lee looked
out into the audience gathered in the meeting room. Her brilliant green eyes were sharp beneath her collapsing twist of
white-washed red hair. She wore an elegant, blue green three-
piece Liz Claiborne suit chosen specially for that moment.

She didn't like stereotypes and didn't intend to become one.

"Asking a person from North Carolina to talk about tobacco *could* be considered an insult these days. Fortunately,
I'm not insulted very easily." The audience chuckled a little
and moved restlessly at their tables. The waiters still hadn't
come to clear the luncheon plates, and occasionally silver-
ware or china clinked as a speaker strove to make his or her
point. Peggy took a deep breath. *Tough crowd.*

But she was prepared. The letter asking her to speak at a U.S. Botanical Society conference in Kennett Square, Pennsylvania, about thirty miles west of Philadelphia, wasn't a surprise. She found time to be there most years. Asking her to specifically speak about the evils of tobacco *was* a surprise.

She was recognized by the society for her work with botanical poisons. She didn't start out in that field, but circumstances brought it to her doorstep. Tobacco qualified as a poison, even if you *didn't* count smoking or chewing it.

Every year, harvesting the plant made a few dozen workers sick from nicotine poison they absorbed from the leaves. Despite the centuries it had been cultivated, people still made mistakes with it. Like every other poisonous plant, it needed understanding and care if the person tending it wanted to stay well.

Asking her to speak about the controversy that had developed between smokers and nonsmokers made her feel like the society expected her to show up in overalls and bare feet to represent the North Carolina tobacco farmer.

But to prove to herself that her fellow attendees were more interested in the botanical view than the political view of *Nicotiana,* when the society suggested visual material, she refused to bring her projector and laptop. She knew she could create a far more stunning visual impact.

She put on a pair of sturdy garden gloves, dug into the insulated bag she brought onstage with her, and pulled out a healthy specimen of tobacco. After plunking it down on the speaker's podium, Peggy smiled at the suddenly quiet crowd. "This plant is probably more maligned than any plant has a right to be. We blame it for everything from heart attacks to warts. Everything people have done to themselves. The truth is, people have smoked and chewed it since the fifteen hundreds in Europe, probably thousands more years in North and South America. While it's been accused of terrible things, modern science has begun to agree with folklore that it may hold the key to valuable healing properties as well."

Peggy was satisfied with the shocked look on her colleagues' faces. She stepped down to the audience with the plant, pointing out the wide green leaves and pretty white flowers. While she rattled on about research and isolating the important properties of the plant for the good of humanity, her friend Debby Moore, who worked for Longwood Gardens, shook her head and smiled. When her twenty-minute speech extolling the benefits of the tobacco plant was finished, Peggy returned to their table to enthusiastic applause from the rest of the audience.

"Thank you, Dr. Lee." Stan Mason, current president of the society, adjusted the microphone as he took back the podium. He dusted some soil from the stand and smiled down at her. "For those of you who aren't aware of it, our Dr. Lee was spotlighted in *Crime Fighter's Magazine* last month for her work with the police on murder cases that involve poison. Very unique for a member of our society. Commendable, Dr. Lee!"

Peggy acknowledged his accolade as she finished putting the long-leafed tobacco plant back into the travel bag. Her normally pink, freckled cheeks were slightly more flushed from the attention, but her stubborn chin refused to let her look away from the interested stares of the group surrounding her. It wasn't like she was wearing her panty hose on the outside or anything. It always seemed she was just a *little* different, something her mother pointed out as being her own fault.

"That was interesting," Debby whispered as another speaker was introduced. "You didn't tell me you had a plant in that bag. You know we don't allow plants from outside."

"It's not like it can escape. And I didn't want you to tell anyone." Peggy zipped the plant into the bag. "Poor thing doesn't like this cold, I'm afraid. I'm going to have a rough time getting it back in shape when I get home."

The next speaker was a botanist from Ohio who spoke about using plants to prevent the infiltration of harmful pests in the garden. He began to speak in a droning, nasal voice that lulled the crowd like a bee on a hot summer day. Eyes shut and heads rolled to one side.

Debby leaned close to Peggy. "I don't think anyone expected you to talk about the *good* qualities of tobacco."

"I guess they were surprised then." Peggy patted an errant strand of hair that was beginning to annoy her. Sometimes she thought it might be better to shave the whole mass off but never really went beyond annoyance to action. She wore her hair the way she'd worn it for twenty years. Mostly she was too busy to pay it much attention. "My father raised tobacco every summer while I was growing up. It was a stable cash crop. He even let us smoke some after it was cured. Vile stuff, but important to the farmers in South Carolina. I wouldn't mind if research developed something to save all those tobacco farms from extinction. I love the smell of it growing after a rain as you go down the road in the summer."

They sat through a few more speakers before the conference was over. While the others were leaving, Peggy walked with Debby to the developmental area of Longwood Gardens. She loved to see what they were working on and borrow some ideas for her own basement greenhouse.

"I'm glad Antares did so well for you," Debby said, speaking of the huge, night-blooming water lily she'd sent her. "Your night-blooming rose was impressive. Thanks for bringing us one. We've been working on a variety of night- and twilight-flowering plants. Besides the water lily and the rose, we also have a dahlia and a hibiscus that are under development. I suppose you'll be turning your eye on the magnolia now. That would be impressive at night."

"Actually I've been working with a local farmer on more pest-resistant strawberries. They've made them big now, but they're having problems with bugs they never had before."

"I guess the bugs didn't notice strawberries as much when they were the size of peas," Debby quipped, "but now they're the size of apples, it's a different story."

"That's always the way it is." Peggy admired a deep purple rose. "When you change one thing, you change ten more things with it. I love playing with flowers, but when I can help in a more practical sense, that's when I really get involved. I'm also working with Darmus Appleby to help establish a community vegetable garden in Charlotte for next summer."

Debby smiled and adjusted a water sprinkler. "When do you have time for that new beau of yours? With everything you take on, it can't be easy to find time to hold hands while you watch a Sunday matinee."

"It's difficult." Peggy's eyes flashed as the image of two old people barely able to move filled her mind. "But don't make it sound like I'm over a hundred and met the man in the wheelchair next to mine. I'm still capable of having a meaningful relationship. Having Steve in my life has been strange and stressful sometimes. I never expected to share my life with another man."

Debby laughed as she held out her hands to protect herself. "I didn't mean anything by it! Relax! You don't have to convince *me*. You've never seemed older than thirty."

"Oh hush!" Peggy smiled at her. "I'm a little sensitive about the whole age thing right now. I told you Steve is younger than me. I never thought about my age until I met him. Now sometimes I feel ancient. Like people look at us strangely when we're together. I'm waiting for the first person to come up and ask if I'm his mother."

"He's not *that* much younger than you," Debby, who'd met Steve at Christmas, reminded her. "As for anyone else, ignore them. You deserve to be happy. Steve is lucky to have you."

"I try not to notice, but you're talking to a woman born and raised in Charleston. When a thing wasn't proper, you didn't do it. I still haven't told my parents about Steve. I know my mother will be shocked and horrified. She thinks the proper mourning time for a wife is still five years."

Debby looked amazed. "You can't *still* feel like that, can you? I thought when I got older I wouldn't care what my parents think. You mean there's no relief? You've taken all the fun out of getting old for me."

"I suppose it might be different with different parents. Or if they die. That's the only way it can get better for me. Not that I'd wish them harm in a million years. They might be proper and fussy, but they're still my parents." Peggy glanced at her watch. "I've loved being with you this weekend. You'll have to come down and see us again. You can help out with the

community garden. With your expertise, we could grow vegetables the size of footballs."

"Maybe after the summer," Debby said. "You know what
my life around here is like once the weather gets warm. I never
go outside the garden. I think by September I'm starting to feel
a little green."

They looked at the huge, sleeping garden outside the greenhouse. The lush green and vibrant colors of summer were
months away. But the brown, drab landscape was full of promise in both their eyes. Gardeners' eyes see more than what ex-
ists at that moment. They always see the possibilities of what
could be.

The first snowflake broke Peggy's dreamy-eyed gaze.
She shivered, looking at the gray sky. Thousands of small,
white flakes followed the first flake, tumbling into the garden.
She wasn't a big fan of cold weather, especially snow and ice.
The idea of driving back to her hotel in Philadelphia made her
cut her good-byes to Debby short. She wanted to be inside before the snow started accumulating on the street.

"Be careful!" Debby waved as Peggy backed her rental car
out of the deserted parking lot. "Call me when you get to your
hotel. I want to be sure you make it safely back."

"I will. Thanks for a wonderful time! Come and see me
when you have a chance."

Despite Peggy's dread of frozen roads, one she had in common with most Southern-born women, the drive back wasn't
as bad as she feared. The snow melted as it hit the ground, creating a slushy mix on the pavement. But the Pennsylvania Department of Transportation was out with trucks and plows.
The slush never had a chance to freeze on the road. She wasn't
sure what it would be like later that night. But by then, she'd
be home.

February in the Carolinas might have some frost, but snow
was unlikely. And if it *did* snow, she wouldn't have to drive in
it. That was one good thing about living in an area that didn't
have much frozen precipitation. The city was never prepared
for it. She could only hope they never would be. Let the people

who moved there from other states complain that they couldn't get out in bad weather. Sensible people didn't want to try.

Her thoughts of home were banished by some kind of commotion at the front of the Four Seasons Hotel where she was staying. The entire street and sidewalk were blocked with people. She thought at first there was an accident, but there was no sign of an ambulance or mangled cars.

She maneuvered her car close to the hotel entrance, wondering what was going on. It looked like a rally of some kind. Her cell phone rang as she noticed the signs and banners. *"Clean up your act! Give life a chance!"* Some of the people were made up to look like corpses with white faces and blackened eyes. They chanted slogans about saving the planet that she hadn't heard since she was in college.

"Hey, Peggy! How's the conference? Did little Nick wow them?" Her assistant, Sam Ollson, asked her across the miles between Pennsylvania and North Carolina.

"They loved him," she told him. "I thought I'd never get through the applause."

"Really?" Surprise made his youthful voice squeak. He was in his second year of college, hoping to go to med school and have a career as a surgeon. He'd worked for her at her garden shop, the Potting Shed, since it opened two years ago.

"No. Not really. But I think I made my point. Now little Nick and I are looking forward to coming home. There's something going on here, Sam," she said as the hotel concierge approached her car. "I have to go."

"What's wrong? Are you okay?"

"I'm fine," she answered. "It's some kind of demonstration or something. I'll talk to you later."

"Sorry for the delay, ma'am," the concierge said as she put away her cell phone. "We've called the police. This should be cleared up shortly."

"What's the problem?" She looked at the angry people as they swarmed around the hotel. A dark limousine pulled up at the hotel, positioning itself directly in front of the entrance. She could hear the police sirens coming closer.

"Protesters. They're holding meetings here at the hotel about drilling for oil and gas in some popular wilderness area. People are pretty worked up about it. But we didn't expect anything like this. If you want, you can leave the car here. I'll have it taken care of once this is cleared up."

"Thanks." She handed him the keys, scooped her possessions out, and headed around the limousine toward the door. As she walked past, the driver opened one of the limousine doors, and her friend, Park Lamonte, stepped out of the car. "Hey there! I didn't know you were staying here, too."

Mindful of the protesters who started pushing and shouting when they saw him, Park took her arm and walked quickly with her into the hotel. "It's nice to see a friendly face, Peggy, but you picked a bad time to visit. These jokers would like to have my head on a platter. Sorry I have to hustle you in this way. I don't want you to get hurt if this gets ugly."

"How are you involved with them?"

"A company I work for is doing some testing they aren't crazy about," he explained. "I'm only one of a dozen lawyers working on paving the way for business to continue. The world has to progress, right?"

Peggy recalled the signs outside. *"Keep the bay clean! Find an alternative to oil!"* "I don't know, Park. Not all progress is good progress. Are you sure you're on the right side?"

He laughed and put his arm around her shoulder. "I'm on the side that makes the most money, like always. That usually decides who's right. How long are you in town? Would you like to have dinner tonight? I have a reservation at the Fountain Restaurant here in the hotel."

"I'm afraid my flight leaves at three." She glanced at her watch. When she looked back at him, she was appalled to notice how gray his complexion was. "You look exhausted. Maybe you should take a vacation with Beth and the boys when you get home."

He rubbed his hand over his face. "I haven't been sleeping well. Damn bed's too soft. The hotel is booked up so I can't trade. I'm only here for a few more days. I'll be okay. But you're looking fine. I'd say that new man in your life is good for you. I still haven't had a chance to meet him."

"That's because you're always so worried about being on the side that makes money. Sometimes you have to be on the right side because it's right. It's not always about the money."

She knew Park long enough and well enough to speak her mind. She knew he was driven to succeed by some inner demon that poked him with a sharp pitchfork every time he tried to sit down and rest. He wasn't a bad man, just misguided sometimes. Knowing his parents, she was surprised he wasn't much worse.

Looking away from his red-rimmed blue eyes as they stepped into the elevator to go to their rooms, she pushed number six for her floor. She sighed at their personal differences that were mostly ignored in the light of their longstanding friendship.

They knew each other in college. He grew up with her husband, John Lee. John was a police detective for twenty years. They consulted on many police cases over dinner at one of their houses. Park didn't leave her side for three days when John was killed two years ago. "I guess I'll have to make an appointment for you to meet Steve."

"Don't be that way, Peggy. Let's go ahead and make plans to get together for dinner. I'm back in Charlotte on Thursday. Can you do dinner Friday evening at seven? I know Beth is free that night. I talked to her this morning."

"I think I can manage that." She smiled at him, not liking the terrible darkness in his eyes. He looked more than tired to her. It had probably been years since he'd even thought of having a medical checkup. "Steve and I will be there. Take care of yourself. Don't leave Beth alone so much if you don't have to."

He hugged her, shifting his expensive alligator briefcase to his left hand as the elevator reached his floor. "You worry too much. Have a good flight, Peggy. I'll see you back in Charlotte. Friday night. Don't forget now."

She watched as Park walked toward his room down the elegantly appointed hallway. A tall, scraggly looking young man in ripped jeans and a red T-shirt approached him as he took out his key card.

"What are *you* doing here?" Park asked, visibly drawing back.

"You *know* why I'm here," the young man returned before the elevator doors closed on the scene.

Peggy stabbed her finger on the three button to return to Park's floor, but the elevator went to her floor first, then back to his. By the time the doors opened again, both men were gone. She thought about trying to find his room but decided against it. Whatever was going on between them was none of her business. That alone wouldn't usually stop her. But there was a long line of doors to knock on since she didn't know the right room number. She didn't want to miss her flight. And Park could take care of himself.

She went back to her floor and used the key card to open her hotel room door. After putting down the insulated bag that held the tobacco plant and her pocketbook, she noticed the flowers that had been delivered while she was gone. They were beside a large gift basket from the hotel that she hadn't opened yet.

She didn't need to read the card on the flowers to know they were from Steve. He was the only one likely to send Queen Anne's lace as a gift. He already knew her so well she felt like they'd been together for years rather than months. Where he'd managed to find the flowers in the dead of winter was another story. She suspected Sam had something to do with it. He had access to most of the greenhouses in and around Charlotte.

She opened the card and saw the broad, masculine handwriting. *"Shakespeare and I miss you. We hope you enjoy this 'fantasy.' Come home soon. Love, Steve."* She brushed her hand across the broad top of the flowers. They were one of her favorites. Most Americans refused to see it as anything but a weed. In England, however, it was cultivated for its lacy beauty. Its traditional meaning in floriography, the language of flowers, was *fantasy*. Steve must have looked that up.

Seeing the flowers and reading the card made her eager to

get on the plane and go home. The Potting Shed was in capable hands while she was gone, but she missed being there, helping her customers get ready for spring. Some gardeners got depressed in the winter. She knew spring was always just around the corner. In Charlotte, North Carolina, the temperate climate meant an early spring. After the one or two obligatory ice storms in January, February was mild, and March would be warm, already beginning the spring growth cycle.

Just thinking about the Potting Shed . . . and Steve . . . made her pack her single bag quickly. The flight home would only be about an hour. Steve and Shakespeare, her adopted fawn-colored Great Dane, would be waiting for her. She couldn't think of anything more likely to get her moving.

Sirens and shouting disrupted her train of thought. She went to the window that overlooked the street and watched as police clashed with the demonstrators on the steps of the hotel. Had she known what was going on, she might've joined them. Being a botanist and a gardener, she had a stake in keeping the major corporations from trampling on everything living to keep their stockholders happy. It wouldn't be the first time she'd taken to the streets to protest, but it had been a while. *Like thirty years . . .*

She thought about Park again. Was he moved at all by the protesters' sincerity that made them willing to go to jail for their cause? Was he watching from his window and questioning his values? Probably not. His single-minded, bullheaded determination made him a top corporate attorney. If it meant he couldn't look from side to side, she was sure he'd find a reason why that was better.

They'd decided a long time ago to keep their individual politics from affecting their friendship. Not that her friend had any ideals or issues he wouldn't compromise for the right price. She didn't know what happened to the free-spirited young man he'd been in college, sneaking away from his tyrannical mother's watchful eye and spurning his father's racial bigotry with already enviable debating skills.

John remained idealistic until he died, despite terrible things he'd seen on the street. Park grew more interested in the bottom line. He could be witty and charming, always gave good parties to the right people, and had a soft heart for his family and friends. But he changed, became harder, more ruthless.

She suspected the three of them had remained friends more because of their shared past than what went on in their present lives. Sometimes those things happened. She always hoped something would open Park's eyes one day. She realized she loved him for what he had been, not for what he'd become.

When her bag was packed, she called the front desk to let them know she was leaving. The concierge offered to call her a taxi since her rental car was blocked by the protest in the street. "No charge to you, of course."

She thanked him and took a last look around her room. She'd already pressed her flowers into some damp newspaper and stuck them in a plastic bag for the flight. The food-filled gift basket she left untouched on the bedside table. Maybe they could give it to the next visitor.

Drawn by the angry scene on the sidewalk and in the street, Peggy walked outside to wait for the taxi despite warnings from the hotel staff. She watched the police load the angry protesters into vans. There weren't many of them, but they were tough and resilient. They didn't so much fight as resist. Most of the signs were lying in the street now, but several television cameras were videotaping the disturbance. She knew they'd scored some airtime for their cause.

The scraggly young man from Park's room ran toward her, wild-eyed. He looked anxious to get away from the hotel. He carried a banner, dropping it at her feet. She couldn't tell what it said anymore. The fat, wet snowflakes had blurred the marker he'd used to make his statement.

He was running from two policemen, who were yelling at him to stop. Peggy started to step aside until she saw the desperate yet determined look on his face. She wasn't sure what made her put herself between him and the police. Maybe it was because he reminded her of her own intense son. Maybe she just got caught up in the moment.

"What's going on?" she demanded, hoping to give the

young man a chance to get away. Even though she seemed to recall it being a badge of honor to be arrested, she didn't think he looked the type. He hadn't lain down in the street with the others. Instead, he reminded her of a terrified animal.

"Get out of the way, lady. This is police business," the first officer warned.

"Is there a problem?" She tried to take their attention away from their quarry. "It seems like you'd have something better to do than chase these young people."

"I won't ask you again." The officer charged, almost running into her on the slippery sidewalk. "This is a police action. You don't want to be standing around out here."

Peggy couldn't tell if the young man got away yet. She bent down and picked up the banner he dropped. "You can't even tell what this says anymore. Give the boy a break. He was only standing up for what he believes in."

"That's it! I warned you!" The officer snarled as he snatched the banner from her. The next thing she knew, the police were lifting her and carrying her to the waiting van. The reporters took her picture as the doors closed on her. *Another fine mess . . .*

2

Jerusalem Artichoke

Botanical: *Helianthus tuberosus*
Family: N.O. Compositae
Common name: Sunchoke

The name of this edible plant is a misnomer, since it doesn't come from Jerusalem and is not an artichoke. The name is from the Italian girasola articiocco, *the sunflower artichoke,* girasola *meaning "turning to the sun," and* articiocco, *"artichoke." In the 1920s, famed American psychic Edgar Cayce extolled the virtues of this plant in treating many medical maladies and brought it to the attention of the public.*

"So the police arrested you?" Sam followed through to the logical end of her story as Peggy explained why she missed her original flight home.

"Not arrested exactly," she hedged. "More like detained. They didn't press charges against any of the protesters. They held us for a few hours, then let us go when we promised to leave Philadelphia. Except for the man with the concealed weapon. They kept him."

Sam laughed as he easily navigated through early morning traffic from the airport to the Potting Shed. "At least you don't have a record. When you called me last night, I thought maybe

I should send Hunter up after you. I hope the experience taught you a lesson."

Peggy raised her eyebrow. "I didn't need your sister's legal defense, but thanks for thinking of me. Exactly what lesson is it that I should've learned?"

"Don't always jump into things until you know what's going on."

"I prefer to think of it as a good deed. Those people had a righteous grievance. That company has no business looking for oil in an estuary!" Peggy's words were as fiery as her once-red hair. Her green eyes gleamed with purpose.

"Yeah? What happened to the protester you were trying to save from the police?" Sam stopped at a red light and grinned at her, the sunlight catching in the golden strands of his long hair. "Did he stop by to say thanks?"

"I didn't see him again." She folded her hands in her lap and looked out of the side window. She shouldn't have told Sam the truth about what happened. Really! She was fifty-two years old. If she chose to join in at a protest, she had the right.

"Case closed. You helped him get away from the mess he created, and the police nabbed *you* instead. You did what you always do: jumped in with both feet, and it put you in a bad place. I don't know what I'm going to do with you."

He was joking, of course. They had a long-standing, easygoing relationship that allowed them both tremendous freedom in what they could say to each other without making the other person angry. Peggy sighed and sat back in her seat. She could take the ribbing.

Sam pulled the pickup into the loading zone behind the Potting Shed. Peggy waited until he turned off the engine. "When did you become a philosopher? It must've been while I was gone, because I could've sworn you're the same Sam Ollson who played that prank on his friend last week. Didn't that put you on the dean's blacklist for the month?"

Sam was a big man, more suited physically to being a construction worker than the surgeon he planned to be. His natural Scandinavian coloring and year-round tan made him look like a surfer. He had large hands that he used frequently to express himself when he wasn't coddling plants or shoveling dirt. He shrugged his broad shoulders covered by a tight-fitting green Potting Shed jacket. "I'm only twenty. People expect me to do things like that."

She burst out laughing at his excuse. "I'm over fifty. People expect *me* to do things like that. It's only the middle-aged people who are supposed to be the sane pillars of society. I guess we'll have to agree not to lecture each other." She looked up at the back of the shop. It was early. Brevard Court wasn't open yet to allow them in the front door. The big wrought-iron gate was still locked. But she couldn't wait. "It's good to be home anyway. Let's go inside."

He was ready for her barrage of questions about the shop and handed her a few printed pages of what transpired while she was gone. "I knew you'd want to see these. I thought this would be the best way."

She took the pages after she opened the back door. The air outside was cool and damp, with the pungent aroma of garbage waiting to be picked up from the restaurant next door. In an hour or two, the smells from cooking would overpower it. Now she hurried inside and was immediately embraced by the smells of new plants and potting soil they kept in large quantities in the back storeroom.

She glanced at the sales figures on the sheets Sam gave her, but they didn't really matter. Her heart was already home as she walked across the squeaky heart-of-pine floors and opened the door into the main body of the shop.

Peggy loved this time before the customers started coming in, before anything was moved or spilled. It was a quiet balm for her soul. Plants she'd started from seeds or cuttings stretched out new tendrils in the gauzy white sunlight coming in from the wide front windows. The oak rocking chair sat squarely on the multicolored rag rug, the display ready with plants and everything a gardener needed for spring. She sat down in the rocker and sighed.

"Orange spice tea?" Sam asked, smiling at her contentment.

"That would be perfect." She rocked the chair a little.

"Now. Tell me how things went while I was gone. Don't leave anything out."

EMIL BALDUCCI WAS CLEANING off some bird droppings from his shop window at the Kozy Kettle Tea and Coffee Emporium just across the courtyard from the Potting Shed when Peggy came back from lunch. "Hey, Peggy! Good to see you! That boy you left in charge while you were gone doesn't have a brain in his head!"

She joined him in the cobblestone courtyard. Emil always had some complaint about how things were done when she went away. She took a deep breath and smiled at him. "Good morning. How are you? How is Sofia?"

"She's fine. I'm fine. You have to fire that boy. Find someone more reliable. I have a nephew, Christo, Sofia's brother's son. He would do a good job for you. And his father is a widower. He's still got his hair and teeth. He's got plenty of money, too. You could sell this place and marry him."

Not daring to laugh, she asked, "Are you talking about me living with Christo or his father?"

Emil took a moment to curl the ends of his heavy gray mustache that he oiled every day. "You make jokes, but it's a hard life for a woman alone. Ask Sofia. She had an aunt who tried to live alone. Three years she was without a man. The first salesman who stopped at her door married her. She was desperate. Now she's happy."

Before she was married off to Sofia's brother or his son, Peggy got to the point. "What did Sam do this time?"

"He got dirt on the stones in the courtyard when he was working with the big flower pots. He came back after a while, when he felt like it, and cleaned up, but three customers noticed the mess. Then he sent people to that new bakery up the street. It's not bad enough I have to compete with Dilworth Coffee House, now I have to worry about my pastry being better than theirs."

"I'm sure he had a good reason, Emil. I've known Sam for years and so have you. He's a hard worker, and I trust him. I'll have a talk with him and let you know what happened."

"Oh! You'll have a *talk* with him." Emil shrugged and shook his head. "I'm sure *that* will take care of the problem. Especially since what he really needs is a boot in his rear. If you had a husband, like Sofia's brother, Angelo, he'd know what I'm talking about." He continued ranting in Sicilian as he walked back toward his shop.

Peggy thanked him, not sure what else to say, then hurried into the Potting Shed to get away from his tirade. With her back against the door, she looked up to find Sam and her shop assistant, Selena Rogers, who'd come in for the afternoon, staring at her.

"What happened?" Selena asked. "You look like someone chased you in here."

Peggy took off her heavy purple jacket, unwound the red scarf from her neck. "Mr. Balducci wants me to hire his nephew to run the shop."

"Does he want you to marry his brother-in-law again?" Sam laughed, his even, white teeth gleaming against his darkly tanned face.

"Of course. I'm sure one day I'll have to meet him." Peggy picked up the mail and looked through it, tossing away some ads for life insurance. "How are you, Selena? How did it go while I was gone? Any strange requests?"

Selena shrugged her thin shoulders, her blond hair sliding against her neck. "It was about like February. It's cold outside. It's hard for most people to think about planting yet. But there was this *one* guy. He wanted to plant a whole yard full of stuff right now."

"Oh yeah." Sam zipped up his jacket. "I forgot to tell you about him. Mr. Crawford. He offered me a thousand dollar bonus if I could get enough plants in his yard to make his wife think they were there already when the house was built. I think it's one of those treeless wonders from over in Pineville."

Peggy stopped opening her garden catalogues. "What did you say to him?"

"It was hard, but we both said no." Selena looked at Sam. "First of all, none of those plants would survive right now. How happy would he be after his wife pulled up into a yard filled with dead plants? It was a crazy, desperate idea."

Sam shook his head. "I offered to plant *anything* that might live, but none of it would have tons of flowers and green leaves. Apparently Mr. Crawford told his wife, who was still out of state, that everything blooms here all the time and their yard was filled with flowers and trees."

"If there had been any way at all," Selena finished, "we would've shared that money. It would've made the Potting Shed's bottom line skyrocket for the month, too."

"It's just as well you didn't do it." Peggy put down the mail and picked up the phone. "It would've ended in disaster. And we all know he would've blamed us. So I guess we'll have to do something the old-fashioned way to remind our normal customers spring is closer than they think. Pull up the customer list on the computer, Selena. Let's come up with a sales flyer to send to everyone. By the way, I love your hair."

The younger woman smiled and fingered her new, shorter cut. "I was mostly trying to get that awful blue color out I put in over the summer when I went to that pool party. I'm thinking about going darker. Dark hair is really popular right now. What do you think?"

"I already told you what I think," Sam responded as he picked up a hundred pound bag of bulbs from the floor like it was a child's toy. "You don't have the coloring to go dark. Unless you're going to dye your lashes and brows. You'd just look spooky."

"Okay, Thor. Thanks." Selena turned to Peggy. "I meant what do *you* think?"

"I agree with Thor, I mean, Sam," Peggy replied with a laugh. "Sorry, honey. Let me make this phone call, and we'll talk." She dialed the number of one of their local distributors and ordered two fifty pound bags of Jerusalem artichokes.

Selena and Sam were still bickering about Selena's hair color when Peggy got off the phone. She ignored it. The two were good-natured, even when they disagreed. "Thanks for taking over for me, Selena. I feel like I haven't been home in a month. And I promised Steve I'd get Shakespeare from him before dinnertime."

"Not a problem, Peggy," Selena added. "But what do you *really* think about me going dark? I think I'd look good."

Peggy glanced at her. "There's only one way to find out. Do it. You can always change it back. It's only hair, after all."

"Thanks, Peggy." Selena smiled at Sam smugly. "At least *someone* has a brain around here!"

"Sam, can you drive me home?" Peggy asked him after they'd gone through a moment of glaring at each other.

"Sure." He shook his head. "Are you still working on changing the engine in your Rolls so it burns hydrogen? If not, maybe you should just get a hybrid car. It's not doing much good for the environment if you ride your bike to work then use our old truck to drive all over the city after you get here."

"I know that." Peggy shot him an irritated glance. "I'm working on it. Selena, please get that list together for me. This place is like a tomb. We have to get some of our shoppers interested in warm spring days and beautiful green plants. I'll see you tomorrow."

They went through the back door to the loading area behind the shop, and Sam asked, "And what are we going to do with all the Jerusalem artichokes? I already got four fifty pound bags in yesterday, and now you ordered more. Any ideas? Are we planting them in Founder's Hall?"

"They're very nice plants and a good way for patio growers to have sunflowers. They're also good to eat and good for you. And they aren't really Jerusalem artichokes, you know. They're calling them sunchokes right now. That's much nicer, isn't it?"

Sam started the truck. "I suppose. But that's still a lot of them. Do you have some plan you aren't sharing? Are you giving them away when a customer buys a *real* plant?"

"Don't be prejudiced," she scolded, buckling her seat belt. "The sunchokes will do very well. You'll see. People are always looking for something different. As long as we give it to them, they won't have to look anywhere else."

"You're the boss." He backed the truck out of the parking lot. "I just don't want to be eating them for the next year. I remember the first year the Potting Shed was open, and you ordered too many tulips. I got tulips for bonuses, my birthday, *and* Christmas."

"You worry too much." She smiled at him and patted his arm. "This is different."

They drove through thick evening traffic from the Potting Shed to Peggy's home on Queens Road in the heart of the city. As usual, there was never a break in conversation between them as they discussed Sam's notes about the shop.

Peggy noticed a problem with her Great Dane, Shakespeare, as soon as she got out of the truck. He had a crazed look in his eyes as he waited in the drive and almost knocked her down when he saw her. "What did you do to him?" she asked Steve as she absorbed the impact of the dog's body slamming into hers.

"He's the same unruly mutt you left behind." Steve kissed her and nuzzled her neck as he handed her the leash. "You smell great! I missed you. But as your veterinarian, I'd recommend obedience classes. Just because he's friendly and lovable doesn't mean he won't pull you down the street while you're holding his leash."

A thin layer of ice from that morning still varnished the sidewalk in her yard where the trees kept the sun from reaching the concrete. Peggy wasn't paying attention as she took the dog toward the house. Shakespeare saw a squirrel and pulled hard to the right as he investigated. Fully recovered from his abuse at the hands of his previous owner, the 140-pound dog almost dragged her into oncoming street traffic. She pulled him back but lost her footing and sat down hard on her butt right on Queens Road.

Shakespeare looked back at her with a goofy grin, his floppy, unclipped ears framing his massive face and black muzzle. He paused long enough to lick her face, then started back toward the house. The leash went with him. Fortunately, he sat down by the front door and waited for her, tail thumping the frosty ground.

Angry and bruised, suffering from several drivers' vented rage as cars swarmed around her, Peggy wasn't in the mood to be lenient or moved by his cute face. "You've become a monster. We're going to have to do something about this before you kill me."

"Are you okay?" Steve reached her side.

Sam hid a smile behind his hand as he grabbed the dog's leash to keep him from running any farther.

"I'm fine, thanks." Peggy brushed herself off while Sam opened the door and took the dog in the house. She didn't want to admit how bruised she already was from her long night in jail as she walked slowly into the house behind them.

Shakespeare galloped through the house to the kitchen and slid across the hardwood floors, waiting to be fed. She followed him past the thirty-foot blue spruce that grew in her foyer. "I have to do *something* with him."

"I'm not surprised. What did you have in mind?" Steve asked. "I know a man who works on a freighter who would be glad to have him. Or we could volunteer him to be the first Great Dane in space."

Peggy frowned. "That's *not* what I mean. I like having him here. I just don't want him to kill me. You've been preaching the gospel of obedience classes almost since I got him. I'm ready now. Where do I sign up?"

"I have a friend who gives classes. She's really good. You'll like her. She has a grooming salon over in the Ballantyne area, unless that's too far for you. I'm sure she could find time to help you with Shakespeare." He gave her the phone number. "Want me to go with you?"

"Thanks. But I think I can handle this. Selena will be at the shop in the morning. I'll give Rue Baker a call."

"You're not teaching tomorrow?"

"Not until the afternoon." She yawned. "Oh, sorry. I'm just exhausted."

"No wonder, after you had to elude the police *and* save the world." Sam laughed.

Steve glanced at her, then took a seat at the kitchen table.

"I was wondering why you were late. Anything you'd care to share?"

"Sure." Sam drew up a chair. "Picture these headlines: 'Peggy vs. the Police.'"

"Don't you have something to plant?" she asked him.

"Oh." He looked at the two of them. "I suppose you'd like some time alone, huh? Three days apart. That's a pretty long time. Even for you old folks."

"Sam!"

"Okay! Okay! I'm going. I'll see you later, Steve. I'll talk to you in the morning, Peggy."

Steve waited until Sam was gone, then got slowly to his feet. "How about some dinner?"

"I'm too tired to go out," she said. "Maybe tomorrow night."

He moved to the fridge and took out a covered tray of cheese and veggies. "I thought you might be. I have this, some salad, bread, and an excellent bottle of sauvignon blanc. I thought we could take it into the basement and picnic beside the pond while you work on your plants. I know you're not going to ignore *them* for a whole night after you've been gone."

"You think of everything." She smiled as she kissed him.

"And you can tell me what Sam was talking about."

"I don't think so."

"Oh, I think you'll talk." He opened a tray of mini éclairs.

"Brute!" She reached to grab one.

"Uh-uh. Start talking." He re-covered the dessert. "I can't wait to hear all about it."

THE NEXT MORNING, PEGGY ate her breakfast and read the paper while Shakespeare ate in another corner of the kitchen. She was just pouring herself another cup of coffee when her son knocked on the kitchen door. "Come in, Paul. I've got a cup of coffee left. Have you had breakfast?"

"You know me." He took off his regulation blue police jacket and hat, his thin frame appearing even narrower in the navy blue uniform. "I'm always hungry." He chafed his hands together. "It's cold out there. I thought it was supposed to be warming up."

"We still have some cold weather left. You need some gloves." She poured him the coffee and fished some powdered sugar donuts from the bread box. "Are you about to go on duty or just coming off?"

He sat down at the scrubbed wood table, tracing the tiny initials he'd carved into it as a child with his long, narrow fingers. Peggy gave him piano lessons when he was four with dreams of him being a concert pianist with those supple fingers. But Paul had other ideas. "About to go in. I thought I'd stop by and see how things are going. I would've stopped last night, but I thought Steve would probably want some time alone with you."

Peggy sat down opposite him. "You aren't still having trouble with the idea of Steve and me being together, are you?"

He shook his head as he sipped his coffee. "No. I like him, Mom. It was weird to begin with, but I'm handling it. I was trying to be considerate."

Her cinnamon-colored brow raised above one clear, green eye so like her son's. "Thank you. But you're always welcome here. I'm glad you came this morning."

He shoved a whole miniature donut into his mouth and kept talking. "I've been moonlighting. Mai and I have been seeing each other for a few months. We're thinking about getting a place together. We need some extra cash. I've been doing some side jobs they offered at the precinct. You know, directing the Bojangles' customers into the parking lot, doing some security work. That kind of thing."

"That's wonderful about you and Mai!" Since Peggy was the one who saw the initial attraction between Mai Sato, the young medical examiner's assistant, and her son, she was especially gratified. Not many people she thought *should* be together ended up together. She squeezed his cold hand across the table. "But you don't have to moonlight. I have some money. I'll be glad to help."

"We're almost set, Mom. Thanks anyway. I want to show

Mai how important this is to me. I've had a tough time convincing her to give up that little packing crate she calls an apartment."

Peggy was very proud of his attitude but didn't say so. She didn't want to sound *too* lofty. She was only recently on secure footing with her only son who had her fiery hair, temper, and independent spirit. After his father's death, they had some bad times together. Paul suddenly wanted to join the police department after studying to be an architect. She didn't want him to get hurt, especially since she suspected he was only interested in finding John's killer. "I just wanted to let you know I'm here if you need me."

"Thanks, Mom." Paul sipped his coffee with an awkward expression on his freckled face. "Anyway, we found a place on Providence Road. It's a little bungalow house. We're going to rent with an option to buy. Mai isn't so sure about the buying part. I asked her to marry me. She turned me down. She said she might reconsider after we live together and share stuff for a while."

Peggy nodded. *Smart girl.* "What kind of stuff?"

"Money. Dishes. Garbage. Dirty clothes. That kind of thing." He shrugged his shoulders under the Charlotte PD uniform and ran his hand across his short, spiky red hair. "I don't know why she doesn't trust me. I'm really in love with her. I don't think she feels the same about me, or she'd trust me, right?"

"Maybe she does." Peggy played devil's advocate. "Maybe she just wants to make sure there's more to it than that. There's a lot more than saying 'I love you' that goes into a relationship. Mai's smart to try it out before she buys it."

He looked stunned. "Most mothers don't want their sons to live with a woman without marrying her."

She waved her hand at him dismissively. "I'm not most mothers. And that was a hundred years ago! Things have changed since I was a girl. Just don't tell your grandparents. We'll never hear the end of it."

Paul ate the rest of the donuts and threw away the empty bag. "I think maybe Mai was married before or at least had a

serious relationship that went bad. She seems a little raw
about the whole idea. But this house will take care of all that.
She'll see I'm okay."

"I'm sure she will . . . *if* she's ready." Peggy smiled at her
handsome son. She hoped he wasn't being overconfident. It
sounded like he was moving too fast for Mai. If she wasn't
ready to commit to the relationship becoming more serious,
Paul would have to wait.

Maybe she'd see if Mai could meet her for lunch, and they
could talk. She knew the girl didn't have a close relationship
with her family. Maybe she needed a sounding board. Peggy
believed her relationship with her was strong enough to over-
look the fact that she was Paul's mother. She liked her whether
she decided to be with Paul or not. She hoped Mai felt the same.

"I guess I'm willing to take that chance." Paul kissed the
top of her head. "I have to get going. It's good to have you
back, Mom. Charlotte and I missed you."

The warm fuzzy that gave her lasted Peggy all the way
through the crowded city streets as Sam eluded icy patches on
the road.

Shakespeare was distracted by every child or bird he saw
along the way. She held him back from jumping at the window of the truck with an iron grip and the gruff voice she'd
used with Paul when he got in trouble as a child.

Interstate 77 was crowded as always. A large part of the
road was down to one lane as they came out of the metro area.
There were orange barrels and flashing signs everywhere
while traffic backed up. The sun was warm, melting away the
small amount of ice that had accumulated during the night. It
still gleamed in the bright light on the overpasses and railings,
but county trucks had spread plenty of slag on the road. No
accidents were causing this holdup.

"Weren't there any dog trainers closer than Ballantyne?"
Sam asked as they waited in traffic.

"I'm sure there are." Peggy glanced at him. "But Rue is
Steve's friend. I thought I'd give her a try. What's wrong with
you this morning anyway? You're like a possum with a sore
tail."

He sighed, his heavily muscled chest sagging. "I'm not sure how that possum part relates to my problem. But you're getting to be as bad as my mother. Unless it's me, and I just can't hide anything anymore."

"You're not a difficult person to understand, sweetie. Go ahead. Tell me what's wrong."

"I'm failing chemistry, and my dad is on my case. He says he's not paying a fortune for me to go to school if I bring home bad grades. Hunter never failed anything. Hunter *always* does the right thing."

Peggy didn't miss the mild rivalry he shared with his sister wrapped up in Sam's words. Hunter and Sam were both over-achievers, spurred on by their father. She'd met him once. He was one of those people who believed competition was good for children. "You aren't Hunter. But I think chemistry is an important part of premed. I'm sure he's just concerned about you. Why are you failing? You're brilliant! You certainly shouldn't be having problems this early in school anyway."

"I'm not anywhere near premed yet, Peggy," Sam declared with a rebellious snarl. "I might change my mind about being a doctor at all."

As if a messenger from heaven came down to deny Sam's words, a shaft of sunlight glinted off of a shiny chrome bumper on a burgundy Lincoln going up on the Interstate 485 ramp. It caught Peggy's eye, like a shooting star set against the clear blue sky.

The car should've slowed down on the sharp turn. It should've curved past the concrete rail. It didn't. She grasped Sam's arm as they watched the car careen off the hundred-foot-high overpass. "Oh my God!"

3

Flowering Dogwood

Botanical: *Cornus florida*
Family: Cornaceae
Common name: Virginia dogwood

The dogwood is a small tree native to the eastern United States. The root and bark were used by Native Americans to treat fever before quinine was available. The tree is steeped in Christian folklore about its use as the wood that made Jesus's cross. The sap is said to have magical properties that bring good luck.

SAM AND PEGGY WATCHED the car as it seemed to hover in the air for a moment, suspended by the forward thrust of the speed it was traveling. It happened so quickly, yet time seemed to slow down around it. Too quickly, the spell was broken. Like something from a nightmare, the car sailed down from the sky, hit the pavement, and rolled across the highway.

When they realized what happened, drivers jammed on their brakes to avoid the accident scene. Car horns sounded as several vehicles slammed into the cars in front of them. Angry drivers yelled and cursed from open windows. Nothing moved on the left side of the road going toward Charlotte, but traffic flowed freely in the right lanes going out of town.

"Pull over!" Peggy was already opening her door. Shakespeare started barking as Sam pulled off on the brown, grassy shoulder. She jumped out of the truck, pushing the Great Dane back as he tried to go with her. "Stay, Shakespeare!"

"Wait, Peggy! Where are you going?" Sam tried to call her back. "You're going to get killed out there." He tried to follow her, but cars whizzed by, honking their horns when they saw his door open. He watched her run through traffic, zigzagging to the tune of angry curses and blasting car horns. The first clear instant, he jumped out to follow her.

Once they saw the wreck, drivers in the three right lanes slowed down or stopped to point and gasp, bringing traffic to a crawl on that side as well. It made it easier for Peggy to cross the road. If traffic had been flowing as it usually did at seventy miles an hour or better, she might be injured or dead.

Not stopping to consider the matter, Peggy got to the left side of the mud and dodged the cars that were erratically trying to move around the steaming wreck before the police got there and shut everything down. Only a few close drivers actually *saw* the car come down from the ramp. Most were still trying to figure out what stopped their commute.

"Call 911," a man called out from one of the cars she passed. The back end of his car was smashed from the violent stop he made behind the car that fell from the ramp. There was a nasty red gash on his forehead.

"I will," she yelled back without stopping. "Stay where you are. Help will be here soon!" She pushed 911 on her cell phone and yelled at the dispatcher when she answered.

Peggy reached the wreck, heart pounding, breath frosting in the cold air. She couldn't see the car clearly on the overpass before it went down. It was just a blur of color and form. But something told her it wasn't a stranger who went over the ramp in front of her.

Intuition swamped her emotions. She *knew* someone she cared about was involved. There was no scientific proof to back her theory; until she looked at the new burgundy-colored Lincoln.

Even then her mind denied it, tried to negotiate with the truth. *There have to be hundreds of burgundy Lincolns in Charlotte. What are the chances this could happen?* Yet even as she clawed at the knowledge, she knew the truth: It was Park Lamonte's car.

Hundreds of pictures of her college friend flew through her mind like squalls passing over the ocean. He was funny. Sarcastic. Playing pranks like Sam. How many times had she told John back in those days she would've married Park if she hadn't met him first?

Then they graduated, and he went on to law school in Chapel Hill. They were still close for a time, arguing about right and wrong late into the night. Even later, their friendship endured. He was there when they came to tell her about John's death. He was there when they buried him.

It couldn't be Park. But she knew it was.

The car had come down nose first, then flipped over to rest on the roof after rolling a few yards. It was a miracle another car hadn't run right into it. Not that it mattered. The damage from the fall was extensive. Metal and plastic were crushed and wrenched into terrible shapes. Smoke came from the engine, but Peggy couldn't see any sign of fire yet. That was amazing, too. It seemed like the impact should've caused the car to explode. The cement was creased beneath it.

She lay down on the cold, wet pavement and looked in through the smashed driver's-side window. The opening was barely a few inches high. She prayed another miracle had occurred and he was still alive. "Park? Can you hear me?"

"Yes." He reached out a hand to touch the one she dared to slide through the shattered glass. "Peggy? Is that you?"

"Yes." Her voice was thick with tears she tried to hold back. She squeezed his hand, felt the warm blood oozing over the cold flesh. "Hold on. I hear help coming."

"That was quite a splash, huh?" He tried to laugh, but ended up making a gurgling noise in the back of his throat. "I don't know what happened. I think I fell asleep. One minute I was up there. Then the car was falling. It smashed down here. It was . . . awful."

"But you're still alive, Park. You're going to be all right."

"It never happened to me before," he continued, rambling, "but you were right when I saw you at the hotel. I've been sick. I guess that's why I fell asleep. Either that or too many carbs. You know what a sweet-eater I am. Beth always said it would be the death of me."

"It's all right." Peggy wished she could see his face, but the angle of the car and the damage done to it made it impossible. She wished they hadn't argued the last time she saw him. She prayed she had more time to make amends. "They'll come and get you out. You'll be fine. Just hold on a few more minutes."

"Tell Beth I love her."

"You'll be able to tell her yourself," she argued. "You're too mean and tough to die this way. Just don't let go. You'll be fine."

"I think my luck has run out this time." She heard him fight to draw a ragged breath. "I don't know how this happened. Beth made me get a checkup last month. The doctor said I was fine."

"I don't know, Park," she admitted. "I don't know how it happened either. We can find out later. The important thing is you're still here. You can make it through this. I'll stay with you until someone gets here who can help. Just squeeze my hand."

She felt him try to move. He was pulling at something, maybe the seat belt, trying to push himself out of the crushed driver's seat. Pieces of glass from the windshield rained down on the pavement as the car shook with his efforts. She clutched his hand, urging him not to move again. She didn't want to think about the damage already done to his body. Where were the paramedics?

"Can you get me out? I have to get out of here!" Park tried to push against the door that separated them. "For God's sake, Peggy, get me out of here! The car is going to catch fire!" His voice ended on a weak, terrible cry. "Peggy, help me, please!"

She sobbed. There was nothing she could do. Sam was beside her in the street. He put his hand on her shoulder. They could hear the paramedics getting closer; smell the strong exhaust fumes from the cars and trucks that passed them.

Peggy held Park's hand even when it went limp and he didn't respond to her calls. She didn't move away from the car. She wouldn't leave him. Tears froze on her face. Her knees ached from the cold, hard ground. She kept telling him to hold on, help was coming. He couldn't die this way.

The firemen, police, and paramedics finally arrived in a loud, busy stream. Sam helped Peggy to her feet as the rescue workers pushed toward them. She could barely hold herself up, numb from the cold. They moved out of the way and stood in the street while the police diverted traffic to the other lanes of the interstate.

The police officers asked about anyone being hit on the ground by the car. Sam told them he didn't see anyone. Peggy heard all of it as a dim fog formed around her brain. She watched as they tried to decide how to free Park from the wreck. Firemen took out the Jaws of Life and pried open the metal body of the Lincoln like a can of peas. Paramedics rushed in as soon as he was visible.

When she looked down, her hand was covered in his blood. Or her blood. She wasn't sure which. Did she cut herself putting her hand through the window? She knew it was too late when they pulled his mangled body from the car. A doctor, stopped in traffic by the accident, pronounced him dead a little after eleven a.m.

"Anything you can tell us about how this happened?" Highway Patrol officers joined the group working at the scene and started asking questions. "Where were you when the car came down?"

"We were in the southbound lane. We saw it happen like everyone else," Sam answered. "We're parked on the shoulder over there. We came over here to see if we could help."

"He was my friend." Peggy's voice wavered as she spoke. She was freezing inside and out. Shock was beginning to set in. Nothing the officer said made any sense to her. "I have to call his wife."

"We'll take care of that, Dr. Lee. You just take it easy, ma'am," the officer told her after getting her name and address from Sam when she didn't answer him. "Could you tell from what you saw if Mr. Lamonte skidded off the ramp? Was there ice up there?"

"We were too far away," she finally said, more to herself than him. "It didn't look like he tried to stop at all. The car flew past the barriers. He told me he fell asleep. It wasn't like him. But that's what he said."

She couldn't bear to have someone tell her this was his fault. It might come out that way later, but she'd feel more herself by then. At that moment, she felt consumed by the event. She turned away from the officer and tried to focus on something else. Park's car was squarely in front of her. She squeezed her eyes tightly closed.

"I appreciate your help, ma'am. We'll finish up here if you'd like to leave." The young patrolman smiled solicitously. He nodded to Sam and walked back toward other witnesses who were standing outside their cars with their arms wrapped around themselves as the icy wind rushed by.

Peggy stared at the wrecked car, not able to believe her friend was dead. Some crazy notion took hold of her half-functioning brain as she recalled they were supposed to have dinner Friday night. She'd have to call Park's wife, Beth, and cancel. Or would Beth call her?

Sam put his warm arm around her shoulder and urged her toward the truck, worry and emotion softening his voice. "Come on. Let's go. There's nothing else we can do here. Let's go back to the Potting Shed and get some tea."

Peggy didn't see the ambulance driver zip the black bag closed over Park's face. But she heard the sound. It shredded across her skin like a knife. She took a deep breath and held tightly to Sam's hand. "You're right. Thanks for staying with me. I'm ready now."

Shakespeare was barking and jumping in the cab of the truck. Sam had to push him down on the seat before he could get inside. He held the dog back so Peggy could open her door. The roar of traffic never ebbed. Horns blared and drivers shouted obscenities as they swerved away from them.

Even after they were safe in the warmth and quiet of the vehicle, Peggy could only stare out the window. She had no words to express the emotions smothering her. She wanted to make polite conversation with Sam. She could feel his anxious glances in her direction.

She got a Sani-Wipe out of her pocketbook and cleaned her hand as best she could. The glass hadn't cut her. But she couldn't force herself past the terrible blackness that wouldn't wipe away as easily as the blood.

They were back at the Potting Shed before she realized where they were. The trip was a blur of sound and color that had no meaning. She kept seeing Park's tired gray face at the hotel in Philadelphia as they argued about the estuary.

"Do you want me to take you home?" Sam's blue eyes were studying her face. He took her cold hands in his and chafed some warmth into them. "You don't have to be here right now. Selena and I can take care of everything. Keeley should be here soon, too."

She patted his hand and forced herself to smile and speak. "I'll be fine. I didn't mean to scare you. It was such a shock. But life goes on, doesn't it? I have to call Rue and let her know I'm not coming. Maybe she'll have another appointment open in the next few days."

"Okay." He scratched his head and opened the truck door. "Maybe it'll be better for you to be here instead of by yourself anyway. Would you like me to call Steve or Paul?"

"Of course not." She stared at him. "I'm fine. There's no reason to bother them. I just need a few minutes to pull myself together. I've known Park a long time. I think I'll go in and have some tea. Then I'll go see Beth."

Sam formally escorted her inside, helping her sit down in the rocking chair that always ended up being part of the seasonal scene they created. In this case, she found herself seated beside the snowman they made with white Styrofoam. There was a robin on his shoulder and crocuses blooming, purple and yellow, from the band of his hat. Underfoot was a white blanket that was supposed to simulate snow. Here and there multicolored plastic flowers bloomed, showing their customers spring was only a few weeks away.

After a brief whisper from Sam, Selena rushed to the Kozy Kettle for Peggy's favorite peach tea. She came back with a large cup of tea, some cookies, and Sofia. "I heard what happened." Emil's hearty blond wife crossed herself several times. "No one should have to die that way. It's like the time my uncle Georgio died after he was crushed by the boulder. Who knew it would roll down and kill him someday, eh?"

Peggy accepted the hot mug, warming her cold hands on it, grateful for the tea and Sofia's distraction. "Boulders falling on you is pretty tough to beat."

"I don't know." Sam shuddered. "I'm never going on another ramp. That was too much like a movie."

Selena put her arm around him and handed him a cup. "I got you some coffee. It has chocolate in it. That should make you feel better."

"I hate it that Park died that way. He was so alone. I know he wanted to see Beth and the boys again. There wasn't time." Peggy ignored the banter.

"Georgio at least got to say good-bye." Sofia shook her head. "Aunt Sarifina was in the house when it happened. She rushed outside to find him under the boulder."

Selena wiped a tear from the corner of her eye. "Poor Uncle Georgio and Aunt Sarifina. What did they say to each other?"

"She beat him in the head with her towel. It was the only part of him she could get to. She said, 'I told you to quit digging under that thing, didn't I? Idiot!' "

Selena rolled her eyes and walked away. Sam held his laughter until he was on the aisle with the fertilizer and mulch.

Sofia took Peggy's hand in hers. "You go through so much for your friends. If you need me, let me know. You could come and stay with us. God knows you should be with someone instead of rattling around in that big old house alone." She paused and narrowed her heavily made-up eyes. "Have you had your house appraised recently? My cousin is in real estate, you know. She could get you a good price."

Peggy almost choked on her tea. "Thank you, but I want to keep the house. I appreciate you coming over, Sofia. Thanks for the tea."

"Anytime. What are friends for, eh?"

When the other woman was gone, Selena left the front counter. "How can you sit there and listen to her? She's crazy!"

"She means well," Peggy told her. "And why did *you* tell her about the accident? You go over there every day for tea. She wouldn't have come if there wasn't anything interesting going on over here."

"You mean nothing she could relate a family story to?" Sam snorted. "She should write a book."

Selena shrugged. "I don't know. She looks at me with those crazy-person eyes, and I can't help it. She asked me what was wrong, and I *had* to tell her. It was creepy."

Sam brought a ripped bag of fertilizer up to the front with him. "Maybe you shouldn't go in there anymore, Selena. Or maybe you should wear dark glasses when you go. That way her 'crazy-person eyes' can't get you." He made extraterrestrial whirring noises and chased Selena around the store.

Peggy focused on their bickering to push herself back to reality. What happened to Park was no less real to her, too fresh in her mind to chase away. But this was real, too. This was life. This was what continued. Even when she was gone, life would still go on. "Selena, can you stay while I go and see Beth? I don't want her to be alone."

"I have some studying to do for a math exam. But the shop's been quiet. I can do it here." Selena glanced up at Sam's thunderous face as she finished. *"What?"*

"I only have one run to make." Sam mouthed the words, *Shut up! Don't remind her the shop has been slow! She feels bad enough already,* to Selena. "I have to take those orchids to the Millers for the party tonight. Then I'll be here, too. Want me to drive you over to Beth's when I get back?"

"That's fine, Selena. Thank you. And thanks anyway, Sam, but I'll take my bike." Peggy started to get up from the rocking chair. Selena and Sam rushed to take one of her hands and help her up. They were obviously overwrought as well. "I think I need some cold air in my face. I'm going to leave Shakespeare here since Beth has so many antiques in her house."

"I'll finish up that customer database when I get done studying," Selena promised, then tried to make up for her previous words. "I didn't mean the shop was going under or anything. I just meant it's slow. But it's always slow in February, right?"

"Pretty much." Peggy put her cup on the counter and realized she hadn't taken off her jacket since she came inside. "I'll talk to you later." She went to the restroom and switched on the light, mindful of them watching her. She remembered acting the same way when her grandmother was ill, before she died. Standing there watching her, wishing there was something she could do. Sam and Selena were like family to her.

The towelette from her pocketbook had cleaned most of her hand. She scrubbed her nails thoroughly with hot water and disinfectant soap, then looked at herself in the mirror. It always amazed her how the most terrible things could happen and never show up on a person's face. Oscar Wilde had the right idea in *The Picture of Dorian Gray*. It was like they all had portraits somewhere that absorbed life's impact.

Before she left, she picked up a small marjoram plant she'd potted weeks before. *Comfort and consolation.* It was all she had to offer Beth at this time.

The sun had already warmed the day when Peggy stepped outside into the courtyard. She unlocked her bicycle, tucked the plant into her satchel, and put on her gloves. Traffic was slow on College Street where Brevard Court and Latta Arcade fronted it. The wrought-iron gate that led into the courtyard was still wet from the melting ice. Not many people were in the shopping area yet. But even in winter, a warm sun and lunchtime brought out the office workers the downtown shops depended on.

Peggy turned her bicycle away from the downtown area and headed toward Myers Park, a well-to-do area of the city. The houses there weren't as grand as they were on Queens Road where she lived, but they were part of the classic heart of Charlotte.

Most were maintained as they were when they were built in the 1940s, still inhabited by lawyers, doctors, and other professionals. Park could have lived anywhere, but he chose to raise his children in the same neighborhood where he grew up.

Riding under the skeletal branches of the huge old oak trees that dotted tidy brick, fenced yards and provided shade in the hot summer, Peggy was struck by the ordinary atmosphere around her. The intense blue sky seemed the same. Mothers put their children into car seats in Volvo station wagons. An errant sprinkler sprayed diamond droplets of water on top of frost-browned grass. Everything seemed the same. Yet everything had changed.

Peggy walked her bike into Beth and Park's hushed front yard. The two-story redbrick house looked shuttered and dark. The sun had gone behind a cloud, making the house appear shadowed and sad. Had the police told Beth about Park yet? She would've called her friend first but didn't want to unknowingly be the bearer of terrible news. The great oaks stood sentinel around the house, a few scattered brown leaves from last fall fluttering in the cold breeze.

She stood outside for a long time looking at the years of work put into the carefully tailored yard. Park was one of the few people she knew who could still get two cars into his garage. Maybe it was because he was rarely home. Maybe he was that organized. She remembered visiting his office once with John. It was as trim and tidy as his house.

The holly and azalea bushes were neatly shaped into rows around the house. Not cut into boxes that looked ridiculous but nicely rounded. Large acorns littered the brown grass at her feet. Fat squirrels chased birds through the tree branches. In one corner of the house, sheltered from the harsh winter winds, a young dogwood was blooming. "Silly tree," she muttered, fingering the delicate white blossoms. "Don't you know we'll have more frost yet?"

A shaft of sunlight rested on the tender green leaves. That's what encouraged the tree to bloom too early. It happened frequently to Charlotte's ornamental pear and cherry tree population. Too much warm weather too early. The trees bloomed, gorgeous white and pink blossoms against the clear blue sky, then another shot of cold weather withered everything to brown. By the time real spring showed up, the trees had only green leaves to brag about.

The dogwood flowers meant *durability* in floriography. And the wood from the small trees was strong and flexible. *Like the area it's growing in.*

It was easy to lose herself in thoughts of her favorite things. But she still had to go inside. Peggy shook herself out of her cold misery and pushed her feet toward the front door. She was devastated by Park's death. But for Beth, it was the end of the life they'd had together. How well she remembered. The loss of dreams and hopes for the future was as awful as not having John beside her in bed every night. She had to be strong for Park's widow.

Peggy knew when she saw Beth's pale, tearstained face the police had done their job. She was relieved but felt guilty at her own cowardice.

Beth made a mewling noise in the back of her throat, then launched herself into Peggy's arms. "I can't believe he's dead," she sobbed. "I can't believe he's gone."

"Let's get inside," Peggy urged her out of the chilly breeze. "I think we'll need some tea."

Beth was pliable, unable to really take in what happened. Fortunately, her two sons, six-year-old Reddman and eight-year-old Foxx, were still at school. "Should I bring them home? I don't know what to do."

Peggy took the cheerful orange kettle off the stove and poured steaming water into two mugs. Immediately the scent of last year's lemon balm mixed with chamomile. She'd sent over a plentiful supply last fall. It was an abundant year for the herbs in her backyard. She knew Park and Beth both loved it. "The boys are fine for now. Take a moment for yourself. Once they get home, there'll be no end to everything. Drink this. It will help."

Beth slumped at the polished wood table. She sipped at the tea and raised empty eyes to her friend. "The sergeant from the Highway Patrol said you were there. He said you stayed with Park as long as you could."

Peggy wrapped her hands around the hot mug for warmth. "I was. I saw what happened. I was on my way south, just before the ramp."

"Tell me." Beth didn't look at her, focusing on the steam coming from the tea. "Tell me what happened."

"I'm sure the sergeant already told you." Peggy tried to convince her not to hear it again, even though she knew she'd

wanted to hear what happened to John more than once. It
seemed to make it more real.

"He did. I want to hear it from *you*. Please."

Peggy took a deep breath and told her everything she knew
about the accident. "I was there with him when he died."

"Good." Beth's sable brown head nodded. "At least he
wasn't alone or with some stranger, wondering what happened."

The silence between their words was as thick as the smell
of the herbs. A grandfather clock in the hallway chimed the
hour. One o'clock.

"Did he say anything?" Beth's brittle voice asked out of the
blanket of silence that enclosed them.

"Yes. He asked me to tell you he loved you and the boys."

"That was Park. Always thinking of us first."

"You were everything to him, especially after that first disaster." Peggy shuddered, thinking about Park's first attempt at
marriage. It only lasted two years, but he put himself through
hell with that woman. People said Beth was too young for him
when they married. She was fresh out of college, and he was
forty-two. But it worked for them.

"The police said he went off the overpass," Beth said carefully. "Was it icy up there? He was always such a good
driver."

Peggy put her hand over Beth's. "He told me he thought he
fell asleep. He said he woke up as the car hit the ground. He
said he'd been ill. Did you know about that?"

"That's hard to believe, isn't it? Park is always so alert. I've
never known him to fall asleep in the car. Most of the time, it's
all I can do to persuade him he needs sleep at all. You know
how he is. That's one of the things I love about him." Beth corrected herself in a flat voice. "Loved about him."

"I know. I thought it was odd, too. But when I saw him in
Philadelphia, he said he wasn't sleeping well, and he looked
ill." Peggy squeezed Beth's hand. "Do you think something
was wrong? Could he have been sick and didn't want to worry
you? He said you made him go to the doctor for a checkup."

Beth smiled slowly. "He's kind of a baby when it comes to

being sick. I'm always glad it doesn't happen often. Even a cold might be pneumonia to him. It's hard to imagine he could hide a serious illness. Besides, I saw the doctor's report. He was healthy."

"Did you notice him being more tired than usual after he came home?"

"No, not really. But he only got home late last night. Do you think something was wrong with him?"

Before Peggy could answer, the doorbell rang. Tears slipped down Beth's cheeks as she took out a lacy handkerchief. "I hate to ask, but I don't want to see anyone else right now. Could you get it?"

Peggy stood up and hugged her. "Not a problem. Shall I send whoever it is away? Have you called Isabelle or your family?"

"Not yet. Although I hope the police called Isabelle. I don't want to talk to Park's mother right now." Beth wiped the tears from her face. "But you know *her.* She won't come over here. I expect her to call me later when she thinks about the boys being here and Park being gone."

"Okay. Don't worry about a thing. I'll take care of it." Peggy smiled at her, then went to look out through the leaded glass embedded in the heavy front door. A large black man with a shaved head stood on the front step. She opened the door. "Al! I'm surprised to see you here!"

"Peggy." He nodded solemnly. "I heard you were there when Mr. Lamonte died this morning. I'm sorry for your loss. Is his wife at home?"

"Beth's here, But she's not in any kind of shape for visitors."

"I'm here in my official capacity." He took out his badge through force of habit. "There seems to be some question about Mr. Lamonte committing suicide on that ramp this morning. I need to speak with his wife."

4

Aspidistra

Botanical: *Aspidistra elatior*
Family: Lilaceae
Common name: Iron plant

*These houseplants grow slowly, but there is historical evidence of
them living close to hundred years! Popular in Victorian England,
they were once a symbol of middle-class respectability. They will
tolerate low light and careless gardening habits. In the language
of plants, Aspidistra means* fortitude.

"MY HUSBAND WOULD NEVER commit suicide." Beth's passionate condemnation of Al's suggestion left the police detective with an understanding and patient expression on his dark
face.

Peggy sat in the caramel and cream colored living room at
the front of the house with them. She offered to wait in the
kitchen for them, but Beth wanted her to stay. After hearing
Al's startling revelation, she was glad she obeyed her impulse
to come to the house. It was ridiculous to know Park and
imagine him committing suicide. She felt as strongly about it
as Beth did.

"No one ever expects a loved one to take his or her own
life," Al explained. He took out a small notebook from the inside pocket of his heavy coat. "Your husband suffered some

severe stock losses the last few years. Maybe that had something to do with his decision. Sometimes men get too worried
about taking care of their families. They opt to let them have
their life insurance. That way, they don't have to see them suffer."

"Life insurance?" Beth scoffed. "How could that *ever* replace him? Will money help my sons grow up without a father? Will it keep me from being alone? The idea is stupid and
irrational!"

"Desperate people do desperate things, Mrs. Lamonte. No
one else can understand what goes through a person's mind
when they think what they're doing is best for everyone.
Those are dark thoughts. Nothing *we'd* comprehend unless we
were in his state of mind. But maybe Park thought about those
things. Maybe that was what was in his mind this morning
when he went over the ramp. There's no way for you to know."

Beth glanced at Peggy with a growing expression of horror.
"Then there's certainly no way for *you* to know! Peggy, tell
him. Park *wouldn't* commit suicide. He was dedicated to his
family, but he wouldn't kill himself for any amount of money."

Peggy didn't know what to say. She knew what Al was getting at. After listening to John talk about suicides and accidents during his years as a police officer and later, a homicide
detective, she knew the psychology behind the difficult accusation. But it was unreal to her. Like everyone else who was
shocked by the death of a close friend or loved one, she
couldn't imagine it could be true.

But even though she knew Park well, she couldn't see inside his head. Neither could Beth. The analytical researcher in
her brain told her to remain objective, even though her heart
was crying out in pain. She still wanted to find some way to
prove it didn't happen the way Al was suggesting.

Maybe this would be a good time to tell him what Park
confided in her before he died. "He said he fell asleep at the
wheel. He was ill. I don't think he *meant* to kill himself. It just
happened. I'm sure it was an accident."

Al's red-rimmed brown eyes narrowed. "What makes you
think that?"

"I was with him for those few minutes before he died." Peggy told him what Park said and about her encounter with him in Philadelphia. "I think he was more sick than he realized. He seemed very tired."

"You know a predeath confidence weighs heavily with the department." He wrote down what she said in his notebook. "I take it you'd be willing to swear to this under oath?"

She nodded. "Beth's right about him, too. I've known him longer than I've known you. You knew him, too. He went to school with you and John, didn't he?"

Al squirmed a little on the caramel-colored sofa. "It's true we were both friends of John's, but Park and I barely knew each other, and *that* was years ago. You know how his parents were. They had a thing about him hobnobbing with us *poor* folk."

He didn't elaborate, but Peggy felt the words *black folk* hovering in the air between them. There was no excuse for it, but prejudice still lingered.

It was worse when Park, John, and Al were growing up in Charlotte. The city changed as people moved there from all parts of the world in the 1970s and 80s, bringing their cultures and traditions with them. But until then, it was a small, tightly closed environment.

"I understand. I guess you'll just have to take *our* word for it. He wasn't the type of man to give up that way. A few business losses wouldn't do that to him."

"I'd like to debate this issue, Peggy. But you know I can't. This is an ongoing investigation until we get some answers. Maybe if he fell asleep at the wheel, it would make sense there were no skid marks on the ramp. He didn't even *try* to stop. We always look into things like this, especially when a ten million dollar life insurance policy is involved."

Beth's slender hand went to her throat, and her brown eyes blinked almost comically. "Ten m-million dollars? Park never told me."

Al shrugged his big shoulders. "He planned well for you and your sons, Mrs. Lamonte. As soon as the insurance company was informed of his death, all the bells and whistles started up. A questionable death brings out the investigators on big policies. I just want to warn you."

"Will they do an autopsy on him?" Peggy asked.

"No!" Beth shook her head as she started to her feet. "No! It's bad enough. No autopsy."

Peggy understood what Beth was feeling, but counseled, "It's the only way to really know what happened to him. An autopsy could prove his death *wasn't* a suicide."

"No," Beth disagreed.

Al took a deep breath. "I'll do what I can, Mrs. Lamonte. But chances are the insurance company will insist. I'm sorry."

"Can they do that? Even though I forbid it? I'm his *wife*. Don't I have any recourse? Can I get a judge to issue a stay?"

"You'll have to ask your lawyer that question." He rolled to his feet. "I'd suggest you get one of Park's associates on board right away. I've worked cases like this. You'll need someone to advise you."

Beth was wild-eyed, bordering on hysteria. "Thank you, Detective. I appreciate your honesty. When Park's mother hears about this insurance policy, it's going to be a lot worse than any investigation. A lawyer can't protect me from *that*."

Al glanced at his notes, "You don't get along with Park's mother?"

"Does *anyone* get along with Isabelle Lamonte?" Beth's tone challenged him to deny her claim.

At that moment, Reddman and Foxx raced through the door, throwing aside their jackets and book bags and calling for their mother. Beth excused herself and went to talk to them while Peggy walked with Al to the front door.

"That isn't much to go on," she told him. "No skid marks, losing some money, and a big life insurance policy. If he fell asleep, he wouldn't have been able to hit the brakes. That's pretty simple. Everyone's lost money on stocks in the last few years. And I'd be more amazed if a man like Park *didn't* have a ten million dollar life insurance policy."

"You know I'm doing what Lieutenant Rimer tells me, and he just does what they tell him. We're all just cogs in the wheel. The life insurance company doesn't want to pay out that ten million dollars if they don't have to. You know better than most how it goes. Maybe you can help your friend." He chuckled. "Wish you could've seen the look on the lieutenant's face when he saw *your* name on the report! He said there was going to be trouble if you were involved. I'm afraid you solving that murder in your shop still rankles him a little."

Peggy frowned. "I help out with one little murder case and I'm branded for life."

"Looks like he was right anyway. You're here *and* there's trouble." Al checked the hallway behind her shoulder. "How well do you know Beth Lamonte?"

"Very well. I've known her since she married Park ten years ago." She stared at him. "Why do you ask?"

"She didn't like the idea of the autopsy, did she? Seems to me like most people would *want* to know the truth."

Peggy was more than a little impatient with what she thought he was suggesting. "A lot of people are sickened by the idea of their loved one being cut open. You *know* that. Don't go getting suspicious about this. I'm sure everything will come out in the wash. Park and Beth are good people. No one did anything wrong here unless you count working too hard."

"I hope you're right. I don't like making the suggestion that something could be wrong any more than you like hearing it. But you know how it is. Sometimes an innocent remark can make a red flag go up in my brain. I'm sure it happened to John, too. Doesn't mean it's always right." He sighed and hugged her. "I have to go. The lieutenant was good enough to send me out to talk to Isabelle Lamonte, too. I'm on my way there now. Lucky me. It's good to see you. Paul's been on his toes since he and Mai got together. They're good for each other. I'm really glad."

"I know. I'm so glad it's working out for them. I'm still hoping for grandchildren before I'm too old to enjoy them." She shuddered, thinking of Al's task ahead. "Good luck with Isabelle. You know, Park used to joke that his mother was the dragon queen. It didn't help when she got that dragon-head walking cane. I *always* think of her that way. I'll talk to you later. Say hello to Mary for me."

"I will. She's still waiting to find out what it's like being a *retired* detective's wife. How's it going with Steve? I assume the two of you are still together."

"As far as I know," she quipped. "I was on my way to get obedience classes for Shakespeare. Our relationship might hinge on whether or not Steve has to take care of him again the way he is."

Al laughed heartily. "I can imagine. The bigger the dog, the bigger the trouble."

When he was gone and the heavy front door closed behind him, Peggy heard the boys crying in the kitchen. Park was so close to them. Even though he was gone a lot, he never missed their important events. They were going to be devastated by his death.

She stood by the door awkwardly, not wanting to interrupt their grief. A large aspidistra was in a tall iron planter behind her. She took a few minutes to pull off some dead brown fronds. Really, it wasn't the best place for the plant. They liked warm, contained areas better. The door opening and closing let in too much cold air.

She finally went into the back of the house. Beth was hugging both boys to her as the three of them sobbed. It had to be one of the most heartrending things she'd ever seen. She wished she could scoop them all up in an embrace that would take away the pain. But nothing so simple would help them.

Knowing there was nothing she could do for them, she tidied up the kitchen. The same large gift basket she received at the hotel was at one end of the counter. It was open, most of the fruit spoiled. She was surprised Park kept it. She'd left hers at the hotel, since it was too big to take on the plane without being a nuisance. She pushed the open jar of jam and almost-empty jar of honey to the back of the cabinet and threw away the rotten fruit.

Looking around for something else to do, Peggy thought about Beth's parents. They lived in Salisbury, about an hour away. Beth was going to need them. Finding the number on the side of the refrigerator, Peggy gave them a call.

• • •

IT WAS AMAZING HOW quickly things could change. Park fell asleep and died on the interstate. Now the police were questioning his death. Could he have committed suicide? She was sure anything was possible. No one knew what was in his mind as he started across the overpass. But she didn't think he'd give up without a fight. It wasn't like him.

But Al could be right. She couldn't deny it, much as she wanted to. Maybe Park was afraid of a continued financial slide. No doubt he drove himself too hard chasing the almighty dollar. But he was very levelheaded, very calm. It seemed to her suicide would take a wild moment of insane passion. Maybe it happened that way. Then again, maybe the insurance company was capable of creating doubt in their minds, but it was only lack of sleep that pushed Park over the edge. She hoped the investigation would be quick, and the answer would be in Beth's favor.

"I sent the boys upstairs." Beth put her hand on Peggy's shoulder. "Thank you for staying and calling Mom and Dad. I know I'm going to need them. I think I'll call Alice and see if she can come over for a while, too. If I'm going to fight this suicide charge, I'm going to need all my concentration. I can't believe this is happening. Everything seemed so normal when I got up this morning."

Peggy agreed it was a good idea to call Alice, the part-time housekeeper and nanny. She was lucky Paul was an adult when John died. It was hard enough for an adult to understand when something like this happened. "You know I'll do anything I can to help."

"I know. You're so dear." Beth's brow knitted, and she stroked it with her shaking fingers. "He couldn't have done this. Not Park. He felt so strongly about suicide. You remember when his father died a few years back. He was in terrible pain. Park's mother thought they should help him die. She even said she knew a doctor who would help him. Park refused to do it. He hated that his father was in pain, but he believed suicide was wrong. He was tortured by not helping him. Isabelle never let him forget. Park wouldn't kill himself over *anything*."

"I'm sure you're right." Peggy didn't want to argue with her. There would no doubt be a full investigation. She believed the truth would come out. She hoped it was what Beth wanted to hear. "Just ignore everything and get you and the boys on an even keel. Let everyone else do their jobs. I'm glad Al thought about you calling a lawyer. Do you know someone?"

"Almost all of Park's friends are lawyers." Beth laughed. "That's one good thing about being married to one, I suppose. I'm sure one of them will be willing to help me."

Peggy waited there with Beth while family and friends began to filter into the house after hearing about Park's death. There was a shocked, stunned look to all their faces when she opened the front door. Whether they were thinking Park had committed suicide or just couldn't believe he was gone was impossible to say. When Beth's parents arrived, Peggy told her friend she'd be back later and left the crowded house.

She took a deep breath of fresh air, clean and sweet, after being closed in the house all day with so much grief. She was exhausted despite the fact that she hadn't really done any physical work. It would be less tiring to go out and plant a thousand tulip bulbs than stand by helplessly and watch death ruin someone else's life.

The weather was worse. Heavy clouds promised snow or sleet. Peggy pulled her coat closer and wrapped her scarf around her neck. It would be unusual for it to snow this month but not unheard of. Somehow it fit with what happened to Park. Snow was the ultimate concealer. It could hide a multitude of sins, changing a brown, drab landscape to a sparkling wonderland.

Let it snow, she prayed with her eyes closed. *Let it help all of us through this terrible time.*

"Margaret," a familiar voice hailed her.

There were only a few people who called her by her given name. Her mother wasn't there. It could only be . . . "Mrs. Lamonte." Peggy took a deep breath as she opened her eyes and faced her.

She knew most of what she felt about the older woman was still tinged with adolescent anger about the times Park's mother wouldn't let him do what he wanted. Parties she wouldn't let him go to. Friends she forbade him to see. It was stupid, really, and she needed to get over it. She and Park joked about it sometimes, but she couldn't keep holding it against the old woman. "I'm sorry we have to see each other at such a tragic time. I'm so sorry about Park's death."

The Dragon Queen looked down her long, straight nose. Her thin lips never came near a smile. Sallow cheeks, sunken in with age and disappointment, lent her face a look usually only accorded death masks. Her elegant black coat enfolded her emaciated body, hiding the skin barely covering bone from view. But the black made her look even more like an evil caricature of a witch. "Never mind all that fine sentiment. Where's his wife?"

"If you mean Beth, she's inside." *Okay. Maybe not all of what she felt about Isabelle was left over from her college days.* "Her parents are here with her and the boys."

"Who else would I mean? Don't be obtuse, girl."

Peggy took a deep breath. She knew Isabelle was suffering. Park was her only child. But she was suffering, too. She didn't want to put up with this woman's rude attitude more than she had to. "I was just leaving. Please let me know if there's anything I can do." She ended their conversation curtly and started to walk away.

"The police visited me," Isabelle called after her. "He didn't commit suicide, you know. That's unacceptable. My son wasn't made that way. I raised him better than that. Talk to your husband. Have him explain to the police."

"I'd be happy to do that if it were possible," Peggy assured her. "But John was killed a few years back. There's not much I can do."

Without a word of sympathy for her loss, Isabelle Lamonte brushed her aside. "You're no good to me then. Might as well go home. Take all those regrets with you. No use for them."

Peggy watched the haughty old woman go into the house after a sharp rap at the door with her ivory-headed cane. Everyone who knew Park well sympathized with him over his mother.

Old newspapers from the 1940s showed a different side to the woman. Peggy had seen some of them once when she was helping John clean out the attic.

During that time, Isabelle was the reigning queen of society in Charlotte. She married Park's father, a prominent lawyer who took over his father's prosperous law firm. They built a life for themselves in Myers Park with their large, showpiece house where they entertained important people from government and the arts. Isabelle was beautiful back then, but there was a harshness to her eyes and mouth even in the black-and-white photos.

After Park's father died in the 1970s, Isabelle mostly kept to herself. She occasionally surfaced to manipulate her son or some other family member. She was behind Park's failed marriage to Cindy Walker, a protégé of hers, as well as his attempt to run for city council. Mother and son were never close, but after those failures, they became even more distant. Peggy actually found herself feeling sorry for the Dragon Queen when she saw her from time to time around the city. It couldn't be easy living her lonely life.

Unlocking her bike, Peggy got ready for the long, cold trip back to the Potting Shed. There were times when she wasn't sure if her commitment to the environment was worth another long ride home. Especially in the winter. But she supposed it was as good for her health to ride the bike as it was for the Carolina blue sky.

A green Saturn Vue pulled up at the end of the drive, and a big, sloppy smile spread across her face. Steve rolled down the car window and grinned at her. "Need a ride?"

"Not really. My bike is fine." She was joking, of course. She was disgustingly happy to see him. Steve Newsome had become very important to her in a very short time.

The grin faded from his handsome face. "I came all this way so you wouldn't have to ride back after everything that happened today." He opened the car door and started around the back of the Vue. "You *have* to come with me. You don't have any choice. The ozone can handle this trip."

She laughed. "I was just kidding. Thank you for coming. It's been a terrible day." She grabbed him and hugged him tight, planting a large kiss on his cool lips right in front of all of Myers Park. Her mother would swoon to see it. A lady never kissed a gentleman in public.

"That's more like it." He kissed her back, then took the bike from her and put it in the cargo space alongside cat carriers and bags of dog food, all tools of his profession. "I'm sorry about your friend. Sam told me when I called. I hate that you had to be there when it happened. Would you like to talk about it?"

"I don't know what to say. I'm not sorry I was there." She walked around to the passenger side. "I'm glad I was there with him when he died. But I know I'll see that car going over the guardrail for the rest of my life. I *knew* it was him. I don't know how. I can't explain it. There are only about a thousand burgundy Lincolns in this town. But I *knew*."

He got in the warm car and covered her hand with one of his. "I'm sure he was glad you were there, too. I know it had to be terrible for you. If there's anything I can do, you know I'm here. Feel free to call me anytime you see the car going over the rail again. I'm sorry I couldn't be there with you."

She leaned over and kissed him again, looking into his clear brown eyes that she thought were so ordinary when she first met him. Why had she thought that? He was the most extraordinary person she knew! "Thank you. I'm really glad you're in my life."

"Coincidentally, so am I!" He glanced at the house. "How's his wife doing?"

"As well as she can." She told him about the police considering Park's death a suicide. "She didn't need that right now. Not that anyone ever does. Why does everything have to be so complicated?"

"You don't think it's possible?"

"Not really." She shrugged, wishing she could be more definite. "But I don't know. John used to tell me people will do anything if they're pushed. He saw some terrible things happen to good people. I don't know all the details yet. But maybe Park was in a bad place. Maybe he felt this was his only way out. I won't believe it until someone proves it to me,

Steve. And I hope it's not true for Beth's sake. It's not just the insurance money either. There's the stigma she'd have to live with and the unanswered questions."

"You're right. No one should have to ask those questions." Steve shook himself free of the events that hung over them both like the dismal turn the weather had taken. "I guess we'll all have to hope for the best. That's all we can do anyway. So. Where are we going now?"

"I need to go back to the shop and close up. Shakespeare is still there, too."

"I got a call from Rue when you didn't show up." He turned right and started down Providence Road. "She was worried about you. I told her what happened."

"I totally forgot about that! Thanks for covering for me. I'll call her back and see if I can reschedule." She glanced at him. "How did you know?"

"Sam told me when I called the shop."

Peggy sighed and shook her head. "I'm sorry he bothered you with this."

"*Bothered* me?" There was a slight edge to his tone. "You're an important part of my life, Peggy. This was a major happening in *your* life. I don't think letting me know would classify as *bothering* me."

She could tell he was a little riled up over being left out. She hadn't thought of it that way. "I'm sorry. It's still very new sharing these things with you. I've been alone for a while. That's my only excuse. And I guess I really didn't want to let on to Sam about how upset I was. Sometimes they treat me like I'm made of china!"

"Okay. As long as you weren't excluding me because you thought *I* couldn't take it. I called the shop to see if you wanted to have dinner tonight. Sam told me what happened. I wish *you* would've called me."

"I know. I promise from now on when really terrible things happen to me, you'll be the first to know."

"Good thing. You know what magazines say men are like when they get their feelings hurt. You don't want to take one of those compatibility tests or anything, right?"

She laughed. "Not right now. But if your offer for dinner is still good, I'd like to do that after we drop Shakespeare off."

"Sounds good to me. I'll help you get the shop closed up."

But when they got to the shop, it was more cleanup than close up. Selena had locked the front door and gone into the back storage area for a few minutes to help a customer load some peat moss. When she came back, Shakespeare had ripped open a few dozen bags of potting soil and dragged them across the old wood floor.

Selena didn't realize she was playing his game as she chased him across the shop, spreading the mess everywhere as planters, pots, and gardening implements fell down in their wake. She grabbed him around the neck and tried to wrestle him to the floor. Shakespeare thought it was a new game. He rolled with her still holding on to him through the spring garden scene.

That's where Peggy came in. "What in the world happened here?"

Selena looked up from under the demolished snowman. "It was a dog quake. I tried to stop it, but it was at least a seven on the canine scale."

Steve picked up a shovel lying across Shakespeare's back. The dog looked up and wagged his tail. "Don't try to get on my good side. I'm the one you dragged through the holly bush the other day."

"We have got to get you those obedience classes." Peggy frowned at the dog.

He whined and hid his head in his massive paws.

"Bad dog!"

They cleaned up the mess and took Selena home first after they left the shop. Dinner ended up at Steve's house. Peggy didn't want to go out. Besides being exhausted mentally and physically, she didn't want to talk to anyone else yet about her experience with Park. The cocoon wouldn't last long; only one night. Then the media would have done its job, and everyone would know. But she knew she'd be able to handle it better tomorrow.

Feeling a little like another Southern woman who thought

she could handle everything better tomorrow, she apologized to Steve for not being better company when he finally took her home. "Maybe you should've let me find my way back without you. All you got for your trouble was a mess at the shop and a lot of silence from me."

He kissed her good night at her door and told her it didn't matter. "I love being with you no matter what. Besides, someday I might need you to be there for me. That's what having a relationship is all about, right?"

"Right. Thank you. I'll talk to you tomorrow." Neither one of them were surprised when she didn't invite him in out of the cold night. Peggy watched the headlights from his SUV fade into the darkness.

She let herself in the house and dragged herself up the curving marble staircase to her bedroom. Shakespeare followed. He jumped on the bed beside her, wagging his tail and waiting for her to complete her nightly ritual of washing her face and putting on her nightclothes before he settled down.

The house was familiar and quiet around her. The sounds from the old furnace in the basement reassured her as she closed her eyes, wishing she could shut out the world so easily. Even the prospect of visiting her botanical experiments couldn't rouse any interest or excitement. She lay under the heavy green comforter, with her arm across Shakespeare's neck, crying. People, good people, died too soon.

Park's death brought back all the old memories of losing John. She wasn't prepared for them, thought they were behind her. But they rose again like terrible specters haunting her, chasing her through the night.

She finally realized she wasn't going to sleep that night. Her hand hovered over the phone as she thought about calling Steve. Shaking her head, she got up, changed clothes, and splashed some cold water in her face. "You'd better get a grip, Margaret Anne. This isn't going to help anyone. Especially not *you*!" She studied her red-eyed, blotchy-faced reflection in the mirror over the bathroom sink. "I don't think you want to see Steve looking like *this*! Let's go take care of the plants."

5

Lenten Rose

Botanical: *Helleborus niger*
Family: Ranunculaceae
Common name: Christmas rose

Also known as virgin's mantle. It is said to be good for breaking spells and curses and should be planted near the front door to prevent evildoing from entering the house. It was used in the seventeenth century as a treatment for insanity and depression.

Not to be confused with lady's mantle, helleborus is poisonous.

IN THE BASEMENT WORKSHOP of her turn-of-the-century home, Peggy kept a botanist's laboratory with various experiments going year-round. A large frame of strawberries was in full bloom under the strategically timed grow lights. She checked her notes. It was in these early stages as the plants started making fruit that they needed help. Slugs, white flies, and other pests looked at the feast and got ready to munch.

Her ideas about introducing herbal remedies, including sprays and complementary plantings of mint and borage, hadn't worked. The fruit ended up tasting like the herb. Her friend at Broadway Farms, who grew two acres of pick-your-own strawberries, tried companion planting to draw the insects and birds to other plants. But the insects were too focused on the juicy red fruit to pay any attention. At the same time, he didn't want his berries to taste or smell like garlic or other strong, natural repellents. It wouldn't matter if the insects stayed away; so would his customers.

They'd taken care of the slug problem by putting diatomaceous earth around the plants. The rough edges kept the snails away by snagging on their slimy little bodies the same way ashes or crushed glass work for many home gardeners. A snail won't cross anything too rough, or its body will tear and it will die. They seemed to understand and stayed away.

For the insect problem, she was working with some different theories from a few colleagues in California. They managed to solve the problem with specially bred "good" insects. These insects were handpicked for their voracious appetites. They ate the offending thrips and mites in massive numbers.

Her friend at Broadway was a little skeptical. Peggy told him she'd test the idea on plants in her lab. Since he was dedicated to using only organic means to protect his fruit, she believed this might work for him. The proof would be in the next few days. The berries on her plants were large, red, and juicy. Yesterday, she dumped some spider mites and thrips on her healthy plants and told them to do their worst. Tomorrow, she'd have the pleasant task of dumping lacewings and ladybugs on the plants to see what their effect would be.

Her friend couldn't use most pests' worst enemy, birds, since they were also his enemy. But if the lacewings and ladybugs worked, he could encourage them to stay with small plates of water and a little shelter from the sun and rain among his plants. That way they'd be less likely to run away when they'd eaten the thrips and mites.

In a normal strawberry garden, she'd tell the owner to encourage the ecosystem this way. Peggy's experiment in her home was limited by a cover to protect the rest of her plants in the lab and by the tiny space she had to work. But if the lacewings and ladybugs did their job here, they'd be effective in the field as well.

Another experiment was in the large pond. The filtration

system hummed as recycled water circulated through the six-by-eight-foot tank. Her showy water lilies from Longwood were still there but in a dormant cycle now. She was working instead with some rice plants, helping a colleague from the University of Louisiana to develop a heartier form of rice.

More than half of the world's population was dependent on the crop for their existence. Certain blights and colder weather had reduced the amount of crop worldwide. If they could get the plants to yield larger amounts of rice in more difficult growing conditions, it would be a boon to everyone.

Her rice paddy, a very recent addition to the pond, was maturing nicely. The fine green shoots were sprouting toward the light source. Some koi she'd introduced were swimming through them and taking a right turn at the tangled water lily roots.

Somehow she'd managed to get a few frog eggs in the mix. They must have been on one of the plants. She thought she got them all out until one night when the sound of a large bullfrog caught her attention, almost startling her into the pond.

He was seated on the edge of the pond, staring right at her as she leaned into the water to plant the rice. She didn't have the heart to put him out in the cold where he'd die, but she promised him a ticket to the backyard when spring arrived.

She sighed, wet and cold after checking her experiments. But she felt more like herself. She didn't bother going back upstairs. Most of the night was gone anyway. Instead, she sat in an old chair she kept in the basement and pored over her well-worn garden catalogues. Almost every page was marked with her wants and needs. Mostly wants. Shakespeare yawned at her feet but was still for a while.

She was thinking about acquiring a piece of land to start a fruit orchard. Fruit trees did well in the area, everything from peaches and cherries to apples and pears. It would give a whole other dimension to her work. The basement of the ancestral Lee home was huge but not large enough for trees. Her backyard was filled with hundred-year-old oaks whose thick branches would keep smaller trees from growing. She wasn't sure where the money would come from yet for the undertaking. It was probably just a pipe dream, but she liked planning it in her mind on nights like this.

She was placing a sentimental order tonight. John had loved sunflowers. He'd talked several times about planting the entire backyard with them. Only Peggy's assertion that they wouldn't grow well under the old oaks kept him from his dream. That and taking away his chain saw! It made her smile to think he'd actually cut those ten-foot tree circumferences. He loved the old trees as much as she did. Still, he yearned for a sunflower garden.

When she was approached to help out with the community garden Darmus Appleby's Feed America group planned for Charlotte in the spring, she went out and bought a hundred pound bag of sunflower seeds. She was having a plaque made up to dedicate that part of the two-acre edible garden to John. She knew it would make her cry when she saw the golden flower heads turned toward the sun, but it would also help her keep his memory alive.

Sometimes in her rush to go on with her life after her thirty-year marriage came to an abrupt, terrifying end, she worried John would be forgotten. It wasn't just Steve or the changes she made to her life or resuming normal routines she'd had before his death. It was realizing she could only *really* remember his face when she looked at a photo of him. He was so dear to her. How was that possible?

Shakespeare got up, stretched, and whined. Peggy glanced at her watch. It was seven a.m. She noticed the gray morning light spilling into the basement from the French doors that led into the backyard. "You're right," she told the dog. "It's time to go out and face the world again."

She barely finished showering when the phone rang. Shakespeare had already been out for his walk. He was at the bedroom door waiting to be fed. Every time she moved, he jumped up and started down the stairs, only to come back, disappointed, when she didn't follow. "Take it easy! I don't get ready as fast as you do. The food will still be there!" She patted his head and turned off the shower.

Peggy wrapped her heavy white chenille robe around herself, shivering a little in the chilly morning air. The furnace kept the basement warm but always had a difficult time reaching into the master bath and bedroom, even though she kept the other eight bedrooms closed off.

It was part of the price she paid for living in a rambling old house that had seen better days. Not that she'd think of moving. John's family hinted occasionally that they'd like to pass the house to the next in line to inherit. Unfortunately, it wouldn't be Paul. The Lee family had the house set in trust for the oldest son in the family. John's brother, Edward, had a son who would live in the house after her. Legally, it was hers until she died or couldn't live there anymore for whatever reason. The young and impatient Lees were just going to have to wait.

"Hello?" She finally, breathlessly, answered the phone. She sat down on the bed to dry her hair.

"Peggy? Can you come over?" It was Beth. Her voice was strained and filled with sobs. "I need your help. Can you come over right away?"

Peggy glanced at her watch. She had an early botany class at Queens University that morning. She might be able to switch classes with another professor if someone could cover for her at the Potting Shed that afternoon. Selena was such a dear. She didn't want to abuse her willingness to help. But this was a difficult time. "I just got out of the shower. I'll be there as soon as I can."

"Thanks." Beth hung up without another word of explanation.

There was a wealth of relief and gratitude in her shaky voice. Peggy knew it was the right thing to do, even if it was a tricky balance of time on her part. She wrapped the thick white towel around her shoulder-length hair and started punching numbers.

WARM, DESPITE THE CHILL, in a heavy autumn tweed sweater and brown pants, Peggy rapped on Beth's door about an hour later. She'd maneuvered her schedule, dried her hair, settled Shakespeare, and called a taxi. No time to waste pumping her way on her bike that morning.

While she was waiting for her ride, she glanced in on her experiment in converting John's father's Rolls to a hydrogen-burning vehicle. It was a work in progress, hampered now by the cold weather. But she'd already been at it for almost a year. The Rolls was always at the bottom of the list. She looked at a few of the new hybrid cars but couldn't bring herself to buy one. She horrified the salesperson by telling him how inadequate the vehicle was, particularly for the exaggerated price. So she humbled her principles and constantly promised herself to get the job done.

Between her part-time professorship at Queens and a growing customer base at the shop, she could scarcely find time to turn around. She was retired from teaching when John died, but financial concerns about setting up the shop drove her back to her twenty-year career. As the Potting Shed surged forward in sales, she knew the time was coming that she'd have to give up her teaching again just to remain sane.

"Thank God you're here!" Beth opened the door and dragged her into the house. She took Peggy in the kitchen and poured some orange spice tea into two heavy glass mugs. "I thought you'd never get here. I never knew a night could be so long."

"I'm sorry I couldn't be here sooner." Peggy took a mug and looked embarrassed when her stomach growled loudly. In her rush to get out of the house, she forgot to feed herself and Shakespeare. Poor dog. A victim of her haste. She silently promised him an extra dog biscuit when she finally got home.

"I have some muffins." Beth shrugged and offered the box from Harris Teeter. "Someone brought them last night. Everybody brought food, of course. Isn't that what we do when people die? It's a strange custom, isn't it?"

Peggy took a blueberry muffin, warm red spots on her cheeks. Beth must've heard her stomach growl. That probably shouldn't embarrass her. It should've been left behind in her proper childhood with always wearing gloves on Sunday. But some things never changed.

She glanced around the cluttered kitchen. There were baskets of fruit and boxes of food everywhere. Casserole dishes and cake plates littered the counters. Beth was right. In the South, at least, the response to death was a smorgasbord of food. "Thanks. This is good. I was in such a hurry to get here, I forgot to eat. I guess people don't know what else to do to express their grief. Food is pretty basic. We either forget it or overdo it."

"I guess." Beth sat down at the table with her but forgot her own mug of tea on the stove and had to go back for it. "Peggy, the police called me this morning and told me their *official* report is going to be that Park committed suicide. The insurance investigator already left Charlotte. That's how sure *they* are. I don't even have the funeral planned, but the report says that Park committed suicide because of some *money*. What kind of investigation is that? How can they know what happened so quickly? I don't understand."

Peggy sipped her tea to cover her sympathy for Beth's problem as she let the other woman rant about the unfairness of the process. She didn't believe Park committed suicide either, but if the police and insurance investigation proved otherwise, there wasn't much anyone could say. "I'm so sorry. Maybe you could appeal it."

"I plan to," Beth assured her. "I'm not going to let them get away with this."

"I wish there was something I could do to help."

"There is!" Beth's drastically stricken face turned hopeful as she slapped her hand on the table. "You found out what happened to the man who died in your shop last year. You have to find out what *really* happened to Park. Did he fall asleep? Was he ill? There has to be *some* way for you to prove it wasn't suicide."

Peggy scrambled to regroup. What could she say? She wasn't *actually* volunteering. Polite phrases could get you into trouble with a desperate person. She had to be more careful what she said in the future. She smiled and tried to find a tactful way to say no. "I'm not a private investigator, Beth. I wouldn't know where to start. Maybe you should hire someone. Maybe one of Park's friends would have some idea."

Beth pushed back her chair with a sudden screech on the wood floor. Her long dark hair was braided but showed signs of her sleeping on it, little dark hairs poking up through the smooth twists. Her eyes were circled with black shadows. "You were Park's *friend*. He needs you now. No one else wants to do anything. No one wants to help him. They all sympathize and pat my hand, but they won't really help. I don't know what you did to prove who killed the man in your shop. But whatever it was, you need to do it now for Park and me. For Reddman and Foxx. Don't let him die like this."

Peggy was surprised by her outburst. Of course, her friend wasn't herself. She didn't really know what she was saying. Still, her heart twisted in pain at Beth's words. Park was always there when she needed him. There was very little she wouldn't have done for him in return. She wanted to help.

But this wasn't something she could do. Mark Warner's death at the Potting Shed was one thing. It was a fluke, a one-time event that wouldn't happen again. "I'm sorry, Beth. I don't know what to say. I don't know what to do to prove that Park didn't commit suicide. There has to be someone better qualified than me. The appeals process is there for a reason, too. You'll be able to get help there."

Beth strode to the stove and threw her cup of tea into the sink. The fragrant tea splashed everywhere, showering the room with the orange herbal scent. The cup shattered in the sink, pieces crashing to the floor. "Then I guess that's it. Park is a suicide. He killed himself because he lost a few thousand dollars. That's what *everyone* will think. That's the legacy he'll leave his sons. He deserves better."

Peggy's hands were shaking as she got up from the chair. "I'm sorry. I wish there was something *else* I could do. Something I'm qualified to do."

"So do I."

It seemed so final, so devastating. Peggy felt she should leave. There was nothing more to say. In time, Beth would understand. The pain and rage would fade. Their friendship was strong enough to handle this. "Let me know if I can help with anything else."

"I will," Beth promised in a whisper, but she didn't look at her. "I'm sorry, Peggy. I don't know what I'm thinking right now."

"I know. I'll give you a call later."

Peggy was numb as she got in the taxi to go to the shop. She supposed she could understand Beth's desperation. How would she have felt if John had been accused of committing suicide? She wanted to help. But what she did after Mark Warner was killed in her shop was purely dumb luck. She didn't think she could do it again if she tried. Besides, that was different. Maybe Park didn't kill himself. She didn't believe he did. But this wasn't a murder. There were no real answers to find.

Fortunately, shop traffic was light that morning. It gave her time to think about everything that had happened. She couldn't close her eyes without seeing Park's car going over the edge of the ramp. Sometimes the sheer horror of it made her physically ill. She knew it would pass in time. At least Beth didn't have to deal with that part.

The weather cleared as it neared lunchtime. Workers in the downtown buildings spilled out into the sunlight like little seedlings turning toward the warmth. A break in the weather was always good for business.

Latta Arcade swelled with people who spilled out into Brevard Court behind it. The sun was magnified inside the restored 1915 shopping area by the high skylight roof used originally for the grading of cotton. Now filled with shops and restaurants, it was natural to extend the area to include the outdoor courtyard.

The Potting Shed, an urban gardener's paradise, was set on the corner of the courtyard across from the Kozy Kettle Tea and Coffee Emporium and beside Anthony's Caribbean Café. Office managers in stiletto heels and Ann Taylor suits browsed through catalogs and ordered faux antique garden implements, seeds, and even professional help in setting up their gardens. It was the only store of its kind in uptown Charlotte.

Peggy was grateful for the patronage of the workers as well as the contracts she received to care for plants in the office buildings they worked in. The Potting Shed also did special orders for parties as well as outdoor landscaping. It kept everyone who worked for her busy. She wished John could've seen it.

But at least he'd seen his son grow to manhood. A luxury Park was denied.

Guilt gnawed at her. She knew there wasn't anything she could do to help Park's family. It didn't keep her from *wanting* to help. She thought about it while she waited on customers and straightened shelves. Beth was right, of course. The so-called investigation was stingy. How could they possibly know what happened on the ramp that morning so quickly?

Keeley Prinz, the daughter of Peggy's best friend, Lenore, came in to work early. A tall, dark, and handsome combination of Lenore and her husband, Keeley was as nice as she was gorgeous. When Peggy explained what happened, the younger woman was outraged. "I can't believe she asked you that! What was she thinking? What were *you* supposed to do?"

Peggy rang up the sale for the *Helleborus* mix Keeley was boxing up. Also known as the Lenten rose, it was good for adding color to the late winter and early spring landscape. "It was hard knowing what to say. Of course, I wanted to help her. But I wouldn't know where to start."

The customer, a new member of the growing uptown condo dwellers, took in their words and waited for an opening. "Peggy? You said these will flower in the shade, too, right? Because I have a shaded area underneath the eaves on my balcony where I need some color."

"No problem." Peggy smiled at her. "These little plants are hearty, and they like the shade as well as the sun. They should bloom for you. If they don't, let me know, and I'll come by and take a look at them."

"Thanks." She knitted her brow as she put her hand on her

hip. "And Keeley's right. Your friend may be grieving, but she had no right to ask you to go through that again. You aren't a police officer or a private detective. I'm sure she'll come to see that later."

Peggy glanced at Keeley. That's what she got for discussing her private matters in public. At least she hadn't mentioned Beth's name. "Thanks. You're right."

"Damn straight. You take care of all of us here. We don't need you traipsing around solving murders all over the place. You're our plant lady. Everyone calls you that."

Plant lady. There were worse names. Peggy thanked her again but didn't tell her it wasn't another murder. The woman, she didn't even know her name because she'd only been in a few times and paid cash for her purchases, didn't need any more information. She could just see the headlines in the *Charlotte Observer:* "Plant Lady Solves Suicide." The police would *love* that!

Keeley giggled as the customer left the shop with her Lenten roses. "That was strange! Guess you have to be careful what you say. You never know who might be listening."

Peggy agreed as she went to help another customer choose a lighted fountain for his backyard. He wanted something with a light sensor so it wouldn't come on until he got home from work and would go off in the morning. There wasn't anything like that in the shop, but she found one in a new catalogue, and he ordered it. She took his payment for the fountain as he bought a new Christmas cactus for his office.

"A friend of mine has one of these," he said as he admired the red-rimmed leaves and inch-long pink flowers on the plant. "She says she barely does anything to it, and it still flowers. That's for me!"

"That's right," Peggy assured him. "They're good little show plants. Water them when they get dry, but be sure they have good drainage. They don't like their feet to stay wet. Then fertilize once a year, and you should be set."

"Thanks." He picked up the plant and tucked away his wallet. "I tried a poinsettia, but it was too much work. I ended up killing it. But the ladies like a man who has plants, you know?

When should my fountain be in?"

"About two weeks, probably. But I'll give you a call as soon as it gets here. We can deliver it if you don't have time to come and get it." She glanced at his catalogue order. "Whatever works for you, Mr. Burnette."

"I'll let you know when you let me know." He grinned at her. "Thanks."

Peggy watched him walk out of the shop. Keeley watched her watching him and nudged her. "Come *on*! He's not all that much. Steve's much cuter. You've got a good thing going with him. Don't be checking out the competition!"

"It's not that." Peggy shook her head, feeling as if she'd seen a ghost. "That was the man who took Mark Warner's place at Bank of America."

Keeley whistled through her teeth. "Really? Small world, huh?"

They split up again to help other customers. Peggy couldn't help ruminating over the appearance of a dead man's replacement in the Potting Shed. She was a scientist by profession but a gardener in her heart. Working in the fields with her father as she was growing up, she heard many strange tales of omens and apparitions. They were part of the Low Country lifestyle in the Charleston area.

Everyone in her family, even her very proper mother, believed things could happen that foretold the future. A pregnant cousin once saw a man lose his leg in a combine accident. Her child was born three months later with one short leg. The rest of the family agreed the combine accident was an omen.

Was the appearance of Mark Warner's successor an omen? Was it telling her she needed to do as Beth asked? It sounded ridiculous. She didn't mention it to Keeley. No one else who wasn't raised as she was would understand.

It didn't help that Beth's words continued to eat at Peggy's conscience as she worked. She knew she wasn't responsible for the accident that killed Park. She certainly wasn't responsible for the insurance company deciding to call his death a suicide. But was there something she could do to help? Before Mark Warner's death in her shop, she probably hadn't thought she could solve a murder either. Yet that's exactly what she did. With a little help from her friends, of course.

What would John do if he were alive? How would he respond to Beth's call for help? It wasn't an easy question. He was a police detective. He had thirty years' experience investigating circumstances that didn't seem right. She had thirty years' listening to him talk when he *could* talk about his cases. That hardly qualified her to investigate Park's death. She was probably foolish to let Beth's words bother her.

The lunch hour went quickly. Many workers couldn't take their orders with them, so they either arranged for delivery or planned to come back. The sunlight seemed to have inspired spring in many winter-weary breasts. If sales continued at that pace, she wouldn't have to worry. Her profit margin would sail into spring.

But a few years' business experience had taught her better safe than sorry. She sent out the sales circulars to all of her customers. She fully intended to retire from her work at Queens once the shop was secure. She always kept that goal in mind.

Keeley stepped out for a well-deserved break as the rush slowed to a trickle. Peggy planned to leave when she came back. She had to stop by her house to feed and walk Shakespeare, then teach the afternoon class she'd exchanged with her friend at the university.

She was organizing a new shipment of vegetable seeds in a display when a hoarse voice took her by surprise. "You're somewhat of an expert on flower lore, aren't you, Margaret?"

Peggy turned to face Isabelle Lamonte. The old matriarch was dressed in her usual black. The sunlight streaming through the tall windows facing the courtyard drew harsh lines in her face. "I've dabbled in it. Is there something I can help you with?"

Park's mother looked around on the smooth tongue-and-groove wood floor. "Where was that man killed? I remember! He was facedown in a basket of anemones. Was he right here? I read all about it in the newspaper. What made you decide to investigate his death?"

"I'm not sure," Peggy answered cautiously. She wanted to

ask: *Why are you here? You've never come in before.* "I suppose it was because he was in my shop, and an innocent man was accused of killing him."

"Suppose you found him lying in a field of orange lilies." The older woman tested her knowledge of flower lore with a superior smugness to her thin lips. "What would you think then?"

Peggy considered the question, wishing Isabelle would get to the point. She gave her the creeps. It was childish. But true. "I suppose I'd think someone hated him. Isn't that what an orange lily symbolizes in the language of flowers? Disdain. Hatred. False pride."

"Exactly." The old woman's head nodded stiffly. "Park might as well have died in a field of orange lilies, Margaret. He was killed just as cruelly."

"I *saw* him die, Mrs. Lamonte. He told me he fell asleep at the wheel. No one killed him." She picked up a small forget-me-not plant in a delft blue china pot. "Please let me give this to you. For the memories you have of him."

Isabelle pushed the plant away. "*She* did it. As surely as if she stabbed him in the heart. And that's what I intend to tell the police."

"What?" Peggy stared at her. "Are you talking about Beth? The police know how he died. They aren't going to believe she had anything to do with an accident witnessed by a hundred people. She was nowhere near that ramp."

"Nevertheless." Isabelle turned toward the door with all the magnificence of the Dragon Queen she was in Peggy's mind.

"Why are you telling me this?"

"Why?" The Dragon Queen turned to stare back at her. "Because Park was your friend before he was *her* husband. If you have any compassion in your soul, you will go to the police and tell them he wanted you to investigate his death. You should tell them it was his dying wish."

6

Aster

Botanical: *Aster*
Family: Asteraceae
Common name: Wild aster

Also called starwort. Aster means "star" in Latin, referring to the shape of the tiny flowers in the wild. The flower was once placed on the grave of French soldiers, as a tribute to their bravery in battle. Burning aster flowers was believed to keep snakes away.

PEGGY KNEW NOTHING ON earth was going to make her go to the police and say anything else about the accident. She stared blankly into Isabelle's harsh face. Losing her son must have snapped her mind. She felt sorry for her but wouldn't indulge in her madness.

On the other hand, if Isabelle went to the police and told them she suspected foul play in Park's death, Peggy knew they would have no choice but to investigate. It would be fruitless for the police to continue to look into his death, and it would be horrible for Beth and the boys.

She considered that Isabelle didn't know about the suicide verdict. Without a stitch of remorse for the old lady's sensibilities, believing that hurting Isabelle would spare others a mountain of agony, Peggy told her about the insurance company's decision.

"At least *she* won't get the money."

Peggy stared at her. "You *know* about that?"

"I do." Isabelle's eyes narrowed. "You don't believe Park killed himself, do you?"

"No, of course not." Peggy put her hands into her pockets and tried to imagine how Isabelle was privy to the insurance information. "I can't imagine him giving up on life. But that's what they decided. Let it alone, Mrs. Lamonte. You can't bring him back by hurting anyone else."

"Let's not worry about such nonsense. We have to cut to the bone, Margaret. We have to help the police find Park's killer before *she* gets away with it."

Sighing over the same entreaty from Beth that morning, she agreed. In order to protect her friend from any more grief, Peggy promised to talk with the police about the possibility of Beth killing Park. It was stupid, the rambling imagination of a woman consumed by anger and sorrow. But if it would keep Isabelle from going to the police, it would be worth it. She just wouldn't say *when* she'd do it. "Let me handle it. I know what to say. Does that satisfy you?"

Isabelle considered her silently, leaning on the dragon-head cane with clawlike hands swaddled in black gloves. "It does. You've always been an honorable woman, Margaret. Thank you for helping my son. I'll expect to hear from you in the next few days. If not, I'll go to the police myself."

Peggy nodded, wondering what she'd got herself into this time. If nothing else, she supposed, she bought Beth a few days to have Park's body released and get the funeral arrangements settled. "All right."

Without saying good-bye, Isabelle limped from the Potting Shed, letting Peggy close the door behind her. A gust of freezing air blew the robin off the snowman's hat as it chilled Peggy's soul. Not that it seemed to have any effect on what happened, but how *had* the Dragon Queen known about the ten million dollar insurance policy? Gossip was rife in the small community, but that information didn't seem as interesting as who was sleeping with who. Beth certainly wouldn't have told her.

She needed to talk to Al. Maybe he'd agree to put on a show for Isabelle. If she were placated, she might leave Beth alone. If not, a homicide investigation would add more darkness to an already black time.

Peggy took a moment to call him before she left the shop. He wasn't in, of course, and she had to leave him a voice mail. It was probably farfetched to think Al would help her fool Isabelle about Park's death, but it was worth a try. He could also think the charge was worth looking into. That was a chance she had to take.

When Keeley came back after her break, Peggy called a few companies for more stock. There was a run on dinner plate asters after an article in the gardening section of the newspaper about the beautiful flowers. People couldn't get enough of them to plant for the summer. She went ahead and asked for another bag of dahlias and Jerusalem artichokes at the same time. Business was picking up!

Peggy wanted to call a taxi to take her home since the weather was freezing and the sky was threatening some kind of precipitation at any moment, but she decided to brave the elements at the bus stop. She waited alone at the corner in the gloomy half twilight that encompassed the afternoon streets. Ice gathered on the bench where she sat and hung like frozen tears from the streetlight above her.

She gritted her teeth when the bus finally got there half an hour late in a puff of black diesel smoke. How could anyone feel that was better for the environment? She climbed on board and rode silently through the almost deserted Charlotte streets.

At home, she shivered as she let herself in the door, dragging her mail with her. Ice coated her jacket and hat just as it glazed anything that kept still outside for too long. As she was shaking them off, Shakespeare's loud harrumphs started in the kitchen and finally ended in the foyer with him running into her. She gripped the edge of the table near the door to keep from being knocked over. It reminded her that she needed to call Rue and make another appointment! This was too much dog to run wild!

There were two messages on her answering machine. One was from Paul, warning her there might be snow or ice that night. She sighed as she deleted it. He was a sweet boy, but she wasn't quite as frail or out of it as he seemed to think. She'd managed to raise him and work for years. But thinking about Isabelle, she supposed it was a nice thing to have someone worry about her.

The other message was from Sam. A shipment of spider plants was lost in transit. The plants were scheduled to be put in place at eight of the Handy Finance buildings around Charlotte the next day. It was a big contract for the Potting Shed and a lot of money over the next three years. Sam was worried about making a bad impression on their first job.

Peggy called the distributor, got a firm date for the new delivery, then called her contact at the finance Company to apologize and reschedule. The woman didn't seem fazed by the news at all. She thanked Peggy for calling and noted the new date for setup.

Sam was out when she called him back, so she left him a message. It was always something. A hundred different contracts meant a hundred different problems. Shipments were late or didn't come at all. Wrong plants or dead plants were delivered and couldn't be used. If they'd managed to get the contract for the new uptown arena, it would've been worse. Their bid was too high on the arena for the new Charlotte basketball team, the Bobcats, but they *did* get the contract on the new mall.

Despite the problems, Peggy knew she had to keep pushing if she wanted to retire from teaching. It probably wouldn't happen this year, but her plan called for her to be done with the university in the next five years. The Bobcats' arena would've helped make that dream a reality. But the mall was a nice step forward.

She glanced at her mail on the floor after the emergency was dealt with. It would happen sooner or later. She loved teaching, but she felt like she was spread too thin. She didn't want to do a bad job at either Queens or the shop. She only wanted to be sure it was possible to support herself by spending all her time at the Potting Shed. Sometimes it seemed too good to be true. Most people her age were thinking about retiring to a nice community where they could learn to dance and do woodworking. She supposed the Potting Shed was her retirement. Although woodworking sounded interesting, too.

After some hot soup and a cup of her own cold-preventing tea mixture—dandelion, astralagus, and lemon balm—she sorted through her mail and put in another call to Al. His line was busy, but she left a message to call her on the cell phone. She walked Shakespeare without mishap by tugging hard on the leash and threatening him. All the normal aspects of her life that she took for granted every day.

She thought about Isabelle, trapped in a cold world of her own making in that big, dark, empty house. She held herself aloof from being involved with her family while Park was alive. With him gone, she was completely isolated. It was better to have Paul call to remind her of the ordinary things than to be that alone.

Dressed in warmer clothes, Peggy went out again. It seemed ridiculous to call a taxi for a few blocks, and the city buses were unreliable, especially in bad weather. The sky was more ominous, but the freezing rain had stopped. She rode her bike through the slushy city streets toward the university. The storm was still closing in on the city. Headlights and streetlights were already turned on at three p.m., illuminating the gloom.

She realized as she saw the nearly empty parking lot that there might not be many students to teach, although most of them lived close by or on campus. But the school hadn't closed down yet. Classes were still scheduled. She assumed she had one to teach.

A young man passed her, leaving the main campus as she was arriving. He looked familiar even with his head down against the wind and a large black scarf bundled around his neck. It wasn't until she passed him that she realized where she'd seen him last. It was the scraggly young man in the red T-shirt from Philadelphia.

Peggy looked back around the corner of the redbrick building when she realized, but he was gone. She was *sure* it was the same person. What was he doing in Charlotte? Was there an environmental event she didn't know about? Her friend, Darmus Appleby, usually gave her a call when anything was set. She didn't always participate, but she gave a donation when she couldn't give her time.

"There you are, Peggy!" Maurice Dillman was waiting for her at the double doors. "I was wondering if you'd make it."

"Did you see that young man who went out just before I got here?" she asked him.

"I haven't seen anyone but you for the last ten minutes."

Peggy didn't press the point, even though she was curious. The young man she recognized could've come from anywhere on the campus. She thanked Dr. Dillman for trading class times with her as they walked inside. He was eager to get home and out of the weather. "Watch out," he warned as he bundled up inside the faculty lounge. "They don't like to close down until they have to. I dismiss class early if I think it's bad enough. I might be from Boston, but I get off the Charlotte streets if there's bad weather. There are maniacs out there!"

Peggy laughed to herself at his response. She'd lived in Charlotte for thirty years after being raised on the mossy, sun-baked shores of the Atlantic Ocean. They never had snow or ice along the coast. But she'd loved the icy crystals since the first morning she saw them outside her window.

As for driving, there were maniacs everywhere. The people in Charlotte weren't as confident or prepared as their colder neighbors when it came to bad weather. But they managed. Everyone bought plenty of bread, milk, and junk food and stayed inside until the storm cleared. It was the perfect thing to do in the cold.

Dr. Dillman's first year biology class was waiting restlessly for her. She looked at his planner and followed his instructions for the class.

It was difficult for the students to concentrate on what they were doing as the darkness settled in outside like a thick blanket around them. Glances out the wide windows for any sign of accumulating snow or ice made normal class procedure difficult. When they finally got through the reproductive cycles of a fruit fly, a large sigh went up from the class.

That's when the first snowflake hit the window followed by a flurry of white that began to cover the cold streets. "It's snowing!" an eighteen-year-old student exclaimed with all the joy of a ten-year-old. They all looked toward the front of the classroom to see what Peggy's response would be.

Before she could comment on the weather, class was over. She dismissed her students, reminding them to read their textbook. She gathered her books and coat for the trek home when the classroom was empty. The local weather channel was calling for six inches of snow overnight when she got to the cafeteria for a cup of coffee. So much for no snow in February!

Already classes and other activities were being canceled around the city. That much snow would paralyze Charlotte. It wasn't so much that the county wouldn't send out plows and salt the streets. Most people were afraid to drive on the stuff, knowing if everyone stayed in their homes, snow days became unofficial holidays.

Keeley called to say she was closing the shop early. Peggy agreed and thanked her as she got ready to leave the school. She almost walked into Al as she came around the corner talking on her cell phone. She told Keeley to be careful going home and put her phone away. "Thanks for coming over," she said to him. "You could've called, you know."

"I could've," he agreed. "But this is a pretty serious accusation from Mrs. Lamonte Senior. Think there's any coffee left in the cafeteria?"

"There's at least something hot and dark that resembles it," she joked, taking his arm as they walked. So much for her plan to keep the Dragon Queen away from the police. "Let's go down and check it out."

"So what can you tell me about Park Lamonte that I don't already know?"

Peggy sipped her hot apple cinnamon tea as she watched

the other people in the cafeteria standing at the windows looking at the snow. It was coming down fast and hard, big flakes
whitening the leaden sky. "I don't think what you need to
know involves Park. It's more what I can tell you about Isabelle."

"Whatever you can tell me might be helpful. Lieutenant
Rimer doesn't think much of her accusation against Lamonte's wife, but you know we have to follow up." Al slurped
his coffee, then opened the package of shortbread cookies he
bought from a vending machine near the door.

"I'm surprised Jonas wanted you to get me involved any
more than I already am." She glanced at him. "He doesn't
know you're here, does he?"

"No, ma'am." Al dunked his stale cookie into his coffee.
"But since you seem to know the family so well, I thought you
might have some answers."

"I'll do the best I can."

"We thought the wife didn't play a part in his death since
she was nowhere near the ramp when it happened. I can't
imagine Beth Lamonte climbing around under her husband's
Lincoln and cutting the brake line or anything. But she
could've paid someone, I suppose."

"Didn't the insurance company check to see if the car was
tampered with?"

Al shook his head. "They checked. But the car is in bad
shape. They're pretty thorough. But not like the ME on a murder case."

Peggy nodded. "What about the autopsy?"

"Despite the grieving widow's objections, the ME will be
doing *that* over again, too." He looked up from his coffee. "I
told you I thought it was kind of strange when she first said
she didn't want to have it done. Always trust your instincts."

"Your instincts are *wrong* in this case," she snapped. "Beth
had nothing to do with this. Isabelle *never* liked her. Beth
wasn't from one of the 'right' families. Isabelle didn't want
Park to marry her. Her people come from somewhere in
Iredell County. Just a bunch of poor farmers. But Park fell in
love with her. His first marriage was a disaster, even though

his mother handpicked the woman. He was disinclined to listen to her when she told him Beth wasn't good enough. There's always been bad blood between them."

Al nodded as he sipped his coffee and ate his cookies. "That's pretty much what I was thinking. Isabelle Lamonte gives anybody who doesn't have a pedigree a hard time. Especially if they came near Park. The lieutenant doesn't realize how things have always been with her."

"It's difficult to explain something like that to someone who hasn't experienced it," she sympathized. "I don't know if my agreeing with you makes your job any easier, but I think you're right about Isabelle." Peggy told him about the Dragon Queen's demand that she tell the police the same thing.

"So the old lady doesn't really have anything concrete against the wife. She knew we'd have to check it out if she questioned it. And there'll be a full investigation from her vague accusation. Especially in this case. Park was pretty famous around here. The DA likes to see well-to-do lawyers who are county commission wannabes rest in peace. But he wants to make sure we don't have to go back and dig up the body."

"It's such a shame about Isabelle. I don't know what she'll do without Park. He was her whole life. She doesn't care much for the children. They're too noisy and messy, you know. She still had dreams of Park running for governor. They argued about it since he was never all that political."

"Unlike his father," Al reminisced. "The old man ran for everything, didn't he? Only problem was, he was still stuck back in the Civil War era. He couldn't understand that people were different. I remember listening to one of his speeches when I was in college. I wondered why someone didn't tell him that times change."

Peggy smiled. "He was a firebrand though, wasn't he? He didn't know what he was talking about, but it didn't matter. He was like a live wire when he got up in front of people."

Al scratched his head. "You might have some fond memory of him, but I was scared somebody might listen to him. According to Park Senior, my kind didn't belong in college.

We belonged behind a mule plowing the back forty. That man was crazy."

"I agree with you." She patted his hand and sat back in her chair. "Isn't it lucky people are smarter nowadays? So what happens now? Has what I said made any difference?"

He shrugged. "I don't know what to tell you, Peggy. We'll go through the investigation. We *have* to. Maybe it will make me feel better about the younger Mrs. Lamonte. I don't know. I just get this feeling she's trying to hide something."

"Gut feeling." She nodded with a smile, recalling how many times John told her his hunches. How many times was he right? She *knew* Al was wrong about Beth. "What will you tell Isabelle?"

"When it's all over, we'll send her an official letter telling her what we found. It might still be a suicide."

"I don't believe that's true either," she disagreed. "Park wasn't the kind of person to kill himself. Beth's right about that."

"Are you saying you think he was killed by his wife?"

"Are those my only two choices? Couldn't it have been an accident? They seem to happen to other people all the time."

"I don't know. The insurance company believes there would have been skid marks on the ramp if Lamonte *wasn't* trying to kill himself. He lost a lot of money the last two years, and the law firm his grandfather founded has taken some hits. One of his friends told an investigator he was 'slightly unbalanced' over those things as well as some problems at home. Know anything about trouble at home?"

"No! And that's hogwash!" Peggy said. "He couldn't stop the car if he fell asleep and didn't wake up until he hit the pavement. As to the other things . . ."

"There may be a lot of mitigating factors you don't understand, Peggy. I'm sorry about your friend. But the case is pretty much closed as far as the insurance company is concerned. His wife can appeal it, and I'd encourage her to do so. Those guys were in and out of here pretty fast. In the meantime, we have to get through this accusation from the elder Mrs. Lamonte."

She was frustrated by his answer. "That doesn't make much sense. I think the insurance company just didn't want to pay off on a multimillion dollar policy."

Al pushed himself to his feet. "I think you're right, for what it's worth. There wasn't a suicide note. He was in a little financial trouble but not as bad as the insurance company made it out to be. I'd like to think it was just a terrible accident, and everyone wants to find someone they can to blame for it, too. I guess we'll see."

She made a snorting sound as she tossed away her paper cup. "Such is the state of society. You can't even have a decent insurance policy without people thinking you killed yourself for it."

"See? I can't please you." He chuckled and glanced out the window at the snow-whitened landscape. "Let it go, Peggy. It'll work out one way or the other. I'm sure the family is all right without the money. Can I give you a lift home?"

Angry with the protocol, not the man, Peggy took him up on his offer. They drove carefully through the streets filled with cars rushing to get home. The wet Carolina snow made the branches of the oaks that lined Queens Road hang down low enough to scrape the tops of trucks that went by. There was already a layer of ice coating the snow that made the street slippery.

Al stopped twice to help drivers who skidded off the road. One of them he called in as an accident since the Honda slammed into the side of a parked Toyota. Watching him help people in the street brought back fond memories of John doing the same thing. Sometimes she was impatient with him when stopping to help made them late for a party or some other function. It was funny how time and sorrow could change frustration to a loving memory.

She got out quickly when Al finally pulled his Ford Explorer into her drive. He helped her get the bike out of the back. They could hear Shakespeare's excited barking inside the house, followed by the sound of something crashing and breaking. "Sounds like that dog of yours is going crazy in there."

"He's having some adjustment issues." Peggy winced as something else crashed.

Al laughed. "Is that what they call it now? My mom called it an 'outside' dog. See you later, Peggy. Stay warm. I'll let you know what happens with the Lamonte case. Thanks for talking to me."

"You're welcome. I know none of this is your fault. I hope I didn't sound that way. Thanks for the ride. I won't ask you to stay since I know Mary is probably waiting at home for you with hot chocolate."

"You got it." He grinned as the snow covered the top of his brown knit hat. "The kind with the little marshmallows, too. Take care. I'll talk to you later."

Peggy let herself in the house. Shakespeare had managed to pull down a set of front drapes that were from the original decorator of the house as well as break a Dave the Slave pottery jug her mother gave her for her wedding. "I think you might need more than obedience classes when my mother finds out you broke an eighty thousand dollar piece of pottery. Go lie down! Bad dog!"

She was trying to rehang the pale green drapes when the doorbell rang. It was Steve, his arms full of plastic shopping bags. "I just got back. I'm loaded up with munchies, tear-jerker movies, and batteries for the flashlight. I thought we could hide from the storm together. You have plenty of fireplaces, and all of yours work, presumably. None of mine can draw smoke. The contractor says they need cleaning out."

"Hello to you, too! You've made your case." Her smile was huge as she took a few of the white plastic bags from him and rummaged through them. "White chocolate cheesecake and what DVD is this, hmm, *Ghost*? I *love* Patrick Swayze! You know the way to a woman's heart."

"They always say that about men. That thing about the way to a man's heart being through his stomach? But I know it's true about women, too." He produced a container of dipping chocolate and a quart of strawberries. "I tried to think of everything." He followed her through the trail of debris toward the kitchen to stow the goodies. "Looks like Shakespeare has been playing with your china."

"Let's not talk about him right now. It will ruin my mellow mood." She put the strawberries into the refrigerator, and he put his arms around her. She turned around and kissed him. "I hope I have something to eat for dinner, or we're just going to be eating a lot of junk food all night."

"That's what bad weather is for. You're from the South. You know that. Who wants to eat what's good for them on a night like this?" He kissed her. "I don't care anyway. I've got you to keep me warm."

"That and my working fireplaces, right?"

"Those were just an excuse." He kissed her neck and nipped at her ear. "I just needed you to let me in the front door. I knew I could convince you of anything after that. You'd be putty in my hands once you saw cheesecake and the right movie."

She laughed as she enjoyed his warmth. "How nicely cliché of you! You sound a little like a vampire."

"A goody-bearing vampire," he reminded her as he lightly bit her neck. "Not the nasty, bloodsucking kind."

Shakespeare started barking and running toward the kitchen door. "He's been so crazy since I got back," Peggy complained. "I thought he'd settle down by now. I hope the obedience classes help him. Otherwise my insurance agent might demand I get rid of him." She told Steve about the broken pot.

His eyes widened with amazement. "Are you kidding me? Eighty thousand dollars for an old jug? Was it made out of gold? Why didn't you keep it in a safe?"

A knock on the door startled them both. "Well at least he seems to be a good watchdog. He knew someone was out there before we did." Peggy went to answer it, ignoring his questions. How did one explain the value of a pot, hand-thrown by a poetry-writing slave two hundred years ago, if it wasn't transparent to the other person?

"Was that the old brown jug by the front door? What kind of jug costs that much money?" Steve demanded, following her. "I mean, did it have gemstones in it or something?"

Peggy had her hand on the doorknob when it opened. "The

door was unlocked," Paul explained with a frown, seeing the surprised expression on her face. "You should keep this door locked. If you won't set the alarm system, you could at least lock the doors. Oh. Hi, Steve. How's it going?"

"Hello Paul. How are you?" None of Steve's disappointment at not spending the evening alone with Peggy showed in his face.

"Fine, thanks." Peggy's son took off his jacket and rubbed his cold hands together. "I thought I'd come over and see how things are going, Mom. I didn't know you had company. I probably shouldn't stay. You probably want to be alone, huh?"

"Company?" She laughed. "Don't be silly! It's just Steve. We were about to have some snacks. It would be wonderful if you could stay."

"And watch a movie about vampires." Steve's eyebrows went up and down suggestively at Peggy behind Paul's back.

"Sounds great!" Paul looked at them both. "I haven't had dinner yet. Are you sure there's enough for me?"

An instant of silence was immediately followed by assurances that he was welcome to join them. Peggy smiled at Steve. He shrugged and smiled back at her as Paul told them about his day. There would be another time for the two of them to be alone.

"I'm glad you're off duty so you don't have to deal with the accidents that will pile up tonight." Peggy looked around for something that *could* be dinner. She needed to shop, something she hadn't done since getting back from Pennsylvania. "Al stopped for a couple of them on the way back from Queens this evening."

"What was he doing at Queens?" Paul asked as he helped himself to an overripe banana from the basket on the table.

She absently explained about what happened earlier in the day with Isabelle, her mind on other things. There was some leftover rice in the refrigerator. If she added some peppers and eggs, that might be enough for a meal. Where were those Bojangles' biscuits she brought home?

"Between you being at the accident scene when Lamonte died and his mother asking you to go to the police, that puts you in the middle, doesn't it?" Steve said as he helped her with the rice.

"I suppose so. Al seemed to think so anyway. But there wasn't much I could tell him." She glanced up at Paul, who was looking at her strangely. "Is something wrong? Have you stopped eating rice?"

"That's pretty weird. I was lucky to get out of the precinct when I did," Paul explained as he helped himself to a piece of cheesecake from the refrigerator. "The news about Mrs. Lamonte was coming in just as I was leaving. Five more minutes and I'd still be there. Between the weather and the unexplained death, everyone who was there will be held up all night. They called Mai in five minutes after I left."

Peggy quit rummaging for biscuits. "What about Beth? What happened?"

"Not *that* Mrs. Lamonte, Mom. The old one. The one you've always called Dragon Queen." Paul looked at her. "Didn't you hear? Somebody found her dead at her house."

7

Camellia

Botanical: *Camellia thea*
Family: N. O. Camelliaceae
Common names: Tea plant

Historically dated back to 150 B.C., the camellia is a native of India but was cultivated very early in China. Both green and black tea come from the same species. Camellia is grown extensively for its beautiful, lush green foliage and multi-petaled flowers in the southern U.S.

"WHEN DID IT HAPPEN?" Peggy waved the spatula she held as she scooped rice into a pan to fry it again. "How did she die?"

"I don't know the details, or I'd still be there." Paul shrugged. "Sorry. I could call Mai, if you like. I know you're a friend of the family. Bad luck to lose two members in a less than a week, huh?"

It seemed like *more* than bad luck to Peggy. It would be different if they both died from natural causes. Of course she didn't know about Isabelle yet. The Dragon Queen was old and frail. She could've had a heart attack in her grief about Park. She itched to know what happened. "No. That's okay. I'm sure we'll all find out tomorrow. I don't want you to have to go in because of my curiosity. Let's get some food and watch a movie."

Halfway through the movie, the power flickered and went out. Paul was already asleep and snoring on the sofa. Peggy and Steve sat together in front of the fireplace. A chessboard was set between them. It was always difficult to say which of them would win the game. They were evenly matched. Steve was up one game at the moment, but Peggy knew the tide would change in her favor eventually.

"Will this cold snap hurt your plants?" Steve asked as he made a move.

"No. I have a small generator in the basement." She examined his move and considered her own. "The power rarely stays off that long. Even after Hurricane Hugo hit here, the power was back on in a few days. I'm close to the university and the hospital. Between them, the city crews move pretty quickly."

"Do you think the old lady was right about her daughter-in-law?" Steve sat back as he stretched his long limbs in the chair. "If anything suspicious happened to Isabelle, it could be bad for your friend, Beth."

Peggy moved her bishop. "Since we don't know what happened to Isabelle yet, let's assume it wasn't anything unusual. She was a terror, but she wasn't healthy. What happened to Park may have been too much for even her iron constitution." She didn't admit that the thought of suicide crossed her thoughts. Isabelle was in a terrible state of mind. She was so alone without Park. It wasn't impossible to imagine the old woman going that way on a cold winter's night.

"Do you think she killed herself?" Steve suggested as he made his next move.

She looked up at him. He was very perceptive. It struck her frequently since she met him that he almost seemed psychic around her. *Had he noticed?* If so, he hadn't said anything. "I suppose it's possible. She didn't have much to live for. But I really can't imagine her doing it before she had a chance to see what happened with the investigation into Park's death. She was aggressive about catching his killer."

They finished the game as the fire in the hearth burned down to red coals. Peggy won. They were game for game and decided to leave it at that. The room was warm and smelled like popcorn. Steve added wood to the coals as Peggy put a blanket across her son. She looked at his sleeping face, thinking how much he still resembled his five-year-old self. He reminded her so much of John, even though people always said he looked like her.

With the portable radio playing weather updates between some old jazz music, Peggy and Steve settled in for the night together on a large green velvet love seat in front of the window that looked out on the street. The drape Shakespeare ripped down was still gone, so they could look outside. There were no cars, just the white flakes covering the trees and houses. The snow illuminated everything, making it easy to see, even without streetlights. Shakespeare came and lay down with a thud on the floor beside them.

"This is a great way to enjoy the bad weather," Steve whispered, his arms around her.

Peggy yawned and rested her head against him. "People up North don't know what they're missing by carrying on."

"Of course, if they didn't, everyone's lives would fall apart since they have snow almost every day over the winter."

She smiled as she closed her eyes, listening to the steady sound of his heart. "That's true enough. I guess we're just lucky."

He rested his head against hers and sighed. "I guess we are."

SHAKESPEARE WAS UP AND barking at four a.m. when the power came back on and the snowplow went down Queens Road. Like a switch turned the world back on, Steve's cell phone went off with an emergency call from the owner of a sick chow. He grabbed some coffee as it perked, kissed Peggy, and was gone.

Paul was barely awake when they called him back to work. He ate the last of the cheesecake and strawberries before rushing out the door.

Peggy sat down at the table to watch television and see how the city fared during the night. "I guess it's just you and me again." She patted Shakespeare's massive head as she fed him.

The snow had stopped a little after midnight. Now everyone was digging out of six inches of ice and snow that locked up all of Charlotte, including the airport. The police were advising that no one venture out on the streets unless it was an emergency. Just seeing the cars skidding to the side of the empty interstate was enough to convince most people. But there was always someone with a Jeep who thought he knew better.

There was a small mention of Isabelle's death during the night. But two other people had died as well, their deaths attributed to the storm, so the station didn't devote much time to it. Maybe it had been resolved. Maybe the old lady *did* die from some natural cause. Peggy closed her eyes and prayed it was something simple, but she knew she wouldn't be happy until she found out.

By the time she checked on her plants, walked the dog, and got dressed in a warm turquoise wool pantsuit, the snow was melting under the bright February sun. The blue sky was blinding against what was left of the white landscape. The frozen night was miserable for police and county road crews who tried to keep people in their homes and out of ditches. They were still up and patrolling the city, blear-eyed with lack of sleep but dedicated to their work.

Most residents of the Queen City were happy to oblige the call to stay home, especially the children who missed school that day. School buses and drivers weren't equipped to handle bad weather. They'd have to make the day up somewhere, probably out of a teacher workday.

Peggy slogged through what was left of the slush, stepping around a frozen camellia bush whose bright red flowers struggled through the cold. *You're a flame in my heart.* She translated the flower's meaning as other people translate French or

Spanish. She brushed some of the snow and ice from it before she crossed the street. With the weight lifted off of it, the glossy green branches sprang back up from the sidewalk. "That's better!"

She made her way to Isabelle's house on foot. It wasn't more than a mile. She missed her bike, forgetting how slow it was to walk, but she was worried the frozen ruts in the road would be too hard to maneuver. And there were the abandoned cars littering the streets, parked on the side and in the center. *A good time to be a tow truck driver,* she mused as she watched some of them at work.

She was hoping not to see police cars and the crime scene van when she finally reached the street where Park grew up, but she was disappointed. It meant nothing was resolved. Isabelle's death was questionable. It was as easy to read *that* as it was to know what the flowers meant.

Park's ex-wife, Cindy, was standing on the steps talking to police officers. Her golden hair was perfectly groomed around her pretty face as she dabbed delicately at her tears. Peggy's eyes narrowed. *What is she doing here?*

"Good morning! Is it all right if I come through?" Peggy ignored the yellow crime scene tape to approach Al and Lieutenant Rimer when she saw them outside the two-story, red-brick home.

"No!" Jonas Rimer stalked toward her, his arms waving like a frantic scarecrow. "It is *not* okay if you come through. This is a crime scene, Peggy. That doesn't mean someone can cross the line just because they know a few police officers."

"Well it's more than that, Jonas," she assured him. "I knew Isabelle. She was at my shop yesterday. I was hoping you could tell me what happened to her."

"Nothing happened to her," he said. "Go home. Read the paper like everybody else. You shouldn't be out on the street anyway. You might fall and break something."

"If nothing happened, why are *you* here?" Peggy's eyebrows raised above impertinent green eyes. She decided to ignore his agitated remarks about her fragility. The man was under pressure and obviously not himself. "Come on, Jonas.

You might as well tell me. You know I can stand here and ask questions until I find out."

"We think she was pushed down the stairs," Al explained as he shrugged. "You might as well tell her, Lieutenant. She's gonna find out anyway."

"So is everyone else in the city." Jonas turned on him furiously. "But we aren't going to go around with a loudspeaker telling *everyone* what happened."

Al put his hands in his pockets. "Sorry. But she *did* help us on the Warner case. And she *did* try to help us with Isabelle Lamonte's accusation."

"Yes she did." Jonas smiled at Peggy. "And I know you're in tight with most of the bigwigs in this city. But you can't help with this one. You should go home and wait for the six o'clock news."

"It's terrible about Isabelle." Peggy pushed past Jonas toward Al as if she hadn't heard him. "But why the police investigation? She always kept the house as dark and cold as a tomb. She probably missed the top stair and fell."

"The lieutenant thinks the *other* Mrs. Lamonte might be involved. We heard about the scene between them over at her house yesterday." Al glanced back at Cindy Walker. "And you know we had that call from the elder Mrs. Lamonte about her daughter-in-law being involved in her husband's death. It didn't make any sense yesterday. Today, it might need some answers."

"It still doesn't make any sense today." Peggy wished she could get inside and take a look around. What could possibly be in there that could make them suspect Beth?

"That was before this happened," Jonas decided to tell her before Al said it all. "We found some suspicious circumstances in the house. Enough to investigate anyway. The crime scene people have been here all night."

"What kind of circumstances?" Peggy looked at both of them.

"Never mind." Jonas checked himself and glared at Al. "And if you know what's good for you, Detective, you won't say anything else about this either."

Al scuffed his shoe on the wet sidewalk. "Sorry, Peggy. That's about all I can tell you."

She had to be satisfied with that verdict. A tumble down the stairs didn't sound very suspicious to her, especially since Isabelle was crippled and losing her sight. What did they find that made them think it was anything but an accident? "Does that mean you're going to question Beth about Park's death again, too?"

"That's none of your business." Jonas took her arm and guided her out of Isabelle's front yard. A large blob of snow fell out of a pear tree right on his head. He brushed it off as he said, "You'll have to wait until our investigation is finished."

"Jonas, you need a good cleansing! The toxins have backed up in your body at an alarming rate," she alerted him. "If you don't go home and drink some milk thistle and goldenseal, you're going to catch a cold at the very least!"

He wrinkled his forehead, obviously trying to figure out what she was talking about and finally waved her away. "Go home, Peggy. *Please!* My toxins will just have to be happy with some coffee and donuts later."

She shrugged. "It's your life." She looked back at the gloomy house that seemed to glower back at her. Only an old red camellia bush at one corner told a different story about happier times the house had seen. Had Isabelle planted it there when she was young and in love?

She hadn't been inside the house for years, even though Beth and Park's home was only a few blocks away. Since Park Senior died, Isabelle kept to herself. She let her world shrink around her until all that existed was her anger and fear. Is that what finally claimed her?

It made Peggy shiver to think she could have been the same as Isabelle after John's death. She could've holed up in her house with her plants and her memories until they came and found her dead, too. She shook off the melancholy thought and pretended to examine an ice-glazed holly bush near the front door. The large bush would shrug off the ice as soon as the sun hit it. She knew that, but made a project out of trying to free some of its glossy green leaves from the cold.

Al and Jonas ignored her as they talked to officers who finished canvassing the neighborhood for anyone who might
have seen a strange vehicle or person at the house before Isabelle died. Peggy listened to the reports intently without being noticed. No one saw or heard anything unusual. The
neighbors were used to Isabelle's house being quiet. They
knew she lived alone and tried to keep an eye on her.

While they were engaged in asking questions and getting
statements, Peggy made her way to the back of the house and
slipped in through the porch. The door into the kitchen was
open, so she let herself in the house. The fifties-style kitchen
and dining room were spotless, almost appearing untouched.

The last time she was in Isabelle's house it was the same
way. Like a museum. That was on the occasion of Park Senior's death. His death seemed to fit the house that was already like a tomb. She and John had left the crowd gathered
there as quickly as possible after paying their respects.

Peggy looked for Mai Sato, Paul's girlfriend, and a member of the crime scene team. She found her at the bottom of
the long mahogany staircase. Her shoulder-length, straight
black hair was covering the side of her face as she worked
gathering samples from the red Turkish carpet.

Mai sat back on her heels and rubbed at a spot in her lower
back. She looked up and saw Peggy's inquisitive face. Startled, her large, black-rimmed glasses almost fell off her face.
"Hi!" She glanced at the door. "How did you get in? I
could've sworn Lieutenant Rimer would rather have an ele-
phant step on him than get you involved in another case."

"You're probably right. He doesn't know I'm in here."
Peggy nodded toward the kitchen at the end of the long, dark
hallway. "I came in through the back door. He was too busy to
notice. What have you found so far?"

The silky black hair swung back and forth as Mai shook
her head. Her pretty mouth pursed, and her brown eyes narrowed. "I can't tell you. You *know* that."

"You can at least tell me why everyone doesn't think this
was an accident," Peggy prompted. "Maybe she had a heart
attack. Maybe she slipped on the stairs."

"And maybe somebody pushed her." Mai smiled at her. "All right. I know how you are. I'll tell you what I know, then you better get out of here before somebody else sees you. Rimer is likely to put us both in jail!"

"Okay," Peggy whispered. "Tell me fast."

Mai explained that Isabelle's housekeeper, Alice Godwin, called to make sure the woman was all right. "That was just after six. She was worried about Mrs. Lamonte getting upset about the snow."

"Really? I wouldn't have thought Isabelle got upset about a little snow."

"Well, apparently she was okay at that point. Anyway, around ten o'clock last night, Mrs. Godwin came to check on her. When she got here, she found Mrs. Lamonte at the foot of the stairs. She wasn't moving or breathing. Mrs. Godwin called 911."

Peggy put her hand to her chest. "Poor Isabelle." *Does Beth know Alice was Isabelle's housekeeper, too? That's too much of a coincidence. No wonder Isabelle knew about the life insurance policy.*

"The ambulance came, and the paramedics pronounced her at the scene, but they noticed a few suspicious things and called the police."

"Like *what*?" Peggy tried to get to the heart of the matter.

"Ms. Godwin said Mrs. Lamonte never walked anywhere without her cane. We found it on that chair over there."

Mai pointed to a heavy gold brocade chair that had been in the alcove beside the stairway for as long as Peggy could remember. She went to look at the carved stick without touching the plastic bag that covered it. "Alice is right. Since she hurt her hip in the seventies when she was thrown from her horse, Isabelle never walked without her cane. Why would she be upstairs without it? And where's the dragon?"

"We think someone was in the house with her. Maybe she fell down, and the person took the cane and put it in the chair. It's just a theory right now. What dragon?"

Peggy pointed to the top of the cane. "There's a large ivory dragon's head that belongs on the top of that stick."

They searched the foyer and the stairs, but there was no sign of it. Mai shook her head. "I don't know. But I saw some hair and blood on the side of the cane. Maybe the dragon's head came off when someone hit her with it."

"Whoever did this might have taken it with her." Peggy couldn't help but recall what John always said about the person who found the body.

"If you're thinking about Ms. Godwin, don't bother. She was at a Church function last night. But look at this." Mai moved aside so Peggy could see the chalk outline of where Isabelle's body had been at the base of the stairs. At the tip of the silhouette of one outstretched hand was a letter. "We think it may be written in her own blood."

Peggy crouched down carefully beside the startling piece of evidence. Just between the stairs and the Turkish carpet was a thinly traced letter on the dark wood floor. It was clearly a *B*. Even though the hand that wrote it was shaking, there was no mistaking the intent. "Good God! I can't believe this is happening."

Mai put her hand on her shoulder. "I know you're friends with Beth Lamonte. I don't know what to say. Maybe the old lady knew what she was talking about when she accused her daughter-in-law of killing her son. And maybe the other Mrs. Lamonte thought she could put an end to the whole thing by trying to make this look like an accident. She didn't realize the old lady was still alive when she left."

Peggy carefully got to her feet. She looked down at the circled spot on the carpet. *When had Isabelle ever called Beth by her given name? If she referred to her by any name, it was "that woman."* "Beth didn't do this. I don't know what's going on, but someone is setting her up. We have to find out who."

"I don't know, Peggy."

"Why is Cindy Walker here?"

Mai shuffled her paperwork, glancing through it. "She's listed as an emergency contact after Park. Why?"

"She's always tried to weasel her way into this family. She had plenty of reasons to hate Beth since she lost Park to her."

Mai groaned. "I can't help you this time. Not like last time.

Paul *really* wants this house. I can't afford to lose my job. You'll have to let the investigation prove if your friend is guilty or innocent. Then there's still the trial. Believe me, the system works if you let it."

"The system also likes to make it simple," Peggy argued. "If you find even the slightest DNA from Beth here, she'll be charged. And what are the chances there won't be a hair or something? She's only been here when she *had* to be, but that was still plenty of times. No one can refuse a direct summons from the Dragon Queen. That won't help her or her sons. There has to be another answer. Who's responsible for this? And how did they kill Park if his death wasn't an accident either?"

The sound of the heavy front door opening and closing preceded footsteps and voices coming their way. Mai opened the nearby coat closet and pushed Peggy inside. "Quick! We can't let anyone see you. Be really quiet. In case I have to leave, wait until everyone's gone to come out."

"Will you help me prove Beth didn't kill Isabelle or Park?"

"That's blackmail!" Mai hissed. But the voices were getting louder. Al and Jonas were coming toward them. "All right! I'll do what I can. But I won't lose my job. Now get *inside.*"

Peggy smiled at her, then backed into the closet. It was completely black when Mai shut the door. It smelled of mothballs and musty old clothing. She wondered if Isabelle had used it at all in the last ten years. She stood very still and listened as Jonas, Al, and Mai talked about what they knew about the case so far.

"I guess we'll be paying the Mrs. Lamonte who's still alive a visit," Jonas said. "Good thing Peggy left before she knew. She'd already have the woman hidden away in her house waiting to sneak her out of the city."

The three chuckled in a way Peggy hoped could be construed as "fondly." Al said, "She's not really like that, you know. She got involved in the Warner case because the man was killed in her shop. She wouldn't necessarily do it again."

Bless his heart. Peggy tried not to step down too hard on the side of a boot lodged under her foot.

"But you wouldn't want to stake your pension on that would you, Detective?" Jonas baited him.

"No, sir. I wouldn't. Peggy gets too emotional, no doubt about it. I just hope she *doesn't* get involved this time."

"I'm sure she won't. Why would she? I mean, she has enough to do, right?" Mai laughed nervously. She cleared her throat when they looked at her strangely and told them her "theory" about the dragon's head missing from the cane.

"Al, get a couple of officers in here to help her look for that thing. Go over everything again, Mai. Let me know if you find it. Then get some help to take these things back to the lab," Jonas told her. "Al and I are headed over to the other Lamonte house. I'll be glad when this is over. Too many Lamontes."

Peggy wasn't sure what to do. She could call Beth and warn her about the police visit. It wouldn't keep it from happening, but it would prepare her. John would've given her a good talking to when she came home if he were still alive. She *shouldn't* interfere in police business.

But she was already involved. It wasn't like she *wanted* to be there, hiding in Isabelle's dark closet. First Beth, then Isabelle, and finally Al put her in the picture. There was nothing else to do but follow through. Anything else would be letting her friends down.

"Forgive me, John," she muttered as she speed-dialed Beth's home number on her cell phone. She didn't dare get out of the closet and could only hope no one was standing nearby.

"Hello?" Beth's voice was strained and tearful.

"There's no easy way to tell you this," Peggy began in a quick, quiet whisper. "The police are on their way to your house to ask you questions about Isabelle's death."

"How? Why?" Beth sputtered.

Peggy heard the doorbell ring from Beth's end of the phone. "Did you contact a lawyer yet?"

"I spoke with one of Park's friends. He isn't here right now. What should I do?"

"Tell the truth. Just not too much of it. Answer their questions, but don't offer any extra information. Call Park's friend."

Peggy tried to think of any other bit of advice. None came to mind. "I'll be over as soon as I can."

"Why didn't you come with them?" Beth asked.

"It's difficult to explain." Peggy glanced around the closet. "Just keep your wits about you. The police are serious about this. I'll explain when I get there."

Mai opened the closet door just as Peggy got off the phone. "Were you talking to yourself?"

"No." Peggy held up the cell phone. "Is it safe to come out now?"

"Everyone's gone. If you go out the back, you should be okay."

"Thanks. Call me if you find out anything else?"

"As much as I can," Mai whispered. "Please don't do anything that would jeopardize either of us."

"Don't worry. I'll talk to you later."

"And thanks for the tip about the dragon's head!"

"You're welcome. You might want to ask Alice why she didn't mention it. Also, in case you didn't know, Cindy is Park's ex-wife. *That* might be something to check into as well." Peggy waved to her and walked quietly back down the long hall to the kitchen. The grandfather clock ticked loudly in the close atmosphere. The house smelled of mold and decay. The estate would probably sell the place. A family would move in and take care of the old house again. It was hard to imagine laughter ringing through these halls, but she knew it would happen.

She noticed Jonas and Al leaving in Al's SUV. She began running, cutting through backyards to reach Beth before them.

Sam called her cell phone as she got outside. "I'm at the shop. I thought you'd be here, too," he said. "I know everything downtown is closed and everyone is home, but you're usually here anyway."

"Normally I would be," she agreed as a thorn on a climbing rose branch caught her jacket as she ran by its trellis. She disengaged it and continued on, waving to an acquaintance as she ran through her backyard. "But everything is crazy, Sam. Beth might be accused of pushing Isabelle down the stairs last night."

"*What?* I knew she was having problems with Park's death because of the old lady, but I can't believe . . . what happened?"

Peggy explained as she rounded the corner of the street Beth lived on. She stepped in one end of an ornamental pond, camouflaged by fallen leaves. She drew back a wet boot but kept going. "It looks pretty convincing. Isabelle wouldn't have tried to come down the stairs without her cane. And the *B* was brilliant. If I didn't know better, I'd blame Beth, too."

"What are you doing?" Sam wondered as he listened to her labored breathing. "You sound like you're running a marathon. Are you really *that* sure about Beth?"

"Yes. She wouldn't hurt anyone. But there must be someone who wants to make it look like she did." She huffed out warm air into the cold morning. "I'm trying to get to Beth's house before Al and Jonas. It's a lot easier to run through these yards when there isn't snow and ice on the ground."

"Okay. I suppose that means you want to prove Beth is innocent. Maybe we should open a detective agency instead of a garden shop."

"I don't think so!" She snorted. "We'll have to talk later. I'm at her house and Al is pulling in right behind me. I'll call you as soon as I can. Thanks for being there, Sam."

"You know me. Always ready to steal a body or break into a funeral home."

Peggy laughed as she closed her phone. She didn't have the breath to assure him that those circumstances wouldn't happen *again*. She might be able to help Beth in *some* way but not so directly. She wouldn't risk so much, even to help her friend. Some of the things she had to do to find Mark Warner's killer were impossible. She certainly wouldn't involve Sam, Steve, or Mai as she did last time.

Jonas was getting out of Al's Ford Explorer that was parked behind an unfamiliar black Hummer as she pushed herself up the sidewalk. "What are *you* doing here?" he demanded.

"I'm here to visit my friend," she replied with as much indignity as she could put into her wispy, breathless voice. Her chest was heaving with exertion. "She lost her husband, you know. She needs support. What brings *you* here?"

"Don't act like you don't know! We're here on official police business, Peggy. Please don't try to interfere." Jonas's look told her he fully expected her to do it anyway.

"Are you here to notify Beth of Isabelle's death?" She stalled for more time for her friend.

"No. And that's all you're getting out of me. I think you should go home."

Peggy drew herself up to her full height and faced him fearlessly. "Despite your official business here, the law doesn't say anything about not being able to visit a friend. If Beth doesn't want me here while you're here, she can tell me."

Jonas opened his mouth to say something else but thought better of it. He turned to Al, "Come on, Detective. We have a job to do."

The three of them went up to the front door together. Al shook his head when Peggy knocked before Jonas could do it. The door opened slowly to a man dressed casually in jeans and a red flannel shirt. His sharp, inquisitive gray eyes searched the faces at the doorstep. "Can I help you?"

"Yes." Peggy pushed past Jonas and Al. "I don't think we've met. I'm Peggy Lee."

"Of course. Mrs. Lamonte is expecting you. I'm Gary Rusch, Park's partner."

8

Gardenia

Botanical: *Gardenia jasminoides*
Family: Rubiaceae

This sweet-smelling flower was first propagated in China and Japan. It has been used for a perfume source for centuries. The Celtic people believed planting it outside the door would make a loving family in the house. The Wiccans believe it represents peace, love, and spirituality.

"I'M LIEUTENANT RIMER, AND this is Detective Al McDonald. We're from the Charlotte-Mecklenburg Police Department. We're here to see Mrs. Lamonte about the death of her mother-in-law."

Gary Rusch's charming smile didn't falter. "Come right this way, gentlemen."

But while Peggy went into the sitting room with Beth, Al and Jonas were detained in the hall by the lawyer.

Peggy shut the door to the hall. "I got here as fast as I could. I thought you didn't have an attorney here yet."

"Actually, I left a message on the firm's voice mail yesterday." Beth shrugged. "Gary showed up this morning right when you called. I feel like the woman tied on the train track and the cowboy on the white horse rides up in the nick of time."

Peggy sat beside her and held her hands. "How are you? How are the boys doing?"

"We're all right. It was such a shock to hear about Isabelle. I think she probably killed herself. She was so damn daunting. But she couldn't live without Park. He was *that* important to her."

"I don't know if your lawyer can keep the police from talking to you. They're going to want some answers, Beth. If not now, then later. Where were you last night before ten?"

"Here, I suppose. I really haven't gone out much the last few days. Everything was closed by that time because of the snow. I can't believe the police think I would hurt Isabelle. What would I gain by her death?"

"It's only questions right now." Peggy squeezed her friend's hand as the lawyer led the two officers into the quiet, comfortable room. "Just do what the lawyer tells you. Don't embellish!"

"Mrs. Lamonte." Jonas glanced at Peggy impatiently. "I'm Lieutenant Rimer, CMPD. You already know Detective McDonald. And I suppose since *she's* here, you know why *we're* here."

"Yes. And I didn't push Isabelle down the stairs."

Gary put his hand on her shoulder. "Don't feel like you have to say *anything*, Beth. These men are here to ask you some questions. You can answer them, if you like. Or not."

Al and Jonas sat down awkwardly in the tiny room. Peggy knew it was Beth's favorite place in the house. The small fireplace was surrounded by brightly colored enamel tiles that created a mural using the fire in the grate as the sun in the sunset scene. The four chairs were in shades of orange, and the burnt orange Shirvan kilim rug on the wood floor enhanced the warm images.

"We appreciate your cooperation, Mrs. Lamonte. Let's start by asking where you were last night between six and ten p.m., Mrs. Lamonte?" Al asked as he shifted uncomfortably in the small chair.

"I was here. I think I was resting after dinner. My housekeeper, Alice Godwin, was here with the children until nine. Then I got up and put them to bed."

"So you were in your bedroom the whole time?" Jonas suggested. "Did you talk to your housekeeper or your children during that time? Did they see you?"

"No, I don't think so. I was exhausted, as I'm sure you can appreciate, Lieutenant. I was in my room with the door closed the whole time. The kids can get pretty loud playing games."

Al and Jonas exchanged meaningful glances. It reminded Peggy so much of Sergeant Joe Friday and Officer Bill Gannon from *Dragnet* that she almost laughed. She controlled the smile she hid behind her hand and focused on what was happening.

"Well, one thing Peggy *couldn't* tell you, since we managed to keep her out of the crime scene," Al explained, "is that your mother-in-law managed to write a single letter in her own blood before she died. It was clearly a *B*."

"That doesn't mean *I* did anything. In the ten years I knew her, Isabelle *never* called me Beth. You can ask anyone. She always called me Elizabeth. She was very formal. But I'm sure there are plenty of people with *B* as an initial. I was home all night last night. I didn't hurt Isabelle."

Jonas got to his feet and paced the tiny room like a caged cat. "Come on, Mrs. Lamonte. You expect us to believe you *weren't* angry at your mother-in-law's accusation about your husband's death? She said you *killed* him. We know she accused you to your face right in your home, in front of your friends. That *must* have made you upset. Maybe you didn't mean to hurt her when you went over there. Maybe you just wanted to shut her up and things got out of hand."

"Isabelle Lamonte meant her accusation *metaphorically*, Lieutenant, I'm sure," Gary intervened. "Mrs. Lamonte and my client didn't get along well, not an unusual relationship in families. When she said my client killed her husband, she meant in the sense that she wasn't good enough for him. But anyone who knew Isabelle knew how she felt about the relationship. It wasn't a secret."

"That's not the impression we were under, Mr. Rusch," Jonas said. "Isabelle Lamonte was explicit. She believed your client *actively* killed Mr. Lamonte for the ten million dollar life insurance policy. She told us that her daughter-in-law *actually* killed her son. There was nothing metaphoric about it."

"Not that it matters, Lieutenant. As my client told you," Gary reiterated, "she was here with the children all evening. I think that's about all we have to say on the matter."

Jonas glared at Beth, clearly not satisfied. "I hope you'll advise *your client* to work with us, sir. This isn't over yet. We're conducting a more in-depth autopsy on Mr. Lamonte *and* checking out the car again as well as continuing the investigation into what happened to Isabelle Lamonte. If we find anything out of the ordinary, we'll be back. Maybe with an arrest warrant. And we want to talk with your housekeeper. I need her name and address."

Gary smiled, unruffled by the threat. "If that time comes, Lieutenant, we'll be here. You're welcome to the housekeeper's name and address."

Al and Jonas left after Beth wrote down Alice's full name and phone number. She wasn't sure about her address. Al remarked on the fact that the two households shared the same housekeeper.

Beth shook her head. "I'm sure you're mistaken, Detective McDonald. I don't think Alice has ever worked for Isabelle."

Checking his notebook, Al replied, "I have her finding Mrs. Lamonte last night. She said she's worked for her for years."

"He's telling you the truth," Peggy chimed in. "I—uh—overheard the same thing outside."

"Overheard, huh?" Jonas remarked.

"I-I don't know what to say." Beth glanced at Peggy and Gary.

"Does this have some bearing on the case, Detective?" Gary asked him.

Al shrugged. "I'm not sure yet, Mr. Rusch. It might. Talk to you later, Peggy."

The lawyer showed Al and Jonas to the front door. Beth hid her face in her hands. "I can't believe this is happening to me. Isn't it enough that Park is dead? Why is this happening?"

Peggy didn't know what to say. Gary came back and sat on the side of the chair beside Beth. "Sorry about that. We don't want to give them the impression we're *not* cooperating. You need to think back, Beth. Maybe Alice saw you some time last night when you went downstairs for some water or you asked how the children were doing. Maybe she looked in on you while you were resting. She was worried about you. It would be a spontaneous thing to do."

His meaning was clear. Peggy's eyebrows raised, and Beth stared at him. "I didn't do anything, Gary. I'm not going to ask Alice to lie for me."

He shrugged, quite elegantly for wearing flannel, Peggy thought, watching him. "You have to know the police will be back whether they find anything wrong about Park's death or not," he informed her. "It isn't a big stretch of the imagination for anyone to think you could sneak out when no one was looking, push Isabelle down the stairs, and come back. Her house is only a few minutes' walk from here."

"It took me about five minutes, maybe." Peggy squeezed Beth's hand again. "I agree with Gary. I don't think it's over either. But there's no reason to lie about it. The evidence will prove you innocent."

Gary got to his feet and glanced at his Rolex. "I'm just trying to help. I would rather nip this in the bud than fight it in court. You know we'll all do whatever we can for you, Beth, but a *B* drawn in the old lady's blood is pretty dramatic. All those friends of yours who heard Isabelle say you killed her son will testify for the DA against you, whether they want to or not. Having Alice say she glanced in and saw you sleeping seems easier to me. But you do what you think is right."

"Thanks, Gary." Beth shook his hand.

Was it Peggy's imagination or did his hand linger on Beth's a little longer than was necessary?

"I wish I could handle this for you, but I'm swamped. I'll send someone from the firm over to help you out." He smiled and hugged Beth, his hands sliding up and down her slender back, pressing her closer to him.

Peggy frowned. Really, the man had no sense of propriety!

Beth closed the door behind the attorney and leaned against it.

"I hope whoever he sends is better than Mr. Rusch," Peggy said.

"Gary's a very good attorney. Park always said so."

"Maybe. But I wouldn't want him on *my* side!"

"What else can I do?"

"I know just the right person," Peggy took out her cell phone. "I'll give her a call."

Hunter Ollson was there in twenty minutes. She was tall, blond, and beautiful, more like a fashion model for *Fitness Today* than an attorney. She hugged Peggy when she saw her, dropping her briefcase on the wood floor. "I'm so happy to see you! You called at just the right time. I was trying to decide if I should give up being a lawyer and go into wrestling. I defended a lady wrestler last month. Do you realize how much money they make? The Warner case made me notorious in this town. All I can get now is DUI sports figures and race car drivers who slap their fans."

Peggy laughed. Hunter was always a breath of fresh air. "Beth, this is Hunter Ollson. She's Sam's sister."

Beth shook Hunter's hand. "I remember your name. You defended Mr. Cheever when he was accused of killing that man in Peggy's shop. Hello, Hunter. I'm Beth Lamonte."

"Hello. I'm so sorry for your loss and this other mess. I hope I can help." Hunter picked up her briefcase, and the three women went into the dining room. From the kitchen, they could hear Foxx and Reddman's laughter as they helped Beth's parents make cookies. "Wow! Something smells good."

"Would you like a gingerbread man?" Beth went into the other room and came back with a tray of cookies.

"Thanks." Hunter munched one, exclaiming when it was hot but continuing to eat. "I didn't have time for breakfast. Sam was supposed to bring pizza by last night and got held up somewhere else or with *someone* else."

"He was probably with his boyfriend of the-month." Peggy rolled her eyes. "I wish that boy would settle down. He told me his grades dropped, and your father yelled at him. I can't believe he'd give up so easy as much as he wanted to be a doctor."

Beth laughed. "I suppose when you look like Sam, it's easy to get distracted."

"That doesn't mean you're supposed to forget your starving sister and drop out of college," Hunter argued. She drank a glass of milk Foxx brought in for her in one gulp, then looked at Peggy and Beth with a white mustache on her upper lip. "Uh—sorry. Did either of you want some?"

Both women smiled and assured her they didn't. Peggy handed her a napkin as Hunter opened her briefcase and took out a pen and a yellow legal pad. "Okay, I'm ready. What happened?"

Peggy let Beth tell the story on her own. Hunter took notes and nodded. When Beth was finished, Hunter glanced up at Peggy. "How did *you* get involved with this? Were you here because you're a friend of the family?"

"Not exactly."

Hunter made a chuckling sound in the back of her throat. "I thought not. Okay, Peggy. What do you know about all this?"

Peggy told her everything she knew about what happened, including the fact that Alice Godwin found Isabelle dead. She also told her about Cindy Walker being at the house. "She could have made that *B* with her blood after finding her. I don't know when she got there but she hates Beth enough to want to implicate her."

After hearing from Peggy, the three women tried to plot a strategy for getting Beth out of trouble. It was difficult since they didn't have all the information on either case. Hunter finished writing her notes in a broad scrawl across the yellow paper. "There's nothing anyone can do until they finish the autopsies on Park and Isabelle."

"Will they do an autopsy on Isabelle even though they know how she died?" Beth looked at Peggy.

"Any questionable death demands an autopsy," Peggy quoted John. "And that could be good for you. Maybe Isabelle died of natural causes and fell down the steps. The *B* might not mean anything."

"That doesn't explain her cane being on the chair," Hunter reminded her. "Or the dragon's head missing from it. Of course, we *still* have the chance the old lady died of natural causes and someone found her and moved the cane. Maybe took the dragon's head since it was probably valuable. Maybe even drew the *B* in her blood to try to implicate Beth. I'll check out Cindy Walker's and Alice Godwin's alibis. We'll have to wait for the autopsy report and crime scene disclosure. But so will the police."

"What do I do in the meantime?" Beth asked.

"Don't talk to anyone unless I'm with you," Hunter advised as she glanced at her notes. "That means the police, the press. Anybody. Got it?"

"All right," Beth agreed.

"What about this life insurance policy?" Hunter's warm blue gaze flashed up to her new client's face.

"She didn't know anything about it," Peggy defended her.

Beth cleared her throat. "That's not *entirely* true."

The other two women stared at her.

"Park told me about it. I-I was just so stunned when he died. I forgot."

"Well, try not to *forget* anything else," Hunter said, closing her briefcase. "Especially if it involves money. The police are looking for anything out of the ordinary."

"Lots of our friends have large life insurance policies," Beth commented. "It's not out of the ordinary."

"When the police think you may be responsible for two deaths, everything becomes out of the ordinary. Your life is going to be scrutinized down to the sheets in your linen closet. Don't keep any secrets for me to find out from them. It will only hurt your case."

Beth looked away but didn't reply. Peggy bit her lip, feeling sure there was something else her friend was holding back. "I think there might be something to Alice Godwin working for both Beth and Isabelle."

"The housekeeper?" Hunter checked her notes. "Wasn't she here with Beth and the boys during that time?"

"She left here at about nine," Beth recalled. "If she went out before then, I don't know about it."

"Isabelle may have paid her to spy on Beth," Peggy explained. "I'm not sure how that would relate to everything that's happened, but Alice had access to both houses."

"I'll check into it." Hunter got to her feet. "If you think of anything else, let me know."

Beth stood and held out her hand. "Thank you for coming. You're a lifesaver."

"You're welcome." Hunter's face turned a little red. "Uh—there's a little thing about a retainer." She named a figure. "I hope that's not a problem."

Peggy was astonished. "That's ridiculous!"

Hunter immediately backed down. "Okay. What do you think is fair?"

"No wonder you don't have money for food," Peggy continued. "Your retainer should be *double* that."

The young attorney glanced at Beth, then back at Peggy. "Maybe we should talk about this later. *Like not in front of the client.*"

Beth laughed as she put her hand on Hunter's arm. "My husband was a lawyer. Peggy's right. I'll get my checkbook, if a personal check is okay?"

"A personal check is fine," Hunter gushed. "Or any other kind of check. Or I take Visa and MasterCard."

After Beth gave Hunter a check for the retainer, almost triple the amount she was asking, Peggy hugged her and told her not to worry. "Hunter is very bright. If anyone can get you out of this, she can."

"Thank you, Peggy." Beth hugged her tightly, tears in her voice. "I don't know what I'd do without you right now. Thanks, too, for not getting angry with me when I asked you to investigate Park's death. I was out of my head."

"Don't worry about it," Peggy said. "I know how hard it is for you right now. But everything will work out. I'm sure of it."

"I'll be in touch if I hear anything, Beth." Hunter shook her hand again.

"Thank you." Beth endured Hunter's hearty handshake. "I'm glad you could represent me."

"Could you give me a lift?" Peggy asked Hunter. "I'd like to go over to the Potting Shed for a while."

"Sure. Are you ready?"

"I am. Thanks. Call me if you need anything, Beth," Peggy told her friend as she put on her purple jacket and scarf again.

"I will. Let's pray the autopsies take care of all of this. I'd like to think Park and Isabelle are at peace." Beth opened the front door for them. "I'll talk to you later."

As they walked to the SUV in the drive, Hunter whispered to Peggy, "Do I have to give back the retainer if the autopsies clear her?"

Peggy laughed as she got in the vehicle. "I don't think so. Don't they tell you what to charge and how it works when you're in school?"

Hunter slammed her door closed and started the engine. "I think that's supposed to come from your mentor, the first person who hires you out of school. You know what happened to *him*. He only taught me older men still want to fool around."

"And you taught him that women today can pack a wallop." Peggy watched Park's house fade behind them. "I remember that. I suppose there wasn't much time for financial lessons."

"Except you don't punch out a senior partner at a major law firm without serious financial difficulties." Hunter turned the vehicle toward downtown, the streets almost devoid of traffic. "Next time, I'll just walk out and sue his ass. That's the *legal* way to do it."

It only took a few minutes to get to the shop. Most of the snow and ice were gone, and the only people out were walking their dogs or taking the opportunity to play in the street. Homemade sleds were everywhere, made from everything from boxes to sheets of plastic. It couldn't be easy to try to glide down the wet slush, but it looked like fun.

Hunter got out with Peggy to go into the shop. "Wish I was a kid again. I used to love snow days."

"I have some black plastic we use to keep weeds from growing around bushes," Peggy volunteered. "You could try it out on what's left of the snow."

"No thanks." Hunter smiled. "I got something even better today. Money! And I'm going to buy myself a new suit as soon as I chew out my brother for forgetting me last night."

"Sounds like a plan." Peggy opened the back door to the shop.

"You *do* think Beth is innocent, right?" Hunter's attractive face was serious as they stood in the shadows of the courtyard and Latta Arcade.

"I wouldn't have called you if I didn't," Peggy assured her. "You're one of the good guys. I know you wouldn't want to represent someone capable of killing her husband and his mother."

Hunter considered the matter. "Probably not. Well, at least not without charging her triple what I got today." She grinned at Peggy but sobered immediately when she saw her brother. "There you are! You are dead meat unless you have a pizza on you!" She hit him hard in the stomach as he transported a hundred pound bag of fertilizer to the loading dock.

Sam groaned but managed to get the heavy bag on top of the pile where he wanted it. "Are you crazy? What would I be doing with a pizza?"

"Remember? You were supposed to bring one over last night. What happened?"

"Oh yeah." He rubbed his stomach where she hit him. "Sorry. I got caught up with something."

"Or some*one*?" Hunter demanded, impatiently tapping her foot. "Mom wouldn't like it if she knew you were letting me starve so you could spend time with your *boyfriend.*"

"He's *not* my boyfriend." Sam started walking toward the front of the shop again. "At least I don't *think* he's my boyfriend. I'm sorry, sweetie. I'll make it up to you."

"Yes you will!" She followed him into the shop where Peggy was already going through the mail. "I got a serious retainer fee today, thanks to Peggy."

Sam made a face that looked like he'd eaten too many pickles. "Are you kidding? You're going to do it again, aren't you? You're going to get involved in another one of Peggy's crazy murder cases."

Peggy heard her name and looked up from an invoice for several tulip trees. "What do you mean one of *my* crazy murder cases? I don't think I've had crazy murder cases. You can't really count this the same way as Mark Warner's death. We're not investigating exactly. Hunter just stepped in to help Beth."

"That's the way it started last time." Sam grinned. "I'm not complaining. I had a good time when we did it before. Hunter was the one who whined and complained when she didn't start picking up expensive clients when it was over."

"This will be different," Hunter agreed with Peggy. "Wait and see. I've already made more money on it than I did on everything last time. How could I charge that poor old man or his daughter for much? They didn't have any more than I do!"

Peggy leaned on the counter beside the cash register. "Beth needs help, Sam. Park's friend from the law firm was a little weird. There's going to be press over this. When Hunter and I get Beth out of trouble, her name will be in the paper and on TV. Her career is bound to take off."

"Okay! Okay! You've beaten me with your plowshares! So what do we do first?" Sam asked as Hunter sat in the rocking chair beside the snowman. "Do we need to steal something? Beat someone up until they tell the truth?"

"Not as far as I know." Peggy laughed. "First, we let the police do their job. Mai told me she'd let me know as soon as the Isabelle's preliminary autopsy is done. In the meantime, I guess we begin by compiling a list of suspects."

"Isn't it still possible the police will come back empty-handed as far as Park's death is concerned?" Sam rearranged the red silk tulips in the spring display. "If his death was *really* an accident because he fell asleep at the wheel, the police won't be able to say anything else to Beth, right?"

Hunter made a pyramid of her fingers as she rocked furiously, the floor creaking beneath her. "That's true. But it won't help with Isabelle's death. The police could still try to say

Beth decided to put an end to the old lady giving her grief over everything. Even if nothing comes of the investigation into Park's death, I think there will still be problems with that."

Peggy agreed with her. "But if we're going to look for Isabelle's enemies, it's going to take us years. No one liked the Dragon Queen. Not even her husband and son."

"That's really sad." Sam shook his head and stared out at what was left of the snow in the courtyard outside the windows. "But there's a big difference between not liking someone and killing them. I don't like Hunter, but she's still alive."

"I'm going to be generous and ignore that remark since you're taking me out for dinner. And not fast food either!" Hunter smiled and hugged her brother. "Peggy, let me know if you hear anything. Otherwise, we'll wait for the police to call us."

"Don't forget about Alice and Cindy," Peggy reminded her. "I think there could be something there."

"I won't." Hunter wrote herself a note on the palm of her hand.

"Where are you off to?" Sam asked her.

"To buy a new suit," Hunter replied with a dreamy expression on her face.

"Everything's closed," Peggy reminded her. "You might have to wait until tomorrow."

"As long as the power is on and my computer is working, I can shop." Hunter grinned. "That's why God gave us credit cards."

Sam shook his head as Hunter left the shop. "I worry about her. It's hard for her to keep five dollars in her pocket without spending it."

"She'll be fine," Peggy advised. "She just needs to get on her feet."

"While we've got a few minutes," Sam said, "let's talk about pruning a gardenia. Mrs. Shultz wants her gardenia pruned. I think it's fine the way it is, and I'm afraid to prune it back any further. I think it might kill the plant. She says it doesn't flower enough."

"Gardenia . . ." Peggy ruminated, glancing through her

vegetable catalog. "A good rule of thumb is to prune lightly. Just look for places where the plant looks uneven or has yellow leaves. You're right about cutting it too far back."

"So what do I tell Mrs. Shultz? She wants it trimmed back to almost ground level."

"You tell her the truth. We don't prune back so far as to cause damage to the plant." Peggy looked at him and smiled. "If *she* wants to do it, that's fine. Our last word should always come from Hippocrates. 'Do no harm.' That's the Potting Shed motto."

"That's what I thought. Just wanted to clear it with you because I know she'll be on the phone with you as soon as I leave."

"Don't worry about a thing." Peggy put on her glasses. "I've got your back, as they say on the street."

Sam laughed. "When was the last time you were on the street?"

"Today. Furiously running from yard to yard. You'd be surprised how much you pick up."

"I'm going to finish putting out this *fertilizer* for pickup tomorrow." He smiled with a hint at her "street smarts."

Peggy stayed at the shop, looking through catalogs and ordering supplies. A few customers actually came up and knocked on the door. She let them in and offered them a cup of hot tea as they explained what brought them out.

One man was looking for a last-minute gift for his wife. Peggy sold him a terrarium kit when he explained his wife liked indoor gardening. They lived on the fifth floor of one of the new condominium units right around the corner. He thanked her heartily. His wife's birthday party was scheduled for that night, despite the bad weather. He promised to come back when they were ready to start gardening on their balcony.

Debra Carson, a longtime friend of Beth's, came into the shop. She was a regular customer at the Potting Shed. Peggy rarely saw her because she mostly ordered online and had her supplies delivered. But since the snow kept her home for the day, she sat down and had tea with Peggy.

"I can't imagine how Beth must be feeling about now." Debra sat in the rocking chair and rolled her eyes. She was married to a pediatrician and lived two doors down from Park and Beth.

Peggy wished she couldn't imagine but didn't bother explaining that to Debra. "It will be hard for her, especially with the two boys."

"Not to mention the guilt." Debra flipped through the flowering tree catalog.

"You mean about Isabelle's death?"

Debra looked up at her, brown eyes open wide. "You mean she didn't tell you about Park and her?"

Peggy put down the catalog she held and paid more attention. "What about them?"

"Beth was going to leave him over the summer. They finally reconciled and managed to keep it together. I think it was mostly for the boys. But it was close for a while."

"What happened?" Peggy couldn't believe it was true. Park and Beth had one of the most stable relationships she knew.

"It was the ex-wife, what's her name?" Debra said the words like they explained everything. "As a second wife, I can tell you they can be a real bitch."

Cindy Walker again. Her name was coming up more and more often. She was always a problem, stalking Park, trying to run Park down with her Saab when he left her for Beth. Maybe she was more than just a scorned wife. "What did she want this time?"

Debra smiled and narrowed her eyes. "It wasn't *what* she wanted. It was *who*. And I guess you could say she got him. Park slept with her. Beth found out somehow and was ready to leave. I don't know what changed her mind. I would've left Kinsley if he ever tried that on me."

"Why would Beth feel guilty about Park dying because of that?" Peggy was confused and concerned about the information. Why didn't Beth tell her? The police were sure to find out.

"Because," Debra explained, "part of her agreeing to stay with him was that big, fat insurance policy. Imagine how she feels now that he's *dead*."

9

Begonia

Botanical: *Begonia*
Family: Begoniaceae

The begonia was first discovered in the rain forests of South America around the mid-1800s. For almost a century, it was considered an exotic plant only owned by the wealthy. Today, the begonia is to Belgium what the tulip is to Holland and graces the windowsills of homes around the world.

"YOU'VE CONSISTENTLY LIED TO the police from the start," Peggy accused Beth an hour later as she paced her kitchen floor.

"Alice, take the boys upstairs, please," Beth requested.

The burly black housekeeper snorted and glared at Peggy. "Seems to me *some* people should have enough to do without getting in other people's business!"

"It's all right." Beth smiled at her. "Peggy and I need to talk."

Peggy waited until Foxx and Reddman were out of the room. She didn't mean to burst in and begin a tirade, but the words just came out when she saw her friend's placid face. "Beth, if the police find out . . . *when* the police find out, it's going to be very bad for you."

"I didn't know what to say," she confessed, hands twisted in her lap. "Park told me we should keep quiet on the insurance.

That's why I pretended not to know about it. Then all these other things came up. I just blanked."

"This makes you look incredibly guilty of something." Peggy continued to pace the old hardwood floor. "I *know* you didn't do anything to hurt Park or Isabelle. But the police won't. They'll come after you about this. You have to tell Hunter so she knows what she's up against."

"I will," Beth agreed. "It's so scary, Peggy. I-I don't know what to say or do. They're accusing me of terrible things. I could lose the boys."

Peggy wanted to hug her. She really did. But she was angry, too. So she stayed where she was, arms folded across her chest to keep from reaching out to her friend. "Just tell the truth from now on. Don't let them catch you in any more lies. This is bad enough without that."

"I agree." Beth looked up at her with tears on her face. "I won't let it happen again."

"Did you talk to Alice about working for Isabelle?"

"I don't see what difference it makes now." She shrugged. "Isabelle probably sent her here years ago to spy on me. It's not surprising. She liked to know what was going on."

Peggy tended to agree with her. With Isabelle dead, those small intrigues would be over. Still, it disturbed her. Did Isabelle know about the insurance policy *and* Park's affair with Cindy, courtesy of Alice? Is that what made her think Beth was responsible for Park's death?

Alice called Beth to let her know the boys were ready for their stories. Peggy said good night to her but waited for Alice to come downstairs.

When the housekeeper saw her, she drew her arms up combatively and her dark eyes narrowed. "What do you want now, Miz Peggy? Can't you leave good enough alone?"

"I suppose not. Not with everything that's going on." Peggy focused on the other woman, who was easily twice her size. "What kind of things did you report to Isabelle?"

"Nothing! I worked for both of them. Don't mean I spied on *either* of them, if that's what you're thinking!"

"So you didn't tell Isabelle when Park had the affair with

Cindy or about the insurance policy Beth took out on him?"

Alice's lip curled. "I didn't have to tell *her* about the insurance policy. Mr. Lamonte's doctor told her when he went in for a physical to qualify. And I *know* you don't think I had to tell Miz Isabelle about Miz Cindy! *That* woman was bursting to tell her!"

"But you *did* tell her things, didn't you?"

"Things about the boys." Alice shrugged. "Nothing important. Nothing that would hurt Miz Beth. She didn't offer to *pay* me for anything, you know. It was like my duty to her. With her it was always like I should be grateful for her letting me work there. When she got me this job, I was supposed to be double grateful. But don't take a leftover potato or a decent Christmas bonus home. No, ma'am!"

Alice's voice was bitter. Peggy looked at the surly housekeeper but decided to leave it. Alice worked for both households, had access to both dead family members. But it was hard to imagine where Park's or Isabelle's death would benefit her.

Peggy called for a taxi and waited outside for it. There was nothing else she could do, and she was tired. She wanted to go home. She left a message on Al's cell phone about Alice and Cindy while she was waiting. Maybe the information would be helpful.

The cold air cleared her head. It was dark at six p.m. The streets were starting to freeze over for the night. All that melting left a lot of water on the pavement that quickly became a glossy sheen under the streetlights' gleam.

She heard some rustling in the bushes close to the house. Thinking it was probably a cat caught in a frozen holly, she went to help. She took a step back when Cindy Walker emerged from the cover of blackness where the lights couldn't penetrate the shadows.

"Peggy! It's nice to see you again." Cindy's pale green ski-bunny outfit was perfect for her. Her blond hair was pushed up under a matching green knit cap with a white tassel on the top. "Cold out here, huh?"

"What are you doing out here, Cindy?"

"Not spying, if that's what you think. I was about to go in

and offer my condolences. Not that she'd come and offer any to *me*! And not that *I'm* not entitled to a few. He was my husband *first*! And he still loved me."

"You can sashay around the truth as much as you like," Peggy said, "but when it comes right down to it, Park was with Beth. Not *you*!"

"Not because he wanted to be," Cindy declared passionately. "He wanted to leave her. *She* wouldn't let him go. He didn't want to lose everything. That's the God's honest truth! Ask *her*!"

Peggy knew the only thing that kept this woman in Isabelle's good graces was that her father was a state senator and she had a pedigree that went back before the Civil War. Cindy had to make the Dragon Queen grind her teeth just to talk to her!

Unfortunately, she could hurt Beth's case with her last declaration. The police would listen to her once they knew the whole story. Especially since Beth had lied to them. "I'm sure you were devastated as well," she finally said to Cindy. "It's been hard for everyone. I'm sorry for your loss."

Cindy's shoulders sagged dramatically. "He was my life. She never loved him like I did. And he loved me. Now she's killed Isabelle, too. I have no one. What am I going to do?"

Peggy sympathized with her for a few minutes, patting her shoulder until the taxi came to take her home. But she thought about her for a long time after she left Myers Park. Cindy could be the prosecution's best witness against Beth. She was also a good suspect. But while she definitely had motive to kill Park, Peggy couldn't imagine her hurting Isabelle, her staunch supporter. *Park,* she sighed, *what a mess you left us in!*

PEGGY WAS GLAD TO be home safely after a five-minute drive became a twenty-minute obstacle course. A car was turned sideways on Providence Road, blocking all traffic. Her driver, David, knew some side streets to take and skidded down them to reach her house. She gave him a large tip and some advice on what to do for the cramps he was having in his legs. "Eat plenty of bananas. That should help. You might need to see a nutritionist."

"Thanks, Peggy. Those eyebright drops you recommended did good for my wife."

"That's wonderful, David! Eyebright will do the trick! Say hello to Agnes for me, and drive safely."

Shakespeare was barking loudly when she opened the door. He ran and slid across the wood floor, taking a rug and a table with him, crashing into the wall. He looked up from his upside down, feet-in-the-air position and wagged his tail.

"You're a mess," she told him as she extricated him from his tangle. "If we don't get over to get those lessons soon, there won't be anything left of the house or the shop."

She made herself a light supper of cheese and crackers while she looked through her mail and watched the news on TV. She was headed upstairs to change clothes and check on her plants when Hunter called. Beth had called her, as she promised.

"This is bad, Peggy," Hunter began. "When the police find out Beth and Park were having problems, then a big insurance policy surfaces after he dies, it will be very bad."

Peggy sighed. "I know. There's nothing we can do about it now. Let's hope they don't find anything suspicious about Park's accident. No matter how guilty Beth looks, if there's no crime, it doesn't matter."

Hunter agreed. "I hope she's not hiding anything else from me. I can't help her if I don't know the truth."

"I know. I'm sorry this happened. But I really think it was a mistake and nothing calculated on her part." She told her about her words with Alice and Cindy.

"I hope so," Hunter said. "On a lighter note, Sam took me out to a nice pizza and spaghetti place for dinner. There was no one there, so we got great service. They closed the place down as we were leaving."

"That's great," Peggy enthused. "But Sam is going to be with his new friends a lot. You need a boyfriend to take you out to dinner."

"Easier said than done. The last date I had was two years ago when a junior partner at a law firm took me out for lunch."

"What happened to him?"

"He was interviewing me for a job." Hunter laughed. "Pathetic, isn't it? But it's the best I can do. It's not easy meeting men when you work twenty hours every day."

"I'll have to see what I can do. You're gorgeous! There's no reason why any man shouldn't be proud to be with you!"

"Thanks but no thanks, Peggy. I don't need to be matched up like Paul and Mai. They knew each other first anyway. I'm going online now to order some clothes. Maybe I'll order up a boyfriend, too! Talk to you later."

Peggy went upstairs to change her clothes. The house was cold. She put on a purple sweatsuit and thick socks. She wouldn't put her hands in the pond and get soaked tonight! That cantankerous old furnace was acting up again. She was going to have to give it a good kick when she got downstairs.

But before she reached the basement, she heard knocking at the door. Shakespeare ran for the front foyer like a tan, furry rocket. He didn't let up until he slammed headfirst into the heavy door. Even *that* impact only stunned him for a moment. But it was long enough for her to answer the door. "Mai! Come in! How are you?"

"I'm fine, Peggy. I can't believe the roads are freezing so fast." She glanced at Shakespeare as he shook his head. "Is something wrong with your dog?"

"Not really." Peggy patted his head. "He's a little wild right now. Thankfully, he's hardheaded, too." She took Mai's coat and hat and hung them on a rack in the foyer. "Would you like some tea?"

"That would be wonderful, thanks." Mai rubbed her cold hands together. "I brought *you* a plant for a change." She handed Peggy a wilted begonia. "My mother gave it to me. Do you think you can help it?"

"I'm not sure." Peggy examined the nearly dead plant. "I'll do what I can. I think you may have overwatered. But you didn't come here just to bring me a dead begonia."

"Not exactly. I hope you don't mind me coming over without calling first. I really need to talk to you."

Peggy frowned. "Is it about Park or Isabelle?"

"No. We aren't finished with that yet. It's about me and Paul."

"Oh!" Peggy led the way to the kitchen. "I'm sorry. I get so caught up in other people's problems. Paul told me you two are house hunting."

"See, that's the thing." Mai sat down at the old oak table. She glanced around the room at the fragrant bunches of drying herbs on the wall and the shelf of seedlings in the window. "Paul wants us to move in together. I don't think I'm ready. But he's insistent. *Very* insistent. I don't know what to do."

Peggy put some water in the copper kettle and set it on the stove to heat. This was exactly what she was afraid of. "Have you told him you aren't ready?"

"Dozens of times. He's as hardheaded as Shakespeare. I don't want to lose him. But I need some time. We've only been dating a few months. I'm not ready to give up my own place yet. Not to mention that he wants to buy a house to prove himself to me. I'm *really* not ready for that."

"I understand. When he told me about the house and the extra job, I was concerned he was pushing a little too hard. He was always like that as a child. He'd make a new friend and want to spend every waking moment with him. I guess he gets *very* attached very quickly."

Mai drew invisible patterns on the tabletop. "And I really like him. He's fun to be with. We have a good time together. But I'm only getting started in my career. I don't know if I want something so serious right now. Neither one of us makes much money either. I know I don't want a house if Paul has to work all those hours to pay for it. It's all we can do to find time together now with both of our schedules."

Peggy nodded as she brought the hot mugs of cranberry tea to the table and sat opposite Mai. "What can I do?"

"I guess I was hoping you'd talk to him." Mai sipped her tea, warming her hands on the mug. "I don't want to break up with him over this. I want us to stay the way we are for a while."

"I'll be glad to try to set him straight," Peggy promised. "His father was the same way. John and I were married within a month after meeting. He followed me around until I thought I'd have to slap him to get him to go away. I told him I never wanted to see him again. He sent me magnolia flowers in the dead of winter. I still have no idea where he got them."

Mai grinned. "So what did you do?"

"I guess I succumbed and married him. I wasn't so sure about it, but he seemed sure enough for both of us. I never regretted the decision. It wasn't that I didn't love him, you see. It was just that it was too fast for me. John was always one step ahead."

"Then Paul *does* take after his father," Mai agreed. "But I can't do this right now, Peggy. Please see if you can get him to understand. I don't want to hurt him."

Peggy agreed, and they talked about other things. They went downstairs to look at Peggy's plants, and Mai tried to catch the bullfrog who laughed at her from the edge of the pond. She never even got close.

Mai left an hour later after more tea and ginger cookies. They hugged quickly, then she disappeared into the night outside. After discussing her problem with Paul, they talked about everything else *but* her son. Peggy wasn't sure if she could convince him to back down from getting the house. If Mai's arguments weren't enough, what good would her words be?

She talked to Steve for a while on the phone while she recorded data on her experiments. He didn't have any advice about Paul. He told her about his animal emergency from that morning. A cat had her claw stuck in the leather collar her owner was trying to teach her to wear. It wasn't much as emergencies went, but everything he did helped his new veterinary practice to grow in Charlotte.

After finishing with her plants, Peggy went upstairs to her room to shower and change. Contrary to her personal pledge not to get wet, she was soaked again. She shivered when she got out of the shower and threatened the old furnace with getting a new one. She didn't want to think what that would cost for a twenty-five-room house. She hoped the trust fund set up by John's grandparents would take care of it. She'd have to approach John's uncle to find out. Not a pleasant proposition, since he'd made it clear he thought she should move out when John died.

The message light was flashing on her computer, sidetracking her from joining Shakespeare in the warm bed. She wrapped her robe a little closer and sat down at the desk. She'd been waiting for a message from a colleague at Berkeley for some help with her strawberries. Maybe this was it.

She waded through the hundred e-mails she normally received in a day. There were ten *phishing* letters from banks and credit card companies. Some she did business with. Some she didn't. They always asked for personal financial information under the guise of helping her in some way.

She knew better but wasn't sure if everyone did. She saw a message about *phishing* for information that could lead to identity theft on a university bulletin board. It was a warning for students, but clearly, anyone using a computer needed to be aware of it.

Four messages were left when she got done with her junk e-mail. One was from her mother in Charleston, asking if Peggy was coming down for her birthday in June. Another was from the university giving her the final dates for exams. The third was from a student who wondered if Peggy would give him a private tutorial in poisonous plants. The fourth was an invitation to play chess.

There was no doubting who the invitation was from. His return e-mail address was different, but his handle was the same. She hadn't heard from Nightflyer in weeks. A tiny thrill ran down her spine even as she debated whether or not she should get involved with him again.

Not that she knew him personally. She'd never met him except over the cyber chessboard. But he was an exceptional opponent. She'd missed playing against him. She thought she might never hear from him again, not sure if he was only in contact with her because of the Warner murder. He was an ex-CIA agent who'd worked with John and was very mysterious about himself, but he'd been right about the incidents involved with the murder.

He'd given her a link to a new chess site. Peggy clicked on it and found she was already signed up to play. This site was different than most she played on. Two opponents were matched all the time unless one asked to change. Most places she waited to find a partner for a game. It could be anyone, anywhere, from Canada to New Zealand.

Nightflyer logged in right after her. As always, it was as though he was monitoring her computer. Or maybe he was just set up to receive a message when she logged in. It wasn't unheard of. She had to stop thinking conspiracy theories about him.

"Hello, Nightrose!" He greeted her. *"Are you ready to play?"*

The board was set up on Peggy's screen with her as the white player. She made her first move: pawn to e4. *"I didn't expect to hear from you again."*

"Sorry I had to desert you for a while. Some old war wounds giving me trouble." He moved to counter her: pawn to c5.

"I hope you're feeling better. I'm not going to let you win because you tell me some sob story." Peggy smiled as she moved her next piece: knight to f3.

"Excellent move. You've been practicing." He slid his piece across the checkered board: knight to f6. *"How have you been? I was sorry to hear about your friend."*

"I'm fine. I just got back from a conference in Pennsylvania. I won't ask how you know about Park. I have this picture in my mind of you sitting in front of twenty monitors, reading news reports from all over the world." She moved again: pawn to e5.

"That's too close to the truth!" He took her pawn. *"His wife will be charged with his murder."*

"Are you psychic now?" Knight to c3. She moved too quickly and bit her lip. *"Park was killed in an accident. I'm sure you know I witnessed it."*

"There's more going on than you realize. I believe Park was killed in the accident you saw, but what caused the accident?" Pawn to d4.

Peggy considered his move before making her own. *"Are you saying Beth is responsible for his accident in some way?"*

"No. I'm saying she'll be charged in the matter. I don't think she's guilty. I'm waiting for a pattern to emerge." Bishop to g5.

"Not in the mood for subtlety, are you?" She surveyed her

position. *"Are you telling me everything you know? Is there something I should look for?"*

"I'll let you know. Your move. Careful not to make yourself more vulnerable. Speaking of which, be careful, Nightrose. This could be dangerous for you."

Peggy was distracted by his conversation and didn't move at all. *"Could you be more precise about the danger? I like riddles as much as anyone, but nice, solid answers would be good. If I'm going to help Beth, I need to understand everything."*

"That's all I can tell you until I know more. I'll get back to you when I do. Do you want to finish the game?"

His evasive answers made her angry. *"I don't think so. I'd like to know more about how you gather your information."*

"Maybe some other time. Good night, Nightrose. Better get that dog some training!"

She sat back in her chair. *"How did you know? Are you monitoring my phone calls?"*

"ROTFL! Or I saw your name and Shakespeare's name on Rue Baker's Web site. What do I have to do to get you to trust me?"

"Lunch?" ROTFL: online chat and e-mail talk for rolling on the floor laughing. So he thought it was funny?

"Maybe. Someday. Oh ye of little faith. I may have to call you Thomas. Good luck with finding out what happened to your friend. I'll do what I can to help you."

"Thanks." She logged off right after him. Men could be *such* a problem!

PEGGY WAS BETWEEN CLASSES the next morning when Mai called her cell phone. "We finished most of the new work on Lamonte's car this morning. Took it apart. There was nothing wrong that would make it unsafe. Just like the insurance company said."

"That's good news," Peggy replied in relief. "What about the autopsy?"

"That's another story. There was nothing overt that we found in examining him the first time. He definitely died from

massive trauma following the accident. But there *was* something unusual in his tox screen when we dug deeper. They sent
the results to Raleigh for more analysis. We couldn't identify
what we found."

"What did you find?"

"Some kind of foreign substance. The ME isn't sure if it
has anything to do with the case. In fact, he's really leaning
toward it being a natural health food kind of thing."

Peggy frowned. Park never used a natural health food
product in his life. The few times they'd discussed anything of
the sort brought snickers and jeers from him. He was definitely a meat-and-potatoes, traditional medicine (if any!) kind
of person. "Can you tell me what the substance was without
endangering your job?"

"I don't see why not, since it probably isn't anything important anyway. It was bee pollen. The kind people take for
instant energy. You know what I mean? Mr. Lamonte had a
high concentration of it in his body."

"Bee pollen?" Peggy was amazed. Had Park finally succumbed to her way of thinking? Was he trying to combat the
fatigue she saw in his face with bee pollen?

"That's it," Mai agreed. "Looks like your friend is off the
hook. At least on her husband's death."

"Thanks for letting me know. May I tell Beth?"

"I think the chances are pretty small that a police detective
will tell her." Mai laughed. "They tend to only want to deliver
bad news. Everything else you get in a report. Does Beth have
a lawyer yet?"

Peggy told her about Hunter being involved. "I'm sure
they'll both be glad Park's death didn't turn out to be a homicide investigation."

"I'm not too sure about Hunter. I think she's still looking
for that big score that will make her famous."

It was past time for Peggy to go to her next class. She half
agreed with Mai about Hunter, thanked her again for calling,
and hurried out of the teachers' lounge. She wasn't able to call
Beth until the Botany 301 class was over. By that time, Hunter

had already gleaned the information from *her* sources and given her client the good news.

"I can't believe it's over!" Beth gushed. "I thought it would be so much harder."

"You were lucky it didn't go any further," Peggy assured her. "Anyway, I'm very happy it turned out this way for you and the boys."

"Thank you so much for your help. Why don't you bring Steve over for a celebration dinner tonight? Is seven okay with you?"

"That's fine. I'll check with Steve."

"Please come anyway, even if he's busy. I feel like there wouldn't be a celebration without you."

Peggy called Steve at his office and asked him about dinner.

"That's fine," he agreed. "I should be done checking out this pregnant hamster by then."

She laughed as throngs of students passed her, spilling out of the school into the sunshine. "What is there to check out on a pregnant hamster?"

"The owner thinks the hamster is past her due date," Steve said then added, "Well maybe not. Here they come now. Call you back later."

There was no sign of the snow or ice that had changed everyone's lives for a few days. Peggy got her bike out of the rack and headed for home. She'd managed to squeeze in an appointment with Rue Baker at Whiskers and Paws right after lunch. Things were looking up.

She watched a noon report on Channel 14 news that included a small bit about Isabelle. The reporter talked about the mysterious circumstances of her death and her life as a social leader in Charlotte before her husband died.

Peggy couldn't believe the police would continue to investigate Isabelle's death as a possible homicide after Park's death was declared an accident. The Dragon Queen's autopsy probably wouldn't be finished for a few days. Hopefully, it would indicate natural causes. The position of her cane, missing dragon's head, even the bloody letter could go away in that light. If Beth was cleared of any wrongdoing in Park's death, it wouldn't make sense for her to attack Isabelle.

Of course those were all *her* concepts. The police brain was different. Especially Jonas's brain!

Keeley pulled up in Peggy's drive a little before one. It took both of them to get Shakespeare into the Potting Shed truck. Once he was inside, he kept trying to get on the floor, wagging his tail and barking at them. "I hope this woman you're taking him to knows what she's doing," Keeley said, pushing the dog away with her foot.

"I hope so, too. Steve thinks Shakespeare's the same as he's always been. But I think he's much worse. I don't know what happened to him." Peggy finished speaking just as they were about to go over the same ramp that she'd watched Park's car plummet from. It seemed to go up much higher than she noticed before. At one point, it looked as though the truck was going to fly off the edge as well.

Peggy gripped the dash as they went past the spot where the safety wall was demolished. In her mind, she could see the Lincoln flying down over the edge again.

"Are you okay?" Keeley asked, her dark eyes concerned.

"I'm fine." Peggy smiled at her and forced herself to let go of the dash. "I guess I'm just a little nervous after seeing what happened to Park."

"I can understand that. My psych professor says the mind plays tricks on us, but usually it's trying to protect us from what we can't deal with."

"I'm sure he's right in this case." Peggy took a deep breath and forced herself to relax. "It's hard seeing something like that happen to a stranger. To find out it was someone I know has been very difficult."

Whiskers and Paws was easy to find once they got to the Ballantyne area. It was a neat little shop with cartoon dogs and cats on the windows facing the street. Rue Baker was as nice as Steve described her. A good thing, since the moment Shakespeare saw her, he ran and jumped on her. His weight pushed her back into a desk and shoved several plastic paper trays clattering to the white tile floor.

"This must be Shakespeare." Rue laughed as she righted herself. She ran a hand across her very short, very blond hair. Her brown eyes summed up the problem. "You need obedience classes more than most dogs, don't you? It would take a poodle a long time to do the damage you could accomplish in five minutes."

Shakespeare woofed deeply and tried to push his nose into the pocket of her jeans.

"Nope. No treats for you, big fella. Treats are for good dogs who don't assault strangers."

Peggy ran up and dragged the dog off of the trainer. "I'm so sorry. He's been such a handful lately. I hope you can help."

They introduced themselves as Rue rubbed Shakespeare's head. "I hope so, too. Let's get an idea of what he already knows. I don't like to overtrain. If he already knows some commands, we'll work from there."

She tried to get the dog to sit. Shakespeare lay down on the floor. She tried to get him to stay, and he ran toward the door. "Let me see what you can do with him, Peggy."

It was the same. "I know he's big and unruly, but I think he listened better before I went to Pennsylvania recently. Could that have anything to do with it?"

Rue shook her head. "I don't think so. Behavior with a dog is learned. You probably noticed it more after being away. I'd like to get classes set up with him twice a week to start. Can you commit to that? It's very important you're here as well."

Peggy agreed. At that point, she would've agreed to almost anything that might help. They set up for that week on Tuesday and Thursday afternoons. She thanked Rue and apologized again for Shakespeare's rude behavior.

"That's okay. We'll take care of it. Right, boy?"

In response, Shakespeare knocked over two plastic chairs in the waiting area. Peggy was sure she felt a headache coming on.

10

Bay

Botanical: *Laurus nobilis*
Family: N. O. Lauraceae
Common name: Sweet bay

Bay is another name for laurel, the leaf of fame and glory. In ancient times, this small tree was endowed with many magical properties including warding off evil and averting lightning strikes. It is now used mainly in the kitchen to flavor meats and vegetables and for decorating purposes.

STEVE PICKED HER UP at the shop that evening. "You'll be happy to hear I have five healthy baby hamsters."

"Congratulations." Peggy smiled at him. "I suppose the owner is very happy."

"You don't get it. *I'm* the owner. The mother hamster's owner doesn't want the babies. Her allowance won't stretch to feeding more than one. She bought the hamster without realizing she was pregnant."

"Oh. What do you do in a case like that?"

"I try to give them away." He turned the car on Providence Road and grinned at her. "Want a hamster or two?"

"I don't think so. I can't even handle my dog." She told him about her visit to Rue's shop. "You were right. She's very nice and seemed very professional."

Beth's house was a riot of light when they pulled up in the drive. Several other cars were already there, including Hunter's SUV.

"Rue *is* special," he agreed. "She has a lot of patience with animals. I'm sure she'll be good for Shakespeare."

"Did you date her?" Peggy asked without thinking. "I'm sorry. That's none of my business."

"That's okay." He smiled and kissed her gently. "I like it when my woman gets jealous. But no, I didn't date Rue. She's married."

"Looks like quite a crowd," Peggy remarked, changing the subject as they went up to the house. She felt like an idiot for asking about Rue. It just suddenly popped out of her mouth. She wasn't *jealous.* Just nosy.

"I hope all the food isn't gone." Steve looked mournful. "I haven't eaten since breakfast. All the excitement of the birth, I suppose."

They left their coats in the foyer and mingled with the other guests. Something smelled good in the kitchen, where a caterer was warming food and getting ready to serve. The large dining room table was set with crystal and china from end to end. A wonderful bay wreath was set in the center with a large, squat, white candle in the middle.

Peggy saw Alice helping the caterer. The housekeeper turned her head when she saw her. She wondered if Al had spoken to her to give her such a sour face. The housekeeper might not be guilty of anything, but it couldn't hurt to have her answer some questions. She couldn't help but wonder what the answers would be.

She left Steve by the fireplace with a group of professional-looking people who were asking about heartworm and went to look for Beth. She glanced at the counter when she reached the kitchen. All the cake boxes and food containers that had been there after Park's death were gone, along with what was left of the gift basket he brought back from the hotel.

A sharp stab of awareness shot through Peggy's mind. Her stomach churned, and her heart skipped a beat. *Bee pollen,*

Mai said. Where is the half-eaten jar of honey Park brought back with him from Philadelphia?

"Peggy! I'm so glad you could come!" Beth threw her arms around Peggy's neck and hugged her.

"Where's the jar of honey that came from the basket Park brought back from his trip?"

"I'm not sure." Beth glanced around the kitchen. "It might have been thrown away. But I have some other honey in the pantry. Would you like that instead? I could go out and get you some honey."

"No." Peggy's brain worked furiously, considering the possibilities. "When did you throw it away? Was your trash picked up yet?"

"I'm not sure when it was thrown away. I can ask Alice. She might know. Or Mom might have done it. But today was trash day. I was surprised they came after the snow and all. Usually it takes a few extra days for them to get back on schedule. It was just as well though. With all the food boxes, we needed a pickup. Peggy? What are you thinking?"

"Did you or the boys eat any of that honey?"

"No, I don't think so. Park ate almost the whole jar. You know how he loved sweets."

Peggy nodded, her mind already raking over the possibilities. "I have to go. Give my love to the boys. I'll talk to you later." She found Steve in the great room sampling some cheese puffs and talking with Beth's parents. "Excuse me." She took his arm and drew him away as she smiled and nodded at Beth's mother and father. "I'm sorry, but I have to go."

"Is something wrong? Did someone call you? Did Shakespeare break out?"

"Something's wrong," she confirmed, going back toward the front door for her coat. "I have to go to the landfill."

"The landfill?" He followed her, weaving through the people who were just arriving. "Please tell me that's a pet name for the Potting Shed and not the place where they take the garbage."

Peggy smiled but didn't wait to put her coat on before she scooted out the door. "I wish it was. But I may have a lead on something Mai told me today. I have to find a jar of honey."

Steve used his keyless remote to unlock the doors on the Vue. "Couldn't we just go to Harris Teeter and *buy* honey? Isn't all honey the same?"

She closed her car door and took out her cell phone. "No, actually, all honey isn't the same. It varies from place to place, according to where the bees gather the pollen. I wish it *were* that simple. You don't have to feel obligated to come with me. It's going to be a nasty job."

"You know I'm not going to let you go by yourself." His voice said he wished he could. "Can we at least go home and change clothes? I just bought these shoes, and I *really* like them."

"Thank you, Steve." She leaned over and kissed him as he started the engine. "Of course we'll go home and change first. I'm going to see who else I can scrounge up to help us. It's a big landfill. We're going to need all the help we can get."

"In that case, why not call the police? Surely they'd have more manpower than we can muster. And it would probably be legal for them to search the landfill."

"I think it's too soon to call them." She squashed his dreams of sitting in the Vue and waiting to see what the police could find. "They have a little trouble believing I know what I'm talking about. Jonas was downright hostile about it. But I don't think it's against the law for people to look through the trash."

Steve accepted his fate with grace and dignity. "I'll drop you off at your house and pick you up again in twenty minutes."

"That works. Thank you. If I'm right, we could find out what *really* happened to Park before he died."

After Steve dropped her off, Peggy changed clothes quickly into what she would normally wear to work with her plants. In a gray sweatsuit and dirty old Reeboks, she called Sam, Keeley, and Selena as she walked Shakespeare. The other three promised to meet her at the landfill and bring any other people they could find.

Peggy spent the rest of the time cleaning up the mess Shakespeare made of a pillow he'd shredded while she was gone. "I don't know what *else* I'm going to do with you," she told the dog. "But if you don't stop being so destructive, I'm going to have to lock you in the pantry."

The dog howled mournfully, as though he understood her threat. He lay down on the floor and put his paws over his face.

She laughed and rubbed his head. "Don't bother looking cute either. It won't save you. You'd better learn something from Rue when we start taking those classes."

Steve picked her up again exactly twenty minutes later as promised. "So where *is* the city landfill?"

"Get on Interstate 77 northbound, and we'll go from there," she explained. "I won't confuse you with other street names, since you're new to the area and probably wouldn't know where I'm talking about."

"There must be more than one," he remarked, turning the Vue toward the interstate. "How are you going to know which one?"

Peggy smiled. "Carlos Gonzales. He drives a taxi now, but he used to work in sanitation. I called him to ask which land-fill Beth's garbage would go to. We should only have to search one. You're in luck."

Steve laughed as he accelerated to match speeds with the other fast-moving cars on the interstate. "Boy, am I *lucky*!"

"You don't have to do this," she told him again. "Sam and some others are going to meet us out there. You can drop me off. I don't think scrounging through the landfill falls under normal dating practices."

"I wouldn't miss it!" He grinned in her direction. "I've never actually been in a landfill. I always wondered what one looked like."

"Okay, *that's* doing it a little heavy."

"Just tell me one thing. How are we going to find a single jar of honey in a whole landfill? That seems impossible."

"I'm banking on the fact that it's fresh trash from today. Whoever works out there should be able to tell us where the trash from Myers Park gets dumped. I hope that will narrow down the search to a few hundred houses."

"When you put it that way, it sounds easy. What do you think the honey has to do with Park's accident?"

She explained about the pollen the police sent away to have analyzed. "It might not be the same, but I know Park loved sweets, and I know he wasn't taking bee pollen for energy. Most of that jar was gone the last time I saw it. By the time the police get the tox report back from Raleigh, the jar will be long gone from the landfill, too. If it shows anything unusual, the evidence that could link it to where it came from would be lost."

Steve understood the concept. "It *seems* like the police would be interested in that."

"It *seems* that way," Peggy agreed. "But if I tell them about it and they decide it's stupid, they could keep me from finding the jar. This way, the worst that will happen is I'll have wasted everyone's time."

"Okay. I'm sold. I brought some pairs of surgical gloves and masks. I hope I have enough for everyone."

The landfill off Lakeview Road was enormous. It stretched over several acres, up and down hills. Trucks were still unloading. Bright lights kept the work possible all night long. Mounds of debris, some taller than houses, filled the horizon with every imaginable household item from mattresses to cookie dough with dirty diapers and empty dog food bags in between.

Sam and Hunter were already there with several of Sam's college friends. They got out of a brown van when Sam saw Peggy. "Wow! This place smells worse than it looks," Hunter said. "What are we doing out here?"

"We're looking for a jar of honey," Sam repeated. "And cheer up. It could be worse. I've brought stuff out here during the summer. It doesn't smell bad at all right now compared to *that*."

Selena and Keeley came up together in Keeley's orange Volkswagen Beetle. They got out slowly when they saw everyone else. "Are you sure this is the right place?" Selena asked Peggy. "I'm sure you didn't *really* mean the landfill, right? You don't *really* want us to search the landfill."

One of Sam's friends, a burly soccer player with the UNCC 49ers gave a loud yell and dove headfirst into a big, steaming pile of trash. He made swimming motions with his legs and arms to show Selena how it was done. "Come on in, gorgeous. The trash is exceptionally fine this evening."

Selena turned her back on him and made a terrible face. "Yuck! Am I supposed to find *that* attractive?"

"Let's get organized here." Peggy drew them all together. "I'm going to talk to that man in the shed over there and see where we need to go."

"Don't we need some kind of special permit to look through trash?" Hunter wondered hopefully.

"Let me find out," Peggy said, taking Steve with her to the guard shack.

The pock-faced man in the guard shack was wearing overalls and a ragged green sweater. He put down his stainless steel Stanley coffee thermos long enough to laugh at her request. "You're kidding, right? You can't just come out here and search for stuff. What if you're a terrorist or something? We gotta keep whack jobs away."

"It's very important," she explained. "We need to look tonight before the item we're looking for is gone."

He leaned back in his chair and sized her up with his eyes. "What's it worth to you? I'm not an unreasonable man."

Steve reached for his wallet, but Peggy refused to believe it was the only way to get into the landfill. "And I'm sure you're a compassionate man as well." She smiled. "A man might be dead because of something out here in the landfill. We need your help to find it. I'm sure that would bring you deep personal satisfaction, wouldn't it?"

The man scratched his stubbled chin. "Probably not as much as fifty dollars."

Peggy's smile changed as she leaned closer and tried another tactic. "There will be television cameras up here from *every* news network in North Carolina. You'll be famous after they ask you questions about what happened."

"Why didn't you *say* so?" The man's face brightened. "People say I sing like Roy Orbison. Look like him, too.

Maybe I could get an audition for *American Idol*! Simon would *love* me! What do you need?"

He told them where they'd find the fresh garbage from the Myers Park area. It covered an entire hillside. There was no other way to get there but to tramp through the muck to the spot. Avoiding potentially dangerous objects, the group walked out through the sea of trash while the landfill manager took out his electric razor to shave before the TV cameras got there.

"Peggy," Hunter began, "even if all of the trash from Myers Park *is* on this hill, how will we ever find a single jar of honey in it? It's impossible!

"There were a good many cake boxes, you know? Those big, square white boxes you get from Harris Teeter. I thought we could look for a group of those, and that would be Beth's trash."

"Oh. I see. Easy." Hunter rolled her eyes and mumbled, "We're *never* going to find this."

Peggy squeezed her arm. "Never is a very long time to spend in a garbage dump. Let's think positively, and maybe we'll be done by morning. That way, it will be so much easier to get the smell out of our hair. Maybe only one or two shampoos."

Hunter groaned as they reached the designated area. "Let's get this over with then. Too much shampooing makes my hair dry and frizzy."

Sam cordoned off individual sections for each person to search through. The trash was knee high on the surface. Fortunately, they didn't have to dig below that level to look for the jar. The large, intense spotlights made the night brighter than day. They illuminated every aluminum pie pan, disposable diaper, and open can in the mix.

Steve passed out surgical gloves and masks to each person, cautioning them not to touch their faces after rummaging through the trash. "These are only good if you don't get the bacteria near your nose or mouth. If the glove breaks open, I have some others. If you get cut, I hope your tetanus vaccinations are up to date."

One of Sam's friends hooted. "What about hepatitis, man? Not to mention a hundred other diseases we could get out here. This place is a germ haven. Don't you love it?"

Steve ignored him as he started looking through his section of trash. He watched Peggy, who was conveniently searching beside him. "He's crazy, but he's right, you know."

"You mean about the possibility of disease?" She kept searching without looking up at him. "There's probably more of a possibility for disease when you push a shopping cart at the supermarket."

"Has anyone ever mentioned the degree of determination that drives you?" He smiled as she slowly looked up and focused on him. "You're *very* persistent."

"If you mean I don't let a few bugs and viruses get in my way, you're right. I'm not sure we can find the honey jar, but at least we can try."

"Well then, have you thought what this might mean to an otherwise *closed* investigation?" Hunter asked from Peggy's left side. "Bringing anything else into the equation could mean more trouble for Beth from both investigations."

"The truth about what happened to Park is more important than Beth staying out of trouble," Peggy told her. "I know she'll feel that way, too."

"I think I found something." Selena held up a small jar from the other side of the hill. "It's definitely a honey jar." She slapped at a few ants who were keeping warm in the trash and didn't want to let go of their prize. "Can we go home now?"

"Does it have a blue label?" Peggy asked.

"No." Selena looked at the jar again, her hopeful smile fading. "It's white. Does it have to be a *blue* label?"

"The jar we're looking for has a blue label." Peggy started sorting through her trash again. "Sorry, sweetie. I forgot to tell you."

"That's okay." Selena tossed the jar over her shoulder. "I'll look for one with a *blue* label until I fall down and die of disease from being out here in this cesspool of human waste."

"Wow! Nice words," the soccer player beside her exclaimed. "Will you marry me and write my next thesis?"

They continued searching past midnight as garbage trucks continued to come in and dump their loads around them. It was cold but thankfully, not raining. The orange sky looked far off behind the glaring lights, bright stars invisible. The stench was overpowering. From time to time, someone groaned as they stepped into a partial cheesecake or a half-eaten chicken carcass.

Peggy's back was beginning to ache and her fingers were numb, but she kept digging. Doubt was beginning to seep in with the cold. Hunter's words nagged at her.

Even if they *could* find the jar and she *could* prove her theory about what happened to Park, who would benefit from it? It could reopen the investigation into her friend's death. She was worried about Beth. A deeper inquiry would bring out some unpleasant facts about the couple that had managed to stay hidden so far. If someone *had* hurt Park, she didn't want him or her to get away. Yet at what price? Foxx and Reddman stood to lose both their parents if Beth went to jail.

It was the scientist in her that kept her from calling off the whole thing. Discovering the truth and understanding what made something happen drove her. She could never put away a jigsaw or crossword puzzle until the whole thing was finished. She couldn't stop wondering until she knew what happened to Park either. She hoped he'd want it that way, too. She prayed they could prove Beth wasn't involved in any way.

Sam yelled from the top of the hill. Weary workers stood up and stretched as he ran down toward them. "I think I found it, Peggy! You said a blue label, right?"

She looked at the jar Sam held up in the light. It was the jar from the welcome basket given to Park by the hotel in Philadelphia. The label was a little messed up with some trash on it, but the jar was intact with the cap on tight. Peggy held it up to the light. The honey was at the same level she saw it on Beth's kitchen cabinet. "You're right, Sam. Good work! We can all go home now."

Steve and Hunter stood beside her and looked at the dark gold, syrupy fluid. The hot, white lights made it seem brighter than it was, showing the small particles in the otherwise clear substance.

"I hope it's worth it," Hunter said, transfixed by it.

"I hope so, too." Peggy put the bottle into a resealable plastic bag for protection. "We should know in a few hours. I have samples of honey and pollen in my collection. If I'm right, this could be what killed Park."

"No matter what, didn't the car accident still kill him?" Steve asked.

"Not if there were contributing factors," Hunter explained. "I mean, technically, the crash still killed him. But if something *made* him crash, something someone did to him, it's a whole other ball game."

Peggy thanked everyone for coming and offered to take them all out for breakfast. No one had the heart to eat anything with the way they smelled. All of them agreed to a rain check on the food.

"Where are the TV cameras?" The landfill manager glanced around the empty drive as everyone was leaving and he was tucking in his clean shirt. "You *promised* me TV cameras."

"They'll be here." Peggy walked by him quickly. "You'll get your ten seconds of fame. Thanks for your help."

He turned away and made a grunting sound. She wasn't sure if he was agreeing or blowing her off. Either way, if she was right, there *would* be television cameras. If she was wrong, she supposed she owed the man fifty dollars.

Steve threw sheets over the car seats in the Vue. "I'm prepared this time. I've learned to expect the unexpected when I'm with you."

"You're a wise man." She sighed heavily as she got in the car with the precious jar they'd all given up a night's sleep for. "I hope to God I'm right."

"Well, it's only a theory. Anyone can make a mistake. You'll have to look at something else if you're wrong."

"No, I mean I hope I'm right doing this. Sometimes all branches of science get so eager to show everyone the possibilities, to find the facts, they forget not everyone might be ready for them."

Steve covered her hand with his. "If someone poisoned your friend, you're right to find out. I'd want my friend to do that for me, even if it made other people's lives uncomfortable for a while. You're doing the last thing you'll ever do for him, Peggy. Don't feel bad about it."

"Thank you. I'm not sure if Beth will feel the same way. But I appreciate the sentiment *and* the support."

Steve dropped her off at her house. "I'd come in, but I have to go home and stand in the shower for an hour or two while I burn these clothes. Let me know if you find anything. I'll be glad to go with you to the police or to talk to Beth. You shouldn't have to do this alone."

"And I'd kiss you for offering." She grinned. "But I don't think we should get that close. With both of us smelling this bad, it could cause some kind of explosion that would destroy the very fabric of time."

He laughed. "No more science fiction for you. Good night, Peggy. I'll talk to you later." He didn't try to kiss her.

AN HOUR LATER, AFTER taking a long shower, Peggy threw away her ancient gray sweat suit. She walked Shakespeare after cleaning up what was left of Mai's begonia, which he'd managed to knock on the floor. There wasn't much, but she found one healthy stem just above a leaf node and cut it off. After dipping the end in rooting hormone, she put the cutting in some moist potting soil and said a little prayer over it as she put it into the kitchen window. It couldn't hurt.

Peggy sat down at the kitchen table when she was finished and looked at the jar of honey in the plastic bag. It would be simple to throw it back in the garbage. Hunter, Sam, and the other kids out there at the landfill wouldn't care what happened now that the adventure was over. Hunter might even welcome not seeing the jar again. Peggy could explain to Steve, and he'd understand.

It was only that nagging voice in the back of her head that drove her to search for the jar once she'd thought about the bee pollen found in Park's system. It was seeing Park's tired face at the hotel when he invited her to dinner when they got home. It was recalling when he stood beside her as they lowered John's coffin into the ground. Sense and reason were fighting a losing battle against those powerful images in her mind.

If she was right and the honey was poisoned, the chances were the police would begin looking at Beth again as a suspect. She had opportunity. They'd argue she had motive. Peggy couldn't offer them a better suspect. She didn't know for sure she ever could. How much satisfaction would there be in seeing Beth behind bars for a crime Peggy knew she didn't commit? To see her children raised by grandparents or strangers?

She roused herself from her slumped, exhausted position at the kitchen table. On the other hand, if the honey *was* poisoned and it *was* responsible for Park's death, someone killed her friend. Or at least contributed to his death. She had a responsibility to him as well. She had to trust her instincts. Beth *didn't* do this. She had to believe they would find the person who did this to Park, even if Beth had to suffer some discomfort while they searched for the truth.

Making the decision gave her the strength to put the kettle on the stove and go upstairs to get dressed. She had no classes that day, but she was due at Whiskers and Paws for Shakespeare's first obedience class that afternoon. Plenty of time to go in and talk to Mai and spend some time at the Potting Shed.

She put on her warm cranberry-red sweater and matching wool slacks, then fussed with her hair before finally covering it with a cranberry wool cap. She drank her tea and ate some orange bread before closing Shakespeare into the laundry room. "You only have yourself to blame," she told the whining Great Dane. "If you'll stop vandalizing the house, I'll let you out. Until then, you're under restriction."

Peggy rode her bicycle through the early morning traffic before rush hour. It was cold, frost making her face feel tight. There was light on the horizon behind the tall buildings that made up the downtown area of Charlotte as the sun began to rise. It would be another hard night for the trees and plants around the city. The heavy white frost lay thick as icing on a birthday cake as she locked her bike in the rack outside the uptown precinct.

"Can I help you?" the sergeant behind the desk asked brusquely when she walked through the door.

She glanced at the three men and one woman already waiting in the outer area. They looked back at her with vacant stares and hostile expressions. "I'd like to see Mai Sato. Is she in?"

"Not yet. Take a seat."

Peggy sat by the side door that led to the offices in the back. John had worked here for twenty years, but everything had changed since he died. Once in a while, she met someone who'd worked with him. Mostly his friends were retired or had changed divisions.

She looked at the ficus she'd managed to save from extinction last fall. The police department didn't have the budget to hire the Potting Shed or any other plant service to take care of the random plants at each of the precincts, according to Al. Moving the plant away from the door helped it survive in the hostile office environment, but it wouldn't last for long without some care. She stuck her fingers in the soil. It was too dry. She'd mention it to Mai when she saw her. Someone had to water the thing once in a while, and she didn't see that task falling to Jonas or Al.

Mai finally came in about forty-five minutes later. "Peggy! What are you doing here?"

"It's a long story." Peggy stood up on stiff legs from her hard wood chair. "Do you have a few minutes?"

"Sure. I have a meeting at ten. But I'd love to talk to you until then." Mai took Peggy back to her office that wasn't much larger than a broom closet.

Peggy explained about her theory and her hunt through the landfill during the night as Mai made coffee.

The assistant ME's eyes widened as she listened. "I can't believe you did that!" She hit herself in the forehead with the palm of her hand. "What am I saying? Of *course* I can. Did you bring the honey with you?"

Peggy pulled it out of her book bag. She set the jar in the plastic bag on Mai's desk. "I haven't tested it yet. I thought it might be better if we did it here."

Mai didn't touch the plastic bag, just looked at it. "You know, even if we find the same pollen in this honey, we won't be able to use it as evidence. Anything could've been added or tampered with other ways."

"I understand the chain of evidence." Peggy's green eyes were thoughtful. "But if the enzymes you found in Park's body match the enzymes in the honey he got from the hotel, it might give you something to work with that you can use as evidence."

"This could bring forward a case against his wife." Mai didn't shrink from telling her the truth. "She had opportunity, since the honey was at home with him. She had motive, ten million dollars' worth of motive. You could be opening up a big can of worms with this jar."

Peggy sighed and looked at the jar. "I know."

Mai put on surgical gloves. "Okay. Let's get started."

11

Sassafras

Botanical: *Sassafras albidum*
Family: N. O. Lauraceae

Sassafras was used by Native Americans for infections and gastrointestinal problems. It was one of the first exports from the New World as a beverage and medicine, the originator of the term "root beer."

"It's definitely horse chestnut honey." Mai looked at the two samples under the microscope. "And it matches the pollen we found in Mr. Lamonte. Is there anything else you can tell me about it?"

Peggy sighed. It was a bittersweet victory for her since there was no way of knowing how it would affect Beth. "The horse chestnut tree is so poisonous, it will kill the bees that harvest the pollen for the honey. But you know how persistent bees are. They keep going, passing it on to the next workers, all the while eventually killing the hive."

"My poison chart tells me these trees only grow in California." Mai took off her glasses. "This honey came from Pennsylvania."

"Your poison chart is partially correct," Peggy agreed. "But the trees also grow in Ohio and a few other states. The horse chestnut is actually in the same family as our own native buckeye. So the honey could be harvested in a good many places. But no respectable honey grower would allow that tree near their bees."

"I suppose the question then would be who put the poisoned honey in the jar. Was it an accident or something done on purpose?"

"We should contact this producer, Elmwood Farms, and see what they know about it. There may be other tainted jars."

Mai nodded. "I'll run this by the ME and see what he thinks. I hope you realize that if this is the *only* jar, the problem is going to fall in Mrs. Lamonte's lap again."

Peggy understood that possibility and hoped it was just a bad batch of honey, as tragic as that would be. "Have you heard anything about Isabelle's autopsy?"

"Not yet. I'm sure that will be another factor." Mai shrugged. "If her death is ruled an accident, the daughter-in-law will be less attractive for a case about the husband."

"Thanks, Mai. Please keep me posted."

Mai squeezed her hand. "I will. You did the right thing. I know it had to be hard for you."

"Let's hope for the best, shall we?" Peggy gathered her book bag and coat. She was almost out the door when she ran into Jonas.

He stepped back out of the way for her to leave Mai's office. Then he recognized her. "Please tell me you aren't here to help with anything." He sneezed and blew his nose on a handkerchief.

"I told you all those bottled-up emotions would give you a cold! I'm here to visit Mai," she maintained. "You act like I wasn't a big help solving the Warner case. You know, you could use a forensic botanist on staff."

He sneezed a few times, then laughed. "We don't have a budget for anything right now, Peggy. I'm not sure what a forensic botanist does, but I'll let you know if the position becomes available. As for the Warner case, that was dumb luck and being in the right place at the wrong time. I hope *you* realize you were lucky you weren't killed."

"I hope *you* realize you'd have the wrong person in jail right now if it weren't for me," she scolded, not caring about the interested onlookers in the hall. "And a forensic botanist can do many things for a police department, including help catch people who use poison to murder people."

"I realize I could've had another dead body to add to my homicide file if *you* weren't so lucky!" he said in a nasal voice, then glanced at Mai, who looked away. "And if I hear of *anyone* from this department helping you, he or she will face suspension. Amateurs don't belong in this business! We're the police, not some Girl Scout group looking to earn merit badges!

"I'm sure he or she is quaking." Peggy moved smoothly past him. "You need to relax, Jonas. You're not doing a bit of good for your stomach, you know. You have to watch that!"

"Look. I like you, Peggy. I really do. You're a good person, and I know you mean well. But this isn't the place for a good person to help out. Try the Salvation Army or the Red Cross."

Before she could speak, Jonas slammed the door to Mai's office with her on the outside. She could hear him questioning the girl from the hall. It wouldn't do him any good. The deed was already done. She knew Mai wouldn't knuckle under to him. Really, he could be such a tyrant!

Peggy unlocked her bike from the rack outside after an unproductive discussion about the state of the plants in the precinct building with the desk sergeant. Why have plants at all if no one wanted to care for them? The sergeant was unsure why the ficus was there, but *he* didn't plan on watering it. He told her he'd be happy to set it out on the street, if that would make her happy. She left before she did any more damage.

Charlotte streets were picking up traffic as the brilliant blue sky beamed down on them. The smells of the city—bus diesel, coffee, garbage, and rubber from a hastily applied brake—assailed her. She was glad to finally reach the Potting Shed and shut herself inside with the aroma of potting soil and old wood. It would be wonderful to lose herself in her plants for a while and not think about death and dying. Plants were the ultimate faith in life. When she planted a small sprout and watched it grow, she knew she was adding to the chain of life.

An order of Hoop's blue spruce and Gold Mop thread cypress arrived as soon as she got her coat off and started getting set up for what she hoped would be a busy workday. She signed the delivery sheet for the driver, then got to work moving the two-foot trees into the back storage area.

All twenty of the trees were on back order from a company in the North Carolina mountains. They were hearty, beautiful trees that would provide their owners with years of enjoyment. The blue spruce wouldn't grow as big here as in a cooler climate, but it would still be a nice ornamental. With its milky blue needles and conelike shape, it would enhance any yard.

Sam came in about twenty minutes later, amazed to find all the trees tucked away and Peggy cleaning the shop in time for it to open. "You've been busy. You're either angry or frantically thinking about something you can't do anything about. Or both!"

She frowned. "You know me pretty well." She stopped organizing the bulb rack. "I gave the honey sample to Mai. I was right. It was horse chestnut."

"Wow! That could account for Park falling asleep at the wheel, right?"

"It could. Drowsiness is one of the side effects. If he'd eaten enough in a short span of time, he wouldn't have had to drive his car off the ramp to die. It can be very toxic to humans."

"What happens now?"

Peggy shrugged. "Mai is talking to the ME. I'm sure they'll compare the samples again. Mine isn't within the guidelines for the chain of evidence, so it can't be used. It can only point them in the right direction. I don't really know, after that."

"Do you think other people were poisoned as well and didn't realize it?" Sam glanced at the delivery schedule for the day.

"I'm sure the police will contact the manufacturer. We'll see then."

"Well, let me know. I lost a good pair of jeans to this exercise. I thought bleach would take the smell out." He grinned. "It did. But it also shredded my new *white* jeans."

"I'm sorry, Sam." She hid a smile and touched his hand. "I'll be glad to get you a new pair."

"Thanks, but I'll manage. Next time I'll just roll around in some manure and save myself the cost of a bottle of bleach. No one will notice the difference." He tucked his hands in his pockets. "I'm off to work in Madelyn Montgomery's yard. Those Gold Mop thread cyprus are going to look great. Anything you need before I go?"

"No, I'm fine. Thanks. Say hello to her for me. Be careful you plant those cypress trees deep enough. You don't want their roots to come out looking for water over the summer."

He laughed and ruffled her hair. "Yeah. Because I've only planted a million of them in the last two years. See you later. I'll keep in touch."

Peggy was ready for customers. But they didn't seem to be eager to rush out into the cold morning. She finally caught up with everything on her list and couldn't find anything else to do. She ran across the way to get some tea from Emil and Sofia, who quizzed her about Park and Isabelle's deaths. She pushed off the interrogation by telling them she had to hurry back to the shop. But when she got back, the shop was still empty.

She missed Shakespeare's presence and hoped he'd be able to come to the Potting Shed with her again soon. Selena wouldn't be in until lunchtime that day. Keeley was helping Sam with the Montgomery yard. With no customers, the shop was too quiet and too empty. Usually she liked it that way, but this morning her mind was too preoccupied with everything else to appreciate it as a haven. She sat down to peer through her gardening catalogs, but her heart wasn't in that either.

Instead, she found herself logging on the computer to look up Elmwood Farms on the Internet. It was possible other cases of poisoning had been reported. If a large batch of honey was bad, hundreds of people could be affected.

She had just put in the name when an instant message popped up for her from Nightflyer.

"*good morning, nightrose. found your culprit yet?*"

"*if you mean the poisoned honey, yes.*"

"*i was thinking more of who gave your friend the honey.*"

"*do you have some idea who that is?*"

"*check out some newspapers for names. maybe other people*

have been poisoned. They might have something in common with your friend."

The small IM screen told her that Nightflyer had gone offline. His cryptic message was annoying. This was important to her. If he had information that could help, she wished he'd just give it to her. Everything seemed like a game to him. It was hard to imagine John liking the man, as forthright as John was. But maybe Nightflyer had changed. Maybe there was more to it than she realized.

The Elmwood Farms' page finally came up. A green, grassy meadow with pretty elm trees and a bright red barn gave the index page a nice profile. Who wouldn't want to buy honey or any of the other products they had? It looked very wholesome and appealing.

She clicked on the product list when she saw no warning signs on the opening page. Was it possible no one else had reported problems with the honey? Elmwood Farms' products included fresh eggs, honey, butter, cheese, and various cakes and breads. There was no sign of anything wrong on any of the Web site pages.

Peggy checked out her normal news sites. She couldn't find any stories about Elmwood Farms. But she *did* find an article about a mysterious poisoning in Dubuque, Iowa. When she clicked on the link to the story, she read about another man who'd been poisoned by substances unknown. He was recovering in the hospital after being treated. She wrote down all of the information about the case and forwarded the link to her home computer.

As terrible as it was to think it, more than one poisoning could save Beth from further investigation. If the bees from Elmwood got into a batch of horse chestnut, that was no wrongdoing on anyone's part. Maybe it was all a terrible mistake.

Except for Isabelle . . .

By that time, customers were starting to come into the store. Her mind seethed with the possibilities as she rang up sales on her new antique garden furniture selection. The unit was designed to look like an 1890s cupboard but was made of treated lumber and wrought iron so it could be used outdoors to store garden supplies.

The beauty of the sales was that she didn't have to stock more than one of the cupboards. The company drop shipped directly from her orders to the customers' homes. She had to do what she could with limited space and an ever-questing market of gardeners looking for new products. The cupboards would be functional and enhance the beauty of the yard as well.

Selena came in at noon. Her morning exams didn't go well. She looked like a little girl who was denied a toy. "Dammit, Peggy!" She slammed her book bag on the counter after seeing there was no one else in the shop. "I did a good job on those essays! Professor Martin hates me. I don't know why, but he's got it in for me."

"From the other side of the aisle," Peggy rebutted, "maybe he thinks you could do better. Have you talked with him?"

"If you're going to get someone to work harder, giving them a bad grade isn't much incentive. Now I feel like coasting through the rest of the year. I've tried hard in that class. What's the point if nothing I do is good enough?"

"You should definitely talk to him, Selena," Peggy advised, picking up her jacket and book bag. "I hate to have to run, but I have that appointment with the dog trainer this afternoon. Talk to Professor Martin. Ask him what the problem is."

Selena pushed her book bag behind the counter and plopped down on the rocking chair. "I *know* what his problem is. He's an arrogant idiot. He's so full of himself he can't see past the end of his nose. And he's got a really *big* nose, so he's probably been that way all of his life! I can't stand him. No one can."

Peggy laughed. "Thinking about him *that* way won't help. I should be back by four. Maybe you can take off early and go see him. Work something out. I'll talk to you later. We've been a little busy in the last hour."

"I get the idea." Selena tied on her green Potting Shed apron. "I think you might be seeing this as a professor instead of my friend. Maybe by the time you come back, you could try to be more receptive to *my* whining."

"I'll do the best I can, sweetie. Take care." Peggy ignored the rumbling in her stomach as she smelled the delicious aromas coming from Anthony's Caribbean Café. She raced home on her bike, grateful for the dry streets under the warm February sun. It was a good day for Sam and Keeley, too. It could be difficult to schedule planting days in the winter between the cold and the rain, but the landscaping business was an important aspect of what the Potting Shed did to survive.

She picked up her mail and let herself in the house. Shakespeare was barking and howling, throwing himself against the door in the pantry. But at least everything else in the house was the way she left it that morning. Measuring his discomfort against her own seemed unfair, but she had to survive, too.

Peggy hoped to have some message from Mai when she got home, even though she *knew* Mai had her cell phone number and the number at the shop. She'd call if anything came up. Obviously, there were no updates on the honey. Of course, for all she knew, the ME could decide it wasn't important enough to bring up the investigation again. She didn't always understand the political aspect of the law. But she knew things weren't *ever* black and white.

Peggy let Shakespeare out and took him for a walk. It consisted of him trying to pull her arm out of its socket. She finally called a halt to the torture as soon as he went to the bathroom in the yard. He whined and looked eagerly at the rest of the yard. "That's not going to happen," she told him. "Not until you learn some manners."

She took the dog back inside. Both of them were eating lunch while she surfed the Internet for more information about any poisoning cases in the last few days. An abrupt knock on the door brought Paul in the kitchen. He was dressed for work in his tidy blue uniform. He'd recently had his hair cut and still smelled of spicy aftershave and soap from a shower.

He hugged her, then took off his jacket. "You're trying to ruin my career in law enforcement, aren't you? You couldn't win arguing with me about not being on the job, so you found another way."

She looked up from her hummus and pita sandwich. "Are you feeling all right? Would you like some lunch?"

"I'm fine. I ate a sandwich on the way over here." He glared at her. "You know I love you, Mom. And we both know you didn't want me on the job because of what happened to Dad. But I thought we settled this thing between us. If you *still* don't want me to wear the uniform, say so. Let's talk it out. Don't try to sabotage me."

Peggy swallowed the pita in her mouth, then took a swallow of lemon tea. "I really have no idea what you're talking about, Paul."

"I'm talking about your new business as a private detective. Did you think I wouldn't hear about your run-in with the lieutenant this morning? And I wish you'd leave Mai out of this. We need her income to afford the house. She can't afford to get fired because of *you*!"

It was the perfect opportunity for Peggy to tackle him about the house on Mai's behalf. But she obviously had a few strokes against her already. She knew he wouldn't appreciate her telling him what Mai couldn't. At least not at *that* moment. "What I did had nothing to do with you, Paul. I knew there wasn't any time to explain all the details to the police or wait for them to come up with a search warrant on my information. I did the best I could to help Park."

"How many times are you going to put your life on the line to help people? You aren't *trained* to search for evidence. You could've been hurt out there at the landfill." He sighed and played with the small, silver saltshaker on the wood table. "Don't worry. I know about you and the lieutenant. Mai gave me all the details. But *he* doesn't know about the ME wanting to reopen the investigation because of the honey you found. *Yet*. He's not gonna like it when he finds out."

"He does?"

"What?"

"The ME wants to reopen the investigation because of the honey I found?"

"Yes. I told Mai this would only encourage you! They don't *need* your help." He took her hands in his. Green gazes collided across the laptop. "Stay away from this, please. For my sake, if not your own."

"I won't do anything I don't have to do," she promised, taking her hands out of his clasp. "That's the best I can offer. I want to know the truth about what happened to Park."

He nodded but didn't look at her. "Fine. I have to go. I just wanted you to know the lieutenant talked about you in our briefing this morning."

Peggy didn't know whether to be pleased or offended. "What did he say?"

"He said no one should give information to busybodies who think they're amateur detectives. He called you a busybody and a snoop, Mom."

She tried but couldn't suppress the smile that sprang to her lips. Really, she knew she should take it more seriously. She just couldn't. "Did he call me a busybody by name? I mean was it like, 'Peggy Lee is a busybody and a snoop. Don't talk to her.' Or was it more general?"

Paul didn't find it amusing. "Everyone *knew* he was talking about *my* mother. It made me feel like an idiot." His voice lowered dramatically. "Think about it. I'll talk to you later."

Peggy watched him leave before she giggled. "He's always had a bent for melodrama." She sighed as she stroked Shakespeare's head, which rested on her lap. "I wish there was a school I could take *him* to. But it's probably too late for him anyway. Some old dogs *won't* learn new tricks."

Carlos Gonzales, the garbageman turned taxi driver, picked her and Shakespeare up a few minutes later. She told him about her trip to the landfill. He laughed when she described the landfill manager. "I know him. He tries to charge everybody for everything. You were smart. Did you find what you were looking for?"

She was careful about what she told him. She liked Carlos but didn't want the information in the newspaper tomorrow. As she described finding the honey jar, she wondered if Paul had something to do with Mai not calling her about the ME's decision to reopen the investigation.

Peggy took out her cell phone as Carlos navigated the

high-speed traffic on the interstate. Should she call Mai? Or should she leave well enough alone? She didn't want her to lose her job or get in any trouble. Maybe she should wait and let Mai tell her that she couldn't do anything else.

Looking down from watching traffic before they came to the ramp she was beginning to despise, she noticed there were four messages on her cell phone. How had she missed them? She checked them and found that they were all from Mai. It was a simple mistake. She turned off her ringer at the police station that morning and forgot to turn it back on.

Mai answered her phone on the first ring. "Peggy! I've been trying to reach you all morning! The ME wants to see you. I told him you had some samples of poisoned honey. He wants you to bring them by. Will you do that?"

PEGGY AND RUE SAT down, exhausted by their workout with Shakespeare. He started acting up when he walked through the front door at Whiskers and Paws. A woman with a new kitten was leaving. Shakespeare saw the kitten and let out a deep, booming bark. The kitten yowled, scratched its owner, and jumped to the floor. In the ensuing confusion, three flowerpots were broken and several chairs were knocked over.

After that beginning, things got worse. Peggy held Shakespeare's leash while Rue took him through a series of commands. When he was told to sit, Shakespeare barked. When Rue pointed to the floor and told him to lie down, he jumped up on her, putting his large paws on her shoulders and almost knocking her over. No matter what they tried to get him to do, Shakespeare did the opposite.

"I don't understand what's wrong with him," Peggy huffed, lying back in her chair. Shakespeare was at her feet. He whined and covered his face with his paws. "I *know* he wasn't this bad before I went to Pennsylvania. I don't know what's gotten into him."

Rue shook her head. "Some dogs have a harder time learning. He's a tough cookie, but we'll work it out. He might've been thrown off by chasing the kitten when he first came in.

Or maybe it's the new surroundings. We're not off to a great start right now, but I'm sure things will get better."

"I hope so." Peggy glanced at her watch, then got to her feet. "I have to go. Thank you for putting up with us. We'll see you Thursday."

"Not a problem. It'll work out."

"And I'll replace those vases my big nitwit broke, Rue. I'm so sorry."

"Don't worry about it, Peggy. Just be careful with him. I'd hate for you to get hurt before we calm him down!"

Carlos came back for them. He laughed and couldn't believe Shakespeare wouldn't follow the trainer's commands at the shop. "He's always so good in the car. Aren't you, boy? Maybe it was the way she was talking to him."

Shakespeare barked and jumped over into the front seat, almost managing to sit on Carlos's lap. Peggy tugged on his leash and ordered him into the backseat while Carlos tried to steer the taxi around the dog that was almost as big as him.

When Peggy finally got Shakespeare to move, Carlos straightened his cap and looked in the rearview mirror at her. "That's a lot of dog, Peggy. You gotta be careful he doesn't break your arm."

Peggy, who was almost sitting on Shakespeare to keep him down in the backseat, was breathing hard when she promised to be careful. "Maybe this is too much dog for me after all. I went from not having any pets to this monster. It would probably have been better if I'd found a poodle."

Carlos let them off at Peggy's house. He promised to come back for her at the same time Thursday. She told Shakespeare what she thought of his behavior as she walked him in the front yard for a few minutes. She didn't let him off of his leash like she usually did when they went into the house. Instead, she walked him into the laundry room, told him to stay, and closed the door.

She made herself a cup of sassafras tea to steady her nerves while she checked her phone messages. The university was asking for all school personnel to attend a training/awareness seminar on how to handle early dismissal for bad weather.

She glanced at the big clock on the kitchen wall. She was already twenty minutes late for that. Not that she saw much point in having a seminar for letting people out of school early.

Instead, she tried to relax as she drank her tea. It was a homemade brew. Her mother went out to find the mitten-shaped leaves on the sassafras tree and dig for the roots to make her own tea back home. There was a railroad track by the house, a place sassafras loved to grow. Her mother walked the track for hours to get enough root to dry and carefully preserved her stock.

Drinking it made her think of home and her childhood. Her grandmother always made them drink sassafras as spring was approaching. She said it was a good spring tonic. It wasn't until later, when Peggy began studying plants, that she knew the science behind it. Sassafras was a stimulant, a poison actually, when used in its purest form. The orange brown tea helped the body get over the human slowdown that accompanied winter. And it was delicious!

She finally called Mai to let her know she'd be at the precinct by three thirty. That would give her plenty of time to talk with the medical examiner, show him her samples, and still be at the Potting Shed before five. She was looking forward to meeting the ME, despite Mai's assertions that the man was obnoxious.

Just when she thought she had everything in hand, the front doorbell rang. She opened the door to find Beth and a young man in a dark gray business suit on her doorstep.

"How *could* you do this, Peggy?" Beth cried and wrung her hands. "How could you do this to *me*?"

"David Rusch." The young man tripped over the edge of the rug at the door as he tried to shake Peggy's hand. "I'm representing Mrs. Lamonte for Lamonte, Rusch and Peterson."

Peggy could see the resemblance between father and son. Same dark hair and gray eyes. Except the elder Rusch was much more sophisticated, smoother, and taller. She watched David try to get his foot untangled from the fringe on the carpet for a moment before turning to Beth. "I did what I thought was right. I'm sorry if that makes it hard for you. I know *you* didn't do anything wrong. I'm sure we'll be able to prove that. You have nothing to worry about."

"I'm sure we can all come to a mutual understanding." David finally freed his foot from the fringe. "We all want the same thing. We just have to get on the same page. Keep our heads together. Fight for the team! Make the problems with this accident go away so Mrs. Lamonte can go on with her life."

"I'm thinking that Park's death *wasn't* an accident, Mr. Rusch. Someone at least wanted to make him sick. They succeeded in killing him. Park was my friend. I want to know who's responsible for his death. Don't you want that, too, Beth?"

Beth nodded. Her hair was a mess, and her face was blotchy from crying. "The police know about the insurance policy. They know Park was cheating on me with Cindy. They asked me to come in and answer some questions."

"I'll need to speak to the attorney Mrs. Lamonte hired without realizing Lamonte, Rusch and Peterson would provide her defense." David frowned and waved his briefcase, almost knocking a vase off of Peggy's side table and rushing to retrieve it." She'll have to sign off on the case unless she wants to second chair. We want to provide Mrs. Lamonte the best possible defense in the light of these accusations made against her."

"I'm sure she has nothing to hide," Peggy defended. "And Hunter Ollson is a good *criminal* attorney, Mr. Rusch. I'm sure she's advising Beth to do the right thing."

"Hunter?" David stopped pacing for a moment and stared at her.

"Didn't I tell you her name?" Beth asked him.

"Hunter *Ollson*?"

The doorbell rang again, this time persistently. It was followed immediately by pounding on the heavy portal. Peggy opened the door and stepped aside as Hunter rushed into the house.

"What the hell is going on here?" she demanded, glaring at everyone. "I thought Beth was *my* client." She paused in midtirade and blinked her pretty blue eyes. "Davey? Is that *you*?"

12

Banana

Botanical: *Musa sapientum*
Family: Musaceae

The banana has a history that follows our own civilization. Called fruit of the wise men, Alexander wrote of it in 327 B.C. Arabian slave traders are credited with naming it banan, *"finger," for the shape of it. The banana tree is actually not a tree at all but a giant herb. Cultivated bananas will not grow from seed, only from rootstock.*

PEGGY DID THE INTRODUCTIONS. The look on Hunter's face didn't change. She glared at the other attorney while Peggy was speaking. "I think you and I should step into another room for a word, Counselor." Hunter opened the door to the small sitting room on the right and waited for David—Davey—to join her.

He shrugged and finally followed her, closing the door behind them . . . *after* closing his suit coat in it and extracting it.

Beth turned to Peggy. "I know what this *looks* like. This thing with Park and Cindy was terrible. I was out of my head when I told him to get that insurance policy before he came back to me. I don't know what difference I thought it would make. I suppose I thought the money aspect would affect him. I don't know. But I didn't kill Park or Isabelle. You *have* to believe me."

"I do. But there are some questions here that need answers." Peggy grasped Beth's hands firmly in her own. "It may be hard on you while they ask the questions, but you want to know the truth about what happened to Park, don't you?"

"You know I do." Beth squeezed Peggy's hands in return. "I'm just terrified. I'm not only worried about myself. I'm worried about Reddman and Foxx. What if I lose them, too?"

"We'll make sure that doesn't happen! But it's not going to be easy for them either. Maybe your parents could take the boys home with them for a while until we get this cleared up."

"I don't want to sound selfish, Peggy, but I don't know if I can stay in the house alone right now. I want to protect the boys, but I'm so alone without Park. The house seems so empty."

"Pack a few things and stay with me," Peggy suggested. "You can answer questions just as well from here. And you know I have plenty of space. It's a little chilly because that stupid furnace is screwed up, but I'd love to have you here."

Beth blinked tears out of her eyes as she wiped her cheeks with the back of her hand. "Thank you, Peggy. You're so strong. I hope you don't mind if I lean on you for a while."

"I'm here for you." Peggy grinned, tears in her eyes. "We'll see this through. Frankly, I'm more worried about Shakespeare knocking you down the stairs than I am you being blamed for Park's death. We just have to find out what happened to him and who *was* responsible."

As Beth was about to speak, the sitting room door burst open, and Hunter raced out, waving her hands and talking so quickly, Beth and Peggy could barely understand her. Her face was red and her hair was messed up. Her burnt-red lipstick was smudged. "Well, I think we settled *that* issue. *I'm* your attorney, Beth. I'm advising you to answer any questions the police have regarding your husband's death. We have nothing to hide, right? I'll be there with you the whole time. You're innocent. You have nothing to be ashamed of."

David walked out slowly behind her. He was straightening his blue striped tie and trying to smooth his dark brown hair back but hadn't touched the trace of burnt-red lipstick by the side of his mouth. One persistent strand of hair stood straight up on his head. He cleared his throat. "I think Hunter will do a good job for you, Beth. We knew each other *briefly* in school. She's a good attorney. We talked, and we'll be talking for a while. I mean, until you get through this. Then we'll probably still be talking, of course. Maybe about different issues. But still talking."

Peggy smiled and offered him a tissue to wipe off the lipstick. "That much is obvious."

The attorney's lean face suffused with pink as he took the hint and scrubbed the tissue against his mouth. "Anyway. I have to go. Hunter has agreed to keep her breast firm . . . I mean to keep the *firm* abreast of the investigation. Don't hesitate to call if you need anything, Beth. We're here for you and the boys."

She thanked him, glancing at Hunter curiously. "Thank you for your help, David. I'll be staying here with Peggy for a while until we get things straightened out."

"Good idea." He cleared his throat and gruffly told Hunter, "I'll talk to you later. Good-bye, Peggy. Sorry for the interruption. I hope you're okay."

"I'm fine," she reassured him, trying her best not to laugh as he almost tripped over a cane chair.

"I'll walk you to your car to fill you in on some of the details, Davey," Hunter volunteered with a wide smile, giving up on maintaining her professional demeanor.

"Thank you." He opened the door for her. "We'll just discuss a few more ideas about the . . . *case* . . . out here," he explained to Peggy and Beth. He grinned and walked outside with Hunter, closing the door behind them.

"Well!" Peggy rolled her expressive green eyes. "*That* was interesting. Do you get the idea they may have been *more* than acquaintances in school?"

"I guess they'll keep each other *well*-informed." Beth sighed sadly. "It's not going to be easy being alone, is it? I know you must be glad you have Steve in your life now. He seems so nice."

"He is," Peggy said. "And you'll find someone else, too. I know it's too soon to see that right now. But at least you have Foxx and Reddman."

"I know." Beth smiled. "And I'm happy I had Park all this time. But now I've lost my ride back to the house. You don't by any chance have another bicycle do you?"

"No. But I'm going to call a taxi anyway, or I'll be late. He can drop you at your house after he leaves me at the precinct." She explained about the horse chestnut honey samples.

"And you really think eating that honey killed Park?"

"I think it was a factor." Peggy called for the taxi, then put on her coat and scarf. "Maybe it was just an accident on the part of the honey manufacturer. Not all botanical poisonings happen on purpose. Most *are* accidental."

They talked about the honey all the way to the uptown precinct. Peggy gave Beth a house key and told her to feel free to come and go, as she paid the driver's fare. "I have to close up the shop when I'm done here. I should be home by seven, but if there's a delivery, I could be later. Help yourself to some food. But whatever you do, don't let the dog out of the laundry room. I'm afraid his lesson in obedience didn't go well today. It may be a while before he can be in the house again."

"Thank you, Peggy." Beth took the key with a smile. "I don't know what I'd do without you."

Waving as the taxi pulled away, Peggy glanced at her watch, then hurried into the police station. The sergeant at the desk sent her back to forensics with a visitor's badge clipped to her sweater. She saw Mai waiting outside a door in the hall and called to her. "Sorry I'm late. I was trying to settle a few things." She explained about Beth, Hunter, and David.

Mai frowned. "I'm not sure you should tell me anything else. This doesn't look good for your friend. I work for the police. I can't take sides. I can't be your confidant in this."

"Is something wrong?" Peggy was surprised by her attitude. Mai was helpful, determined to find the truth whether it was good for the case or not.

"I found out that I'm up for promotion," Mai whispered with a shy, proud smile. "I might be the next senior assistant medical examiner. That means a lot to me, and I don't want to do the wrong thing and mess it up. I'm sorry."

"That's all right." Peggy smiled and patted the younger

woman's arm. "You work hard. You deserve the promotion. I'll try not to make this bad for you."

"Thanks. I'm glad you understand. The ME is waiting for you. We should go in."

Peggy paused. "Would the promotion affect the situation with you and Paul?"

"You mean about the house?" Mai shrugged. "I don't know yet. I still have so many doubts that have nothing to do with finances. I don't know what to say. Have you spoken to him about it?"

Recalling her last visit with her son, Peggy shook her head. "No. He was upset with me about the honey. I thought it might be best to catch him when he's more . . . amenable."

Mai opened the door to the ME's lab. "When it comes to talking about this house," she told Peggy, "he's never more amenable. Don't worry about it. We'll work it out. I'm sorry I tried to involve you. It was wrong. You're Paul's mother."

"I'm also your friend, I hope."

Mai smiled at her. "You are. Sorry. There's just so much going on right now. I think I'm getting confused."

Peggy didn't have a chance to assure her she could handle it. When they walked into the spotless lab, there were people walking back and forth, some stopping to talk to Mai. The lab area was huge. Mai pointed out various aspects of what they could do with evidence that was collected. A new DNA processor stood proudly in the center of the room.

"We still don't have all the resources the state crime lab has in Raleigh," Mai explained as they passed a shower for washing off chemicals. "But we're finally catching up. We handle evidence here from several counties besides Mecklenburg. Hundreds of cases come through here, everything from burglaries and shoplifting to rape, arson, and homicide."

"You must be the infamous Peggy Lee." A tall, stout man in a white lab coat joined them. He wore heavy glasses that were reminiscent of the ones so popular in England thirty years ago. He held out a hand to her. "I'm Dr. Harold Ramsey, Chief Medical Examiner for Mecklenburg County."

"I don't know about the infamous part." Peggy put her

hand in his and squeezed. "But the name is right. How do you do, Dr. Ramsey? I've heard a lot about you."

He ran a hand across his thinning dark hair that was swept forward to cover an obvious bald spot on top of his head, then held his hands behind him and rocked back on his heels. "You know, you're alternately a devil and an angel around these parts, depending on the day and the person speaking. You don't sing, by any chance, do you? There's no real connection between you and the other Peggy Lee, is there?"

"No, I'm afraid not. I didn't even come upon the name until after I was married. My husband used to beg me *not* to sing in the shower."

He nodded. "That's right. Wife of Detective John Lee. Mother of Officer Paul Lee. Any other relatives on the force?"

"Not that I know of. Really, two is more than enough. I did everything I could to discourage my son from taking the badge after his father died. But you know how it is when you're young, Dr. Ramsey. You see everything in black and white."

"I thought everyone saw *everything* in black and white at *all* ages, Mrs. Lee." He peered at her quizzically down the length of his broad nose. "I know I do. I thought it might be a common failing."

"I'm sure it comes in handy with your job. But life has taught me there are colors, shades, variances, as well. I wanted Paul to see that."

He laughed. "Maybe he will someday. In the meantime, I believe you have some samples for me. Horse Chestnut honey. Killing someone with honey! What a concept!"

"We don't know yet if it was deliberate or an accident, do we?" She gave him the samples. "I collected these from various places. You'll see the locations marked on the slides. I'm not sure how they'll help you in this case."

Dr. Ramsey set one of the slides in place on his microscope and stared into the lens. "They give us a source of reference, actually. You're a respected botanist. I've read some of your work on botanical poisons. I think we can use you as an expert witness on this case. Are you up for that?"

Mai looked at her, too, encouraging her with her large,

almond-shaped brown eyes. Peggy wasn't sure what to say. Not that she believed her testimony about the honey would have any impact on Beth, since her friend wouldn't be on trial. But what if she was wrong? What if she couldn't help Beth prove her innocence? Would she want to face her across a courtroom giving evidence for the prosecution?

"I didn't realize it would be such a difficult decision." Ramsey continued to look at the sample under the microscope. "Surely you've done it before?"

"Not really." Peggy looked away from Mai. "I've answered some questions about poison for one or two police departments, but I've never testified in court."

Ramsey looked up and focused on her. "Let's say I won't call you unless it's necessary. Would that work?"

"I suppose so. It's not that I don't want to help. It's just that—"

"Yes, I know. Your *friend*." Ramsey put another slide on the microscope. "I know about your personal involvement in the case. But sometimes, we have to put our personal feelings aside in the pursuit of justice. As the widow of a police detective *killed* on the streets, you must agree."

She took a deep breath. From the corner of her eye, she could see Mai. She was pleading with her eyes not to make a scene. She was afraid it was too late for that. No wonder the poor girl didn't like the ME. He *was* an obnoxious man! "I don't think I can be your expert witness in this, Dr. Ramsey. I wouldn't be pursuing justice if it didn't involve my personal feelings and my *friend*. I don't believe she killed her husband. I'm sure she'll be exonerated. And that has nothing to do with my husband's death, though I appreciate your *tact* in reminding me."

Ramsey swiveled back to her, taking off his glasses to look at her. "The lieutenant may feel differently. I contacted Elmwood Farms this morning. There haven't been any other cases of poisoned honey reported to them. It looks like this is the only one."

Peggy took the information in stride. "That doesn't make Beth guilty of anything. A hundred other people could have put that honey in the basket. Including their housekeeper. And Park was eating it *before* he got back from Philadelphia."

"Can you prove that?"

"Not yet. But—"

"I'm sure you know as much about the process as I do, Dr. Lee. I hope you're right, and your friend isn't guilty of this. But I believe your conclusion about the honey and the pollen we found in Mr. Lamonte's system is correct. I'm going to hand over our findings to the lieutenant and the DA's office. Good luck to you. Thank you for bringing in the slides. I'll have Mai call you if we need you again."

Ramsey went back to study the slide. Peggy realized she'd been dismissed when Mai gently took her arm to lead her out of the lab. Annoyed, she stood her ground. "Is that it?"

He looked up from the microscope, one dark brow arched. "Yes. Unless you have some other *crucial* evidence to share."

"Not really, but—"

"Then I have to get back to work." He frowned at Mai.

"I came all the way over here for you to tell me what I already knew," she challenged.

He shrugged. "I'd be willing to share more, but you obviously aren't interested in working with us because of your friend's *supposed* innocence. Good day, Dr. Lee."

"Good day, Dr. Ramsey!" She huffed and strode quickly out of the lab with Mai trailing after her. "You were right about him. He's *very* annoying!"

They paused in the hall, Mai twisting her fingers together as she looked at Peggy. "I'm sorry. I didn't know about him contacting Elmwood Farms. It sounds bad for your friend."

"That's all right. As you said, you deserve this promotion. Don't do anything to jeopardize it. We'll find our way. I'll talk to you later."

Mai reached over and hugged her quickly. "I have to go. I hope it works out."

Peggy hugged her back. "It'll be fine. You'll see."

But on the way over to the Potting Shed in the taxi, Peggy wasn't so sure. Someone gave Park poisoned honey. With the information from Elmwood Farms, that meant Park was the *only* one. Beth *had* the opportunity to add the poisoned honey to the jar Park brought home from the hotel. She *had* the motive of ten million dollars and her husband sleeping with his ex-wife.

Except for the gray look to Park's face in Philadelphia, Peggy might be tempted to suspect Beth as well, at least on an objective level. She *looked* like a good suspect in theory.

But Peggy firmly believed Park was already eating the poisoned honey before he came home. She had no way to prove it besides her own instincts. Those wouldn't impress anyone. She had to have more. There had to be some way to prove the honey was poisoned *before* it came to Charlotte.

By the time Peggy reached Brevard Court, Selena was in the middle of a last-minute rush at the Potting Shed. It happened frequently just before the shop closed. Together, they managed to get the last ten customers out the door and lock up before anyone else could come in.

"Wow! They must've been waiting for the cold weather. It zapped them into buying supplies for spring." Selena sat down hard in the rocking chair, one hand automatically stabilizing the snowman beside her.

"Sorry I was running late." Peggy started cleaning out the cash register, getting the cash, checks, and credit card receipts ready to go to the bank. "I seem to be chronically late recently. I think I'm trying to do more than I can handle. Who knew the shop would pick up so much business so quickly?"

"You could make this your last semester at Queens," Selena suggested. "You're only part time there anyway. I think there's plenty to do here now. The shop could use a full-time owner."

"That's never been the problem," Peggy said. "I guess I'm just afraid to give up my professorship again. I'm not a spring chicken, in case you haven't noticed. They may not take me back if I need the money again."

"That's true, I suppose." Selena laughed. "Except the chicken part. If anyone is a spring chicken, it must be you."

Peggy sighed. "No matter what, I'm under contract until June 1 with Queens. I guess I'll see how it's going by then. I may have to make a leap of faith."

Selena got up and stretched her long, thin body. "Just be careful Shakespeare doesn't make that a *nudge* of faith that knocks you down the stairs." She glanced up and saw Steve at the door. "Hey there! I think I should be going. I'd offer to stay and help, but I'm going to study with some friends. Trying to get those grades up, you know."

"You've done plenty anyway. I can never really pay you what you've been worth to me. Without you and Sam and Keeley, I wouldn't have been able to keep up with everything."

"You're right." Selena picked up her jacket and book bag. "You definitely owe me dinner at the Capital Grill. Bye, Steve. Nice talking to you!"

"Bye, Selena." Steve stood aside and held the door as she left. He smiled at Peggy. "I haven't talked to you all day. I thought we could have dinner."

"That would be wonderful," she replied, closing her bank bag. "But I have an hour cleanup and stocking here." She consulted the delivery log. "And it looks like I might have a delivery."

"Anthony does food to go. If he won't deliver, I think I can manage to go over and get it."

Her eyes lit up with his offer. Was there another man who was willing to be as flexible as Steve? "Thank you. I'm thinking about giving up my classes at Queens at the end of the year. Maybe that would keep things like this from happening."

He hugged her and kissed her lips. "I have this feeling your life has always been hectic and always will be. Maybe you just never noticed before."

"So you don't think I can simplify?"

"I think anything is possible. But I don't care either. I like your hectic life. I enjoy being part of it. Even when I'm burning my clothes after following you through mountains of garbage. So, on that note, what do you want to eat?"

While Steve went next door to the Caribbean Café, Peggy began straightening up the shop. There were always tulip bulbs mixed in with the jonquils and vermiculite with the fertilizer. People browsed, picked things up, and put them back down wherever they were in the shop.

She enjoyed walking through the aisles, the feeling of the worn wood floor under her feet. The old boiler kicked on, steam heat hissing through the vents. It reminded her that she was going to have to tackle the issue of having her furnace replaced at the house. That might help her make the decision about giving up her classes. If she had to purchase the furnace herself, she'd be teaching at Queens for another ten years!

The phone rang several times after she dialed Dalton Lee's phone number. She wished John's uncle would either get an answering machine or keep the phone with him. Instead, she knew the fifties-style, heavy green phone sat in a corner between the foyer and the kitchen downstairs. Dalton spent most of his time in the library upstairs. With his arthritis, it could take ten minutes for him to get down there and answer it.

"Hello?"

"Hello, Dalton. It's Peggy. John's wife."

"I know who you are. And don't you mean John's *widow*?"

Peggy took a deep breath. Dealing with Dalton was never easy. "I was wondering if I could come by and discuss something with you. Anytime you have free would be fine."

"Just come to the point, Peggy. What do you want *this* time?"

Ignoring his curt rudeness, as always, she did as he asked. "I need a new furnace at the house. The old one died about twenty years ago, but we made do. I can't do anything with it anymore. It has to be replaced."

"Why are you telling *me*? Call a furnace man."

"You know why I'm telling you, Dalton. I'd like the trust to pay for the furnace. It's not like it won't be good for whoever moves in after me. If it stays in the house as long as the one I have now, there won't have to be another one for a hundred years. I'm not planning on living there that much longer."

"How long *are* you planning to live there, Peggy? I think you've already overstayed your welcome. It's not your house. If you want the trust to repair it, you'll have to give up the place. Then we'll do major renovations before the new owner moves in."

"I didn't say I was planning to move. But I probably won't be alive in a hundred years either," she rebutted. "I'm not ready to give up the house. But I'd like you to replace the furnace."

"Replace it yourself. Or move out."

The phone line went dead. Peggy knew he'd hung up on her. Not surprising. Most of their conversations went that way. How could John have been related to such an obnoxious old coot?

Steve brought back spicy rice and grilled vegetables for dinner. He served it with hibiscus tea and cheddar biscuits. They ate sitting on stools at the checkout counter while the other shops in the courtyard and the arcade closed down around them.

Peggy told him about her disastrous first obedience lesson with Shakespeare and her meeting with the medical examiner. He was surprised they would ask her to testify in a case where a friend was involved.

"There aren't many experts in botanical poisons for the taking in Charlotte." She wiped her lips with a napkin. "I suppose Dr. Ramsey was being expedient."

"What are you going to do?"

"Prove that Beth is innocent. I hope."

"What if she isn't?" He took a sip of tea and held her gaze over the glass.

"There's no doubt of that in my mind, Steve. I *know* her. She didn't kill anyone."

"Maybe she's banking on you feeling that way. On most people feeling that way. No one wants to think someone would kill their spouse. But she's got a lot against her, Peggy. Isn't it at least possible? She *did* lie about the insurance and kept quiet about the affair. Why would she do that if she were innocent?"

The delivery truck driver honking his horn in the back of the shop kept her from answering. She knew Steve was being hypothetical. But she couldn't bring herself to see Beth as a killer. No matter what it looked like, she didn't believe her friend was capable of adding poisoned honey to the jar.

Besides her own belief that Park was already being poisoned in Philadelphia, there was Peggy's other intuition about people that refused to admit Beth had any part in this. But Steve was a typical person who didn't know Beth. She could imagine many people feeling that way, especially a jury.

As Steve helped her stow away the boxes of flowerpots, garden implements, and other items, he glanced at her. "I'm sorry if I upset you by saying that about Beth."

"That's all right," she answered, checking out a dozen baby banana trees a customer ordered for her sunroom. The big leaves were drooping, but the plants seemed to be in good shape. "I'm not upset. You're right in many ways. But I'll have to be shocked and amazed if she's guilty of anything more than a little anger when she learned Park was having an affair with his ex-wife."

"I can see that. If she were *my* friend for years, I'm sure I'd feel the same. I just wanted you to see there could be another point of view."

"Thanks. I appreciate you exercising my brain." She grinned at him as she took off her gloves to sign the delivery slip for the driver.

"That about does it," the big man said, hitching up his jeans. "See you next time, Peggy."

"Thanks, Joe. See you next time. Say hello to Maria for me."

"Will do!"

She locked the back doors and turned off the lights when he was gone. The shop was clean and ready for the next day. It was time to leave. Sometimes, when she was alone, Peggy sat in the rocking chair for a while reading new catalogs and listening to NPR. But tonight, Steve was with her. It made her conscious of the change her life had taken. It was good, but it was different.

"I don't see what else you can do to help Beth," Steve said as they got in his SUV. "Besides proving Park didn't commit suicide, I don't see what else you *can* do."

"I'm not sure right now. I got some obscure information from Nightflyer. I was trying to follow that up."

The distaste that name brought to him was evident in Steve's voice. "Nightflyer? Are you still talking to him online?"

"He knows something about what's going on," she explained. "I don't know why he can't just come out and say it plainly, but it's a game with him. Like chess."

"Peggy, this guy is probably dangerous. I don't know how he knows what he knows, but I don't like it. He gets too personal with you."

"I think you're jealous!" She laughed. "I can't believe it. But it's true."

"I'm not jealous of a crazy man who makes things up and plays a good game of chess," Steve defended.

"Yes you are! Otherwise you wouldn't care."

"I'm concerned. Not jealous. You don't really know who this man is. He might just *seem* to be helping you."

"I told you, he worked with John. He's not a threat," she argued. "Except maybe to *your* ego."

"*My* ego?" Steve demanded, turning on Queens Road. "I don't have an ego. I'm just worried about you. If this guy is so smart and wants to help, why doesn't he show himself? That's all I'm asking."

Peggy reached across the seat and hugged him when they stopped at a traffic light. "I'm not complaining. A woman my age doesn't expect to have men fighting over her. It's wonderful!"

He put his arms around her and kissed her fiercely until the light turned green and the car behind them honked its horn long and loud. "That guy doesn't have a chance."

Peggy sat back in her seat, a rosy glow on her face, her heart pounding in her chest. "Not at all. But if he can help me save Beth, I'm going to exploit our relationship."

Steve pulled into Peggy's drive. "What does that mean? Exploit your relationship. What relationship?"

She wasn't listening. "What is Hunter doing here?"

"Never mind her," he continued. "How do you plan to *exploit* your relationship with Nightflyer?"

But Peggy had already unfastened her seat belt and was out the door, walking quickly toward Hunter as the attorney got out of her vehicle. "Hunter? What's wrong?"

"They got the results of the old lady's autopsy back, Peggy. I went in ready for their questions but not ready for them to charge Beth with a double homicide. They arrested her. There was nothing I could do. Her bond hearing is in the morning. I'm sorry."

13

Strawberry

Botanical: *Fragaria ananassa*
Family: N. O. Rosaceae

This type is the most widely used today. Not a true fruit but a pseudocarp because of the way the berries form. Native to Eurasia and North America, it was cultivated in Europe in the fifteen hundreds. All parts of the plant are used medicinally.

"HOW DID IT HAPPEN?" Peggy demanded. "What did they find that made them take such drastic action?"

"Apparently, one of Mrs. Lamonte's bumps and bruises didn't come from her fall down the stairs. Her skull was cracked, and the ME says it was done by the walking stick. They found some of Beth's fingerprints. They're testing her DNA for other evidence. It was an ambush." Hunter finished and drew a deep breath.

"We have to get her out of there. What kind of bond do you think they'll ask for?"

"I'm not sure. It could be high. I can't see how she'd be perceived as a threat to the *community* exactly, even if they think she killed her husband and mother-in-law, but I suppose they *could* consider her a flight risk."

"What time is the hearing scheduled?"

"Nine a.m. I'm going to talk with her before that." Hunter lowered her head. Her hair gleamed like gold in the streetlight's glow. "I'm so sorry, Peggy. I thought I was doing a good job. But I didn't see this coming at all. Maybe Davey was right about not letting Beth answer questions."

"You did the best you could. You didn't know what was going on." Peggy put her hand on the younger woman's shoulder. "Is there any way I can get in to see her?"

"Not before the bail hearing tomorrow. But with any luck, I should be able to get her out then."

Shakespeare was barking frantically from inside the house. Steve's cell phone rang, and he turned away to answer it. Peggy sighed. No matter what kind of trouble went on, the everyday aspects of life continued. "I suppose there's nothing more we can do tonight. I'll meet you at the courthouse tomorrow, Hunter. You can only do the best you can, sweetie. I have complete faith in you. I know Beth does, too."

Steve put his arm around Peggy's shoulders. "Is there anything I can do to help?"

"Not really," she responded. "Was that an emergency call?"

"Yeah. A woman's dog was hit by a car on South Boulevard. She's bringing him in to the clinic. I can come back when I'm finished."

A cold breeze rustled through the oaks that surrounded them, and Peggy shivered. "I don't think there's anything anyone can do tonight except pray. Maybe tomorrow we'll need everyone to help out with something. Tonight, I think all we can do is get a good night's sleep."

Hunter crossed her arms protectively against her chest. "I *hate* feeling stupid!"

"Go home!" Peggy advised. "You're not stupid. And you'll come up with something."

When Hunter was backing her SUV out of the drive, Steve's eyes focused on Peggy. "You're going to get a good night's sleep tonight and not try to exploit your relationship with the crazy man online, right?"

She stared back. "I'm going to do the best I can to help Beth, Steve. I'll see you tomorrow."

She could tell he wasn't happy with her answer. But honesty compelled her not to swear she wouldn't contact Nightflyer. If he knew anything that might help Beth, Peggy wanted to know, too.

Steve looked away first. "Just be careful. I kind of like our relationship, even if you can't exploit *me* for information unless it has something to do with cats or pregnant hamsters. This guy could be dangerous."

She hugged and kissed him as Hunter's headlights flashed on them. It reminded her of a night in Charleston when she stayed out too late with John, and her father had come out to look for her. She was kissing John when he found them behind the smokehouse. Her father blew the horn several times, then used the high beams on them.

Recalling that moment, and the embarrassment that followed, made her smile. It was amazing how the events of a lifetime could be encapsulated and brought back in a single flash of memory, even thirty years later. But she wasn't twenty anymore. She didn't care who saw her kissing someone.

Well, at least she didn't *think* she cared. Without her father trapping her in his headlight beams, it was hard to say.

"I'll be fine," she finally assured Steve, the man presently in her arms. "Don't worry so much. It will give you frown lines. Go and take care of your patient. I'll let you know as soon as something changes."

"I wish I could go with you in the morning. But I have a surgery scheduled for nine. Call me and let me know what happens."

"I will," she promised. "Good night. See you tomorrow."

PEGGY E-MAILED NIGHTFLYER AN invitation from the new chess site. He didn't respond. She waited half an hour in front of her computer before finally changing clothes and going downstairs to check on her plants. Tonight was the night she was scheduled to release the hero bugs that would save her hapless strawberry plants.

Sometimes it disturbed her sense of empathy with the plants

to experiment on them. There they were, going along thinking they lived in a perfect world. Then suddenly, a plague of biblical proportions was released on them. It didn't seem fair, but such was the nature of experimentation.

The thrips and spider mites she'd released had gnawed hungrily on the strawberries. But their damage was contained, in this case, by limiting the number of bugs. In a normal strawberry patch, the damage could be catastrophic. She looked at a half-eaten strawberry that had fallen off the plant and shook her head.

Making note of everything, she released the lacewings and ladybugs she'd bought from the insect warehouse. Many places had begun growing their own helpful insects to sell to gardeners. The only problem was keeping them around. Once the food supply was gone, the insects typically flew off to find more. That's where the right environment came in, encouraging them to stay.

Thankfully, her enclosure around the strawberries seemed to be containing what was sure to be an epic battle. Thrips and mites would play havoc with her other plants as well if they escaped. This way their only food source was the strawberry plants.

After recording the progress of the rest of her experiments and watching the frog in the pond, Peggy went back upstairs to check for Nightflyer. There was still no response to her challenge. Maybe his old war injury was bothering him again. She left the chess site and went on to look for poisonings in the daily papers online.

She followed up the story about the man in Dubuque. The poison was still unknown, but the man was alive and listed in fair condition. She took note of his physician's name and sent an e-mail to the hospital for further information on the case.

Two more unknown poisonings caught her attention. One was in Syracuse, New York, and the other was in Staunton, Ohio. Both were men. One was in serious condition in the ICU. The other was in serious but stable condition. She e-mailed both hospitals for updated information on the cases.

She needed a list of people who stayed at the hotel in

Philadelphia and received the gift baskets that contained the honey. The police probably already had that information but weren't likely to share. With Mai's anxiety about her job, she couldn't ask her to check. But if there *were* other cases of poisoned honey, Hunter could use that in Beth's defense.

They needed a way to prove the poison was already at work before Park returned home. That would, at least, clear Beth of any wrongdoing where Park was concerned. It wouldn't help with the charge against her for what happened to Isabelle, but like any other sequential event, one step at a time.

She sat back in her chair; still no word from Nightflyer. She supposed she could only depend on a mysterious stranger for so long. If he *really* wanted to help, he'd come out of hiding and work with them. He'd explain how he did his research and where he got his sources. A good scientist always shared with colleagues. Steve was right. Nightflyer skulked in the shadows. She would have to find her own answers to help Beth.

She didn't realize she fell asleep at her computer until her alarm clock went off and Shakespeare started barking in the laundry room. She hated that forlorn sound and wished he was still sleeping in her bed. Maybe it sounded crazy, but she missed him. She yawned and stretched her aching back. She was still willing to give the obedience classes time and hoped they would help him. God help them if the first class was a model for the rest of their time with Rue!

Peggy took Shakespeare out into the cold, foggy morning. Icy mist hung low in the crape myrtle trees, dripping to the ground and on the heads of unwary walkers. Shakespeare seemed better this morning. He walked sedately at her side, looking up from time to time with a strange expression on his face. She brought him back inside and fed him, but he lay down beside the food bowl and for once, refused to gulp down his food.

"What's wrong?" She scratched behind his ear, feeling guilty. It couldn't be plainer if he sat up and told her. He wasn't happy living in the laundry room. He wanted to be with her.

"If you'd stop breaking things and acting like an idiot, you could come back upstairs and to the Potting Shed with me."

She answered him as though his words of complaint were spoken aloud. In response, he laid his head on the worn wood floor and groaned.

She tried everything to get him to eat. He wouldn't look at the food. Finally, she let him go back upstairs with her. He bounded happily up the sweeping marble staircase, leapt into the bedroom like a gawky gazelle, and broke the lamp on her bedside table. The lamp that had been a wedding gift from John's mother. She rushed in after him, but it was too late. "I knew it! I shouldn't have trusted you!"

The phone rang as she began picking up the pieces of the lamp. Shakespeare snuffled her head as she worked. She sat on the floor, shooed him away, and answered the persistent summons.

"Dr. Lee?"

"Yes. Who is this?"

"My name is Alan Richards. I'm the head of forensics at the University of Iowa Hospital at Dubuque. I received a message that you were interested in one of my cases. I'm sorry it's taken a while for me to get back with you. We've had a bad flu season this year."

"Sorry to hear that. Yes, that's right." She struggled to get to her feet, pushing Shakespeare out of the way as he lay down on her. "If you could give me a moment to get to my desk, Dr. Richards."

"Of course. I've read some of your work on poisons, Dr. Lee. It's exciting to speak with you. We don't get many poisonings. At least not of this type. Once in a while, a child will drink bleach or eat some fertilizer, you know. It happens. But this is something out of the ordinary, isn't it? How did you find out about the case?"

Peggy made it to her desk and pulled out a yellow legal pad while she hunted for a pen. The only one she could find was half-eaten. "I read about it in the newspaper. Have you been able to identify the toxin Mr. Hollings ingested?"

"As a matter of fact, we just found out this morning that the substance is horse chestnut honey. We determined that the patient ingested a large quantity in a few hours prior to being admitted. I don't know if this is an accident or something else. I've called in the police. Unfortunately, Mr. Hollings died during the night from complications."

Her heart raced. Maybe she *was* on to something. She could hear Shakespeare chewing behind her. She glanced back and groaned. He had her chenille bathrobe, the one John gave her for her birthday the year he died. "Put that down!" She got up and shoved the dog away. Too late. There was already a large hole in the back. She stifled the urge to scream and locked the whining dog in the bathroom.

"Dr. Lee? Is everything okay?"

"It's fine, Dr. Richards. I'm having some problems with my dog. I apologize. Please go on. I'm sorry to hear about Mr. Hollings."

"I understand. I have a puppy, too. She's a shepherd." He laughed. "I've had a time with her."

"I wish my monster was a puppy. He's a fully grown Great Dane, and he's decided to behave like a rebellious teenager."

"I've heard training works wonderfully for some cases," he advised. "Of course, not every dog responds. Sometimes you just have to get rid of them."

"Well, I hope it won't come to that." She took a deep breath and pushed her hair out of her face. "As to the poisoning . . ."

"Yes, of course." He shuffled his papers. "We think Mr. Hollings ingested the honey at home. The police are checking it out. He ate almost an entire jar of it and lapsed into a coma before his organs failed. He had congenital heart disease, which may have contributed to his death. The CDC might get involved with this. We don't know yet if this is an isolated case or something more widespread."

"Do you have a sample of the honey? Do you know where it came from?"

"Let me see." He checked his notes. "Yes. It came from a small town in California. The label on the jar says Yellow Hills. Are you working on this case, Dr. Lee?"

"Please call me Peggy. I'm working on a similar case." She told him about Park and the honey at the hotel. "Could you check and see if the Yellow Hills honey came from a hotel in

Philadelphia? Do you know what Mr. Hollings's occupation was?

"He was an attorney," he responded. "I'll check with Mr. Hollings's family and try to find out where the jar of honey came from. If this is true, we could have a major epidemic on our hands. Maybe there's more poisoned honey being produced. Perhaps the honey growers need to be alerted."

Peggy made notes. "That may be true, although here in Charlotte, we have a second death linked to the first that has nothing to do with honey. I'm sure the police will want to ask questions and follow up. They should get an idea of who's involved quickly. I'd appreciate it if you would keep me updated. Do you have my e-mail address?"

"Yes I do, Peggy. Thanks for your input. I'll let you know what happens. Please keep me advised about your situation as well. And call me Alan."

"Thanks, Alan. Maybe if we work together, we can find out what's going on. I'll let you know if we learn anything else here." Peggy hung up the phone thoughtfully. She glanced at her notes. She'd have to take them to Al this morning. The police should know the poisoning might be more widespread than just Park. It could get Beth out of trouble as well. At least for Park's death. The DA could still contend that Beth killed Isabelle just to keep the old lady from making any more accusations.

She walked into the bathroom and found soap and bubble bath spread everywhere over chewed-up towels. "Shakespeare! What have you done?"

BETH WAS PALE AND tightly poised in the crowded courtroom. Her hair was pulled back from her thin face that was devoid of makeup, and her black suit was demure. She looked young and helpless, more like a grieving widow than a killer.

When her name and case number were called, Hunter and David stood up for the defense and pled not guilty on Beth's behalf. They gave their summation of their client's innocence after the damning words from the assistant district attorney.

"We ask for the court to release Mrs. Lamonte on her own recognizance. She holds no threat to the community and is an active member of many charities and other groups that benefit the city. She was born in this area, has two children who reside here, and has lifelong ties to Charlotte. She doesn't pose a flight risk."

The judge looked at the young ADA in the ill-fitting brown suit who consulted his file and shook his head. "We disagree with counsel for the defense, Your Honor. Both of these acts were heinous and perpetrated solely and coldly for profit. We ask for no bail."

"Your Honor," Hunter argued. "The defendant is the mother of two small children. She isn't going anywhere and isn't guilty of these crimes."

"Save the arguments for court, Counsel," the judge advised. "Bail is set at five hundred thousand dollars." She banged the gavel and moved on to the next case.

"Your Honor, Gary Rusch for the defense." The senior attorney glided to the front of the courtroom. He wore his conservative gray suit and white shirt like a fashion model. Heads turned at his entrance. "If I may? Mr. Lamonte's former associates at Lamonte, Rusch and Peterson would like to stand bail for Mrs. Lamonte as a testimony to our belief in her innocence."

"That's fine, Mr. Rusch. I'm sure you know how it's done. Next case." The judge purposefully turned away.

Peggy was surprised and pleased by the move. She watched from the back of the courtroom as Beth hugged her savior. There was that disturbing intimacy again between them that bothered Peggy. It seemed to be one-sided. Beth didn't cling to Gary, but he bent his head close to hers and brushed his hand across her cheek. Was there something else Beth hadn't told her?

Beth was led away by a guard and wasn't released until about an hour later. Peggy waited inside the courthouse for her. The press was everywhere outside, snapping pictures and demanding answers from the district attorney. Beth's father was waiting with a car around the side, hoping to get his daughter away from their prying eyes.

Peggy led the way when she saw Beth walk out of the holding area. "Let's duck out the side entrance."

Beth was still in shock. "This is unbelievable, Peggy. Not only have I been charged with Park's death but Isabelle's, too. I don't know what to do. I don't know how I can go through this."

"You let us worry about that," Gary told her, joining them with Hunter and David at his side. "We'll take care of it. David assures me this kind of incompetence won't continue."

"Incompetence?" Beth frowned. "I thought they were fine."

"They should have been able to get you out on your own recognizance. But David will try harder next time, right son?"

"Yes! I'm sorry I was incompetent, Mrs. Lamonte."

Peggy thought Rusch Senior was a little hard on his son but didn't say so.

Gary glanced at his watch. "I'm sorry to have to leave you right away, but I have to get back to work. I'll talk to you later. Just hang in there."

"Thank you again, Gary." Beth hugged him again. "I don't know what I'd do without the all of you."

Peggy nudged Hunter, whose blue eyes were focused on David. "Is there anything we should know, Hunter? *Hunter!*"

The young attorney shrugged, but her face was pink. "Not really. Davey and I grew up in Chatham County together before his parents moved to Charlotte. We dated for a while when we met again later in law school. I haven't seen him in a few years."

Peggy glanced at Beth, who smiled and looked away. "I mean about the *case,* sweetie!"

"Oh!" Hunter's face got *really* red. "Oh, no. Not really. Not right now anyway. I'll look over the evidence the DA has in the case."

"*We'll* look over the evidence," David reminded her with a gentle smile on his face.

Hunter pressed her cheek to his. "Yes. Then *we'll* interview witnesses and take statements. We're thinking about starting a new practice of our own!"

Peggy smiled. "I'm happy for you. That was some pretty fast work."

"Yeah." She laughed. "It was. One minute, everything was normal. The next minute, I was on the floor looking up. I never saw it coming. But wow! I like being hit by trains."

David put his arm around her shoulder. "Rusch and Ollson."

"Ollson and Rusch," Hunter corrected.

Beth walked between Peggy, Hunter, and David as they ushered her quickly out to her father's Buick. "I guess I'll do whatever the two of you decide is best. I have faith in you. Maybe you can find some way to get me out of this mess."

"Maybe," Peggy half agreed. "But best not to depend on any one strategy or person. I'm sorry I got you into this, but I'm working on a theory to get you out." She opened the car door for her. "I should be done at the shop by six. We'll meet at your house to strategize, Beth. Hunter, can you and David be there, too?"

Hunter's eyes and brain were still focused on the man beside her. When she realized Peggy was talking to her, she started and smiled. "Sorry. What did you say?"

Peggy repeated her question, while Beth laughed. "Of course." Hunter put her hand on Beth's arm. "Don't worry. We'll work this out."

Waving to Hunter, David, and Beth, Peggy got her bike and started riding toward the university. The morning was still cold and damp. By the time she reached Queens, she was cold and damp, too.

She grabbed a cup of coffee as she dialed Al's number on her cell phone. He was out, but she left him a voice mail asking him to call her as soon as he could. She wished there was time to do more research into the poisoned honey, but her class was just about to start. It would have to wait until lunch.

She was halfway through a lecture on hybridization when her friend, Darmus Appleby, stopped by. He'd promised to come in at some point and talk to her students about composting.

Darmus was also the organizer of the Charlotte community garden, his favorite subject. He nearly danced when he was talking about it. Composting eventually turned into an appeal to help with the garden project, the first of its kind in uptown Charlotte. But then *everything* Darmus did turned into an appeal to help with the community garden!

The students were interested and enthusiastic about the garden. They signed up to help with it after class. Darmus gave out literature from the US Composting Council as well as flyers for the community garden. His dark eyes glittered in his lined black face as he hugged Peggy when all the students were gone. He was short, barely reaching five feet. His hands and feet were crippled with arthritis, but his appreciation for the miracle of life glowed about him like a halo.

"That went very well." Peggy smiled as she righted herself after his bear hug. "I think you got some volunteers."

"The Lord provides! You and I know that better than most people. We are so blessed!"

"You're right, sir! Can I buy you lunch?"

"If you can find me some decent veggies," Darmus agreed, "I'd be happy to join you. I'm so glad you agreed to help me with the garden. I'm going to be interviewed on *Charlotte Talks* later this week. Think you could be there?"

"I'd be glad to, although you know more than I do about anything to do with gardening. I can be there for moral support anyway."

"Great! Thank you, Peggy. Now where's that lunch?"

LUNCH WAS OVER QUICKLY with two garden lovers talking about their favorite subject. Darmus was a strict vegan who ate only vegetables, fruit, and rice. He always managed to tweak Peggy's conscience about buying organics and not eating foods grown in areas served by slave labor or under political sanctions.

She adored him, but even at sixty-seven, he was difficult to keep up with. Born in a desperately poor farming community in South Carolina, he'd still managed to go to school and support fourteen brothers and sisters while he was growing up. He'd become politically active in Charlotte while teaching at UNCC. In the course of that time, he'd traveled around the world as a UN ambassador to hungry nations and been awarded medals by the president of the United States.

"Here he is!" Darmus hailed someone from behind her left shoulder. "Peggy, I want you to meet my friend and coconspirator, Fletcher Davis. I finally convinced him to come to Charlotte."

Peggy turned around with a smile that quickly vanished from her face. *"You!"* she accused the young man who stood behind her.

"The lady from the rally who saved my butt," Fletcher acknowledged her, still wearing raggedy jeans and T-shirt with a threadbare jacket that looked the same as the day she'd seen him at the hotel in Philadelphia. "How was jail?"

"Someplace I don't want to go again, thanks." Peggy's brain raced. *What are the odds he'd be here with Darmus?*

"That's wonderful! I can't believe you've already met!" Darmus laughed. "Fletcher is the head of a huge coalition for conservation, Peggy. It's called Tomorrow's Children. He's teaching a few classes right here at Queens as well. But I suppose you already know that, eh?"

"Not really." Peggy tried to stop frowning at Fletcher. "What brings you to Charlotte, Fletcher? Another rally?"

"No. I'm here to help Darmus with fund-raising for his garden. But we put a serious crimp in those legal eagles' plans in Philly, didn't we? They won't recover for a while."

"Someone poisoned one of those legal eagles," Peggy told him, wanting to see his reaction. "He died."

Fletcher's expression didn't change. He shrugged, his longish brown hair raking his shoulders. "Better him than the bay, right? What's one man compared to a generation losing what's important? Clean air and water. We *all* need that to survive."

PEGGY TRIED CALLING AL again after meeting Fletcher Davis. It seemed *very* convenient to her that he happened to be at the hotel in Philadelphia *and* in Charlotte. Al didn't answer, so reluctantly, she went about her day.

Could Fletcher be the one who gave Park the poisoned honey? He was outside his hotel room in Philadelphia and could have been running away from what he did when she got arrested trying to save him from the police. He didn't seem upset by the idea that Park was dead. Was he fanatical enough to kill Park over the estuary?

If so, how would that tie in with Isabelle's death? Maybe the two events *weren't* connected, as the police believed.

She took Shakespeare out for his walk, relieved to find the laundry room intact. He still refused to eat, even when she offered him a treat. Feeling guilty, she let him stay in the kitchen with her while she checked her e-mail on her laptop. She'd heard back from the other two physicians treating the poison victims. Neither one of them knew what type of poison was involved yet. She replied, suggesting they look for the poisoned pollen and asking for more details about their patients.

There was still no word from Nightflyer. She put Shakespeare back in the laundry room despite his pitiful look and whining. She reminded him that it was his own fault. Maybe next time he'd behave better with Rue and learn something.

Steve called her on her way to the Potting Shed. She told him what happened at the bail hearing and afterward with Darmus. He offered to take her to Beth's after the shop closed that evening. Peggy agreed quickly as she raced her bike around a car that was looking for someplace to park.

She reached the Potting Shed only a few minutes before the city was hammered by heavy rain. Shoppers hurried to shelter, some running in from the courtyard to stand near the door and wait for the shower to pass. "Hi Selena! How's business?"

"It's been good," her assistant told her. "It'll probably be slow from here on in with the rain. Why doesn't it ever rain like this when I'm working?"

"Weren't we just concerned about not having enough customers?" Peggy asked, checking the bills and catalogs that came in the mail.

"Yeah, but they *could* come in when *you're* here to prove how well we're doing." Selena picked up her book bag and got ready to leave. "Sam and Keeley called in from that new mall over off of Harris Boulevard. They said it's been raining there for the past two hours. They're not getting anything done, so they're coming in."

"Okay. The mall will have to wait." Peggy sighed, hoping they didn't get backed up. As they inched closer to spring, more work was likely to come in. She might even have to hire another crew this year to help them with the landscaping. "I'll see you later. Thanks for holding down the fort."

Not wasting any time, Peggy gave out free catalogs to the trapped shoppers. She didn't recognize them as regulars and decided it was a good time to promote. She was surprised when Al ran in out of the downpour, his jacket pulled over his head.

"Peggy." He nodded to her as he took the jacket off. The look on his face reminded her of a child getting caught doing something silly. "I got your messages and thought I'd stop by."

"Would you like some hot tea?" she asked, taking out the hot plate and the kettle for herself.

"Sure. That would be great." He glanced at the shoppers who were huddled near the door. "A captive audience, huh?"

"Something like that. I'm sure Emil would've liked them more. People are more apt to buy pastries and coffee while they're waiting than bulbs and shovels."

He laughed. "Peggy, you're amazing! I know your schedule. Where do you find time to examine honey between teaching and pushing shovels on unsuspecting shoppers?"

"There's always time to do the things that are important to us." She smiled. "John taught me that."

"Okay. I'm a captive audience, too. Tell me what you know about the honey."

"And a young man named Fletcher Davis."

"Okay." Al got comfortable in the rocking chair. "Let's have it."

14

Horse Chestnut

Botanical: *Aesculus hippocastanum*
Family: N.O. Sapindaceae

*This is part of the buckeye family of trees, native to many parts of
North America. Chestnuts are thought to bring luck when carried
in the pocket, especially sexual fortune. All parts of the horse
chestnut contain the poison esculin, which has been used to make
rat poison.*

"SO FOUR PEOPLE WERE poisoned?" Hunter raised her eyebrows. "Maybe by the same person?"

"Maybe," Peggy cautiously agreed. "But you have to remember, I don't have all the data in yet. Mr. Hollings's poison
has been identified. The other two haven't been. But his jar of
honey came from a different source. That makes it more difficult to trace, *definitely* more difficult to link to Park's poisoning."

"But that's good for *my* case, right?" Beth sat in her colorful sitting room and looked hopefully at the other two women
with her. "I mean, this proves I didn't kill Park, doesn't it? I'm
clear of that anyway."

"Absolutely!" Hunter was emphatic. "Having this information can make all the difference."

Peggy wasn't as sure. "It's too early to tell, Beth. We haven't made the connection yet between Park and the other three men. And there are still the charges against you for Isabelle's death. She wasn't killed with honey. And that *B* in her own blood was pretty convincing. That isn't going to go away, no matter what we find out about Park's death."

Beth frowned, the movement puckering her forehead. "That's true. What can we do about that?"

"We'll have to find out who killed Isabelle." Hunter closed her notebook and zipped it shut. "But let's be happy with *any* victory right now. The DA is saying you killed Isabelle because you killed your husband. Taking away your motive to kill her weakens the basis of the second charge."

"Why *would* someone want to kill Isabelle?" Peggy glanced at them. The room was a little too warm with the fire in the hearth blazing brightly. The house seemed too quiet, too empty around them. But she was glad Foxx and Reddman had a place to get away from what was happening.

She couldn't imagine how Beth was coping with the empty house, but the DA had insisted she had to stay in her own home and not with Peggy. It didn't make any sense to her, but Hunter's arguments had been tossed aside like last summer's tomatoes. "I mean, besides the obvious reasons. I assume someone would've killed her years ago if it was because she was a mean, arrogant old lady. Why kill her *now*, so close on the heels of Park's death?"

Beth shrugged and burrowed more deeply into her amber-colored shawl. The bright red chair made her look smaller, paler. Her dark hair was loose on her shoulders. "I don't know. I've thought about it. I haven't thought about anything else the last two days. Isabelle was harmless. Maybe she was annoying, but surely no one would kill her for that."

"Maybe it was unrelated." Hunter looked at them as she ramped up her thoughts. "Maybe whoever did this was going to rob her. They heard about her being alone when the press talked about Park's death. It made her a target. They didn't mean to kill her. It was an accident. Then after it was over, they grabbed a few trinkets, one of them being the dragon's head from her walking stick, and ran."

"As much as I'd like to believe that," Peggy said, "it's too coincidental. No one is going to believe Park died under suspicious circumstances, then his mother was attacked and wrote a *B* in her blood while she was dying, but Beth wasn't involved. She's my friend and I *know* she didn't do anything wrong, but I don't buy it. Besides, the police didn't find anything missing *except* the dragon's head. While that might be valuable, I'm sure she had jewelry and cash somewhere, too."

"Then we have to find the killer's motivation." Hunter got to her feet and paced the room. "Why *would* someone kill Isabelle? At least in relation to Park's death."

"Maybe she knew something about Park's death." Peggy shrugged. "Maybe she was involved with the killer in some way."

Beth was horrified. "There's no way Isabelle would have helped *anyone* kill Park. He meant *everything* to her."

"I'm not saying she *knowingly* did something," Peggy corrected. "But she might not have realized what was happening."

Hunter nodded. "Like what?"

"Maybe if we understood why someone gave Park poisoned honey, we'd understand why Isabelle was killed." Peggy shifted in her chair.

"Why not give Isabelle poisoned honey, too?" Beth questioned.

"Maybe she wasn't as easy to get to as Park with that basket at the hotel." Hunter stopped pacing. "Let's say it was this man from the environmental group who wanted to kill Park because of the estuary issue. If he's here in Charlotte, he had opportunity to kill Isabelle, too."

"But why would he?" Peggy queried. "She didn't have anything to do with the law firm representing the oil company."

"What about Alice then?" Hunter changed suspects. "She obviously didn't like the old lady."

"But why would she kill Park?" Beth wondered with a cry in her voice. "He was always generous with her."

Hunter shrugged, her forehead furrowed. "To torture Isabelle before she killed her?"

Peggy could see from the look on Beth's face that this conversation was torturing *her*. Besides, they were just going around in circles. There was some piece missing in the puzzle. Something they weren't taking into consideration. "It's late." She glanced at her watch. "I have to go. I can only imagine what trouble Shakespeare has managed to get into. We'll have to keep thinking about this and try to come up with some other answers that make sense. It would be nice if we could find the dragon's head. That might give us Isabelle's killer."

Beth rose lightly to her feet. "I appreciate you coming anyway. Steve, too. I'll try to think of anything that might relate to this. Right now, my brain is on overload. I just need to sleep for a while."

The doorbell rang as Peggy was going to get Steve out of the kitchen. She tried to get him to sit with them, but he said he felt the three women needed the time together alone. "Ready to go?" she asked as Beth answered the door.

Steve shut off the small TV on the counter. "Yes! Thank God you came for me. I hate football."

She laughed. "I'm sorry. Beth said she was having some trouble with her cable. She can only get ESPN. Thank you for waiting for me anyway."

"Did you get everything sorted out?" he asked as they walked out of the kitchen.

"No," she answered briefly before they reached the others. "I wish we'd been able to come up with *any* answers for what's happened. We just can't figure it out. And everything points to Beth."

David was standing in the hall with Beth and Hunter. He had his arm draped casually around Hunter's shoulders . . . after almost knocking over the fern by the door. "We're getting David caught up with what we discussed tonight," Beth told her.

"I wish I could've been here, but I'm doing extra work until we can get in a new person at the firm." He glanced up at Beth and frowned. "I'm sorry. I shouldn't have said that."

Beth put her hand on his arm. "Don't worry about it. I know life goes on. I can't hide from that."

Hunter slipped her hand through David's arm. "I suppose we should get going. I'll talk to you tomorrow, Peggy. If you come up with anything else, let me know."

Peggy smiled. "I will." It was good to see Hunter with someone in her life so she didn't have to depend on Sam for companionship. "Good night, Beth. I'll talk to you tomorrow. If you need me for anything, call."

"That goes for us, too," David told her.

"We'll be prepping for the trial," Hunter said. "I'll call you tomorrow, Beth. We have a lot to do."

Steve and Peggy walked out of the house behind Hunter and David. Steve nodded at the couple, his voice a murmur near Peggy's ear. "That happened pretty quickly, didn't it?"

She glanced at him and smiled. "Some people said that about us, you know. I guess all relationships don't have to take years to develop."

"I suppose that's true." He opened the door to the Vue for her. "What's next with Beth?"

She explained everything they talked about in the tiny sitting room. Maybe he'd be able to make some sense of it. "We have to find out who killed Isabelle. Whoever it was wanted to throw suspicion on Beth. If we find *that* person, I think we've found the person responsible for Park's death as well."

"You don't think the poisoned honey was accidental? How could people control what plants their bees get honey from anyway?"

"Beekeepers are more careful than that," she told him. "No good beekeeper would allow this to happen. They know how far their bees fly, and they're careful about what's allowed to grow in that area."

"But why would someone want to kill Park *and* his mother?"

"I'm not sure. I haven't been able to think of a single reason. I considered his ex-wife. But even if she hated Park enough to kill him, what reason would she have to kill Isabelle? The two of them got along like mud and flies. She was Isabelle's choice for Park."

"What about money as a motive?" he suggested. "Will anyone strike it rich from this besides Beth?"

"I suppose we can assume Isabelle didn't have time to change her will after Park's death. That probably means that everything she had went to Park."

"Which means it goes to Beth."

She nodded. "That's right."

"Okay. What about the housekeeper?" Steve questioned. "She had the opportunity to poison Park *and* kill the mother."

"But what would she gain?"

"Maybe just satisfaction." He shrugged. "I don't know. But she makes more sense as a suspect than your environmental leader from Philadelphia. I can see him killing Park. But he probably didn't even *know* his mother."

"I don't know. My brain feels like it's full of mush." Peggy told him about the relationship she noticed between Gary Rusch and Beth.

"Do you think it relates to what happened?" he queried. "Have you said anything to her about it?"

"Not yet," she confessed. "Some things even *I'm* reluctant to bring up."

"You mean you'd rather *not* know," he guessed. "I don't blame you."

Peggy's cell phone rang. It was Paul. "How far are you from the house?" he asked.

"Only a few minutes. Why?" She glanced at Steve as he turned the Vue from Providence Road to Queens Road.

"They called me from burglary about twenty minutes ago," Paul told her. "Someone broke into the house."

"We'll be right there." Peggy's heart raced as she closed her cell phone. "Someone broke into my house."

"Was anything taken? Did they catch who did it?" Steve drove a little faster down the empty street.

"I don't know yet. Paul's there." She looked out at the houses that lined the street. "I should've set the alarm." She thought about Shakespeare, locked in the laundry room, and sat forward. "Can we go any faster?"

They parked on the road. There was no way to get in the drive through the bevy of police and crime scene vehicles. It looked as though every light was on in the house. Peggy pushed open the car door and ran up through the wet grass.

Her neighbor, Clarice, and her apricot poodle, Poopsie, met her halfway to the house. "Oh Peggy! Imagine something like this happening here. In *this* neighborhood. What's the world coming to? I'm so sorry. I hope all of your valuables were insured."

Peggy brushed by her without a word, focused on the house. Steve smiled at the woman whose hair matched the color of her poodle and patted Poopsie's head as he ran after Peggy. Clarice continued to fret as she followed the two of them.

"Mom!" Paul waited for her at the front door. "I know this looks bad, but it could've been worse. These home invasions can be dangerous, too. Thank God you weren't here."

"What about Shakespeare?" Peggy asked immediately as she continued through the house toward the kitchen. She ignored his attempts to soften the blow for her, focused on her concern for the dog. "Have you seen him?"

"No." Paul shook his head. "I heard him when we first got here. He's here somewhere. Hello, Steve."

"Hi, Paul." Steve kept up with Peggy's frantic pace.

"I thought she'd be worried about the antiques or her jewelry." Paul shrugged. "Go figure."

"Your mother's not an ordinary person," Steve explained with a grin.

"You noticed that, huh? I thought I'd learned to live with it. But she always manages to surprise me."

Peggy rushed by them and finally reached the kitchen, skirting the small groups of crime scene people rummaging through her house. She opened the laundry room door, and Shakespeare jumped down from the top of the dryer. Dropping to her knees, she threw her arms around his broad neck. "Thank goodness you're all right." She looked around the small room. He'd knocked over detergent and fabric softener, almost made his way through the wall near the door in his quest to get at the person who broke into the house. "I wish you could talk. You probably know who did this, don't you?"

The dog wagged his tail and licked her face, almost twisting his body around her as she stroked his head and back. She apologized to him for leaving him in the laundry room, even though it may have saved his life.

Peggy got to her feet. "I guess you might as well come out. There's not much that hasn't been damaged out here."

"If you could get us the insurance list you keep in case of fire," Paul said awkwardly. "I've got Crime Scene looking for whatever they can find that might help. There may be some fingerprints or some other DNA evidence that was left behind. I don't think professionals were responsible for this. You didn't set the alarm, did you?"

"No." Peggy was embarrassed by her lack of responsibility. It wasn't that she forgot to set the alarm. It was easier not to set it. No one bothered houses on Queens Road. She couldn't even remember the last time anyone had a break-in. "Have you noticed anything specific being gone?"

"Just a few things." Paul shrugged. "And I'm not sure if anything was taken. There must've been more than one of them. The place is a mess."

"Have you gone in the basement?"

"Yeah." He looked away. "You aren't going to like it."

Steve walked with her into the basement, Shakespeare staying a sedate step behind them. Paul excused himself, not wanting to see the look on his mother's face when she realized how much of her work was ruined.

The pond was emptied. Plants and dirt were scattered everywhere. The container that was keeping the thrips and spider mites in the area with the strawberries was tossed aside. Even the plants themselves were torn up and tossed on the floor. The red berries were crushed. The French doors going to the backyard were smashed and left open to the cold night outside.

Peggy picked up a few water plants and put them back in the violated pond. The frog croaked at her from the edge. She smiled at him as she shivered. "At least you were smart enough not to run outside. I'll have to get something up over those doors until they can be repaired."

"I've got some tarps at my house. We could use those," Steve volunteered.

"That would be great." She tried to inflect some excitement into her voice. She really appreciated his help. It was just overwhelming to see everything so devastated. It looked more like a tornado hit there rather than a break-in.

Steve hugged her. "Don't worry. I'll help you clean up. There isn't anything here that can't be replaced. I know you have a lot of work in this, but Paul is right. At least you weren't here. At least *you're* all right. Shakespeare, too."

Peggy sat down in the basement with her ruined experiments. She could hear Steve talking to someone on the stairs as he left to get the tarps. Shakespeare curled up on her feet, trying to get as close as possible.

At least you weren't here. The phrase kept echoing through her mind. It bothered her. Not that it was unusual for her to be gone at night. Was someone watching the house and learning her habits? She thought about Nightflyer but immediately took him off of her list. He was far too secretive to leave a mess behind. If he *did* break in, she felt sure she'd never know.

"Hi, Peggy." Mai joined her, glancing around the basement. "I came as soon as I heard. I'm so sorry about this."

"Thank you." Peggy's lips were tight with the effort it took not to cry. Everyone was right. She wasn't hurt. Shakespeare wasn't hurt. Everything else could be redone and replaced. "I haven't looked upstairs yet. Is it like this?"

Mai nodded. "I'm afraid so. I don't know if I've ever seen a mess like this at a break-in before. It's like it was trashed by a horde of barbarians. I don't know how they could see what they wanted to take. It had to be kids."

"I suppose you're right." Peggy got up from her chair. There was no point feeling sorry for herself. She had to move on, move through this. "I guess I should check out the important stuff."

"I'll walk around with you, if you like. I'm not working. Paul called me, and I wanted to be here."

Peggy squeezed Mai's hand. "Thank you. I'd like that."

BY THE TIME PEGGY and Mai had conducted a thorough tour of the house, Al and Jonas were there. Al put his arm around her. "Sorry this happened to you, Peggy. Do you have a list of what's missing?"

"No." Peggy looked at him in amazement. "There's nothing missing. At least nothing I can think of. Every room was rummaged through, but my jewelry, John's coin collection, antiques. Nothing's missing."

Al exchanged glances with Jonas. "Probably just kids. Was the door forced open?"

Mai nodded. "The French doors in the basement were knocked open."

"It's like someone was searching for something." Peggy looked around herself in the trashed-out television room. "Why else would someone do this but not take anything? Even kids would've taken something or spray painted graffiti. Something."

"Don't worry, Peggy." Jonas smiled at her. "I'm sure the burglary unit will be able to give you some answers. We just wanted to check in on you after we heard the call. Sorry about your place. Do you need a hand getting things straightened up?"

"I'll be fine," she assured him. "But I know it's almost impossible for you to find suspects on something like this."

Al cleared his throat noisily. "That doesn't mean *you* should go out and look for them."

"You don't have to worry about that." She laughed. "I think I'll have my hands full here. Thanks for stopping by."

Al lingered behind a moment while Jonas walked outside. "About the information you gave me regarding the honey."

Peggy's eyebrows lifted. "Yes?"

"There may be something to it. I checked out Mr. Hollings with the Dubuque Police Department. He was a lawyer working on the same case as Mr. Lamonte. He got the same gift basket at the same hotel. We're trying to contact people at the hotel and find out where the baskets came from."

"That's great, Al! Thanks for telling me. And Fletcher Davis?"

"I don't know. We can't find the boy, for one thing. He's impassioned, that's for sure. He's been arrested a dozen times for stunts he pulled. Nothing violent."

"He's right here in Charlotte," Peggy informed him. "He's staying at UNCC with Darmus Appleby."

"And you think he seems like a killer?"

Peggy repeated what Fletcher said when she told him about Park's death. "He was pretty cold about it."

Al grunted. "I'll see what I can find out."

"Does that mean Beth isn't on the suspect list anymore? Are you dropping the charges against her?"

"Not yet." He eyed a green velvet drape that was about to fall on the floor. "Even if we do, that won't change my mind about her killing the old lady. Even if she didn't have a hand in what happened to her husband, it's clear she was involved in Isabelle's death."

Peggy rolled her eyes. "That's ridiculous! Whoever did it *wanted* Beth to be blamed for Isabelle's death."

"Well, like you said," Al's gaze took in the demolished room, "you've got plenty to do. We appreciate everything you've done to help. Now stay out of the rest. *Please.*"

Angered by his tone, she nodded. "Better get going before Jonas has to lean on the horn. I'll talk to you later."

Steve and Paul came in after Al left. "We tacked up those tarps over the French doors," Paul told her, sitting beside her on the brown sofa.

"Thank you." She hugged him and smiled at Steve. "Remind me that I owe you two tarps."

Steve crouched down beside her and took her hand. "Don't worry about it. Let's get this place cleaned up. Where do you want to start?"

"You don't have to do that." She got to her feet. "I'll take care of it later. It's almost midnight. We both have work tomorrow."

Paul stood up. "My shift ends at midnight. I agree with Steve. Let's get this place cleaned up. I *know* you, Mom. You won't sleep tonight. You'll be up all night putting things back together. This way, you can get done sooner."

"I'll order the pizzas and beer," Steve added. "I already called Sam. He said he's on his way over with Keeley. They called Hunter, too."

Peggy's eyes brimmed with tears. "Let's get started then."

Sam and Keeley were there a few minutes later. Hunter didn't show up for almost an hour.

"You're always giving me hell about being late," Sam ribbed her as he shoved a slice of pizza in his mouth. "Where have *you* been?"

Hunter smiled at him. "You're just jealous because *I* have a life." She looked around the wrecked kitchen. "Any idea who did this?"

"Not yet." Sam opened a bottle of beer. "Paul lifted some prints they're checking out. I just finished helping Peggy in the basement. Whoever did this took out months of her work down there. I'd like to get my hands around his neck."

"Why assume it was a man?" Keeley asked. "Crimes committed by women are the fastest growing group of offenses. Maybe some women broke in here and did all this. It looks like it took more than one person to make this mess."

"Doesn't she have video cameras or some kind of security monitoring company for the house?" Hunter wondered. "A house this size, it seems like it would be protected."

"It would've been if I'd left the alarm system on," Peggy said as she joined them in the kitchen. "It always seems like a wasted few minutes to set it. No one breaks into these houses."

"They did tonight." A short, thin man with a large nose on his swarthy face walked in through the kitchen door.

Sam, Hunter, Keeley, and Steve stared at him. "He must be a security alarm salesperson," Hunter whispered.

"Uncle Dalton!" Paul greeted his great-uncle as he entered the kitchen. "How are you? How's Aunt Sarah?"

"She's fine, Paul. Thank you for asking." But though Dalton spoke to his great-nephew and shook his hand, his narrow brown eyes were focused on Peggy. "I'd like a moment of your time, Peggy. I know you're busy, but what I have to say won't wait."

Peggy knew why he was there. He'd heard about the break-in on the news, and it fueled his resolve to get her out of the family estate.

She tried to stiffen her back, but it hurt from leaning over the pond, cleaning up the mess. She was in no mood to accommodate Dalton's demands or his rude manner. Steve moved closer to her. She wanted to lean on him and absorb some of his strength, but she knew she had to do this alone. "Not right now, Dalton. Neither one of us wants to do this right now."

The old man pulled his heavy black coat closer around his emaciated frame. "Very well. If you don't mind a public forum, I certainly don't mind. You aren't able to take care of this house anymore. You need to give it back to the trust."

"The trust is set up so that the widow of the man who inherits the house can live here until she dies," Peggy reminded him. "I'm not dead yet."

"If I can't appeal to your *generous* nature in letting go of the estate so my son's family can live here, I'll take it to court. You don't need a house this size, and you certainly aren't able to care for it. You just admitted you don't have time to set a simple alarm system. Do you think John would want you living in his family's ancestral home and destroying it?"

Peggy squared her shoulders, the only part of her that wasn't aching. "I don't care. I love this house, and I intend to live here as long as I can. I'll fight you in court if necessary. It won't make for pleasant family holidays, Dalton. Think carefully before you take that course of action."

He put his black felt hat on his head. "I'll see you in court, Peggy. Good night all."

His departure was as sudden as his entrance, leaving behind a stunned silence. The group turned to look at Peggy, who shrugged and grabbed another box of trash bags from the cabinet. "Are you going to stand there and eat pizza or are you going to clean?"

Everyone followed her back upstairs. "Can he do that?" Paul asked. "Can he kick you out?"

"I have a friend who can help you," Hunter said. "All he does is inheritance law. He could take that guy out with one hand tied behind his back."

"Let's not talk about *that* right now," Sam urged. "I'd like to get home sometime tonight. What else needs to be done?"

"My bedroom and the kitchen," Peggy answered, relieved that they stopped talking about her losing the house. It was one of her greatest fears. If she lost the house, it would be like losing John all over again. So much of her life was here. She wouldn't let Dalton take that away from her without a fight.

"We'll go downstairs and tackle the kitchen," Hunter and Keeley agreed.

"I'll go downstairs and supervise," Sam said. "Otherwise nothing will get done but a lot of giggling."

"You're just jealous," Hunter accused. "I have friends *and* a boyfriend."

"How's that going?" Keeley asked her.

"Wait until I tell you . . ." Hunter's voice trailed down the long stairway.

"Great!" Sam threw up his hands. "Not only do I have sleep to catch up with and hundreds of philodendron to plant tomorrow, I have to listen to Keeley and Hunter gossip about David."

"You could be more supportive," Peggy reminded him. "You didn't want to spend all your time with your sister. She found someone who wants to be with her."

"Yeah, thanks for reminding me." Sam grinned and followed the two women downstairs.

When all three of them were gone, Steve shook out a trash bag and smiled at Peggy. "Where do you want *me* to start?"

"Could you start with Dalton?"

He laughed. "I could. But I'd probably need your help getting rid of the body. You're better at that kind of thing."

"Dalton doesn't really bother me," Peggy admitted. "This break-in is a lot more confusing."

"How so?"

"Because it seems so pointless. Nothing stolen. Nothing written on or abused except for things that were in the way."

She shook her head. "Someone was looking for something. But *what*?"

"I don't know. You said nothing was missing. I tend to agree with the police. This looks like something kids would do."

"Nothing that I *know* of is missing. But the timing is too perfect. I don't believe kids did this. And I don't believe this was a random happening. Someone *knew* I wasn't here and they had plenty of time to search the house from top to bottom. Maybe someone thinks I have something that could incriminate them."

Steve looked bewildered. "You mean something to do with the murder case? Someone knows you've been poking around. What could you possibly have? If someone wanted to keep you from discovering anything else, they should've smashed your computer."

"What if they think I have more than that?" She sat on the side of her bed and pushed her tired thoughts forward. "I was in Isabelle's house while the crime scene team was still working. Isabelle's body had just been removed. Maybe they think I found something and kept it."

"The dragon's head is still missing." Mai suggested as she and Paul joined them in the bedroom. "Maybe whoever did it thinks you have the dragon's head from Isabelle's walking stick. We haven't been able to find it. Maybe he or she can't find it either."

"Wouldn't they think she gave it to the police?" Paul wondered. "Most people give evidence to the police."

"They'd know better if they knew your mother." Steve frowned as he picked up shards of broken glass from the floor.

"I know," Paul agreed with a thoughtful glance at Peggy, "but that would imply that whoever it is knows her that well, too."

"That's scary." Mai shivered.

The thought sobered them, and no one spoke for a moment. Then Peggy shook her head and stood up, stretching her back and shoulders. "We're never going to get this done just standing here speculating. It's late, and we all need to get to bed. Let's save the scary thoughts for tomorrow, huh?"

15

Lemon Balm

Botanical: *Melissa officinalis*
Family: N. O. Labiatae
Common name: Balm

This plant grows one to two feet tall and has a strong lemon smell when touched. It also has a strong lemon taste that translates well to tea and mixes well with other herbs. The plant dies down in winter, but the root is perennial and will spread easily. The name is from the Greek word for "bee" because bees also love this sweet plant. It is beneficial for colds with fever and has a calming effect on the nerves.

"THERE'S ONLY ONE PLACE the top of the cane can be," Peggy said to Steve as they walked up to Isabelle Lamonte's empty house the next morning. Their breaths came out in frosty puffs of air. Yards of yellow crime scene tape still crossed the porch and doorway. "If I don't have it and the killer doesn't have it and the police don't have it, it *has* to be here."

Steve looked up at the impressive brick house with an uneasy expression on his face. "The police already looked for it, didn't they? How are *we* going to find it if no one else can find it?"

"I don't know." She started to walk around the back of the house. "But it's got to be in there. The killer must realize it, too, since he or she didn't find it at my house. We have to find it first."

"Don't you think the killer looked *here* before breaking into your house?"

"Maybe. But not if he or she was convinced I had it. I talked to Mai early this morning. The crime scene teams finished up here late last night. They've been in and out a lot since the murder. Maybe the killer couldn't get back into the house."

"Shouldn't you have told Al or Jonas about your theory? Maybe even Paul could check into it." Steve dragged his feet as he followed her across the brown winter grass.

"I called Al. He said they searched everywhere for it. He doesn't think it's here. He thinks the killer has it. But the killer wouldn't break into *my* house to look for it if he had it."

"*If* the killer broke into your house." Steve put his hands in the pockets of his dark blue jacket. "That's just a theory, Peggy."

"But it makes sense, doesn't it? Besides, what have we got to lose by looking around? We might even find something else important to the case."

"Okay." Steve finally gave in with a sigh. "How do we get inside? I take it you don't have a key."

"We used to sneak in here sometimes. It was a long time ago. Park was still living at home. His mother was very strict. We'd wait until his parents went out and sneak in through the basement. I'm sure nothing's changed. Isabelle probably hadn't been down there in years."

"Park had to sneak into his own house?" Steve asked.

"He was still in law school at Chapel Hill, living in a dorm. His parents took away his house key because he had a big party here while they were out of town. We sneaked into the basement and raided his father's wine cellar for revenge. The Lamontes had very good taste in wine."

As she spoke, Peggy was pushing aside huge old azaleas and altheas to get to the tiny door in the foundation. When she finally managed to get past the overgrown foliage, she dropped to her knees and looked at the moss-covered wood door. "Here it is. Probably just the way we left it after snatching the Chateau Petrus and drinking it all."

Steve knelt beside her in the orange Carolina clay. "Was it good?"

"It tasted like old wine to me. Kind of musty." She shrugged. "The point was that his father paid a lot of money for it at an auction. That's the only reason we drank it."

"I'll bet he loved that." Steve helped her hold back the plants so she could get her hands on the small door. "We're going in through there?"

"It's big enough," she assured him, trying to move the door. "John was larger than you, and he got through."

"Well if *John* could get through . . ."

Peggy looked at him sharply. "I didn't mean it *that* way. Just that his hips and shoulders were broader than yours, even when he was younger."

Steve moved closer to the house and pushed open the warped door in the foundation. He shoved it against the bricks beside it. The doorway behind it was little more than a three-by-three-foot aperture covered in spiderwebs. "I hope you brought a flashlight. I thought we were going in through a *real* door."

She brushed past him and turned on the penlight attached to her keychain. "This should be plenty. There's a light switch on the opposite wall. All we have to do is get to it." She used the light to peer into the blackness. It really didn't look like anyone had been down there for thirty years.

"I'm right behind you," he said as she seemed to hesitate.

"That's comforting. Watch your knees. You have to crawl through this first part. There are some nails and jagged cement pieces on the ground."

"Was this part set up to be some kind of booby trap for a would-be robber?" Steve pushed himself in through the hole in the wall behind Peggy. "If so, it's original, but an alarm system would probably be better."

"No. There's an alarm system in the house. Just not down here. Mai told me it was off, so that shouldn't be a problem anyway. This used to be a coal chute. They closed it off when they switched to gas heat." Peggy moved awkwardly across the rough ground, mostly feeling her way. She bumped her knee against one of the cement chunks and scraped her hand on a nail. The light from the flashlight bounced on the walls around them. "Thank goodness it's winter, or those awful cricket spiders would be down here, too. I hate those things. They jump up at you when you least expect them."

"I didn't know there was some kind of bug you didn't like," Steve said, scratching the palm of his hand on a rough piece of wood that jutted out into his path. "I didn't think that kind of thing bothered you."

"Of course," she countered. "Everybody doesn't like something."

Steve grinned. "But nobody doesn't like Sara Lee?"

"That's the truth! I wish I didn't. Thank goodness I ride the bike everywhere. It's the only thing that keeps me small."

"That," Steve grunted as he scraped his knee on some concrete, "and the fact that you *never* have any food in your house."

"Where's that light switch?" She felt around on the wall. "It was right here somewhere."

"Maybe someone found out about you getting in this way and took it out. How many times would you let someone crawl into your house from the basement before you took care of the problem?"

"Shh!" Peggy unerringly found his mouth with her hand. "Did you hear that?"

"What?" he managed to whisper around her hand.

"Someone's in the house."

They sat in the dark crawl space and listened as footsteps and voices came closer until they were right above their heads.

"We have to do this now." The woman's voice was muffled but understandable. "If we don't, the executor will or they'll hire someone to sort through it. If we want *anything,* we better get it now. Otherwise, all this has been for nothing."

"I *know* that voice," Peggy whispered. "It's Cindy. Park's ex-wife. What's *she* doing here?"

"She's going through the house." Steve moved, trying to

find a spot that didn't have something that poked into his butt. "I suppose the old lady had plenty of stuff to steal."

"Plenty," Peggy confirmed. "But Cindy was always such a *dear* friend of Isabelle's. Even after she and Park broke up. I can't believe she'd steal from her."

"People will do anything they think they can get away with, I guess."

"But who's with her? She's not talking to herself."

"Her jewelry is locked in a chest upstairs." Cindy spoke again. "Those are probably the most valuable items. We should start up there."

"I guess you better start believing Cindy could steal from Isabelle," Steve remarked. "She knows exactly what to look for and what she wants."

"But who's she talking to?" Peggy wondered again. "We need to know who the other person is before we call the police."

"There's those eggs, too. Those Russian eggs are worth some money. She was always so particular about those. They had to be turned every day. Glad I kept them clean now!"

"That's Alice Godwin!" Peggy started crawling back toward the crawl space door.

"Wait a minute!" Steve hit his head on a floor joist as he tried to stop her. He groaned but kept going. "These women might be responsible for killing Isabelle. They're probably not going to like it if you interfere. Let's call 911. Are you listening to me at all?"

But Peggy wasn't listening. She pushed past the spiderwebs and climbed out of the small doorway in the wall. The two women Isabelle trusted most in the world had turned on her. As cranky and unbending as Park's mother was, the thought of those two women hitting her in the head and pushing her down the stairs to steal from her struck a chord in Peggy. Maybe it was because she lived alone, too. She wasn't going to let the two traitors get away.

Steve was frantically dialing 911 on his cell phone as he followed her outside. "I'd like to report a possible homicide. And maybe one in progress." The woman who responded at the switchboard asked for the address. He couldn't remember it. "A woman was killed here recently. Isabelle Lamonte. I'm at her house. Can you send someone, please?"

Peggy was already angrily pounding on the front door as Steve rounded the corner of the house. He put away his cell phone, hoping the police would respond quickly. Before he could reach her, the heavy front door opened, and Peggy confronted Alice Godwin.

"What do you want now?" the housekeeper demanded. "You're always butting into other people's business! I think you should leave, or you might have a serious accident!"

"You can start by handing over the ivory dragon's head from Isabelle's walking stick." Peggy pushed past her, not intimidated by her words. She stood in the foyer, tapping her foot impatiently, covered in dust and spiderwebs. "And you can come out, too, Cindy. I know you're here."

Park's ex-wife peeked around the corner from the library. She blinked nervously. "Peggy? What are *you* doing here? I just came here with Alice to help her . . . uh . . . clean up. I knew the place would be a mess. You know Isabelle hated that."

"I've been listening to murderers and thieves!" Peggy glared at her. "Don't bother to deny it, either one of you. I heard every word from the crawl space."

"The crawl space?" Alice couldn't believe it. "You *must* be crazy! What were you doing down there?"

"We didn't kill anyone," Cindy persuaded. "She called me when she found Isabelle. Maybe *she's* responsible. But I'm not. I took a few things, but I would *never*—"

"What are you saying?" The housekeeper turned on her. "I told you I found her dead. I didn't kill her." She glared at Peggy and Steve. "It was Cindy's idea to steal her stuff. She said she had plenty, and the family wouldn't miss a few trinkets. God'amighty, Miz Isabelle had enough of it! Not like she'll miss it now!"

"Like the ivory dragon's head?" Peggy's chest was still heaving from running up to the house, but she considered the two conspirators calmly. "Did you take that after you hit her in the head with the cane?"

The other two women stared at each other. Steve stood behind Peggy, glancing out the open front door, wishing the police would get there quickly.

"You bitch!" Cindy launched herself at the housekeeper.

Alice screamed and fell backward under the younger woman's impact, but she was broader and stronger. It only took a moment for her to get the upper hand. She pulled Cindy's too-fluffy blond hair and punched her in her pretty blue eyes. Peggy stepped aside, watching them roll across the foyer.

"Aren't you going to do something?" Steve asked.

"Like what? They're getting what they deserve. I say let them kill each other."

With a heavy sigh, Steve stepped in to stop the women from hurting each other. Cindy raked his face with long, red fingernails. Alice landed a punch to his right eye. Peggy was about to step into the fray to save him when the doorway was filled with several police officers.

"What the hell is going on here?" the first officer demanded, pushing back his hat. "This is a crime scene, in case none of you noticed. Are any of you related to the deceased?"

"You need to arrest these two women for the murder of Isabelle Lamonte as well as stealing from her," Peggy told him. "I heard them talking. They're responsible for what happened here."

"And who are you? Don't tell me *you're* a private investigator?" The officer stared down at her.

"I'm Dr. Margaret Lee from Queens University. I'm here on behalf of the family."

"Are they teaching crime solving at Queens now?" the officer half smiled at her. "If they are, maybe I need to go there and brush up on my basic skills." The other officers laughed with him.

Peggy glanced back at the two women, who had stopped fighting. They were both sitting on the floor, nursing their wounds, breathing hard, *probably wondering how they were going to get out of this mess.* "I teach botany," she declared proudly. "But I can testify against these two women."

The officer looked past her at Steve, whose clothes were dirty and ripped, his hair standing almost straight up on his head and covered with spiderwebs. "And where do you fit into this? Are you a student or a murder suspect?"

"I'm a vet," he answered. "And I was just trying to keep these women from killing each other until *you* got here! What took so long?"

"What's going on here, Officers?" Al's booming voice broke through the sarcasm and explanations.

"We got a call about a possible homicide here, Detective," the lead officer explained.

"I know that, son. That's why *I'm* here." Al saw Peggy's face and put his hands over his eyes. But his voice was calm. "Okay. I can handle this from here."

The officer looked at the two women on the floor. "I don't know. This is a pretty rowdy crowd, sir. Maybe we should call in SWAT."

Alice started crying and rocking her body back and forth. "I didn't do anything anyone else wouldn't have done. Do you know what she gave me every year for Christmas, the rotten old miser? A plate of cookies. That's it. Twenty years of service. I was there for her when no one else would bother with her. She gave me cookies. I *deserve* the head on that cane. I deserve some compensation."

The foyer was suddenly silent after her outburst. No one was expecting her to confess to what happened while they were standing there.

Al nodded. "I guess I was wrong about not needing your help, Officer. Would you please take both of these women to the precinct? I think I might have some questions for them."

"What about *them*?" The officer inclined his head toward Peggy and Steve.

"I'd like to take them in, too, but they probably weren't doing anything wrong except snooping around where they don't belong. I don't think the DA would prosecute them for being annoying, much as he'd like to. Although if it *keeps* happening, that might be another story."

Steve straightened his shirt and hair as he got to his feet.

Peggy cleared her throat and tried not to look smug as Cindy and Alice were escorted from the house.

Al turned on them. "What are you *doing* here? Didn't we agree you'd stay out of this?"

Peggy held her head up high despite the dust and spiderwebs covering it. "I knew the ivory dragon's head had to be part of this. You wouldn't even have known it was gone if it wasn't for me."

"I see," Al replied. "I guess that clears both women of murder then, right? If they've had the top of the walking stick all this time, they wouldn't have bothered looking through your house, would they? You *did* say the killer looked through your house?"

Peggy opened her mouth to argue, then stopped abruptly. What he said made sense. Why hadn't she seen it? Too emotionally involved, she supposed. Too eager to find any different conclusion that would clear Beth that she didn't realize she had the wrong one.

"Or the break-in at your house wasn't involved." Al chuckled, seeing her at a loss for words. "That's why they pay us the big bucks to find out how these things happen. Go home, Peggy. Steve, I'm surprised at you getting involved in something like this."

"Me, too." Steve was sure he looked as ridiculous as he felt. "I'll take her home, Al. Thanks."

"I shouldn't tell you this, but you *did* help with figuring out the whole poisoned honey thing," Al gave Peggy a bone. "We picked up Fletcher Davis this morning and took him in for questioning. The Philly police found his fingerprints all over the rooms Mr. Lamonte and Mr. Hollings stayed in. Security cameras picked him up going in and out of the rooms. I think we've got *that* part dead to rights. He poisoned the lawyers who were involved in the estuary case to stop the oil company."

"What about Beth?" Peggy wondered.

"I'll let you know." Al shrugged. "This looks bad for the housekeeper. Maybe it will get your friend off the hook for that killing, too. Maybe we were wrong about the two killings being linked. Maybe it was just coincidence."

"Thanks, Al." Peggy followed him out of the house. "Were all of the men who were poisoned working for the same company as Park? Were they all poisoned by horse chestnut honey?"

"Three of them, all staying at the same hotel as Park. The fourth man we're not sure about yet. We're still waiting for more information." He put his arm around her shoulders. "You've done your part now, Peggy. You pointed us in the right direction. Please stay out of it. Read the papers or watch TV news like everyone else."

Peggy's glance snapped up to his broad face. "Shouldn't I be getting some sort of stipend for helping out instead of threats? You know, the next time you can't figure something out, I might not be so willing to help."

Al took a deep breath and rolled his eyes. "Get her out of here, Steve. I don't think I can take any more."

"Yes, sir." Steve hurried Peggy toward his SUV. "I think *now* might be a good time to make a strategic retreat."

"AND THIS IS LIVE footage from Queens University this morning as the leader of a left-wing conservation group known only as Tomorrow's Children, is shown being put in a van by local law enforcement. He's being identified as twenty-five-year-old Fletcher Davis, a graduate student at Yale who was working at Queens on a sabbatical assignment. Mr. Davis is a suspect in an apparent murder in the death of Park Lamonte, the attorney killed when his car went off the Interstate 485 ramp. There will be more on this as events unfold. This is Mark Shipton in uptown Charlotte. Back to you, Marvin."

David and Hunter sat in the Potting Shed with Sam and Peggy as they watched the news at noon on television. "It looks like that part is over anyway," Sam said as he finished his turkey sandwich.

"I was right about Park being poisoned in Philadelphia. I can't believe I helped that man escape the police." Peggy anguished. "It might have saved Park's life if they'd picked him up then."

Hunter swallowed the last of her diet Pepsi. "Sometimes you can't see all the puzzle pieces until you get them together."

"What the hell is that supposed to mean?" Sam demanded. "Peggy did the best she could in the situation."

"I'm not saying she didn't." Hunter shrugged and looked at David for backup. "I'm just saying things aren't always the way they appear."

"That's true." David rose to the occasion. "But even though this might solve what happened to Park, it doesn't explain what happened to his mother."

"You weren't here when Peggy first came in," Sam said. He explained about the two women who were in Isabelle's house that morning. "I think the chances are pretty good one or both of them did it for the money."

"I suppose that makes sense." David shrugged. "That should help Beth."

"The break-in at your house must've been random," Hunter gently suggested to Peggy. "Maybe they didn't have time to steal anything. You were lucky."

"Maybe," Peggy said, not sure if she agreed about the random part.

"Since there were two of them, maybe the housekeeper and the ex-wife went through your house to throw off the investigation," Sam suggested. "You remember? The police thought it might be more than one person who did that to your house. That would make sense."

"At this point, anything is still possible," Peggy agreed. A customer came in, and she left her place behind the counter where they'd been watching TV and eating lunch.

"We need to go." Hunter nudged David. "Not much time before you have to get back to work."

"You're right." He kissed her forehead. "We better get going."

When they were gone and Peggy's customer was done ordering a hundred Jerusalem artichokes, Sam shook his head. "I don't know if I can get used to seeing them together."

Peggy smiled as she processed the order into the computer. "Jealous?"

"No! Nauseated. Disgusted. Not jealous." He pushed back his blond hair with an impatient hand. "They're sickening together. I mean, nobody *really* acts like that."

"You haven't been to the park on a nice day, have you?" She laughed. "Lots of people act like that. They're called lovers. I acted like that when John and I first got together."

Sam fidgeted with the notepad on the counter, lowering his voice as the beginning of the lunch crowd came into the shop. "I guess the people I know are more *discreet*."

Peggy put her hand on his shoulder. "Maybe they feel they need to be."

"Maybe. The chances are nobody is going to beat Hunter and David for flaunting it."

"Life isn't fair. I'm not saying you're not right about the possible consequences," she said, "but maybe it's worth the risk. People have to speak out. They have to be who they are. It might be scary, but it's worse to keep everything in the dark."

He smiled at her. "Thanks, Peggy. I hope we're talking about the same thing."

"I think we have customers." She laughed and hugged him. "You're crazy, Sam, but I love you."

Because the morning mist and cold were burned away by the warm sun, a flood of customers spilled into the Potting Shed. Sam manned the cash register and took orders. Peggy worked the wood floors, answering questions and finding what her customers needed. She signed one woman up for landscaping her rose garden, promising a variety of old-fashioned, fragrant roses for warmer planting.

A young man asked, red-faced, about starting a water garden on his fifth floor balcony. Peggy led him to the pond kits and pointed out the water plants in a catalog. She was careful to stay away from fairies and other "cute" garden items when he confessed to feeling a little unmanly setting up a pond. They agreed on an alligator fountain and some dwarf cattails to start with. She knew he'd get over his feelings as soon as he saw the water garden in place.

One woman was interested in planting lemon balm in her small patio herb garden. Peggy cautioned her about the prolific tendencies of the plant. "You can try to keep it in a pot, but it probably won't stay put. If you had a larger space, you might be able to grow some and keep it in check. In a spot this small, it could take over your other plants."

"I drink a lot of it and thought it might be good to grow," the young woman explained. "If I keep it in a pot away from the garden and cut it back regularly, do you think I could manage it?"

"I think that could work," Peggy agreed. "The worst that might happen is you'll begin to see sprouts of it in your garden. You can always pull them up right away."

"Good. I'd like to get some plants though. I'm hopeless with seeds."

Peggy ordered three plants for the woman and a half-dozen Jerusalem artichokes. She also ordered some faux antique gardening implements and a Charleston bench. "If you have any other questions, just let me know. I'm online at this address, or you can call." Peggy gave her a business card. The woman thanked her, smiled at Sam, and left after writing a check for her deposit.

Mai came into the shop a little after two. The crowd was gone, and Sam was leaving for afternoon classes. "Can you talk for a few minutes?" she asked Peggy after they said goodbye to Sam.

"Of course." Peggy didn't like the look on Mai's face. She gave her a cup of dandelion tea and sat her down in the rocking chair. "What's wrong?"

"Paul and I decided to break up. It just happened. One minute we were talking about the house, and the next minute, I told him it wasn't going to work." Mai held her bright yellow cup with both hands and stared into the pale tea inside of it. "Don't they say you can read a person's future in tea leaves? I wonder what mine would say right now."

Peggy scooted her chair from behind the counter so she could be closer to Mai. "I don't think this kind of tea would work for that. I'm sorry about you and Paul. But he's been such a butthead about your feelings on the house, maybe it's for the best."

"He hasn't been *that* bad," Mai defended. "He just wants us to have a stronger relationship."

"A relationship you aren't ready for," Peggy reminded her. "He should've been happy with what you were willing to offer."

"But how would we ever progress from dating to anything else?" Mai argued. "If neither one of us ever wanted more, we'd be the oldest dating couple in America."

Peggy sighed. "I'm sure you won't have any trouble finding someone else."

Mai got to her feet. "But what if I don't want someone else? What if I made a terrible mistake?"

"Give it some time," Peggy advised. "Paul isn't going anywhere. Maybe a short break will be exactly what both of you need to clear your heads."

"I hope so. I care a lot about Paul. Maybe I even love him. I'm not really sure." Mai shrugged her thin shoulders. "I guess that's part of the problem, huh? Were you sure about your husband when you got married?"

"No. Not at all. I had all these dreams and goals for my life," Peggy admitted. "I was afraid if I got married I'd lose them all."

"And did you?"

"No." Peggy smiled at her. "At least not all of them. I had to give up my aspiration to sing on the Broadway stage, but I think I managed everything else."

Mai's eyes opened wide, and she laughed. "Did you *really* want to sing?"

"From the time I was five and my grandmother told me I had a voice like an angel."

"Did anyone agree with her?"

"Is that the polite way to ask if I can carry a tune? If so, then yes. I can carry a tune in the shower. That's about all. But I think I've accomplished all the real things I ever wanted. John was never an obstacle. He was always my biggest fan for whatever I wanted to do."

Mai drank her tea and put her cup on the counter. "Thanks, Peggy. I hope you're right, and time is the answer for my problem with Paul. I appreciate you listening to me."

"You're always welcome."

"I have to get back to work." Mai picked up her pocketbook. "Oh yeah. I thought you might be interested. Officers found the ivory dragon's head at Alice Godwin's home. It's clean. She claims she cleaned it because it was 'dirty.' Whatever she used did a good job. Not a trace of blood or anything else. It matches the wound in Mrs. Lamonte's head. So we know it was the murder weapon. There were some other personal effects that belonged to Mrs. Lamonte there, too."

"What about Cindy?"

"Ms. Walker has an airtight alibi for the period the ME established for the time of death. She was in Raleigh at a fundraiser. So with Mrs. Godwin's impromptu confession and all the other evidence against her, the DA is filing charges against her for the murder."

Peggy took a deep breath. "So Beth is clear."

"It looks that way to me."

16

Rabbit's Foot Fern

Botanical: *Davallia fejeensis*
Family: Davalliaceae

This plant gets its common name from the stiff, hairy rhizomes that grow on it. It is native to Fiji but named botanically for Swiss botanist, Edmond Davall. Avoid direct sun! This plant is nonflowering. Popular as a houseplant worldwide.

IT WAS WEDNESDAY MORNING. Time for Peggy's weekly garden club meeting at the Kozy Kettle. It was originally held on Thursday mornings, but Emil insisted Wednesdays were better for him. Peggy changed the day rather than move the group. With a smile on her face and a small knife in one hand, she faced her garden club members.

"The thing we all love about the rabbit's foot fern are the fuzzy rhizomes that trail over the sides of the pot or basket that holds it. Early spring is really the best time of year to cut this plant back, but as you can see, Gerda has a problem with this one that won't wait that long."

Gerda Laint smiled and nodded in the audience. She'd brought Peggy her overgrown fern, wondering what to do with it.

"Naturally, we're going to spread out some newspaper first to try to contain as much of the mess as we can. Then we're going to take the plant out of the pot." The fern stubbornly refused to budge from the plastic pot that held it. "Shaking it a little might be necessary." Peggy demonstrated what she meant, and the plant finally came out. "Go ahead while you're holding it and give the plant another good shake to get rid of any dead leaves or other debris that might be stuck to it."

The fifteen women in the garden club watched intently as Peggy cleared away the old leaves and set the pot to one side. She put the plant down in the middle of the newspaper, then held up her knife. "Make sure you have a good sharp knife so you aren't sawing at the plant. Separation is traumatic enough for the poor thing."

"Carefully cut between rhizomes and make sure you get the roots." Peggy cut the first furry tentacle that gave the plant its name. "Try to cut so you keep some leaves. You should end up with a smaller but complete plant with each cutting. The leaves should be at the top, rhizome in the middle, and roots at the bottom. Put each separate plant in its own pot of new soil. Water them thoroughly." She demonstrated. "Don't fertilize them until midsummer or so. And don't expect to see new growth until the roots begin to develop."

After scribbling down notes on what Peggy was saying, the women rushed to ask questions. One woman even took pictures. Peggy answered patiently and held up the plant for a picture.

"We've got some fresh buns ready," Sofia said, noticing that the group was about to break up. "I know you all want those, right?"

After the garden club, the women were always thirsty and took home some fresh baked bread or cinnamon rolls. That's why Emil graciously allowed Peggy to hold her meetings there. Wednesday mornings were quiet at Brevard Court. The meetings brought in some business.

"You lucked out with your friend," Emil said, watching the news as Peggy was getting her things together. "Looks like they got some other people in mind now for those murders."

She agreed with him and thanked him for the use of his shop as she always did. She didn't gossip with him about anything

that had happened. It was still too fresh, too painful for her to
do anything but mull it over in her mind.

A shipment of hyacinths, daffodils, and tulips waited for
her at the Potting Shed. Their bright colors and sweet smells
brought the heart of spring into the shop. It was enough to lift
her spirits, even though she sold out by midafternoon.

Peggy closed up the shop after a flurry of last-minute phone
orders for plants and services. She looked at her spreadsheet
for February with satisfaction. The Potting Shed was doing all
right. It still terrified her sometimes to be in business for herself. A lifetime of regular paychecks left her unprepared for
the fitful irregularities of money a shopkeeper could expect.

Business was slow after Christmas, but things were starting
to pick up. If the trend continued, she would definitely give up
her place at Queens. It was going to take some faith and
courage, but she felt it was the right thing to do. The Potting
Shed was getting more and more demanding. She didn't want
to shortchange her students either. It had always been her goal
to narrow her focus down to her botanical projects and the
shop. Maybe spring would be the right time.

Peggy spoke with Beth for a few minutes before leaving
the shop. She was glad to hear Beth was as disgusted by Gary
Rusch's advances as she was. "I didn't want to mention it. I
thought maybe . . . but it was none of my business. Park *did*
fool around with Cindy after all."

"Please!" Beth begged, "Give me credit for good taste! If
I was going to fool around, it wouldn't be with him. And it
wouldn't be on the heels of my husband's death. I loved Park
even though he was unfaithful. That's why I took him back. I
really wanted our marriage to work."

"I'm sorry. I didn't know what to think."

"I didn't either," Beth admitted. "And I was scared at first
to say anything. But I warned him off. There won't be anymore of *that* going on!"

Peggy was glad to hear it. When Beth said she had to go,
Peggy put the phone down feeling better about her friend. She
bundled up and went out into the night.

With cold winds blowing down the dark streets of Charlotte, there were few people lingering after work uptown. The smell of fresh bread baking told her someone was working in one of the restaurants. But all she could see were empty windows and closed doors as she rode past the buildings between her and home. She kept her head down against the biting wind and pedaled as fast as she could.

Shakespeare was barking, and the telephone was ringing inside the house as she stepped up to the door with her mail in hand. She shivered as she put the key in the lock. For just a moment, she wondered if she'd find the house ransacked again. But Isabelle's killer was behind bars. She was just being paranoid.

She forced herself to finish the act of opening her front door. Her emotional side argued with her logical side. She couldn't go on standing there, dreading what she might find. And the alarm was set. No one was in there. The house had to be as she left it.

With the door open, the alarm system added its warning sound to the clamor of phone and dog. Peggy quickly turned off the alarm and closed the door behind her. She reached the phone and answered it breathlessly. "Hello?"

"Hello, sweet Pea! We haven't heard from you in a while. Thought I'd give you a call and see what's going on up there in the big city."

Peggy dropped her backpack on the table and collapsed into a chair near the door. "Hello, Daddy. I'm doing fine. Staying busy. How's Mama?"

"She's doing good. Had that surgery on her ankle a few weeks back. She's been a little ornery, but I just make her stay out on the porch when she gets that way. Got a good crop of broccoli and some sweet potatoes for you. I'll bring 'em up when we come."

"When you come?" Peggy sat up and opened her eyes. "Are you coming to visit?"

"Of course. You can't seem to find the time to get down here. So even though Aunt Rachel and Uncle Stripey can't make it, Mama and I and Cousin Melvin and Aunt Mayfield are coming up to see you in April."

"What about planting, Daddy? Won't you need to plant in April?"

"I took care of that, angel. I hired a few boys to help me out this year. I'll get them started at the first of the month, so by mid-April we should be able to spend a few weeks up there with you. You'll have to give your mama and Aunt Mayfield a place on the ground floor of that big old house of yours. Neither one of them can get up those grand stairs. But otherwise, nothing special. I know you have grits in your cupboard. That's all we need. Well, maybe some chicken would be nice, too. But we could always visit the Colonel for that!"

Peggy digested the information. She panicked just *knowing* her parents were coming. They hadn't been there since John's funeral. She always tried to be the one to visit *them*.

Aunt Mayfield was a difficult, complaining woman at best. Cousin Melvin had sleep apnea and fell asleep at dinner, in the bath, and during conversations. He snored loudly enough to be heard from one end of the house to another, and she didn't even want to think about how bad his feet smelled.

"Are you still there, pumpkin?"

"I'm here, Daddy. That sounds great. Maybe Paul can get some time off, and we can all do some sightseeing or something." She was careful to keep any doubt out of her voice. At least this way she had time to prepare for them coming.

"Don't put yourself out, Margaret. We're just coming to see you and Paul. Nothing fancy. What's that sound?"

Peggy listened to Shakespeare's alternate barking and howling. "That's my dog. He's waiting for his supper."

"Got yourself a beagle? They make a good hunting dog. You remember Maisy. She could track anything. Remember that time your mama lost her car keys? Maisy found them."

"Shakespeare is a Great Dane, Daddy. He doesn't track much."

"Great Dane, huh? What kind of name is that? No wonder he doesn't track. You have to give him a proper name for a hunting dog. Call him Skippy or Yeller. Then he'll track for you."

She sighed. "I don't want him to track anything, Daddy."

"He's not gonna be much of a hunting dog if he can't track, Margaret."

"I don't really want to take him hunting. I don't hunt. I'm a vegetarian, remember, Daddy?"

"Thought you'd grown out of that by now. Oh well. It still wouldn't hurt you to give that dog a decent name."

Peggy didn't argue with him. "I'm looking forward to seeing you and Mama anyway. We'll have a good time while you're here."

"Okay then. I'll talk to you later. Give Paul a hug for us."

"I will. Kiss Mama for me. Bye, Daddy." She put down the phone and threw herself back in the chair. Her family was coming up to see her. The house was dirty. They hated Charlotte. She knew they'd try to convince her to come back home with them as they had after John's death. And what about Steve? They were bound to notice that he was younger than her. And what would they think about the Potting Shed?

Peggy got to her feet and went to rescue Shakespeare. She took him out for a walk, then fed him and made a grilled cheese sandwich for herself. He still refused to eat. He lay down beside his food and groaned, looking up at her every few minutes. She tried to get him to eat by offering individual pieces of food. He covered his eyes with his paws.

Glad that he had another obedience class tomorrow, Peggy sat down at the kitchen table to eat her sandwich and drink her sassafras tea. She made it with plenty of sugar and milk until it was pink rather than red. It was the way her mother made it when Peggy was growing up. That thought brought on a whole group of issues she'd have to face when her parents came to visit.

Refusing to face those problems right away, Peggy watched the news for a while, then went upstairs to change clothes and check on her plants. Her Antares water lily was barely alive. She wasn't sure if it was going to survive. Her experiment with the strawberries was completely destroyed, and she had mites on all of her plants. She was probably going to have to spray for them since she couldn't use complementary planting to control them in that environment.

Sighing over the loss of time and her companions, she spent two hours trying to straighten up the mess and check on all of her plants. The frog helped himself to some of the mites, and she thanked him. "If I had a few more like you, I could clean them up pretty easy."

She went back upstairs to her room and showered. Shakespeare was already in her bed when she came out. He hadn't eaten anything or ripped anything apart, so she collapsed in bed beside him. His coat felt smooth and warm under her hand as she petted him. Her eyes were just closing when her computer made a loud beeping noise. Immediately, she jumped out of bed and checked her e-mail.

Nightflyer sent her an instant message: *"r u busy? if not, let's play!"*

Peggy almost didn't go. He'd ignored *her* summons. But curiosity finally won over impatience. She sat down in her chair and went to the new chess site. When she was logged on, she found Nightflyer waiting for her.

"Hello, Nightrose! Are you ready to play?"

"I'm ready. What happened to you? Are you okay?" Peggy made her opening gambit: pawn to e4

He returned: pawn to c5. *"I'm fine. Just a little trip I had to take. Sorry I couldn't let you know. I was off-line."*

"No computer? That's awful. How did you survive?"

"It wasn't easy. What have you been up to?"

"Don't you know?" She moved her pawn to e5.

"I have a few ideas." Knight to d5. *"How is your friend doing?"*

"Beth? She's going to be fine. The police have made arrests for Park and Isabelle's murders." Knight to c3.

"The conservationist and the housekeeper. I know. But I don't think Davis is responsible. Do you?" Nightflyer moved his pawn to f6.

Peggy shrugged and moved her pawn to d4. *"He was at the hotel. He had access to the gift baskets. He had motive. It makes sense."*

"He only poisoned four baskets. There were ten lawyers

*staying at the same hotel. Why not put poisoned honey in all
the gift baskets that went to the lawyers representing the firm
that wants to drill for oil? Why only poison four of them?"*

"Good point. Why do you think he would only poison four
of them?"

*"He wouldn't. If Fletcher Davis is passionate enough about
his cause to poison four men, why not all of them? Hotel videotapes show he had access to all of the baskets. But they don't
show him touching all of them."* Bishop to g7.

"He could've tampered with the videotapes." Bishop to e3.
*"Or maybe he didn't have time to poison the others. Maybe he
panicked."*

"That's possible. Or he didn't do it." Knight to d4. Nightflyer took Peggy's pawn.

"Then who did?" Knight to f6.

"Perhaps someone who wanted to throw the blame on Tomorrow's Children. Maybe even someone who wanted to murder Park and get away with it. Park is the only lawyer who
also had his mother killed."

*"Which the police speculate Alice Godwin did, since she
had the murder weapon, motive, and opportunity. She has no
alibi between the time she left Beth's at 9 and the time she
found Isabelle at 10 and called Cindy Walker."*

"But just a few days ago, the police thought your friend
committed both crimes. How reliable is that?"

"I don't know."

"And you don't want to know since your friend is safe?"

*"That's not fair! I didn't have to tell the police about the
poisoned honey. I already jeopardized Beth and the children
by being objective."*

"But you want to know the truth, Peggy. Who stands to gain
by Park and Isabelle's deaths? There may be someone besides
Beth who fits the bill. Something still seems wrong to me.
There are too many unanswered questions. I believe Cindy
Walker is involved in some way."

Peggy considered the questions as she poised to make her
next move. *"Maybe I'm too close to this. Everyone involved is*

like family. Beth is free now. The cases against Mrs. Godwin and Davis are strong. Why stir the pot because of a few unanswered questions?" She finally moved her queen to e2.

"That makes it difficult. But you're a good researcher. You can't quit until all the answers are there." Queen to a5.

Peggy changed the subject. *"You seem preoccupied tonight. Is anything wrong?"*

"Nothing much. I may be going away again for a while. Don't try to contact me. I'll let you know when it's safe."

"Safe? What's going on?" She asked him. *"Can I help in some way?"*

"No. Thank you for asking. I'll contact you when I can. Thank you for the game."

"But we haven't finished . . ."

Nightflyer logged off, and the phone rang. She glanced at the clock on the computer. It was almost midnight. He was calling to explain the rest.

Instead, it was Beth's parents in Salisbury. "We've been trying to contact Beth since ten when the kids went to bed," her father told Peggy. "She's been calling every night at ten to tell them good night. We had a time getting Foxx and Reddman to sleep. I don't think it's our phone line."

"Have you tried her cell phone?" Peggy asked.

"Yes. We've been calling her all night on both phones. We even e-mailed her."

"Let me see what I can do. I'll let you know as soon as I get in touch with her."

"Thanks, Peggy. We're coming down there in the morning with the kids since this thing seems to be over. I know there's nothing wrong with her. Maybe she went out."

Peggy agreed and hung up the phone. Something in the tone of Beth's father's voice told her he was lying when he said he knew there was nothing wrong with her. She dialed Beth's phone number. When she didn't get an answer, she called her cell phone. When there was no response there either, she put on a sweater and jeans, then peeked in at Shakespeare and decided to take him with her.

It was only a short ride down Providence Road to Myers

Park, but it would make her feel better if he was with her. "Promise you won't trash the house once we get there. And you won't pull me through a tree."

The dog wagged his tail and barked enthusiastically. Peggy took that as a good sign and slipped on his leash. She put on her purple jacket and scarf, slipped heavy purple gloves on her hands. "I hope there's nothing wrong either," she told the dog as she worried out loud. "But let's go see."

Queens Road was completely empty. The traffic lights blinked yellow, glittering on the damp pavement. Peggy raced her bike through the silence, between the shadows of the empty oak trees and the slumbering houses. Shakespeare kept pace with her in his long, loping stride.

All the stores at the corner of Providence Road were shuttered and sleeping. Two police cruisers were parked in the empty parking lot. They were turned so that the driver's side windows were facing each other as they watched her go by. Peggy would have waved. She probably knew them. But with one hand holding Shakespeare's leash and the other holding the handlebars, she didn't think she could manage it.

Providence Road was empty, too. The big Presbyterian church sat squat and solid on the corner. Light showed through the stained glass windows and spilled into the street. Peggy looked at the window where Jesus was tending the flock of sheep. It was comforting somehow to see that image as she rode through the night. Beth was fine. Probably just sleeping heavily. Lord knew she needed a good night's sleep.

Riding through Myers Park without the standard walkers, runners, baby carriages, and Volvo station wagons was much easier. It gave her a different perspective. She could've been in her house asleep like these people. This was what it was like on the outside looking in. She felt like the only person alive in the world. The wind blew through the streets, rattling the winter bones of the trees. She'd be glad to see morning slip over the horizon.

She parked her bike on Beth's front porch. Shakespeare panted and furiously wagged his tail but otherwise stood at her side as she rang the doorbell over and over. Beth might be angry to be woken up this late. But they'd have a good laugh over some hot tea while she called her parents to let them know she was all right. She'd understand their concern and regret that she missed talking to her boys before bedtime. She was a good mother.

When there was no response to the doorbell, Peggy went around through the wet grass starting to gather frost to the back of the house. She pounded hard on the door and yelled for Beth. There was still no response. She looked up at the dark windows in the house. Beth must be exhausted. She was sleeping like the dead.

The thought caused a shiver to slip down her spine and added renewed vigor to Peggy's attempts to get in the house. When trying to wake her friend from outside didn't work, she reached up over the light for the spare key. It was gone. With all the turmoil of recent days, it wasn't surprising. But the knowledge made her feel even more uneasy.

She looked at the kitchen window, gauging how thick it was. Park had all new windows put in last summer. He wouldn't thank her for what she was about to do. And insurance might not pay for it. If it didn't, she'd pay. It was worth it to get into the house and find out what was going on. She was going to feel like a fool if she walked upstairs and Beth was asleep in her bed. But that was a chance she had to take. Too much had happened to this family in a short time to ignore the doubt gnawing at her stomach.

Peggy had never purposely broken a window in her life. She wrapped her scarf around her hand as she'd seen on some television show or movie. It made sense to protect herself from the glass. Shakespeare barked and whined at her side. She shushed him and moved intently toward the window. It was low enough for her to scramble through once she broke it.

Shakespeare barked and whined again, tugging hard at the leash. "I told you that you had to be good." She turned to him, realizing she might have to tie him up on the porch. He was sitting beside a large, heavy shovel. She looked at her hand, bound in her purple scarf, then back at the dog. "If you're trying to tell me there's an easier way, you're right."

She took the scarf off her hand and snatched up the shovel. Shakespeare wagged his tail at her choice, then stood quietly beside her as she closed her eyes and smashed the shovel through the window.

Half expecting an alarm to go off, Peggy stood back for a moment. When nothing happened, she used the shovel again to clear all the glass fragments away from the ledge. She tied Shakespeare's leash to the water spigot under the aperture and pushed herself up and in through the window. Shakespeare started barking as soon as he realized he was about to be left out of the adventure. Peggy ignored him and ran up the stairs to Beth's bedroom.

Beth was asleep, one arm sprawled above her head. There was a small lamp spreading light across the table and the bed. Peggy looked at her friend's face. Relief made her sag into a chair beside the table. She was sleeping so peacefully. No hint of all the trauma she'd been through. There were still dark circles in the hollows of her eyes. Tracks that might have been tears stained her face.

Beth was fine. Of course she was fine. Peggy had broken into her house for nothing. She was going to have to buy Beth a new kitchen window because she acted impulsively instead of thinking the matter through. Some researcher!

But she realized as she watched Beth sleeping that she was *too* still, *too* quiet. No one slept that deeply. Not naturally anyway. The lamplight caught on a small plastic bottle on the brown carpet at her feet. She reached down for it. It was a prescription bottle. The top was gone, and it was empty. She looked at the information on the label. It was Nembutal, a barbiturate sleeping aid. The date was from yesterday. *Yesterday!* All the pills were gone! "Oh my God! Beth!"

Peggy frantically dialed 911 on the bedside phone. She barked her location at the operator who answered, then went to help her friend.

If she'd been in bed since before ten p.m., if she'd taken that many pills five hours ago, would she be able to survive?

"Wake up, Beth! You have to wake up!" Peggy jumped on the bed with her friend, pulled back the comforter, and tried to get some response. Beth's pulse was slow and weak. She roused briefly, trying to speak, but didn't open her eyes.

"You can't do this! Think about Reddman and Foxx. They need you. You have to call them." Peggy grasped at straws. She had to do what she could until the paramedics got there. "You didn't call them last night. They're still up waiting for you. You have to call them."

Beth opened her eyes a little as Peggy forced her into a sitting position. "Peggy?" Her voice was slurred and heavy.

"That's right. You have to wake up now. Where's the phone? Foxx and Reddman need to talk to you."

"Park . . ."

"I know." Peggy heard the sound of a siren in the street below. "I know you loved him. But you can't leave yet. You have to hang on. Things will get better."

The phone on the bedside table rang. The paramedics were pounding on the front door. Peggy left Beth on the bed and ran down to let them in. She answered the phone as the paramedics examined her friend. It was Beth's parents. Peggy briefly explained what happened and told them they should come quickly.

"She still has a chance," one of the paramedics said. "We have to get her to Presbyterian Hospital fast. Are you her mother?"

"No," Peggy answered. "Her parents are on the way."

Peggy rode in the front of the ambulance with the driver while the other paramedic stayed with Beth in the back. She watched him continue to check Beth's vital signs as he reported to the hospital.

We have to get there in time. Those boys can't lose both their parents. Beth has to live.

"Who found her?" The doctor at the emergency room demanded when they finally got to the hospital. "What has she taken?"

Peggy produced the empty bottle from her pocket. "I found her. I think she took these."

The doctor shook his head. "Jesus Christ! What could be that bad?"

"Her husband was murdered, and she's been on trial for his death." Peggy looked at the doctor and shrugged. "Help her, please. I *know* she wants to live."

"We'll do what we can. I'll let you know when I have some idea of what's going to happen."

"Thank you." One of the paramedics showed Peggy to a waiting area. She sank down into an orange plastic chair and buried her face in her hands. She suddenly remembered Shakespeare and reluctantly called Steve to go and rescue the dog after she explained what happened.

"Is she all right?" Steve asked in a voice heavy with sleep.

"I don't know yet. Shakespeare is tied up in the back of her house. Can you go and get him for me?"

"I'll get him. What about you? Are you okay?"

"I will be. I'll talk to you later." She sat in the chair after shutting the cell phone. She was freezing. Her hands trembled with reaction. She stuffed them into her pockets to warm them. Was there some warning this would happen? Was there something she missed? Some way she could've helped that she didn't see in time?

Beth's parents called on their way down from Salisbury and managed to find the hospital. They got there about two hours after Peggy. There was still no word on Beth's condition. The three of them huddled together on the sofa and prayed. The morning that Peggy had wished for as she rode through the night slipped in through the hospital blinds, gilding them gold and pink. She peeked through them, admiring the sunrise but wishing it brought better news with it.

Hunter joined them halfway through the morning. Beth's close friends and other family members came and went as news seeped out about what happened. They asked about the children, asked if they could do anything to help. Beth's parents answered that they left the boys with family, their voices hushed and leaden. Everyone said they would pray for the family. No one said the word they were all thinking: *suicide.* The very thing Beth wanted so desperately to erase from Park's name. When the doctor finally came out, everyone got to their feet, hands joined.

"I think she's going to be all right. It was a close call, but I think you managed to find her in time. It's going to take a while for her to recover." He shook his head. "I realize the tragic circumstances behind this event. But I have no choice but to report any attempt at suicide to the authorities. She'll have to spend some time in the psych ward. Obviously, she needs help."

The family thanked him. He was leaving as Al and Jonas showed up. They spoke with the doctor briefly before returning to the family.

"I'm sorry about all this," Al said to Beth's parents.

"Like hell!" Her father turned away from his handshake. "You've persecuted my daughter. If anyone is responsible, it's you and this police department."

Jonas tried to smooth the waters. "We were only doing our job, sir. We did take the blame away from your daughter, too."

"My daughter would never hurt another human being," Beth's mother sobbed. "Not even that evil old woman who loved to give her a hard time. You've had the wrong person since the beginning."

"That appears to be true, ma'am," Jonas replied. "I'm afraid we all make mistakes sometimes. We do the best we can."

"Get out of here, you vultures," Beth's father demanded. "Leave my daughter alone!"

Al took Peggy to one side. "We actually came to see *you*. We'd like you to come to the precinct and take a look at Davis in a lineup. You said you saw him at the hotel in Philly and again here in Charlotte."

"I thought you had him on videotape and you have his fingerprints in the hotel room." Peggy shook her head. "You don't need me."

"Truth is, we need this case to be as strong as it can. We don't have the boy touching the baskets. He walks right by them on the videotape. But that doesn't mean the tape isn't wrong or just didn't catch him doing the deed. Come down to the precinct, Peggy. You always want to help. Now's your chance."

17

Thrift

Botanical: *Armeria*
Family: Plumbaginaceae

This widely spread carpet of colorful flowers blooms slowly in the spring for a short time. It is perennial and grows to cover a larger area each year. It was once believed that it could cure lead poisoning, hence the family name.

AFTER A QUICK CALL to Selena at the Potting Shed, Peggy got in Al's car. He and Jonas sat in the front seat for the ride.

"I'm sorry about your friend, Peggy," Jonas said when they were out of the hospital parking lot. "I hope *you* don't feel like we were responsible for what happened to her."

"Not at all." She put on some cherry-flavored lip gloss and rubbed some cream on her hands. She was drained of all emotion. She couldn't even summon up enough to be thrilled that Beth was still alive. "I was a detective's wife for too long not to understand the process. Beth looked guilty. You did your job."

"Well at least it looks like she'll be okay," Al added. "Once she gets through this, anyway. These things aren't totally unexpected."

"So now the theory is that this boy—" Peggy began.

"Fletcher Davis, the head of Tomorrow's Children," Jonas interrupted her. "He's twenty-five. Not exactly a *boy*."

"All right. Fletcher Davis is guilty of poisoning Park and the other lawyers to get back at them for helping pollute the bay they're trying to save."

"That's right," Al agreed. "They thought it was a good way to hold up the negotiations."

Peggy thought about Nightflyer's questions. "Why didn't he poison all the lawyers' baskets? If he had access to four of them, he had access to all of them. Have you asked him where he got the poisoned honey? Has he confessed?"

"We wouldn't need *you* to ID him if he'd confessed," Al told her. "This guy is too sharp for that."

"We don't have all the answers yet," Jonas admitted. "That's why we're still working on the case."

"But you're comfortable with the idea that Alice Godwin killed Isabelle." Peggy pulled her jacket closer and shivered. *Why am I asking? Why aren't I just happy that Beth will be cleared of all charges? I'm taking Nightflyer's ideas too seriously. It's all settled.*

"Comfortable? What do you want from me? I thought you'd be happy we got the murder charges taken away from your friend." Jonas cleared his throat and shook his head. "Some people are *never* satisfied."

She didn't answer. He was right, much as it disturbed her to admit it. Just because all the pieces didn't add up for Nightflyer didn't make it wrong.

"If you're mad about us thinking she killed her husband in the first place for the insurance money," Al said, "she wouldn't be the first. And considering her state of mind, that wouldn't be surprising."

"What do you mean, 'her state of mind'?" Peggy demanded.

"Isn't it obvious?" Jonas snorted. "She tried to kill herself. She's not capable of making rational decisions."

Peggy nodded slowly, her thoughts taking her in another direction. "That means she won't be able to control the money from the insurance policy or the Lamonte estate now. Someone will have to be appointed as executor, since Foxx and Reddman are too young."

Al turned the car into the police parking lot. "That's probably true. What are you thinking, Peggy?"

"The state will appoint a guardian *ad litem.*" Jonas waved his hand to dismiss the subject as he got out of the car. "Who knows who that will be? But since she knows so many lawyers . . ."

"What if that's what someone has been after from the beginning?"

"What?" Jonas asked, opening her car door.

"Look," she explained patiently. "Someone knows Park has this large insurance policy. He or she kills him with the poisoned honey. They poison a few other lawyers in Philadelphia to make it look like Tomorrow's Children is responsible for it. Not *everyone,* because they don't need to go that far. But Park doesn't die there. He dies here going over the ramp. The insurance company jumps in and yells suicide. That would be bad for the killer. No money."

"Peggy . . ." Jonas tried to stop her.

"So she, maybe Cindy Walker, passes on the information about the policy and her affair with Park to his mother. Isabelle calls in the police and raises questions about it being murder. The killer is confident enough to take it in stride. After all, murder still collects on the policy."

"Can we just go inside?" Al asked as Jonas paced the parking lot.

But Peggy was on a roll. "But then the killer had to get messy. There's no time for poison. He or she takes matters into their own hands and knocks Isabelle in the head with her walking stick, bless her poor old soul. It doesn't stop the murder investigation, but that's okay. With Beth in prison, now he or she can get at the insurance money plus Park's and Isabelle's estates."

"If you're still thinking about Ms. Walker," Al said. "How would *she* get at the money? I'm sure she's not in the will or on the Lamonte's list to care for the children."

"Good question." Peggy tapped her cheek. "I don't have the answer to that. But she *was* at Isabelle's house during the crime scene investigation and saw me there. She could've trashed my house looking for the dragon's head because she thought I had it."

"Nice theory." Jonas held out his hand. "Can we go inside? They're waiting for us."

"Wait! There's more. I see it now!" Peggy started to pace with her head down and her forehead furrowed. "I don't know why I didn't see it before! Cindy didn't know Alice had the dragon's head. Alice hid it away before she got there. She wasn't trying to frame Alice for the murder. It didn't suit her purpose for anyone but Beth to be charged with it. So when it looked like Beth was going to go free, she gave her the Nembutol. Beth is discredited or dies. Either way, the money is free game again."

"Once again, the question is: How would Mrs. Walker expect to collect on her crime?" Al questioned. "I could see her having motive to kill Park but not the mother. Especially not for the money."

"Excuse me? Have we all been transported to never-never land?" Jonas snarled. "We have viable arrests in *both* of these cases. Peggy, all we need from you is a simple ID. Can you do that?"

"I think you should question Cindy Walker again." She stopped pacing and looked at him. "I know there doesn't seem to be a link to her and the money, but I'm sure it's there."

"She wasn't in town that night. A hundred people, including her father, Senator Walker, were with her," Al reminded her as Jonas gave up and went inside the building. "We can't bring her in and question her again when there isn't any real evidence she was involved besides agreeing to call the police after Mrs. Godwin set her up to try to take the blame away from herself."

"Is *that* what you think?"

"That's what we think." Al put his arm around her shoulders. "Peggy, we have all the answers already. Just ID Davis for us. Please."

They walked into the precinct together. "Beth could have died, too, because we didn't see it in time. Who else might be involved if it goes on? Her parents? Foxx and Reddman?"

He didn't answer. "Sergeant, will you get Dr. Lee a cup of coffee? We're going to get a lineup for her to look over."

"Yes, sir!" The sergeant came to stand beside Peggy. "Right this way, Dr. Lee."

PEGGY CALLED STEVE TO make sure he found Shakespeare at Beth's house. "I got your bike, too," Steve answered. "Where are you?"

"I'm at the uptown police station." She explained about the lineup. "They've got it all wrong. I'm not sure what to do."

"Is Davis the one you saw talking to Park and the one who ran out of the hotel?

"Yes, but . . ."

"Then I don't see where you have any choice. They aren't asking you to *solve* the crime, Peggy. Just ID the man they have for it. They've already made up their minds."

"I know," she admitted, suddenly exhausted.

"Want me to come and get you when it's over?"

"Yes, please." She sighed. "I'm so tired I can hardly focus. I might not be able to ID *you*. Could you make a sign with your name on it?"

"I'm on my way," he answered. "You've been up all night. We'll have breakfast, and then you can decide what to do next."

"Thanks. I'll see you shortly."

She put away her cell phone, leaned her head back, and closed her eyes. She needed a few minutes of peace, not thinking about Beth or anything else.

Al and Jonas came into the little room where the sergeant put her. She didn't need Steve tweaking her conscience. Guilt and remorse were starting to rip her head off as it was.

"Okay, Peggy," Al started, taking a seat beside her. "If you're ready, we'll open the blind. There are five men behind it. See if you can identify any of them. You can point or you can say the number he's holding. It's your choice. We'll ask you to confirm that you know him. That's it."

She nodded, not speaking as she wrestled with what she should do. She'd been part of the process for so long. She could hear John's voice urging her to do what was right. But what *was* right in this case? She didn't believe Fletcher poisoned Park and the others. She couldn't prove it. But what if she was wrong? What if she didn't ID Fletcher, and they couldn't hold him? What if he *was* responsible?

Jonas opened the blind, and Peggy looked out at the group of men. She knew him immediately. He was wearing the same old jeans and red T-shirt. They seemed to be the only clothes he owned. He didn't look up at the window, but he did turn from side to side on command.

"Well?" Al asked her after a few moments of waiting patiently. "You don't have to rush. If there's any question in your mind that one of those men *isn't* Fletcher Davis, the man you saw at the hotel in Philadelphia, just say so."

She took a deep breath. "That's the man I saw outside Park's hotel room, during the demonstration, and again here in Charlotte." She pointed to him. "I don't think he did it. But that's him."

"Thank you, Peggy." Jonas hurried to shake her hand and usher her from the room. "You did what we needed you to do. We'll take care of the rest."

"May I speak with him?" she asked impulsively.

"Peggy . . ." Jonas motioned for an officer to escort her out.

"Wait!" she appealed to him again. "He knows me. Let me talk to him. He might tell me something about the poisoning. Something *you* can't get from him."

Jonas ran his hand under the back of his shirt collar. "It's not procedure. I don't know what good it would do. I don't even know *why* I'm talking to you about it!"

"Please let me try," she persuaded. "Who knows? He might confess to a friendly face. He looks scared and alone to me."

"All right." Jonas looked around the empty room. "Let me find Al. If anything goes wrong, this will be his fault, since he wanted to bring you here for the lineup."

Fletcher was taken to an interrogation room. Jonas and Al watched from a two-way mirror while Peggy was escorted into the room by an officer. She sat down at the scarred wood table and smiled at the young man across from her. "I'm Peggy Lee. Do you remember me?"

"Darmus's friend." The young man nodded and glanced at the officer who stood inside the doorway. "Are you with *them*? Gestapo pigs! They don't understand!"

Peggy searched his face. "You look exhausted. I'm sorry you had to go through this. If it's any consolation, I don't believe you poisoned those men."

Fletcher sat forward. His face became animated, and he put his cuffed hands on the table between them. "Thanks. Don't get me wrong. I would do almost *anything* to keep the bay from being polluted by those idiots. But murder is a little too much. What difference would it make anyway? By now the corporation has hired ten new lawyers to replace the ones who died. That's *their* mentality. I don't think people or places can be destroyed on a whim and replaced."

"I'm a botanist and somewhat of a conservationist myself. Darmus is as impassioned as you are. But he would *never* kill someone."

His eyes suddenly showed signs of life as he leaned closer to her. "Then you *know* what I mean!"

Peggy touched his hand. "I'll let Darmus know that you're in here. Anyone else I can contact for you until this mess is cleared up?"

"No thanks." He smiled at her. "But I appreciate you stopping by. I don't have much faith the police will find me innocent. I believe this whole thing was a setup so that they could plunder the bay without having to worry about me trying to stop them. They're afraid of me, you know. But it was nice seeing *you* again, Peggy."

"You, too, Fletcher. I think you'll get out of this. When you do, stop by my shop." She tucked a Potting Shed business card into his shirt pocket. "I make a mean cup of chocolate mint tea."

Peggy nodded to the officer at the door, and they walked out of the room together. Fletcher slumped over the table when she left him.

"What was *that* all about?" Jonas demanded when they closed the door. "I thought you were going to get him to confess."

"He can't confess to something he didn't do," she explained. "You heard him. He wouldn't go that far to save the bay. He didn't even know how many lawyers were poisoned."

Jonas hit himself in the forehead with the palm of his hand. Al hid his smile with a ragged cough as he turned away.

"Go home, Peggy," Jonas pleaded. "You're going to make me take early retirement."

She didn't argue with him this time. She was still too unsure in her own mind to have any idea what was going on. Everything since Park's death was a confusing blur.

She didn't like herself for helping the police, but when the answers were finally found, she was sure Fletcher would be acquitted. Until then, she felt closed in by the system. John frequently disagreed with things that happened when his cases went to court. But he upheld the law because he said it was the only thing that made men civilized.

Peggy ignored everyone as she walked out of the precinct. Steve was waiting for her outside, holding Shakespeare on his leash. She kissed and hugged him without a word of explanation, patted the dog's head. "Can we go now?"

He nodded and opened the passenger door for her on the Vue. "Let's go over to IHOP and have some breakfast."

Before they could leave the parking lot, Paul hailed them, running up to the driver's side window and smacking it with his hand. Steve opened the window, and Shakespeare came up from the backseat to see what was going on.

"Hey! Where are you guys going? I'm just getting off duty. How about some breakfast?"

"That's exactly where we're headed," Steve answered. "Hop in the backseat if you can push the dog over."

Paul glanced at his unusually silent mother. "No dog, even one the size of a pony, is going to keep me from breakfast."

Peggy called the hospital to see how Beth was doing. She explained what happened to Paul as they rode to the restaurant. "They expect a full recovery, thank God."

"But she'll be confined for a while for her own safety," Paul said. "That's the law."

"I know." Peggy acknowledged. "Unless we find out it *wasn't* an attempt at suicide." She told Paul and Steve her theory.

"I suppose that could make sense," Steve agreed, his eyes on the crowded streets.

"Do you have some idea who would be in line for the money?" Paul asked.

"No," she admitted.

"It seems like it would be Beth's family with Isabelle out of the way. Do you think they had something to do with this?"

"No! Of course not!" Peggy looked at her son for the first time. He was thinking intently about what she said, but his eyes were shadowed and his mouth was a grim line. "Oh, sweetie, I forgot. I'm so sorry about you and Mai. I wish it could've worked out differently."

"That's okay." He shrugged. "I guess it happened too fast, huh? These things take time. At least that's what she said."

Steve glanced at Peggy. "I don't know about that. It all depends, doesn't it?"

Paul's laugh held a bitter edge. "I'm not saying anything about the two of you. Just don't mention marriage or getting a house together, and maybe you'll be okay."

Peggy reached over and squeezed her son's hand. "If it doesn't work out with Mai, there'll be someone else."

"I think you can say it's over between us, Mom. You're always too optimistic."

"We'll see," she said as they pulled into the restaurant parking lot. "Thank goodness we're here! Now that I'm feeling better, I'm starving!"

The three of them went inside together and sat down at a booth. The waitress took their orders and brought them orange juice, coffee, and water. The restaurant wasn't very busy at that hour. The rush had come and gone before nine.

Peggy's mind was still busy with things other than eggs and pancakes. Even the sun-deprived ivy, still in its little Christmas container on the window ledge, only caught her attention for a moment. She gave it some water from her glass and found a single shaft of sunlight for it to bask in. "Is there some way I could find out who would be the executor or guardian for the children?"

Paul sipped his coffee. "It's not easy to find a legal guardian sometimes. It might be the first person a judge appoints for the job."

"What about Beth's parents?" Steve asked, sitting forward. "Wouldn't they be the logical choice since they already have the boys?"

"From what limited information I know about the law," Paul began, "the people who take care of the children and the person responsible for the purse strings can be different. You might have to see a copy of Park and Beth's will."

"Let's give Hunter a call and see if she can find anything." Peggy took out her cell phone as her breakfast arrived. "Maybe she can solve this riddle for me."

STEVE DROPPED PAUL OFF at the police parking lot, then drove Peggy back to her house. She just finished feeding Shakespeare a piece of biscuit she'd saved for him from breakfast. She hated leaving him in the car and wouldn't have considered it if the temperature was warmer. It wasn't always best for the pet to ride with the owner.

"I'm free today if you need to do any sleuthing," Steve offered.

"I'm only planning to go to the Potting Shed until one, then I'm taking Shakespeare back to Rue for his next lesson. I'm hoping it goes better this time."

"He seems calm today." Steve patted the dog's head. "I'll take you over to Rue's. Unless you have other plans."

She smiled and kissed him. "It sounds like the highlight of my day. I'll see you at one. Thanks, Steve."

He put his arms around her and extended the brief kiss she'd started to give him. "I don't want to get married or buy a house. Don't worry."

"That makes me feel so much better," she assured him sarcastically. "But I'm sure there were other issues involved in Mai and Paul's breakup."

"I'm sure you're right. That's the way it happens."

"You sound like you have prior experience." She yawned and tried to hide it behind her hand.

"*You* sound exhausted."

"I am. But we'll take this up later. You know all about *my* past life. I don't know anything about your old flames."

"They're all ashes," he quipped. "Really. Not worth discussing."

She raised one eyebrow above a curious green eye. "We'll *definitely* be talking about it later."

Steve frowned and shook his head. "You're going to be disappointed. I'm not as colorful or ambitious as you, Peggy."

"We'll see!"

"I'll see you later." He finally gave up. "Keep me posted if you hear anything else about Beth."

Peggy dragged herself to the house, unlocked the door, and disarmed the alarm system. The house was cold. She definitely needed a new furnace, with or without Dalton's help. She went upstairs with Shakespeare running up before her. It wasn't until she pulled herself up the long stairway that she realized her mistake.

Shakespeare had stripped the sheets, pillows, and comforter from her bed in the few moments she lagged behind him. He was chewing on one of the pillows when she reached him. Furious, she grabbed his collar and dragged him back downstairs. He whimpered and barked when she locked him in the laundry room. "It's for your own good," she yelled at him. "It's either the laundry room or I'm going to strangle you!" *And Steve had to mention how calm he seemed.*

Sheer force of will got Peggy back up the stairs and into the shower. The phone rang, but she ignored it, letting the hot water flow down her face and body. She tried to push everything that happened out of her thoughts. She couldn't reach a rational conclusion when her emotions were overwhelming her.

She stood in the shower until the hot water was gone, then wrapped a towel around herself and ran, freezing, into the bedroom. There *was* one conclusion she reached during her shower. Teeth chattering, she picked up the phone before she bothered dressing.

When Dalton answered in his slow, deliberate way, she blasted him. "If you don't get this furnace repaired from the trust fund, I'm going to have it repaired out of my own money and sue you *and* the house trust. This is stupid, Dalton. You know I have every legal right to be in this house."

"What about being fair to the next one in line, Peggy?"

"When the next Lee moves in here, he'll have a garden most people only dream about. I've taken good care of this house. This is my home. I won't let you force me from it. It's all I have left of my life with John. I'll fight you to keep it."

She heard a long, indrawn breath. "All right, Peggy. I'll have the furnace repaired. But you'd better keep that alarm system on. If you have another break-in, I won't be moved by any pretty words. Understand?"

"Yes. I'll take care of it." She hung up the phone, shaking with cold and temper. She'd won . . . at least for now.

Peggy dressed quickly and warmly. She fed Shakespeare, but he still wouldn't eat. She was getting concerned about his lack of appetite. Maybe it would be better to dog-proof her house and let him out. She loved him. She didn't want him to get sick. But how could she dog-proof everything?

She stroked his head as he lay on his massive paws. "I love you, you know. Otherwise I wouldn't put up with you. I have to go now, but I'll be back after lunch to take you for your next lesson with Rue. Try to eat something while I'm gone."

Riding to the Potting Shed was slow, heavy traffic on all the roads. She thought about the night before as she rode past Myers Park Presbyterian Church. The image of Jesus with the lambs didn't seem so comforting now. Even though Beth survived what happened to her, her life would never be the same again.

And what would happen when it was time for Beth to go home? They wouldn't keep her forever. The killer would have to act again to secure the money. Unless he or she were long gone with all of it. *Unlikely,* she considered as she rode her bike up to the back of the shop. Beth's life could be in danger again. She had to prove what *really* happened. But where could she start?

"Good morning, Peggy!" Selena sang out from behind the cash register. "I hope your friend's doing better. It's a great morning, isn't it?"

Peggy took off her coat, scarf, and gloves. "Either your grades have come up, or you're dating someone new."

Selena laughed. "How about both? I finally found a good way to get tutored. I'm dating the professor!"

"Don't tell me who it is," Peggy urged, holding out her hand. "It's not ethical to date a student. I have enough secrets in my brain right now. Wouldn't it be easier to learn the material?"

"Those old rules for not dating professors are stupid," Selena told her. "I'm an adult. He's an adult. What we do isn't anyone else's business. This is working for both of us. Can't *anyone* just be happy for me?"

Peggy assumed from Selena's tone that she'd already been chewed out by someone else, probably her mother. Glad it wasn't her job to rein the girl in, Peggy started her day as she always did with a cup of tea and a look at the delivery book. It was early for customers. The silence in the shop was only broken by the sound of the radiators fighting the chill that tried to creep in from outside.

There was a full day ahead of her. She was glad about that. It made her feel better to call the customers who had benches coming, clear out space for some pansies, and stock shelves with seed packages. She had pussy willows and blue Dutch irises for Diane Walters who practiced ikebana, a Japanese form of flower arranging. But the pink thrift that meant *sympathy* brought her right back to the muddle in her brain.

Hunter came by with David a little while later. She looked as pale and hollow-eyed as Peggy felt. "I just left the hospital. Beth is still unconscious. Her parents are with her." David slipped his arm around her shoulders.

"She'll come out of it," Peggy predicted. "She'll be embarrassed about all the fuss. I know I would be."

"I'm not sure where to go from here," Hunter confessed. "I know she's not crazy. This could happen to anyone under the kind of stress she's had to deal with."

"Unfortunately, the law doesn't care about the circumstance," David reminded her. "She's your friend. You'll just have to stand by her through everything that's going to happen. People can come out on the other side of something like this. Mental illness is a treatable disease."

"I know you're right." Hunter kissed his cheek and hugged him. "I wish I could crawl under my bed for a while, but I can't. I have a wrestler with a bad attitude waiting for me. I'll talk to you later, Peggy. Let me know if you hear anything about Beth. I'll be in court, so I won't have my cell phone on."

"I'm making dinner tonight for Hunter," David said as they were leaving, "why don't you and Steve join us? I'm sure we could all do with a bottle of wine and a little conversation over some good food. Around seven?"

Peggy smiled. "Thanks, David. I'll talk to Steve and get back with you."

When they were gone, Selena shook her head. "You didn't give Hunter a hard time about dating someone so quickly."

"My problem with you dating your professor has nothing to do with dating someone *quickly*," Peggy explained. "But I'm sure you've heard all the arguments already. You're an adult. You get to make these choices for yourself. You also get to cope with the mistakes you make."

"Why does everyone *assume* it will be a mistake?"

"Because the ethical question rubs up against the notion of romance in this case," Peggy answered as she put on her work jacket to go into the warehouse space in the back of the shop. "Would you want *your* daughter to date her teacher?"

"Oh, Peggy." Selena frowned. "You sound like my *mother*!"

Customers began filtering into the shop, and a delivery driver needed help dropping off a load of apple trees in the back. Contrary to what most people thought, winter was a good time to plant trees. As long as they were healthy and well-footed, they should thrive.

Gratefully, Peggy left Selena in the front and went to help

him. She certainly wasn't in any frame of mind to offer advice to the girl. She had all the peace of mind that a ticking time bomb in her pocket could bring her.

Lunchtime came quickly. Peggy felt like she looked up from a delivery of carrots and animal sculptures with solar batteries that made them glow at night when Steve was there with Shakespeare, waiting to go to Whiskers and Paws. She picked up her coat and gloves, smiling at Selena. "I should be back in a couple of hours."

"Good luck with the horse," Selena said. "Peggy?"

"Yes?"

"Thanks for caring about what I do anyway." She smiled self-consciously and glanced at Steve. "I know I get to make my own choices now. Maybe they won't always be right. But I appreciate you taking the time to listen to me."

Peggy paused and looked at her. "Are you all right? I can skip the lesson today if you need me to stay."

"I'm fine." Selena opened the shop door for them. "We'll talk when you get back."

"What's with her?" Steve asked as they left the shop.

It was her words to Selena about the *ethical* question of romance that struck Peggy like a bolt of logic. Suddenly, she knew the answer. She pulled out her cell phone. "I have to cancel Shakespeare's lesson for today."

"What's up?" Steve wondered, herding the dog into the SUV.

"I think I know what the link is between Cindy and the money. And I'm sorry, Steve, but you can't help me find it."

18

Amaryllis

Botanical: *Hippeastrum*
Family: Amaryllidaceae

The amaryllis is a relative of the daffodil. It is native to the Andes mountains of Chile and Peru. It was discovered in the eighteen hundreds by Dr. Eduard Poeppig. This showy plant is one of the greatest treasures of the gardening world. It can be grown indoors or out with great success and minimal effort.

STEVE WASN'T SURE IF he should be offended or glad he had to be excluded. "What are you planning to do?"

"I'm going to take a look around Cindy's condo."

"You're going to ask her first, right?"

She glanced at him, eyebrows raised.

"Never mind." He started the Vue's engine. "I don't want to know. But you can't go in alone."

"I have to. It's the only way." Peggy outlined her plan. "I know where she lives. We've done work there. I think I can get the doorman to let me in."

"I could be there with you, taking Sam's place," Steve volunteered. "I won't let you go in alone."

"All right. You wait downstairs. If you see Cindy, call me on the cell phone, and I'll get out."

"I don't like it," he maintained. Shakespeare barked to agree. Or disagree. It was hard to tell. "What are you hoping to find?"

"The link Al told me has to exist. Cindy can't get her hands on the money and probably isn't doing this for herself. She's always had bad taste in men. If I'm right, she's involved with Gary Rusch. He could access Park's money. It would be easy for him to 'take care of' the estate and the insurance. And Beth's suicide attempt came on the heels of her telling me she said something to him about it. I'm betting he gave her the Nembutol when she was with him."

"I can't believe I'm going to say this." Steve shook his head as they stopped at a light. "But if you actually suspect Gary of being the killer and Cindy of being his accomplice, wouldn't it make more sense to go through *Gary's* place? He might still have some of the poisoned honey. Or something else incriminating."

Peggy leaned over and kissed him. "*That's* why I love you!"

The light changed, but Steve didn't move the Vue forward. "You *do*?"

She cleared her throat and rearranged the folds of her scarf, carefully not looking at his handsome face. "Yes, I suppose I do. It happened so fast that I—"

He took her in his arms and kissed her while car horns blared and drivers either laughed or cursed as they went around them. "I love you, too, Peggy. For different reasons, probably. I've wanted to tell you for a long time."

"You mean all three months we've known each other?"

He grinned. "Every minute since you crashed into the side of my car."

She stared into his wonderful eyes, almost forgetting her plan to find Park's killer. She never thought she'd see that look in another man's eyes. "Well! I don't really know what to say."

"Don't worry." He started the Vue off again down College Street. "I'm not asking to go house hunting or hit the bridal registry at Belk. What we have right now is enough for me as long as it's enough for you."

"It is." She smiled and squeezed his hand. "Thank you."

He squeezed back, then sobered, his eyes glued on the road. "So where does Gary Rusch live?"

Peggy didn't know. "But it should be easy to find out." She used her Internet connection on her cell phone to access the Charlotte Yellow Pages. "Well, *that's* cozy!"

"What?"

"Gary lives in the same condo complex as Cindy. What a coincidence!" She glanced at Steve. "So Plan A still works, except I get into Gary's condo instead of Cindy's, and you keep watch downstairs for either of them."

"Why don't you let me go and *you* keep watch?" Steve suggested as they pulled into her driveway.

"As you've said before, I have a talent for this. Jonas might call me a busybody, but I prefer to think of it as research."

"All right." He gave in as he let Shakespeare out of the Vue. The dog whined and pulled at the leash, trying to reach Peggy.

"Let's get him settled in and take care of it." She patted Shakespeare's head. "With any luck, we'll have our answers and still be done in time for dinner."

PEGGY GRABBED A THRIVING red amaryllis from her kitchen before they left and put a Potting Shed tag on it as they drove back downtown. It was as simple getting into the condo as she thought it would be. The doorman knew Sam and the Potting Shed name. He was glad to finally meet Peggy.

"I'm glad to meet you, too." She endured his hearty handshake after she put the amaryllis on the bench near the door at the entrance to the plush, expensive condos.

"You know, I've heard rumors the owner here is going to hire a new landscaping service, inside and out," Tommy, the doorman, confided. "I was wondering if you might be interested. I was planning on giving Sam a call."

"That would be great." She smiled, thinking how life worked in strange ways. "Should I get in touch with the owner or give you my card?"

"Let me give you the owner's number." He wrote it out on a piece of paper and gave it to her. "I think he'll be interested."

"Thanks!" She tucked it away. "I'll give him a call."

"Nothin' at all. I hope you get it."

Peggy walked quickly to the elevators after a peek at Steve waiting outside the building. She called Tommy when she reached number 17 on the seventh floor. He buzzed her into the luxury condo unit.

Inside the elegant condo, nothing was out of place. Not even a smell of any kind. It was more like a high-dollar hotel room than a home. She put the amaryllis down on a table, not planning to leave it behind. With all the glare protection on the windows, there wouldn't be enough light to grow a shade plant. Amaryllis loved sun. In this environment, it would shrivel and die. She couldn't imagine anything *living* there anyway.

What was she looking for? Contrary to her confident manner with Steve, she wasn't really sure. She searched the kitchen for any sign of honey. There wasn't *anything* edible in the room, poisoned or not. But it was very shiny and glamorous. Lots of chrome and beautiful inlaid black marble on the countertops. Like a kitchen from a magazine. She wondered if Gary had ever been in there. He didn't seem like the type who cooks.

She tackled the bedroom next. The bed was huge, with a large portrait of Gary on the wall behind it. There were mirrors everywhere. The black carpet muffled any sound as she walked into the room. She accidentally touched a switch by the door, and a cascade of light and sound streamed into the room. Multicolored strobe lights flashed across the bed.

"So this is the way the other half lives," she mumbled to herself with a wry smile.

Peggy checked through the closet carefully. There was no sign of women's clothing or shoes. There were no personal photos on the bedside tables. Nothing that could tell her if Cindy had been there. The immense bathroom with the black marble tub was the same story. It was like no one lived there.

"I love you, Steve," she said as she dialed Tommy's number at the front desk, "but you're not a great detective."

Tommy was totally understanding of the fact that she for-got to mention she had something for Cindy Walker as well. Apparently it happened frequently with multiple deliveries to the building. She picked up her amaryllis and carefully shut Gary's door behind her.

The buzzer sounded, and Peggy pushed open the door to Cindy's condo. She knew she was at the right place as soon as she peeked inside. Clothes were strewn everywhere. Some of them were Cindy's, but there was also some men's clothing. Two wineglasses and two empty take-out boxes proclaimed the fact that Cindy had been there with someone else. Sta-tionery from Lamonte, Rusch and Peterson had a shopping list scrawled on it.

"Let's take a look in the kitchen." Peggy left everything like she found it. As soon as she saw enough, she planned to go back downstairs and call the police. She wasn't sure how she was going to explain what she knew about Cindy, but she trusted it would come to her when the time was right.

There were two quart jars of honey under the kitchen sink. Both were labeled with the handwritten date, September 9. She held the golden syrup up to the light, but there was no way to tell if it was poisoned without testing. On the kitchen table was one of Beth's pretty tea mugs. It made her blood freeze to see it.

She'd seen enough. She couldn't quite make the connection between Cindy and Gary, but it was obvious it existed. If the police found the poisoned honey in Cindy's condo, she had no doubt it would be a short walk to arrest Gary, too. Cindy wasn't made to be a hero. She'd crack under questioning.

"Peggy!" Cindy's voice was accompanied by the distinct sound of a safety being released on a revolver. "How *nice* of you to visit!"

"Confess now and save yourself." It sounded quaint, even to *her* ears. But Peggy refused to be bullied by the younger woman in the pale blue designer dress just because she had a gun. "I know *you* didn't make this honey." She opened the cabinet door. "Help the police get the *real* killer."

Cindy looked confused for a moment. "What is *that* doing under there?"

Quick to catch on, Peggy shrugged. "He was probably setting *you* up to take the fall in case something went wrong. Did he just hide these here today?"

"Damn, worthless piece of crap! I *knew* I couldn't trust him!" It was easy to see Cindy's brain working hard enough to blow steam from her delicate ears. "Never mind. Pick those up. And give me your cell phone. We're going for a ride."

There was a side door to the condos only used by the residents. Peggy went out of it ahead of Cindy while her cell phone rang just out of reach. It was probably Steve, wondering what was taking her so long. There was no way he could have seen the woman pull into the side street and use the private entrance. Some plans didn't work out.

"Where are we going?" Peggy asked her, conscious of the revolver pressed into her side under Cindy's jacket. She carried both jars of honey carefully. One slip, and the evidence would be gone.

"You'll see when we get there," Cindy vowed as she opened the door to her Cadillac Escalade and pushed Peggy inside. "Just sit there and hold the honey and you won't be hurt."

Peggy did as she was told. She wasn't in fear for her life so much as worried Cindy and Gary would get away with the murders they committed. She didn't believe they wouldn't hurt her. They'd already killed two people. What would stop them from killing her?

But if she dropped the honey on the ground or if she tackled Cindy as she drove through the deepening dusk that enveloped the streets of Charlotte, she might never make the connection between Cindy and Gary. This way, she'd look them both in the face. She'd be able to accuse Park's killer of his terrible crime.

Just before they kill you. Her cell phone rang again. Steve would find some way to get upstairs at the condominium complex. When he did, he'd realize something happened to her. He'd see the amaryllis she left in Cindy's condo. *But will he realize Cindy kidnapped me? Will he know where I'm going? Will he get there in time?*

Peggy wasn't sure how much satisfaction she'd get knowing the truth if she couldn't do anything about it because she was dead. She wasn't *afraid* to die, but she wanted to see the couple brought to justice. Unfortunately, it seemed she couldn't have it both ways. At least not at that moment.

Cindy drove the Escalade down Providence Road to Myers Park. Peggy frowned when she parked the SUV in front of a redbrick house, like Park's, close to the Presbyterian church. "Get out."

"Where are we going?"

"You're going to have to see our little lover's spat, Peggy." Cindy smiled as she shifted the gun to her free hand. "I hope you won't be *too* offended. Bring the honey with you. You can be my witness."

Peggy picked up the jars of honey. The wind whipped her purple scarf free, and it fell to the ground. She didn't move to retrieve it. Maybe it would help them find her if she had any chance of surviving.

Cindy walked up to the heavy oak door and pushed it open without knocking, nudging Peggy inside the foyer before her.

"Peggy!" Hunter greeted her. "You made it! I was beginning to wonder what happened to you. Where's Steve? Who's that with you?"

"Move, bitch!" Cindy waved the revolver so Hunter could see it. "Where is that *snake*?"

"So it was Davey all along." Hunter sat beside Peggy in the dining room while they listened to the heated argument going on between David and Cindy in the kitchen. "He didn't want to be with me. He used me. And he was sleeping with *her*. All I got were a few kisses and some worthless promises."

"Don't feel too bad." David had duct taped them to the dining room chairs after taping their hands together. Peggy squirmed, trying to get her hands free as a loud *whack* and a dull *thud* came from the kitchen. "I thought Gary was the killer."

"Dear old Dad." David rejoined them *without* Cindy at his side. "He'd have a heart attack if he knew I took money from Lamonte, Rusch and Peterson. Point of honor and all that. Park came to me as a junior member of the firm to work with him on his will. It was like God sent him to me on a golden platter. He even confessed to me about Cindy. It was easy to get her to help me with the details."

"So you decided to poison him." Peggy wanted to ask him about Cindy but decided *now* wasn't a good time.

"*After* adding myself to the will as executor in case Beth was unable to carry on. It was always my intention that the police would think Tomorrow's Children killed him over the estuary battle. Poor Beth would succumb to her grief soon after."

"And you learned all about horse chestnut." *Keep him talking until Steve can find you.* Although she had no idea how that was going to happen. Steve would probably go to Gary's office looking for her. By then it might be too late.

"Brilliant, wasn't it?" he gloated. "I knew a man when I was growing up who lost all his bees to horse chestnut. Remember him, Hunter? Old man Jackson. He told me all about it."

"Yes. Davey, please—"

"Shh." He kissed her. "It will all be over soon. I've been working on this house for a while. But I've decided I don't like it as much as I thought. And I'm thinking about taking a long trip somewhere. Just as soon as I transfer the Lamonte money to my name. In the meantime, I think there might be a tragic fire here. Three women. Only identifiable by their dental work, no doubt."

"But why Isabelle?" Peggy asked. "You were going to lose the money because it looked like Park committed suicide. She kept that from happening. Why kill her?"

"It occurred to me Beth was going to inherit *that* estate as well. Why not have it, too? I made a big dent in the firm's money. But now I find I'm not inclined to repair it. I have enough to start over. Maybe in Costa Rica. That's a beautiful place. Have you ever been there, Peggy?"

"No. But my mama always says what goes around, comes around. Killing us won't end it."

"I thought you loved me," Hunter whispered. "I thought we were going to be partners."

David was still just as clumsy, getting his foot caught in the white drape as he walked past the window. "I know you did, angel. Cindy thought I loved her, too. In a way, I love both of you. You were both *so* helpful."

"And you searched my house for the dragon's head." Peggy tried to keep the conversation going. How long had it been since they left Cindy's condo? Thirty minutes? An hour?

"That's right," he agreed. "My girl in the kitchen didn't do a good job on that, did she? Alice had it all along. But I did have a helluva time going through that screwball place of yours, Peggy! Thanks for leaving it wide open for me."

"Not that it did you much good," Peggy yelled as he started to walk toward the basement door. "You've done a lot of tail chasing."

He paused and smiled at her. "That's true. But it all ends here. Good-bye, ladies!"

As soon as the door closed behind him, Hunter fell sideways across Peggy, who thought she must be sick. "Hunter, it's going to be fine. We'll make it through this."

Hunter spat out a mouthful of silver duct tape. "I'm trying to get us free. Keep still. I don't want to bite you. But I hope that gun is still in the kitchen. I want to shoot him right between the eyes!"

"Good idea!" Peggy noticed the sound of his footsteps on the stairs after a few minutes. "He's coming back!"

Hunter sat upright quickly and spat out another piece of tape. "What do they make that stuff out of anyway? I mean, what is it supposed to be used for *really*?"

"I started a little fire in the basement so you won't get too cold waiting around here for help." David grinned at them, madness lurking in the depths of his gray eyes. "Maybe the fire department will even get here in time. But with all the fresh paint and floor sealers, I doubt it."

Peggy could already smell the smoke, hear the popping of fire in the walls and floors beneath her. He was right. Even if they weren't caught in the fire itself, the smoke would kill them. There was probably enough polyurethane in the house to choke a horse!

David started to walk by her on his way to the front door. Without really thinking about what she was doing, Peggy put out her feet and tripped him. He fell hard and knocked his head on the corner of the table. He came up slowly, blood starting to run down his face. "What did you do, Peggy?"

He put up his hand to stop the bleeding, and Hunter kicked him hard in the face. Without a word, he fell back down on the floor. This time he didn't get up. Hunter didn't wait to see what was going to happen. She growled and kicked him savagely again.

Smoke was starting to fill the room. "Forget him! We have to get out of here." Peggy coughed on the noxious fumes.

Hunter leaned down and started biting at the tape that held her. "I can't reach mine. I can try to bite yours again." But she coughed, choking, and couldn't manage to break through the tough tape. "It's no use."

Peggy heard a new sound. Not the one she wanted to hear, sirens, but a good sound anyway. "Do you hear that? It's Shakespeare! Come on, boy! We're in here! Steve? Is that you?"

"Peggy!" Steve yelled back through the dense gray smoke.

"Mom!" Paul added his voice to Steve's as they ran into the room. "We have to get you out of here!"

"Cindy Walker," Peggy choked out her name, eyes streaming from smoke. "She's in the kitchen. She might be unconscious. Or dead. I don't know."

"I'll find her. The fire department is on its way," Paul yelled over the noise of groaning wood and burning plaster. "Get them out, Steve.

Steve used his pocketknife to cut through the duct tape that held them. Hunter and Peggy staggered from the house as the first fire truck pulled into the drive. Steve dragged David across the floor and out into the yard.

He started to go back in to check on Paul, but the fire chief pushed him back. "No one's going back in there, son."

"There's a police officer," Steve coughed as he tried to explain, "and another woman."

"We'll get them out. You all stay right here."

Peggy saw Paul come out of the backyard with Cindy in his arms. He collapsed on his knees in the wet, brown grass, and firefighters rushed to his side. Paramedics held oxygen masks for Peggy, Hunter, and Steve.

Another paramedic started toward David, but Hunter stopped him. "Don't bother. You'll save the state some money."

Peggy laughed until she choked, and the paramedic cautioned her. She smiled at Paul, and he nodded. Probably angry at her. But it was all right. They were alive. Everything else was manageable.

"How did Steve know where to find you?" Sam wanted to hear every detail the next day.

"He was smart and called Paul. They tracked my cell phone. Lucky for me Cindy brought it with us," Peggy answered.

"I still can't believe David killed Park and Isabelle. Little weasel. I knew there was a reason I didn't like him." Sam stood behind the counter at the Potting Shed, pruning a tea rose for a customer.

Hunter smacked him in the arm. "You were just jealous."

"Of a boyfriend who murders people? Yeah, right!"

"Of *any* boyfriend?"

"What happens with Beth now?" Sam asked Peggy. "Will she still have to be in the hospital for observation?"

"No," Peggy answered. "She's home with Foxx and Reddman. She's talking about moving to Salisbury with her parents."

"With that kind of money, she could live anywhere." Sam shook his head. "Why live in Salisbury?"

"It's where she grew up. Having her family close by will be good for her and the boys."

"What about David?"

Hunter crossed her arms protectively in front of her. "He

goes away for a long time. And I give up Tae Bo for karate."

"And always carry a pocketknife," Peggy finished.

"In my boot!" Hunter laughed. "And I'm thinking about buying one of those garter belts that hold knives."

"Too much information!" Sam put his hands over his ears, lowering then slowly as Al and Jonas joined them in the shop.

"Peggy," Al said with a nod at the other two. "If we could have a minute?"

Sam and Hunter went back into the storeroom, closing the door behind them. Peggy felt sure they were listening at the crack. She smiled as she said, "What can I do for you?"

"Dr. Ramsey has suggested," Jonas cleared his throat, "*suggested* we hire you to work with the CMPD on certain cases."

"Really?" Peggy took up Sam's pruning shears. "What kind of cases?"

"*Peggy!*" Al shook his head.

"That's okay." Jonas put out his hand. "She wants her pound of flesh. I can handle it."

She stopped pruning. "Not really. I'm joking. I understand what you're offering. And I'm flattered, really. But I'm afraid I can't help you. At least not yet. It's all I can do to keep up with what I have going on now."

"The job would pay," Al added. "It's not a lot, but it's decent."

"I'm thinking about giving up my place at Queens in May," she compromised, looking out at the rainswept Saturday afternoon in Brevard Court. "Who knows what might come after that? Let's talk about it in the spring. In the meantime, gentlemen, I'm late for an obedience course for my dog. Try not to get into any trouble while I'm gone."

RUE, STEVE, AND PEGGY sat down in the hard plastic chairs after Shakespeare's obedience lesson was over, defeat etched on their faces. Shakespeare wagged his tail and looked at them like he was wondering what was wrong.

"Maybe there's boot camp for wayward dogs like they have for teenagers," Steve suggested.

"I'm sure he'll catch on," Rue assured Peggy. "He needs a few more lessons."

Another woman came into the shop. She was in her fifties or early sixties. She carried a large orange tabby cat who eyed them all suspiciously. The woman was dressed in clothes that almost matched the color of her cat. Her streaked blond hair blended into the whole look.

Shakespeare immediately stood at attention with his tail stuck straight out behind him. He stared at the woman and the cat until Peggy got up from her chair to hold his leash, afraid he'd take a running leap at her.

"Don't worry." The woman laughed. "He's fine. Just a little nervous. And very unhappy with someone named Peggy. Is that *you*?"

Peggy smiled and extended her hand. "That's me. And you are?"

"Mrs. Roberts, pet psychic. And before you get any ideas, how do you think I knew your *name*?"

"My dog told you?"

"Exactly. Rupert is having some issues with you."

Peggy glanced at the dog, then at Mrs. Roberts. "His name is Shakespeare."

"Maybe to you. We don't always name our pets appropriate names, do we?"

Not sure what to say, Peggy patted her dog's head. "What kind of issues is Shakes—Rupert having with me?"

"He isn't crazy about you leaving him all the time. And he wishes you'd buy him a different kind of food. He's eating Purina now, right? He'd really like to try Iams."

Peggy wanted to laugh, but Mrs. Roberts was impossibly right. She was in awe. "I *did* leave him to go to Philadelphia. He hasn't been the same since I got back. But I couldn't take him with me."

Rue had been sitting there with her mouth open. She closed her jaw and stood up. "Peggy, you can't believe this woman is communicating with your dog. Shakespeare needs obedience classes. Not a *psychic*."

Mrs. Roberts smirked. "Take it as you will. Rupert says

next time he'd like to stay at the man's house." She looked at Steve. "I believe he means you. He says you did a good job taking care of him, but he doesn't like being in the big house by himself. He says it's haunted, and he doesn't like ghosts. Even nice ghosts."

Peggy swallowed hard. She was trained to be a skeptic. But her Low Country upbringing included tales of witches and ghosts. As a child, she'd believed all of those stories. Something of that crept into her voice as she said, "Does he know the ghosts' names?"

"No. Apparently, he only knows your name. He really loves you. He'd give his life for you. He just wants to stay with the man if you have to leave. And he wants Iams dog food. He says he wants the lamb and rice." Mrs. Roberts smiled and gave her cat to Rue. "He needs a bath and his nails trimmed. I'll be back at four for him. Mind you, be careful with him. He's a little peeved today. There's a cat outside he'd like to be friends with, but I just don't want him hanging around with that street trash."

With a last glance at Shakespeare, Mrs. Roberts disappeared back through the door, leaving a cloud of Chanel behind her.

"Well!" Rue sat down with the cat in her lap.

"Pet psychic, huh?" Steve looked at Shakespeare. "My name is Steve. You're welcome to stay at my house anytime Peggy goes away."

Peggy crouched down and looked into Shakespeare's eyes. "I wish you could talk to *me*. Do you want me to call you Rupert instead of Shakespeare?"

The massive head shook negatively, the uncropped ears flopping up and down.

"I guess not." Steve laughed. "The dog has spoken."

"You're still going to bring him back for the rest of the lessons, aren't you?" Rue asked.

"I will," Peggy agreed. "Maybe he'll be better next time."

Steve and Peggy left with Shakespeare a few minutes later. "So who do you think is haunting your house?" he asked her.

"The house is almost a hundred years old," she mused. "I suppose it could be anyone who lived there."

The sunshine was bright on their heads as they walked out to the SUV in the parking lot. "Do you think John is there?" Steve suggested, opening the door for Shakespeare to get into the backseat.

"He could be." She looked up into the brilliant blue sky and smiled. "It wouldn't surprise me."

"I'm not sure how I feel about that," Steve said. "What do you think he thinks about the two of us being together?"

"I think he'd be happy about it." She got into the vehicle and closed the door. "Everyone seems to think he wouldn't want me to be alone. I think if John were still alive, he'd like you. It stands to reason he'd like us to be together."

"That works for me." Steve kissed her after he got behind the steering wheel. He smiled up at the sky. "Thanks, John."

Peggy's Garden Journal

Winter

The cold weather months are always the hardest for gardeners. Nothing is blooming. The color is gone, and for many, so
is their enthusiasm. We curl up on cold winter nights with our
catalogues and wish for spring.

But now is the best time for you to take a good look at your
garden. What shapes are in *your* garden?

Studying our gardens when there is no foliage can give us
an opportunity to appreciate graceful limbs and soaring
branches. Take a moment to notice the subtle shades and patterns of bark. The bare-bones shape of our trees and bushes
should be as alluring to us as their leaves and flowers. If
they're not, this is a good time to change that image.

Deadwood can be removed at any time during the winter.
Pruning live wood should be avoided during the coldest times
but can be done in late winter. No need to apply a dressing on
these cuts. The trees will be fine. This is an excellent time to
determine how tall you want those bushes to be and examine
positions for new growth. Create a charming path or stake out
a new flower bed.

Winter can be a time of growth and beauty, if we allow it to be. As your garden slumbers, roots dig deeper to sustain spring and summer foliage. Take some time to acknowledge the cycle of life going on around you. Spring will come with its color and magic. But don't allow the charm of winter to escape you unnoticed!

Peggy

Care and Feeding Guide

AMARYLLIS

This exotic, winter-blooming plant will provide huge, colorful blooms just when you need them most. It requires very little maintenance and will bloom within five weeks of planting. You can choose to buy them already planted or buy the bare bulb.

If you choose to plant, get a pot slightly larger than the bulb, put in some good soil, and set the bulb so its top will rise slightly above the rim. Tamp down well to remove air pockets. Water carefully at first, more as the stem begins to grow. Be sure extra water drains out of the pot.

You can also grow the bulb with water in a glass vase. Amaryllis vases are curved so that the bulb sits securely with the roots in the water.

Either way you decide to plant, keep your plant cool, about 68 degrees. It needs plenty of sun to flower. After it blooms, cut the flower from the stalk. New leaves will grow, although the plant will not flower again until next year. Water and fertilize regularly.

LENTEN ROSE

These dark green leafy plants with small, saucer shaped red, white, or green flowers will deliver a nice, colorful reprieve for winter gardens. They will herald spring, even in the snow!

They bloom from February to April and are extraordinarily

hardy. The species is perfect as a ground cover and loves shady areas, even under trees. The soil can be slightly alkaline. It enjoys a generous amount of mulch and requires fertilizing every spring after blooming.

They look wonderful in pots as well as out in the open. They will grow to be about two feet tall and prefer to be left alone once they are planted, so be careful where you decide to put them.

Lenten roses can be planted during the winter months and still thrive in your garden!

CAMELLIA

Camellias are gorgeous, versatile shrubs with pretty, long-blooming flowers and shiny green leaves. They can grow up to ten feet or be trimmed back to grow in a pot. They grow outside from Long Island, down the Atlantic coast and back up the Pacific coast to Washington. They can survive temperatures as low as 0–10 degrees. They grow best in partial shade and well-drained, slightly acidic soil. They prefer to be wet but not soggy.

Camellias can be planted late fall through the early spring. Allow at least five feet between plants. Dig a hole at least two feet wider than the root ball. Fill the hole around the roots with a mixture of good soil and organic matter. Mulch with straw after planting. Water well and soak once a week during dry weather. Flowers will bloom in late fall to early winter.

The American Camellia Society has a wealth of information for camellia lovers. Check them out here: http://www.camellias-acs.com/

GROW RADISHES!

In warmer areas, sow radish seeds in winter for an early spring harvest. Sprinkle seeds and cover them with ½ inch of potting soil. Keep the bed moist and thin seedlings to 3 inches apart. Harvest in six weeks.

COMPOSTING

Keeping your soil healthy should be every gardener's concern. Poor, tired soil will give rise to tired plants. Consider composting as a good way to refresh and revive your soil. Compost improves soil texture, helps provide drainage, and supplements nutrients by encouraging earthworms and microorganisms. This should be done throughout the growing season, but a good time to start your compost pile is in the winter as you're waiting for the warmer months.

What goes into a compost pile? Chopped-up leaves, dry grass, dead plants, weeds without seeds, and old potting soil. You can provide fruit scraps, vegetable cuttings, tea bags, crushed eggshells, coffee grounds, and shredded paper from inside your house. Don't use meat, fish, bones, plastic, metal, fats and oils, dairy products, or pet waste.

To store your compost, you can build a pile on the ground if you have room, or you can use a composting bin that will cleverly create compost on your deck or porch without anyone knowing what's inside. Compost should be damp but not wet.

How will you know if your compost is finished? It will have a dark, earthy smell, and the ingredients will be unrecognizable. In warmer weather, this happens faster, but your compost will break down in cold weather, too. There is no exact time frame. Just be patient.

What should you do with your compost when it's finished? Use it as mulch in and around your plants. It will fertilize and protect your soil. Be sure to start filling up your compost pile or bin as soon as you empty the old one.

For more info on composting: http://www.compostingcoun cil.org/

CONTROL WINTER PESTS

Warm, dry indoor air can lead to problems with spider mites on houseplants. The mites are barely visible to the eye. You'll have to look for the problems they cause: stippling on leaves and fine webbing on new growth. They attack almost any houseplant. To control them, spray the plants with insecticidal soap two to three times a week. Be sure to spray the undersides of the leaves as well as the tops.

ADD EXTRA LIGHT

Grow lights or high-intensity discharge lamps can be a very good way to give your plants enough sunlight to thrive over the winter months. Sometimes, even a window setting might not provide enough light for your plants. Consider setting up a grow light to add to the natural lighting.

This can also help when you don't have enough windows for all of your wintering plants. Grow lights can make any shelf or other space a plant-friendly area. A good way to know how much light your plants are getting is to put your light on a timer to simulate the natural hours of sunlight.

FROST HEAVED PLANTS AND BULBS

Alternating freeze/thaw cycles can "heave" perennials and bulbs out of the ground. Wind and extreme temperatures can damage exposed roots. Watch for frost heaved plants and bulbs. Replant them or push soil around exposed roots. To minimize damage, cover beds with lightweight mulch or evergreen boughs after the ground has frozen.

Botanical Gardens at Asheville
Asheville, North Carolina

"Dedicated to preserving and promoting our Native Plants. We are an independent non-profit organization housing a collection of plants native to the Southern Appalachian Mountains. Our admission is free, but donations are appreciated and memberships are encouraged. We are located in the Southern Appalachian Mountains, one of the most diverse temperate ecosystems in the world. Our mission is the preservation and promotion of the native plant species and habitats of these mountains. We hope to increase public awareness of this region's unique botanical diversity by maintaining gardens for the enjoyment of the public and by providing educational programs and research resources for the community. The BGA is open year round from sunrise to sunset for the enjoyment of the community, and no admission is charged for entrance."

The Botanical Gardens at Asheville
151 W.T. Weaver Boulevard
Asheville, NC 28804-3414
Phone: 828-252-5190
http://www.ashevillebotanicalgardens.org

Tree and Shrub Catalogs

Wayside Gardens: http://www.waysidegardens.com

Reeseville Ridge Nursery: http://www.wegrowit.com

Meadow Lake Nursery: http://www.meadow-lake.com

Seeds for unusual trees and shrubs:
   http://www.raingardens.com

River Rock Nursery:
   http://www.rdrop.com/users/green/plantit/index.htm

Outdoor Accessories

Patio and outdoor accessories:
   http://www.kitchensource.com/pau

Yard and garden accents: http://www.plowandhearth.com

Outdoor living solutions: http://www.brookstone.com

Cedar furniture: http://www.cedarstore.com

Home of the outdoor armoire: http://www.krupps.com

Happy Gardening!